THE BALLROOM CLASS

09/09

BAM
CII

- 8 MAR 2010

- 3 AUG 2010

9 AUG 2010

1 7 AUG 2010

22·09-15

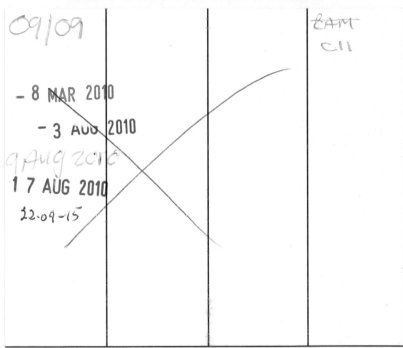

Please return on or before the latest date above.
You can renew online at *www.kent.gov.uk/libs*
or by telephone 08458 247 200

Libraries & Archives

00884\DTP\RN\07.07   LIB 7

THE BALLROOM CLASS

Lucy Dillon

WINDSOR
PARAGON

First published 2008
by Hodder & Stoughton
This Large Print edition published 2009
by BBC Audiobooks Ltd
by arrangement with
Hodder & Stoughton

Hardcover ISBN: 978 1 408 42843 6
Softcover   ISBN: 978 1 408 42844 3

British Library Cataloguing in Publication Data available

Printed and bound in Great Britain by
CPI Antony Rowe, Chippenham, Wiltshire

For my mother, and her lovely dancer's legs,
that I wish I'd inherited.

ACKNOWLEDGEMENTS

Thank you to Mrs Cowper, for the first tap lessons, and to Diana Wykes, for turning four left feet into something approaching two matching pairs.

I'm indebted to Carolyn Mays and Isobel Akenhead for their help and encouragement, and to Lizzy Kremer, for pretty much everything, really. Most of all, thanks to my own Fred Astaire, who made the ultimate sacrifice and learned to cha-cha. Greater love hath no man.

Angelica Andrews, British Open Ballroom Dancing Champion 1974, 76–78, British Ten-Dance Champion 1977, and European Ballroom finalist more times than she cared to remember, did not do rusty keys or locks.

Even without her beaded dance dresses and flicked cat's eye liner, Angelica wasn't the sort of lady who needed to open any door for herself. A man usually got there first, rushing to get it, so she could sweep through. However, there was no man around today, and the key she was grappling with didn't just open a peeling door, it opened her entire monochrome childhood, before she could dance, before she was beautiful, before she was even 'Angelica'.

This wasn't something she wanted company for, so she gritted her teeth in solitary majesty and jiggled the rusty lock to the Longhampton Memorial Hall.

'Damn!' she hissed, as one crimson nail split with the effort. According to Mrs Higham, who might well have been one of the Memorial Hall's original 1921 board of trustees, there was 'a knack' to it. The 'knack' itself was not explained to her. Mrs Higham handed over the key with an air of suspicion, despite the fact that not only had Angelica got full permission to teach a class the following evening, but she distinctly remembered Mrs Higham from her own lessons there, fifty years ago, when she came to collect her bat-eared daughter, Vanessa. Mrs Higham had seemed pretty suspicious, even then.

'I see you're back, Angela,' she'd said, as

ix

Angelica signed the book, with a grim satisfaction that suggested she'd been waiting thirty years to say it.

Angelica made sure she signed Angelica Andrews, not Angela Clarke. She was back, but she wasn't *that* back.

With a final shove that put a fine layer of dirt on her wool jacket, she pushed open the Hall's heavy front door and stepped into the tiled vestibule. Nothing had changed. She'd been here a few times since she moved back to Longhampton, for Friday night dances, but then the place had been filled with bodies, modern bodies fixing it firmly in the present. Now she was here alone, it felt like stepping back in time, with her own past drumming its fingers, waiting for her in the ballroom inside, some of it in crisp black and white, some in high eighties' gloss.

Angelica's eyes closed, and she breathed in a smell that sent her rushing back into the sixties, the fifties: beeswax polish and wood panelling, and decades of dust tramped in from the streets. There'd always been something about the Memorial Hall that made Angelica feel you could slip back in time, if you turned down the lights and put on the right kind of slow waltz music.

Like now, she thought, letting her ears pick up the faint clanks of the ancient plumbing. You could almost feel the brush of satin skirts swishing past in the dark, each creak of the wooden rafters a gentleman's excuse me echoing back from the drab thirties.

Angelica opened her eyes, and looked slowly round at the oak plaques commemorating Longhampton's war dead, the carved finials, and painted friezes of Morris dancers and ballroom ladies in gossamer dresses, now faded like old pressed flowers. The glass panes in the doors that joined the vestibule to the main ballroom were cobwebby, and though the place was obviously still in use, from the stacked chairs and fire safety notices, the hall seemed asleep without music. In her head, she could hear blaring horns, and perky dance-band strings, and the echoing shuffle of drums played with brushes.

It gave her a tingle of memory, almost like déjà vu, but not quite. She *had* been here before. It was an eerie feeling—her past coming back to life, after all those years of pretending it never happened.

Music did that. Angelica had always thought it was so easy to touch your fingers to ghosts when you danced to music recorded years before you were born. When you were moving to the music you were sharing that thrill with shy men and hopeful women who'd done exactly the same thing, in the same place, on the same warm summer evenings and crisp early autumn days like this one. The world might move on, but the steps and rituals, and the lead and follow of the dance, stayed exactly the same.

She sat down on the bench where she'd tied on her red ballet slippers as an eager six-year-old, and reached into her bag for the red leather heeled lace-ups she wore to teach in, battered and butter-soft. Even now, Angelica didn't want to step onto that sprung floor in everyday courts.

If she was going to step into the past, she wanted to do it in the right shoes.

She looked up at the joining doors, as she

pushed her feet into the lace-ups. A fresh shiver of anticipation ran over her tanned skin. If she pushed the doors open now, would the ghosts of her old life be dancing there, waiting for her, in a chorus-line of disapproval?

Mrs Trellys, the first ballet teacher, with her walking stick, and her stories of *nearly* going to Russia to train with the Kirov, and her sharp words about little girls with rrrrround shoulders.

Sweet but dull Bernard, her first proper ballroom partner, awkward in his father's dinner jacket, with his hair slicked back and his ears pink with nerves, still hoping she'd changed her mind.

Her mum and dad, now reunited in that great ballroom in the sky where only classic waltzes were played, and her mum's roller-set never wilted before the last dance.

Angelica swallowed, suddenly tense.

Would Tony be there? With his seductive Spanish eyes and too-tight-for-competition trousers? Holding out his hand, requesting her pleasure in that old-fashioned way that looked gallant to everyone else, but unbearably exciting and tormenting to her?

She closed her eyes, and let the wave of longing and regret and still-sharp disappointment roll over her. She'd kept those feelings at arms' length for years, just like she'd kept most strong feelings safely battened down beneath her fixed ballroom smile, but now she was back in Longhampton, they had returned with all the disorientating intensity of a bereavement.

God alone knew where Tony was. But in her imagination, he was always thirty-four, hair as jet-black as his polished dancing shoes, and they were always three quick steps away from a fight or falling, kissing wildly, into bed.

Angelica shook away the memory, and got to her feet. With a deep breath, she pushed open the doors, solid dark wood with sixteen small panes halfway up, enough to glimpse the dancers when you were putting your shoes on, and to get your own pulse racing and your feet itching to join in. Just enough glass to see if your man was dancing with someone else, or if the floor was emptied by some show-off couple strutting their new steps.

Her footsteps echoed on the wonderful wooden floor. Sprung maple, just like the finest ballrooms she'd danced in, an unexpected jewel of sophistication in the nondescript town. Angelica lifted her gaze up to the rafters, taking in the elaborate friezes, washed out and peeling in places, but still ambitious and proud. It was still as magical as it was in her memory, more so for having survived. When she was a little girl, living round the corner in Sydney Street, her mother had often told her about how the Memorial Hall had sprung up like a glorious mushroom behind Longhampton's lacklustre High Street, and though Angelica found it hard to lay her mother's descriptions over the concrete she tramped along, even then she wanted to believe in a glamour she couldn't actually see.

Since way before the turn of the century, according to Pauline, Longhampton had been the place to go for a dance on a Friday, being the old market town and the centre of social activity for the outlying farms and villages. It had a market hall that was used for whatever dancing could be arranged, and its own band. Of course, losing nearly all the town's men to the Western Front had put a stop to that, but after the war had ground to a numb halt, the people of Longhampton, who weren't badly off in those days, thanks to the cider mills, had scraped together enough money to build a Memorial Hall, instead of a gloomy statue to the husbands and sons who'd spun round the floor in happier years. The ramshackle old market hall was demolished, and the lovely Memorial Hall was built in its place, with stained-glass windows that spilled fruit-jelly-coloured pools of light on to the polished floor, and wrought-iron radiators like stacked Nice biscuits along the walls.

The sprung floor was donated by Lady Eliza Cartwright, for whom Angelica's great-aunt Martha had cooked. Lady Eliza's husband, Sir Cedric, had been a keen Scottish reeler who even reeled with staff at Christmas parties, but he was killed on the first day of Ypres, and Lady Eliza, widowed with three young girls, 'turned white overnight', as Martha liked to recall gloomily, when she'd had a sherry or two. She sold his handmade shotguns, gave the money to the fund, and threw herself into leading the committee of widowed volunteers, stumbling through their grief with over-busy diaries. Lady Cartwright was one of the dancing ladies in the subscription stained-glass window right by the door, her blonde hair flying as she swung round as the mother of the Three Muses, with little Clementine, Ada and Felicity making up the foursome. She was still there eighty years later, her pale arms entwined with her children's.

Angelica stepped across the floor to gaze up at the Cartwrights. They were still exactly as she remembered, though now dulled by age and dust and old smoke. She had used Ada's right foot when she was learning to pirouette, concentrating on it, spinning, then catching it again with her eyes for balance. In a way, it made her feel as if Ada was joining in the lesson, despite the fact that 'that poor scrap of a girl' (Martha again) died in the flu epidemic in 1919, up in St Mary's hospital, when the windows were still sketches on the draughtsman's board.

Through the twenties and early thirties, the widows and their daughters had had to dance together in the new hall, and for a while there'd been a vogue for ceilidhs, because it wasn't so bad to take the man's part in a dance that was more breathless exercise than romance. But as the sons grew tall enough to dance with, proper ballroom nights had started up again, and the glitterball, imported specially from Europe, sparkled over foxtrots and bustling quicksteps, especially when the smooth-talking GIs arrived at the base down the road during the next war.

Then at the end of the fifties—and Angelica remembered this herself, partly from her father's absolute horror—rock'n'roll filled the hall three nights a week, jostling for position with the die-hard ballroomers for alternate Friday nights.

Longhampton's deep-rooted passion for a swinging beat took a long time to wither; even when punk was raging in London, couples still trailed to the Memorial Hall in their C&A best to *fleckerl* and *chassé* of a Friday night. Fashion took so long to spread to the middle of nowhere, and there wasn't that much else to do. Angelica was long gone by then, but Pauline wrote to her to tell her about the success the formation team were having locally, and how sequence dancing was all the rage again. It seemed like another life to Angelica, star of the professional ballroom, stepping out on polished floors all over the world, under the red and gold rococo splendour of the Tower Ballroom, Blackpool, in cruise-ship lounges and night-club stages, spangled and glittering like a Fabergé peacock, transformed into someone else as the music began.

In those days, when anyone asked, Angelica usually said she was from London. And in a sense, that's where Angelica *was* from. That's where she became Angelica, shrugging off provincial Angela's past like an old dress. Who wanted to know about Longhampton? She certainly didn't.

Now she was back, though, Angelica wasn't so sure she could shrug things off so easily any more. Scanning the local paper one evening, in her mother's quiet, empty house, she saw there was a social dance night two or three times a month, on a Friday. She guessed *Strictly Come Dancing* was to thank for that. Of course, she'd gone along to the social—how could she resist?—and it was surprising, given that no one was offering lessons, that the dancers there were so good, even by Angelica's standards. Not competition standard, obviously, but that lovely proficient amateur level where you could have a chat and a dance and not worry about getting your toes mangled. The older generation, of course, not many youngsters.

You're older generation now, she reminded herself, with a wry smile. Nearly bus-pass age.

Angelica could think that, because she knew she didn't look it. Not by a long way.

Once you started dancing, you always wanted to improve, she knew from experience, so she'd put up her own advert for lessons, ballroom and Latin, teaching in the very same hall where she'd learned to tap and *plìe* herself, a little black crow in the line of chubby-legged Longhampton girls.

And here she was. The first lesson tomorrow.

Angelica took a broom and swept the dust off the wooden floor, smiling to herself as she remembered that gorgeous younger Angelica, all slicked-back hair, and false Dusty Springfield eyelashes. How horrified she'd be to think of herself back here, offering a dancing class to complete beginners, of all things, when she could be enjoying her alimony in Islington. Teaching people who didn't even know she'd spent the best part of twenty years as half of one of Britain's top professional couples. People who didn't even remember *Come Dancing*, let alone her magnificent regular appearances on it, making the Tower Ballroom crackle with applause as she and Tony swept and glided like swallows in sequins.

She shrugged and swept, stepping backwards in an unconscious lock step, her feet crossing neatly in their red shoes, trying not to let herself slip into the tempting showreel of Tony memories.

Angelica paused at the stained-glass representation of a matron less picturesque than Lady Cartwright. Poor Mrs Dollis Fairley had always seemed wrapped in bandages rather than draped in Grecian garb—the Mummy, as they'd joked in tap class. Now Angelica was surprised to feel a flash of sympathy for her. For her heavy sadness.

She was offering a class for the same reason

she'd come back to Sydney Street in the first place. Now that Mum was buried next to Dad in the bleak cemetery on the outskirts of the town, there was no real reason to come back, and yet there was part of herself in Longhampton, part of her past that she'd never quite squared up to, and now she couldn't put it off. It wasn't to clear out her mother's terraced house herself—she knew she could have got movers in to do that—it was to make up for all the years of running away.

Besides, Angelica liked teaching, especially now she'd mellowed a bit. It was hard to deal with incompetent learners, and she wouldn't put up with students who didn't listen, or practise, or look for some starry-eyed glamour in themselves, but she enjoyed seeing that moment when the steps clicked in their heads, and a couple discovered they were wound into the music, moving together without thinking.

After all, music was music—it had the same magic here as it did in the ballroom at the Ritz. The moment when suddenly lightened feet moved by themselves, and the dance and the music and the moment launched you round the floor like a boat's sails catching the wind—that was lovely to see. It was almost more rewarding to watch beginners transform and improve under her instruction, than it was coaching the snappy, competitive pros she'd been teaching in London these past few years.

When she could be bothered. It had got harder and harder lately.

Angelica propped the broom against the ancient radiator. That was another thing the old Angelica wouldn't have believed—that the desire to dance might eventually leave her, and it would have nothing to do with her bad neck. It was her heart that seemed to have lost its bounce, not her stiff knees. And Angelica hated going through the motions. She sighed, and told herself that the only thing worse than having a chequered past was not having a past at all.

Then she closed her eyes, hummed the first bars of 'Let's Face the Music and Dance', and began to quickstep smoothly around the hall, her feet moving with a swift sure grace, her arms poised weightlessly, one on an imaginary shoulder, the other held high in the air as her head leaned elegantly first to the left, thcn swayed, as she paused, suspended like a feather in the air, to the right.

And though Angelica started, in her imagination, with Bernard, by the second verse Tony, as always, had cut in and her steps took on a sleeker line.

CHAPTER ONE

'. . . Seventeen, we agreed when I went back to work that Ross would get the kids bathed and in their pyjamas by the time I got home, so we could both put them to bed, but nine times out of ten, they're still running around, which I think is unfair because it means I end up having to take charge and be the mean shouty parent, even before I've got my coat off. Eighteen, he never ever cleans the bath. I know that seems petty, but it means I have to clean it before I can get in, and I'm knackered most evenings. Nineteen, he makes me feel like his mother, or his sister, but definitely not his wife.'

Silence.

Katie looked up from her notebook. That last one might have been a bit much. 'Though his legs aren't bad for a man who doesn't go to the gym,' she conceded.

Ross and the marriage guidance counsellor were slumped in their chairs, not responding, and she felt an unwelcome flicker of frustration, the sort she got when her team weren't on the ball at work. Katie hated herself for feeling it, but then again, if she stopped feeling annoyed at Ross's chronic passivity, she'd start feeling mortified about being here in the first place.

Before she could rein it back in, she heard her own voice snap, 'Look, we're here to get things thrashed out, aren't we? You told us to write a list of the things that weren't working, didn't you?'

'A *list*,' muttered Ross. 'Not a bloody *novel*.'

Peter, the counsellor, shook himself. 'Well, yes,

1

it's good to get everything out in the open. But now let's have your *positive* list about what makes you *happy* in your marriage.'

Katie turned the page, and swallowed. 'One, Ross is a great dad. Two, we've got a nice house. Three . . .' She turned the notebook nearer her so Ross couldn't see she'd only managed to put three things on her list. He'd gazed at her with his puppy-dog eyes when she'd said he was a great dad—which, to be fair, he was—and he might as well have stabbed her. She wished he *would* sometimes. Anything but the wishy-washy predictability that was turning their marriage into a bickering brother–sister arrangement.

Katie Parkinson didn't know what made her happy in her marriage any more. She'd worked hard to get everything she thought she needed for a contented life—decent, faithful, good-looking man, three-bed house with off-road parking, job within a shortish drive of said nice house, two beautiful children—and everyone seemed to be happy except her. She'd pinned her hopes on the therapist diagnosing what exactly was wrong, then fixing it (or confirming it was unfixable), but so far, all he'd done was nod annoyingly while the pair of them squirmed.

Ross looked over at her. 'Is that it?'

'Three,' she went on, playing her final card, 'we have two wonderful children. They make me happy.'

He nodded his agreement, eager as ever to please.

He reminds me of a spaniel, thought Katie, wishing he still reminded her of a bloke. A floppy-eared, soppy, chocolate spaniel with big feet.

2

'We do,' he was saying to Peter. 'Jack's just two and Hannah's four, and they're both wonderful kids. Bright, friendly, really loving and happy.'

'Which he's implying I don't notice, because I'm working full-time, but I do,' said Katie, unable to resist. Stop being such a *cow*. 'Um, four,' she improvised quickly, to compensate, 'Ross has done a lovely job on the garden. We're thinking of getting a conservatory if I get promoted this year. I mean, there are some advantages to those *anti-socially long hours* I work in a planning department, Ross—I do know about building work applications!'

She meant it as a joke, but it came out more barbed than she intended.

Ross and Peter didn't smile. Now she slumped into the hard plastic chair.

There are no problems, only solutions, Katie told herself. It had always been her mantra at work. For the first time in years, she was starting to wonder if it might not be entirely true.

'Ross?' said Peter, turning his kind face towards her husband. 'Why don't you read your list? Why not start with the positives this time?'

Ross shot Katie a dark-eyed look and got out a sheaf of paper. 'OK. We've made the best out of a tricky situation, considering—when the kids were born we did the sums and childcare was going to cost more than I was earning.' He looked up at Peter. 'I'm a graphic designer. I work on contract, and I was doing pretty well, but, you know how much daycare costs these days. Katie's job had better prospects and she earns twice what I did . . .'

When you could be bothered to go out and *get* contracts, thought Katie, though this time she

3

managed to stop herself saying it.

'. . . so it made sense for me to stop at home. I think it takes a strong marriage to cope with a role-reversal like that, but it's working out. Well, as far as I'm concerned, anyway,' he added, with a resentful shrug. 'And the kids seem happy.'

'No, it's *not* working, Ross! Why else would we be here?' protested Katie. Ross was such an *ostrich*. 'It might be working for the children, but it's not working for *us*. You can't just ignore the fact that we only talk about the school run or what bills need paying! And as for . . .'

She brought herself up short. Maybe they should save their dead sex life for round two.

'Finished?' Ross looked annoyed.

'Yes.'

'Carry on, Ross,' said Peter, as if he was used to that kind of impotent squabbling. 'It's good to get all this out into the open.'

How does he put up with it, wondered Katie. Much less find positive things to say?

'Secondly, I feel lucky to be married to such an intelligent, successful woman. I'm very proud of Katie, and what she's achieved. I know there aren't many female town planners, and she's done really well. Her job gives us a good quality of life, and I appreciate that.'

Ross sounded so calm and reasonable. Katie bubbled inside with resentment; Peter would be getting a totally unrealistic view of their life, but the more she protested, the more bitter she looked. And she *hated* this dirty laundry-airing.

'Three, we used to have fun together, and I know we still can, when we make the effort. Four, Hannah and Jack are both healthy and happy, and

4

it's great for them that they've got one of us with them at home.' Ross looked up from his notes. 'They want to see you before they go to bed, Katie, but your overtime's so unpredictable. How am I meant to give them a routine about Mummy and bed if it changes every day?'

'Oh, right, so *that's* why there's no routine in the house,' spat Katie. Ross really knew how to push her guilt buttons. 'It's *my* fault for being a working mother.'

Ross glared at her and his mouth went into a thin petulant line. 'They do have a routine. My routine. It's just *your* life that doesn't have one.'

'But if you're so proud of what I've achieved at work, why can't you see how tough it is for me to do all that and get home by seven? Especially in an office full of blokes just looking for an excuse to accuse me of slacking?'

'Focus on the list,' Peter reminded them.

It wasn't as though she wanted to work overtime. Once she was out of the office, even a ten-minute traffic hold-up felt as if she was being cheated out of precious time at home with Jack and Hannah.

But Ross was talking again, and hitting on the sorest spot of all.

'Five, we've got enough money, so I wish Katie would stop chasing promotion after promotion and just take some time to enjoy what we've got.'

'Yes, but you're not the one looking at the credit-card statements every month!' she interrupted, unable to let Peter think that was the case. 'We *don't* have enough money! You're so short-term about everything—if we want the kids to go to uni, we have to start saving now. Besides, you know I can't *not* go for promotions. It's not as easy as—'

'Isn't it?' Ross flashed back. 'Anyone would think you didn't want to come home of an evening.'

'Well, maybe I don't, when the place is such a pigsty and the kids are running wild,' she snapped.

'They're playing! They're children!'

'Can we get back to your list, Ross?'

'Six, Katie has the most beautiful mouth of any woman I've ever seen.' Ross put the paper down. 'Or she did. Before she started bloody yelling at me all the time.'

Katie was about to respond, more out of guilt than dead desire, that Ross too had lovely brown eyes, or used to, before he started looking like a kicked dog all day, but she shut her beautiful mouth like a trap and glared at him instead.

'Well, there are some very *positive* things there,' said Peter soothingly. 'I think it's helpful for you to listen to each other, rather than go round in circles, as a lot of couples do when there's conflict.'

Katie nodded. That was exactly how she and Ross argued these days: round and round on their own little train-set tracks of resentment, never crossing or getting anywhere.

'OK, good,' said Peter. 'Shall we . . . ?'

Ross waved his papers. 'Don't you want my negatives list?'

'Um.' Peter glanced nervously between the two of them. 'Do you think it would be helpful?'

Ross held up his list. It had just one thing written on it in his sprawling designer's capitals. Capitals that Katie knew she used to find so charmingly creative.

6

What was that awful truism? It was the thing that first attracted you that ends up driving you mad?

'We've stopped trying. Katie has decided it's over, and when Katie decides something, that's it.'

'You're being childish,' she protested, still stinging from the stab of remorse his handwriting had given her. 'I'm here, aren't I?'

'Only because you're trying to audit our relationship! I know what you're doing, Katie, you want someone else to assess us, just like you'd assess some . . . derelict building!' Ross looked furious and pathetic at the same time. 'You want someone else to tell you if we should just knock our marriage down! Well, that's not the way it works!'

'Isn't it? You won't listen to anything I say about making things better . . .'

'That's because it feels like you're the only one capable of making a decision about my life, and yet you're not prepared to try to—'

'Shut up, the pair of you!' roared Peter, then looked stricken. 'Sorry. Sorry. Let's calm down, shall we?'

Katie shook her head in frustration. Her hair swung back into its neat honey-blonde bob, cut every six weeks on the dot—but only because the salon was right next to the council offices. Couldn't Ross see how hard she *was* trying? Forget leaving work early, it had taken all her energy just to find a babysitter, and she wasn't sure she really trusted Gemma Roberts longer than two hours.

Peter rubbed his beard. He was a beard and cosy jumper kind of counsellor. Kind eyes, and real ale. And steely home truths wrapped in warm smiles.

7

'It strikes me, as an observer, that the only positive things you can find to say about your marriage, Katie, involve your house. Is that fair? That your *house* is what makes you happy?'

Ross looked at her, ready to be wounded.

She took a deep breath. The best thing was to be honest about their squabbly mornings and deathly nights. Maybe Peter would be able to decide straight away that they should just cut their losses and split up. That would save everyone time and tears. Knock it down, like Ross said, to save the painful falling apart.

But even as Katie thought about Ross moving out, her family breaking up, her dreams for their perfect life broken, and their seven years together *wasted*, a lead weight of misery plummeted in her stomach.

'Yes,' she said, recklessly. 'My *house* does make me happy. I feel as if I pay all the bills, give out all the discipline, work all the hours, and have none of the fun . . .'

Peter moved in swiftly. 'And how do you feel about your house, Ross?'

'It's our home,' he replied. 'Where we've brought up the children.'

'So you're more of a homebody than Katie?'

'No,' Katie interrupted. 'No, no, no. It's not like I'm *not* a homemaker! I love being at home—I just don't get the chance any more!'

Peter fiddled with his glasses. Katie had already noticed he fiddled with something before making a casually devastating observation. She braced herself.

I don't like who I've become, she thought. Neither does Ross. But what choice do I have?

8

Someone had to go back to work to pay the bills, and if we were living on Ross's income, we'd never . . .

She put that upsetting image out of her mind. Not only was Ross's salary insufficient, he had a lack of ambition that was getting less attractive by the day, and even less idea, apparently, of how much two kids cost. He got the fun of playing with them, teaching them, while she got the shouty, tired end of parenting. It was turning her into someone she didn't know.

'Marriage isn't marked out of ten,' Peter said mildly. 'I'm not going to sit here and award you both points for who's the best spouse, you know.'

'So what are you going to do?' Katie felt got at. She always felt got at these days, one way or another.

Peter smiled. 'I'm going to help you talk through the issues that you have between you, encourage you to listen, and hopefully that'll help you put them right.'

'And how long will that take?'

He shrugged. 'As long as it takes. It's not a quick fix, you know. We recommend six sessions, to give you some focus, but it might take a few more. If you can't fit them in weekly, then we'll try fortnightly. But you've taken the hardest step just by coming here. Don't you feel that?'

Katie felt her frustration tighten like a coil. 'But surely you'll know after a few sessions what we should *do*?'

'Katie, it's not up to me to decide. It's your marriage. But . . .' Again, the glasses. 'The point of coming here is to learn to listen to each other again, and to be honest about what you're feeling.

9

It's not unusual—I see lots of parents who've just stopped making time to be a couple. And if you want to be good parents, which you obviously both do, then there's nothing wrong in investing time in your own relationship, outside of the family. You need to spend some time on your own.'

'Not much chance of that,' snorted Ross. 'Unless I start taking her lunch to work?'

Peter ignored his petulance with an ease Katie wished he could teach her. 'Did you ever have a hobby you took up together? A sport, maybe?'

Katie and Ross looked each other in the eye, properly, for the first time since they'd sat down, and she noticed how tired his face was. She always used to describe Ross to people as 'boyish': chestnut-brown hair that spiked up naturally, large brown eyes with long lashes, a sharp nose that he rubbed unconsciously with his left hand when he was nervous. Ross was wiry, with olive skin that was unexpectedly soft, and Katie used to think, adoringly: when he gets to thirty-three he'll look like that for the rest of his life.

He was thirty-six now, and didn't look boyish any more; he looked slightly crazy. He obviously hadn't had time to shave that morning, and the lines around his mouth were tight with the stress of talking about their marriage. Ross, she knew now, was a denial specialist. He preferred to say nothing and hope she'd guess.

That wasn't Katie's way. Katie was a discusser, a debater, but more and more, she found herself swallowing her questions, knowing she'd get nowhere in the quagmire of Ross's silent emotions, and instead she tried to organise them out of their rut. Which was how they were here.

10

'We used to play a bit of badminton, before Hannah came along,' he admitted. 'We stopped when Katie got pregnant and . . .' The faint glimmer of a smile twitched at the corner of his lips. 'We were pretty good, weren't we?'

'You let me win,' Katie reminded him.

The smile vanished. 'Only until you got better than me.' He looked at Peter. 'Katie's very competitive. She has to win.'

'Great!' said Peter hurriedly. 'Well, I'd recommend you try something new together. Something neither of you have done before, that you can commit an hour or so a week to. Use that time to work together, help each other, let go of the daily stresses, OK?'

'OK,' she said, reluctantly.

'Great! Now, for next week, I'd like you to tell me—separately—about how you met, and what first attracted you to each other.'

What's the bloody point, thought Katie, as they got up and said their goodbyes. We're not those people any more.

*　　　*　　　*

It seemed like a hundred years ago, but it was only seven years since Katie Rogers met Ross Parkinson in a crowded pub in Manchester. She'd got her first town-planning job and was living in a tiny flat in Castlefield; he worked in a design studio round the corner from the pub. Their first conversation, about nothing much, felt to Katie like meeting someone she'd known as a child; though they seemed so different on the outside, on the inside there were little connections that drew them

11

together like magnets—connections that were about taste and touch and look, not logic. Ross had the right boy-smell, the right arty glasses, a shy way of pushing back his fringe—then long and floppy—that twanged some forgotten teenage crush, a sense of humour that made her quiver when he arched his eyebrow, tentatively sharing a joke with her that he didn't think other people would get. There was always something else, something extra that made her feel suddenly she was completed, and that she completed Ross. Something even super-analytical Katie couldn't define.

The first night in the pub led to other dates, not in restaurants, where she used to go with her friends from work, but at gigs, sweaty indie clubs, slow walks along the canal. That summer had been long and sweltering in Manchester, and every memory Katie had of that time brought back a physical tingle: talking into the early morning as the wail of sirens carried on the stifling curry-scented air, or feeling the delicious itch of too-hot sheets on naked skin, while they listened to music in the dark, their arms and legs entwined, happy to be silent together. Ross wasn't her usual type, but she fell in love without reason or explanation, which only made it seem more right.

Back then, Ross hadn't seen her career as something to get angry about. Although Katie might have taken to the suits and Starbucks lifestyle, she wasn't a townie—she'd grown up near Tewkesbury—but she was on a fast-track graduate scheme that had meant she'd stayed in Manchester after her degree course. Her parents hadn't exactly encouraged her to go back, emigrating to Spain almost as soon as she'd qualified, and Katie was nothing if not ambitious.

She'd always wanted to work in town planning, sorting out people's homes and buses and lives, but it was tough, and she'd realised quickly that to get ahead, she had to work twice as hard as the male graduates. After she and Ross had been seeing each other for six months, out of the blue she was offered something better, more money, with more responsibility—but back in the countryside, not too far from where she'd grown up, in a middling-size market town, Longhampton.

It had been a dilemma: Katie had never really adjusted to Manchester, and its busy, chippy attitude made her feel provincial, no matter how slick she looked on the outside. She'd stuck it out for the sake of getting on—something her parents had drilled into her—but leaving Manchester wouldn't be a problem, especially for a job as good as this one. For Ross, though, always busy with design jobs for media companies, dragging him to the middle of nowhere—that was different. That was a lot to ask.

And yet Ross had been decisive.

'Take it,' he'd said, almost before she'd finished explaining.

'But what about . . . us?' They were on the delicate point between spending four nights a week together, and Moving In. 'You have so many media clients, you need to be in Manchester.'

'Ever heard of the internet? Anyway, there are other clients. I'll freelance,' he'd said, and cupped his hands round her face. 'Katie or job? Katie or job? Hmm. Katie.' And he'd kissed her.

Suddenly their relationship was on the same fast track as Katie's career. Within eighteen months

13

they were married, and then Hannah came along, and it had seemed logical for Ross to stay at home for a year, because he could take time out and she couldn't, then when she discovered she was pregnant with Jack, and although she hated leaving Hannah, things seemed to be working . . . Well, why not?

It happened so gradually, like a photo fading in strong daylight, as work, babies, the house, bills shuffled those memories of sticky Manchester nights further away. They pecked kisses at each other instead of lingering over them, they fell exhausted into bed each night, joking about how unsexy they felt, and somehow it was easier to be annoyed with each other about the state of the house than to arrange babysitting for a 'date night' neither of them really had the energy for. Ross and Katie, the beautiful energetic Manchester couple, turned into Hannah and Jack's parents. Two tired people, who loved each other, but not as much as they loved an early night.

One morning Katie trudged to work as usual, handed over a tenner for someone's wedding collection, then when she went to the loo to reapply her make-up at lunch, she found she couldn't stop crying. Her shoulders felt weighted down with some invisible burden, because so many things weren't quite right with the life that seemed ideal on paper.

And now they were here. With just five more sessions to put it right, or finish it off.

*   *   *

When they left, another couple were already

14

waiting on the orange plastic chairs outside Peter's room, their arms tightly folded, heads tensed, not speaking. Without making eye contact, Katie and Ross made their way down the dingy corridor of the community centre, only the sharp clicks of her work shoes breaking the silence between them.

It was hard, she thought, to hear Ross say some of things he'd said, things he obviously hadn't been able to say to her without someone else there. How he knew she wasn't trying. How taken for granted he felt. She thought she'd been covering up fairly well, but though he didn't say much, there was a bottomless well of hurt behind his eyes. No one could suffer like Ross. That was, if she was being truthful, why she couldn't look at him in the counselling session. She wondered if all-seeing Peter had noticed.

She stopped walking and watched him go ahead down the corridor, his shoulders slumped with dejection. He was tall, good looking, and his hair was as thick and dark as when she met him. So what was missing?

The answer was one she didn't allow herself to think often, in case she found herself saying it out loud. It was sexist, selfish, and totally unfair. But it was true: Ross had lost his manliness, the thing that made her want him, the unexpected remark, the feeling of being protected. And it was all her fault.

I used to fancy him so much, Katie thought, as if she were remembering something someone had once told her. I used to stop breathing when he pulled off his T-shirt at night and I saw that prickle of hair on his stomach leading into his jeans. Now I feel like I've got two toddlers and a sulking

15

teenage son, and I feel about as sexy as my mother, and according to the magazines I'm meant to be in the prime of my life.

Ross had come to a halt in front of the noticeboard. Katie noticed that his jeans had flecks of poster paint on them. It didn't look arty any more. It just reminded her that he never sorted the laundry properly.

'What about this?' he said, pointing to a handwritten advert.

'What?' she asked, unable to summon up even pretend interest.

'Singing.' He flashed a brave, fake smile like he would to Hannah. 'Join a choir, no karaoke experience needed!'

'Singing? Seriously? No, thanks.'

'Pottery, then?'

She pulled a face.

'Do you have to be so negative?' he complained. 'The whole *point* is that we try something neither of us can do.'

'Sorry.' Katie shook herself. 'How about . . .' She scanned the jumble of kids' gymnastic lessons and AA meetings. 'Ballroom dancing? Starts tomorrow.'

Ross peered more closely at the ad; unlike the others, it had been created neatly, on a computer, and had silver glitter sparkling around the edges. The harsh strip lights gave it a pretty, animated look. 'Ballroom dancing. Huh.'

'Although you'll have to listen to what the teacher says instead of drifting off and getting me to explain,' she added, waspishly, before she could stop herself.

Ross covered his face with his long, pale hand.

'God, Katie, why are you always trying to pick a fight these days?' He removed the hand and looked at her seriously. 'Listen, I know you think counselling is a huge waste of time, but I really want to try to make things better again. It's just a rough patch. We've got to try. For the kids' sake? Let's do the ballroom dancing. On the proviso, mind,' he added, raising his eyebrow, 'that we only learn dances that don't involve tight satin pants or those fancy fishnet shirts you see on the television. The world's not ready for that.'

'On you or me?' she asked deadpan.

'On either of us.' He paused. 'Although you know I've always had a thing for Olivia Newton-John in *Grease*. So if you want to wear the tight satin pants . . .'

It was a bit lame, but she appreciated his trying. She just wished the trying wasn't so obvious.

'OK,' she said, capitulating. 'Ballroom dancing, then.'

'Great. How hard can that be?' Ross jotted down the details and looked up from his notebook with a hopeful smile. 'Come on. We don't want Gemma to run into a third hour, do we?'

They walked down the echoing corridor in silence, until Katie asked, 'Was that as bad as you thought it would be? The session, I mean.'

'It was what I expected,' he said, stoically. 'Not easy. But, you know . . . Nothing worthwhile is. I want to fix things,' he said, stopping and taking her hand suddenly. 'I really want us to get back to where we were.'

But I don't know if I can, Katie thought. *I don't even know if I want to!*

'A lot's changed,' she managed.

17

'But a lot's stayed the same,' Ross insisted, and they stared at each other for a long moment. 'And we've *gained* so much. Think about all the things we have now that we only dreamed about when we met, Katie.'

Re-mortgages. Love handles. The ability to have sex without waking up. A growing sense of 'is this it?'.

Something cold gripped Katie's stomach, and she heard herself say, 'When did we stop loving each other?'

Ross's face registered painful shock. Then he said, '*We've* stopped?'

Katie looked at him, stricken.

'I haven't stopped,' he said, stubbornly. 'But thanks for the memo about how you feel.'

'Ross!' Katie grabbed for his arm, but he was already storming towards the car park.

CHAPTER TWO

Lauren Armstrong hadn't played netball since she left school four years ago, but in her head, she was still, and always would be, Goal Defence.

'Just stand there, Lauren,' Mrs Hathaway used to yell from the sidelines. 'Stand there, stick those gangly arms out, and don't try anything fancy.'

Lauren didn't need to do anything fancy, because since the age of fourteen she'd been five foot ten, at least three inches taller than everyone else, nine inches taller than her mother, one inch taller than Mr Huddart, the headmaster. And the reason Mrs Hathaway didn't *want* her trying anything fancy was because whenever she did, something usually fell over. The goal post, the other team's Goal Attack, sometimes Lauren herself. But because Lauren did her best, she blocked more goals than she knocked over other players, and was thus nearly always picked for the team, sealing her rather ambiguous self-image for life.

Lauren was now twenty-two, and the Reception Manager/Lead IT Administrator at Longhampton Park Surgery. In a belated moment of revelation, just after her sixteenth birthday, she'd realised that her lanky legs were something to be grateful for, especially coupled with long blonde hair, but sadly her clumsiness wasn't just an adolescent phase. Things kept on getting knocked over. And that was why, now she was months away from being Mrs Christopher Alan Markham, she was determined to be the bride she'd always dreamed about, throughout those freezing-cold matches where she hopped from one long leg to another to keep warm, and everyone giggled about her beanpoles.

On her wedding day, Lauren 'Big Bird' Armstrong promised herself, she was going to be a Disney princess: gorgeous, elegant, graceful and totally, one hundred per cent non-gangly.

Not that it was working out quite as easily as she'd thought. Lauren was a cheerful organiser at work, and an enthusiastic wedding researcher at home, but she hadn't reckoned on her co-planner being even more dead-set on fairy-tale romance than she was. Not her mother, Bridget, who was happy to let her do whatever she wanted, as usual, but the other mother in the picture: Irene 'Call me Mum!' Markham, her mother-in-law-to-be.

Or, as she referred to herself in the wedding notes, MIL2B. Lauren was B2B. Bridget was MOB. And so on.

Lauren was sitting at Irene's marble-topped breakfast bar right now, with a mountain of magazines in front of her, through which Irene was flicking methodically, searching for the glass-slipper cake topper they'd been discussing.

She checked her watch discreetly. They were meant to be waiting for her mum, who was coming over after she'd finished at school, but it was almost impossible to stop Irene. It's almost as if, Lauren thought, she's picturing herself in those dresses, not me.

'If you go for the Sleeping Beauty theme, then you've got your carriage, you've got your lovely big gown, plus you'll get to waltz to "Once Upon a Dream" at the reception.' Irene gave Lauren a meaningful nod. 'Whereas, with Snow White, OK, it's a more distinctive dress, what with the corset and the overskirt, like you say, but everyone'll be wondering, where are the dwarfs?'

'It is my wedding,' said Lauren, in what she hoped sounded like a joking tone. You had to start where you meant to go on with mothers-in-law. And Irene went on and on and on. It took all of Lauren's extensive nice reserves to keep nodding and smiling. 'Mum's Year One class can be my dwarfs!'

'Yes, but do you really want your mother to dress up as the Wicked Stepmother?'

Lauren blinked. So that was it. 'I wasn't planning on making the guests dress up too. But if you think it would be a good idea . . .'

'Ooh!' Irene scrambled for her 'lookbook',

already heavily Post-itted and clogged full of pages ripped out of bridal magazines. 'Apples! I suppose if you go for Snow White you can have apple-themed desserts . . .'

'And if I go for Cinderella, I can have one of those wedding cakes that turns pink, then blue, then pink again like in the film,' said Lauren brightly. 'Irene, can I make myself another cup of coffee, please? I think Mum must be running late.'

'Let me!' Irene leaped to her feet before Lauren could push back her chair. She remembered too late that the last time she'd tried to make coffee at Irene's, she accidentally pulled the handle off some designer storage jar. 'Latte or cappuccino?'

'Whatever's easiest,' said Lauren, blushing at the memory. 'Instant's fine.'

'Proper coffee's perfectly easy when you've got the right machine.' Irene ran her fingers over her latest bit of kitchenware, tapping her shell-pink nails proudly on the chrome. 'Weren't you going to start cutting back on the lattes, though? What about that detox plan we were talking about the other day?'

'We aren't getting married till June,' Lauren pointed out. 'It's only just September.'

'It's never too early!' said Irene as the machine hissed and gurgled. 'You'll be looking at those photographs for the rest of your married life, and you don't want to be wishing then that you'd given up wheat and dairy for a few months.'

'Well . . .' Lauren's stomach freaked out at the thought of no hangover McDonalds till she was a married woman, but she steeled herself. It's not for ever, she thought. Cinderella would not have wheat bloat. 'Did you say you'd got a diet sheet from one of the magazines?'

'I'll dig it out for you.' Irene finished fiddling with the coffee, and set a clear glass cup down in front of Lauren, the cappuccino capped with thick white foam. It smelled delicious.

I'll give up from next week, she thought. 'Ooh, that's lovely. Are you having one?'

'I'm sticking to peppermint infusions,' said Irene and gave her a reproachful smile.

The thing was, Lauren thought, Irene *wasn't* a Wicked Mother-in-law. She meant well, and was quite stylish for someone in her fifties, and nothing was too much trouble when it came to her and Chris's wedding. She just had far too much time on her hands. Since Chris's dad died and the life insurance paid off the house, she hadn't had to work, unless you counted her three mornings a week at the charity shop on the High Street, which Lauren didn't.

'So, have you spoken to Christopher about him learning to ride a horse?' demanded Irene, picking up her pen again. 'Because he'll need to get started with that if you want him riding into the ceremony to wake you up.'

'Um . . .' Lauren hadn't worked out how best to broach that with Chris. Chris still thought— *hoped*—they were having a simple church wedding and sit-down hotel meal. His idea of a big night out was the pub with his mates, followed by an all-you-can-eat at the Peking Tiger, followed by half an hour at Diamondz, the club at the far end of the High Street. But then it was all right for Chris: all his life he'd been the rugby-playing, in-crowd-leading, first-one-to-have-a-car, school-fit-lad type. It wasn't a dream for him, like it was for her.

Irene's pen paused, mid-note. 'You haven't told him about the horse, have you?'

'Um, sort of . . .' Lauren fumbled. She hadn't actually told her own mother about the horse yet, but there had been such a gorgeous photo in one of the wedding magazines, of a bride about her height, mounted on a pearly-white pony, looking so elegant and magical . . .

'Would you like me to have a word?' suggested Irene with a sympathetic half-smile. 'I am his mother, after all.'

The doorbell rang and saved Lauren from answering.

'That'll be Mum,' she said, hastily getting up. 'I'll let her in. She'll have a strong coffee, if there's enough there—three sugars.'

Lauren didn't miss the sotto voce tut that escaped from Irene when she thought she was out of earshot, but said nothing. After a long day wrangling with five-year-olds, her mum needed two cups of coffee in a row, three sugars in each, just to summon up the strength to get her shoes off.

Irene's detached house was big enough to have a front porch, but not a single stray shoe or plastic bag escaped the wicker storage solutions lining the wall. Through the frosted glass, Lauren made out the small, round shape of her mother Bridget. As she opened the front door she caught her hurriedly stuffing the last chunk of a banana in her mouth while juggling a bulging Tesco's bag and her battered leather tote.

'Oops! You caught me—I was ravenous. Haven't stopped all day. Hello, Laurie, love,' said Bridget Armstrong, leaning forward to embrace her daughter.

Lauren hugged her, breathing in the familiar smell: primary-school children, and fresh wipes, and the Chanel No 5 which her dad bought her every birthday and Christmas. 'For the femme fatale beneath the sensible shoes,' he said, every year, and every year Bridget laughed in the same rueful way. A couple of times Lauren had suggested to him that maybe a foot spa or a gift certificate for a manicure might be more up her mum's street, and he'd nodded and agreed, and given exactly the same thing.

She'd begun to wonder if it was some kind of a shared joke.

Bridget hesitated with the empty banana skin for a moment, saw nowhere to hide it in Irene's pristine porch, then stuffed it to the bottom of her school bag. 'So, how's it going?'

'Not so bad,' said Lauren, stepping back to let her in. She and her mum used to talk about Lauren's fantasy wedding in the little kitchen at home, to cheer her up when she'd traipsed home after another miserable netball match. The only problem was that, now it was all real, Bridget didn't seem to grasp the first thing about the sheer scale of what planning a dream day actually involved.

Lauren didn't mind cutting her mum some slack because it wasn't as though she'd ever had to organise one before. Billy, Lauren's older brother by fourteen years, emigrated to New Zealand when she was eleven, and married there, totally doing her out of being a flowergirl, which was what she'd dreamed about before graduating to bridal fantasies. David, her other brother, had got married up in Scotland when she was fourteen, and his wife Vivienne had sorted out the whole thing, up to and including her foul tartan outfit. Vivienne was an event manager and wouldn't even let Bridget choose her own corsage.

No wonder Mum's a bit out of it, Lauren reminded herself. She hadn't even heard of bridal showers.

'I've got one bit of good news.' Bridget unwound her scarf and hung her parka up next to Irene's white wool wrap coat. 'I spoke to Marjorie in the canteen about the cake. You know, the sugarcraft lady? She does lovely wedding cakes, with homemade marzipan, and she'd give me a staff discount.' She winked, her bright brown eye vanishing, then sparkling open again, like a dormouse. 'Three tiers for the price of two! And a sugarcraft bride and groom thrown in. If you tell her what your dress is like, she can make them look like you and Chris.'

'That'd be nice,' said Lauren automatically. It would have been nice too, if she hadn't seen the enormous tower of heart-shaped croquembouche enmeshed in golden spun-sugar Irene had ripped out of *Central Brides* magazine.

Enmeshed. Croquembouche. God. Getting married really expanded your vocabulary.

'Shall I tell her yes, then?'

'Tell who yes?'

Irene emerged in the doorway to the diner-kitchen, brushing imaginary dust off her immaculate cream trousers. Not for the first time, Lauren thanked her lucky stars that the chances of the two mothers wearing the same outfit were low to minimal. Although the chances of Irene turning

25

up in something white and bridal were worryingly high.

'The cake, Irene! I think that's one thing we can cross off the list. How are you? What a lovely pair of trousers.'

'Mwuh.' Irene squinched her face round to airkiss Bridget, who did not, as a rule, do social kissing. 'Jaeger. All in the cut.'

'Very nice. Ooh! Is that a cup of coffee I can smell? I'm just about ready to drop.'

'I'll put the machine on again,' said Irene.

'Poor Mum,' said Lauren, following her through to the kitchen. 'Kids playing up?'

'And the rest. If I put all the little devils on the naughty step every time they deserved it, we'd need a four-storey infant school. Oooh!' She sank down on to a stool, and sighed with relief. 'You've got that to come, Lauren.'

'Mum! I'm twenty-two! I've got years before we even *think* about having kids,' Lauren protested. Then she saw Irene's face freeze as she frothed milk in her special silver jug, and she added, 'I mean, all in good time, eh?'

Irene tipped her head on one side and gazed balefully at her. 'Well, I hope you won't make us wait too long,' she said. 'I can't wait to be a grandmother. Of course, you are already, aren't you, Bridget? It must be wonderful.'

'Of course it is,' agreed Bridget, eyeing the coffee.

'Aren't you sad they're so far away, though?' Irene paused, the cup and saucer held within tantalising reach. 'That's a terrible shame.' She sighed and put the cup down. 'Would you like some sugar?'

'Yes, please.' Bridget stirred the foam into the coffee with brisk movements, then sipped it straight away, not even stopping to comment on the loveliness of the Italian deli cups, bought by Irene on holiday in Milan. 'Ah, lovely—I needed that. So, where have you two got to?' asked Bridget, cheerfully, unaware of the faint moustache of foam on her upper lip.

'Well, we're definite about the fairy-tale theme, but which one *exactly* is still under discussion.' Irene drew her notebook towards her and reviewed what she'd written. Twenty years as an executive-level PA didn't vanish overnight. 'Did you have any thoughts?'

Bridget directed a straight primary-school teacher look at her daughter. 'So we've abandoned the Jane Austen wedding idea now?'

'Yes,' said Irene.

'Er, yes,' said Lauren, wishing Irene wouldn't make it sound as if she was the one making all the decisions. 'Thing is, I tried on some of those empire-line dresses that were in that magazine and they . . . To be honest, they weren't that flattering.'

'I think what Lauren means is that they made her look as if she was four months gone,' explained Irene. 'And that's all very well for those girls that *are* four months gone, but there's no point making things look bad when they're not. Isn't that right, Lauren? We were both agreed, weren't we, and so were the girls in the shop. White just doesn't do much for you, not with your colouring. You want to look peaches and cream, not Bride of Dracula.'

Lauren's head jerked back and forth between Irene and her mother.

Bridget stirred her cappuccino with a deliberate

27

casualness that Lauren knew at once was put on. 'I didn't know you'd tried them on.'

'I popped in on my lunchbreak,' she said, quickly. 'The dress shop was just round the corner from Irene's charity shop, so she dropped in to give me a second opinion. It was just a spur of the moment thing. We can go again this weekend if you want to see for yourself. But honestly, they were grim.'

'Very much so,' agreed Irene. 'Not that you won't look fabulous in the *right* dress, Lauren. We just need to find it. At least we can cross empire line off the list now.'

'It's just difficult,' sighed Lauren. 'They look so lovely in the magazine spreads, but then when you get them on . . .' She grimaced. '. . . it's not what you hoped.'

'You'd look gorgeous in a bin bag, love,' Bridget insisted. 'I still don't know how we managed to produce such a stunner in the first place.' She beamed proudly at Irene. 'I always told her that she'd be grateful to be tall like a model when she grew up. Not a shrimp like me.'

Lauren squeezed out a little smile. That was typical of her mother. Always looking on the bright side. She'd never had to stand with the lads in school photos.

'I know,' said Irene. 'It's a great comfort to me how much our Christopher looks like Ron. He's the image of him in his youth. Anyway . . .' She looked pained, and drew the notebook towards her. 'So to recap, Snow White's Lauren's theme preference, or Sleeping Beauty. Which I myself think would be more romantic.'

'But I've had this idea about the dwarfs . . .'

28

Lauren tried, to no avail.

'Whichever—you're going to need to sign up for some dancing classes now,' Irene went on. 'According to this magazine, most people leave it far too late to learn, and then they make a mess of it on the big day, what with nerves . . .'

'And champagne, if I know Lauren,' Bridget added.

Irene looked up at Lauren. 'Now you don't want that, do you? I've been looking into it and apparently there's a class starting tomorrow in the Memorial Hall in Inkerman Street. Shall I get you and Christopher signed up?'

'You think Chris'll go to dancing lessons?' asked Lauren, dubiously. 'They'll love that at work.'

Chris was the assistant showroom manager at the car dealership his dad had run for years, before dropping dead of a heart attack just after the speeches at his lavish sixtieth birthday party ('The way he'd have wanted to go,' Irene insisted. 'Surrounded by his friends, with a drink in his hand.') Chris was just as natural a salesman as his dad—good at chatting cars and rugby with male customers, just boyish enough to make the ladies want to mother him. The blond good looks and cheeky smile didn't hurt, either. But ballroom dancing wasn't something the lads at the rugby club were going to let him get away with.

'Well, why not tell him about the horse-riding lessons, and if he won't do that, suggest dancing instead,' said Irene, briskly. 'One or the other?'

'Horse-riding lessons?' enquired Bridget. 'Have I missed something?'

'We were thinking about creating a Sleeping Beauty theme with Chris arriving on a horse, like

29

the prince in the story,' Lauren explained. 'Then we could both leave on it, at the end of the ceremony.'

'And what would you do with the horse while you were in church?'

'Ah,' said Lauren. 'Well. I was thinking we could have the service in the park? They're licensed to do ceremonies and we could get that pagoda bandstand whatsit, and cover it in roses so it looks like a bower, or we could do something with thorns that Chris has to cut his way through to get to me, and . . . What?'

She looked up to see her mother glaring at her as if she'd said something stupid. The smile had vanished from her mother's eyes.

'What?'

'Lauren,' Bridget said firmly, 'your dad and I are happy for you to plan whatever you want for your reception—eight-tier cakes, bridesmaids dressed up as rabbits, whatever you like—but you're getting married at St Mary's. You're not getting married in the park.' She raised her hands. 'Isn't that right, Irene?'

'Well, as a matter of fact, I don't think there's anything wrong with going down a less traditional route,' murmured Irene. 'I mean, yes, a church is very nice, but it does rather limit you in terms of putting your own stamp on your special day.'

Bridget looked stunned, but managed to keep a tight smile on her face. 'But, Irene, it's not just about the—'

'It is only the once.' Irene's large blue eyes drooped sadly. 'The one special day in a woman's life, something to look back on and remember for ever. If I had my time again, I know I'd make every

30

possible effort to have the day exactly the way I wanted.'

Bridget softened. 'Yes, well, wouldn't we all, Irene, but . . .' She turned to Lauren. 'You can do whatever you want for the reception, love—I'm sure we can have the whole thing as romantic and fairytale as you want, but for the service . . .'

'Mum, I can hardly do a romantic fairytale with Chris waking me up to symbolise the beginning of our lives together if the vicar's going to make a big fuss about having a horse in church, can I?'

'Well, if you think the *horse* is more important than the actual service, Lauren, then I see your point.'

'You're twisting what I've said.' Lauren's lip jutted out.

'It's not the same as it was in our day, Bridget,' agreed Irene. 'Things have moved on. Young people now, they want to make their own special day.'

With horses, despaired Bridget. When neither of them can ride? The trouble about Lauren's dream wedding was that it was just that—dreams. In her opinion, too many of these weddings set up the happy couple for the worst kind of reality check when they got home and the cake had gone and the bills started to come in. Not that Lauren and Chris were paying for this wedding; she and Frank were standing most of it, at Frank's proud insistence. But then Frank seemed to think it would cost about the same as their modest sit-down-meal-and-one-round-of-drinks affair had done.

Lauren was looking hopefully at her, still holding a magazine advertising Edinburgh Castle

31

as a venue.

It's not real life, thought Bridget crossly. And we shouldn't be encouraging her. But it was something she'd dreamed about so long, through all that teasing at school . . .

'Well, maybe I'm old fashioned,' she said. 'But if you ask me, there's a lot to be said for sticking with tradition, and getting married locally, with your family, in a church.' She paused, and pursed her lips. That hadn't come out right.

Lauren held her breath. The last thing she wanted was for her mother and her mother-in-law-to-be to get into some kind of massive fight even before they'd got the blessing venue booked.

A tense silence filled the kitchen-diner.

Is Irene going to cry? Lauren wondered. She looked on the verge of it. Poor Irene, she thought. It's not that long since she lost her husband. This must be bringing it all back for her.

It was Bridget who spoke first. 'Oh dear. Sorry!' she said, over-brightly, waving her hands in the air. 'I've had a very long day. Don't mind me. Now, what was that about dancing lessons? Eh? Maybe we should go along too, Irene? Brush up on the old foxtrot for the first dance. Frank's not a bad mover, for all he moans about his knees!'

Lauren winced—what was Mum thinking, being so insensitive? There'd be no father of the groom for her to dance with, but the tears had vanished from Irene's eyes as if by magic. 'I'll look into it. Now, have we had any more thoughts about numbers?'

*   *   *

32

On the way home in the car, bought and fixed up for her by Chris, Lauren drove too quickly for Bridget, and she knew her mother was trying to be diplomatic because she didn't say anything.

On the other hand, she could tell she was brooding about something too, on account of the occasional little sigh escaping from her.

Lauren racked her brains for a way of currying favour.

'Do you want to go round to the big Tesco's while I'm in the car, Mum?' she asked, as inspiration and guilt struck at the same time. 'It's my turn for the shopping, isn't it? And I think we're out of cereal. And crisps,' she added.

Before Chris and Lauren got engaged, they'd been sharing a house on the outskirts of the town with two friends from school, but in an attempt to save up for a deposit of their own, Lauren had moved back into her old room at home, while Chris had moved in with his mate, Kian. Lauren missed cuddling up on the sofa, but if she was being really honest, the thrill of 24/7 sex was starting to be balanced by 24/7 cleaning duties. Happily, the old frisson of illicit quickies had returned, just in time to make the wedding seem even more romantic and old fashioned, and Chris certainly made it clear how much he missed her then.

Plus, her mum was mad keen to spoil her, as usual, which Lauren didn't object to at all. There were a few bumps, of course, what with Bridget seeming to think she was thirteen sometimes, not twenty two, but on the whole it wasn't so bad, considering she'd been living away for a few years now. Lauren thought she was pretty lucky to have such a good relationship with her mum and dad. The longer she spent going over wedding plans with Irene, the more Lauren understood why Chris had been so quick to take up Kian's offer rather than go home himself.

'No, it's all right,' said Bridget, as Lauren had known she would. 'Your father and I'll go late-night Thursday. You know what he's like now he's retired—he likes to take charge of something.'

'Well, let me give you some money, then,' Lauren persisted. 'Towards it.'

Bridget flapped a hand. 'Get away. You're barely eating anything anyway. You need to save up, don't you?'

She wasn't saying anything odd, but there was a funny edge to her voice: a sort of tightness. The outward show of normality wasn't quite covering something beneath, especially when Lauren knew her mum so well.

'Mum,' she said, 'what's wrong?'

'Nothing's wrong.'

'There is. I can tell.'

Bridget sighed, then said, tetchily, 'Since when did we start calling weddings *Special Days*?'

'What?'

'Is it one of these non-denominational PC things? If Irene refers to it as "Your Special Day" one more time . . .'

'Mum, it *is* a special day for her. She's only got Chris left, and this is the only wedding she'll get to help with.' Lauren looked across with some surprise at her mother. It really wasn't like her to be catty. 'Can't you give her a break? She was showing me photos of her own wedding the other day—poor Irene had a register office do, in 1978,

34

in Guildford. Pink suit, a bridesmaid with massive glasses, Babycham, and ten guests. She just wants me to have what she didn't.'

Yes, but Irene isn't paying for it, thought Bridget. *And it's not her wedding.*

Instead, she said, 'Lauren, this is your day, not some re-run of hers. I don't want you to end up agreeing to some three-ring circus, just because you're too nice to tell her to, I don't know, *calm it down.*'

'Well, maybe if Ron was still alive, she'd be able to have some kind of vow reaffirmation, but she can't.' Lauren paused, not liking the feeling of her mum sounding jealous. 'Mum, you've got Dad, you're lucky. And you know I've always dreamed of a lovely wedding.'

Bridget sighed. 'I know, Laurie. I want you to *have* a lovely wedding.'

'Well, then, let's just be grateful I vetoed the contract she wanted the ushers and bridesmaids to sign. Fines for unauthorised weight gain, tattoos or hair colour changes? And that was just the men.'

Bridget laughed, and nudged her daughter—carefully, since Lauren's driving was still a bit unpredictable—and they drove in companionable silence for a few minutes, passing the big new supermarket, the posh white villa that Bridget usually told her she'd like to buy if they won the Lottery, and even the 24-hour Donut Diner where Lauren sometimes pulled in to treat them.

'Sorry,' said Bridget, as they turned into Chestnut Grove. 'Sorry for being such an old bag. I don't like it when we fall out.'

'That's OK, Mum,' said Lauren. 'I just feel a bit torn. I don't want to upset Irene, but I don't want

35

to upset you, either. And I'm sorry about the dresses. I wasn't leaving you out. We can go this weekend if you want? I've got plenty I need to see.'

'Don't be silly,' said Bridget. 'There's no need. Irene knows more about things like that than me. I just . . .' Her voice trailed off.

Lauren parked outside their house. Her dad's Rover was in the drive, and lights were on in the kitchen. She could see him pottering about, making a pot of tea, his red jumper making a splash of colour in the little square of light. She'd bought him that jumper a few Christmases back. Lauren was willing to bet he'd never had it on till she came home, and was only wearing it now to please her. 'You just what?'

Bridget sighed and looked wryly across the car. 'It's silly, I know, but I just . . . I just want to be there when you pull back the changing-room curtain, and there you are—my little girl in a bridal gown. I need to get used to seeing you standing there, all grown up and beautiful, or else I'll cry buckets on the big day and set you off, and set your father off, and then where will you be? You'll have to get Irene to find some mother-of-the-bride-proof mascara.'

Lauren heard a wobble in Bridget's voice and tears sprang into her own eyes. 'I know,' she said, taking her hand off the wheel to squeeze her mother's. Bridget immediately clasped it in her own, so Lauren felt the diamond and gold band squeeze against her solitaire. If she had a marriage as solid as her parents', she and Chris would be OK. Forty years, next April, despite her mother's terrible driving, her dad's gardening obsession, and the foot height difference. 'I've got a list of shops I need to go to—will you come with me, on Saturday?'

'I'd love to, Laurie.'

Bridget blinked back the tears threatening to spill. She wasn't a crier, normally, but this wedding was worse than the menopause for hormonal mood swings. Lauren was grown up, with her wedding file and her mortgage leaflets, but not so grown up that she didn't sometimes remind her of the cheery little girl she used to be, so eager to make her mum happy. She seemed very young to be getting married.

A year older than you were, she reminded herself. But things were very diffcrent for her and Frank. Very different.

Maybe it was just the shock of realising how much time had passed without her really noticing, until Lauren was now the age she still felt she was herself, inside, anyway. Maybe that was why it was so hard to say no, as the costs stacked up, and the mad wishlists got ever madder.

'Mum?' said Lauren, concerned. 'Are you OK?'

'Fine. I'm fine,' she said, smiling away the mingled emotions rising up her throat. 'Just hoping your dad hasn't started to make the tea on his own.'

Lauren smiled. 'It'll be the first time in years if he has.'

'Right.' Bridget ran a quick hand through her dark cropped hair, putting the wedding out of her head, and trying to remember if she had everything in to make her emergency tuna bake thing. 'Better go and stop him before something gets burned, eh?'

As Lauren watched her mother bustle up the

path, calling out to her dad as she unlocked the door, she resigned herself to trying on every wedding dress in a twenty-mile radius—for the second time.

CHAPTER THREE

At twenty to eight on Wednesday night, Katie drew up next to an unprepossessing block of concrete 1960s flats and pulled on the handbrake. 'Are you sure it's here?' she said, for the third time.

'*Yes*,' said Ross.

'Did you phone ahead, though, to make sure? It wasn't clear on the poster.' She looked up at the tall, featureless council blocks. 'It *can't* be here . . .'

I should have done it myself, she thought. Then I'd know everything was sorted.

'Katie! I *know exactly* where it is!' He glared at her resentfully, and for a moment she wondered what on earth an hour of stupid dancing was going to do to bridge the cold, echoing space between them. It was so obvious in the car that there might as well have been plate glass between them, even though she'd tried to fill it by telling him all about her problems with the new contractors. 'There's a softplay group in the same place once a week—I sometimes take Jack.'

'OK, OK.' She undid her seat belt, feeling caught offside as she always did when he told her something she didn't know about her own kids.

'It's a Memorial Hall, behind the flats,' Ross went on, getting out. 'The houses round it must have been bombed or demolished or something,

38

but it survived—it's rather nice.'

'I didn't think there was anything like that round here.'

'Really?' Ross replied in his annoying passive-aggressive voice, the one he knew wound her up.

'What do you mean by that? If you've got something to say, then say it! If it's some kind of dig about not taking the kids to bloody softplay, then just say so!'

Katie realised she was standing still, nearly yelling in the street-lit silence of the estate.

Ross stopped too, and looked at her. He didn't raise his voice and his self-control only annoyed her more. 'It's not always about you. I don't *mean* anything. All I meant is that you work in a planning department. I'm surprised you haven't come across it. Is all I meant. Will you stop trying to pick fights and just calm down?'

'I am calm,' she snapped. 'I've just had a stressy day, all right? Remember that regeneration meeting over-running, like I told you?'

Ross said nothing, which was the most irritating response in his armoury of irritating responses. It meant he was thinking something too enraging to speak aloud.

'What?' she demanded. 'Come on.'

'We've *both* had stressy days,' he said. 'Did you even ask how mine went? No.'

Immediately she felt bad. 'OK. How was your day, then?'

He gave her a look, then said, 'Doesn't matter. Forget it.'

Great, thought Katie, it's going to be one of those evenings. One of those evenings where everything we do winds the other up, no matter how hard we try not to let it.

A moment or two passed while they glared at each other in the unflattering yellow light.

We're getting old, she thought. I used to look forward to us getting old together. And if I have to start again with a new man, he won't even have seen the *young* me to make up for these crow's-feet and flab I've got now.

As usual, Ross cracked first. 'Sorry. Come on,' he said, cajolingly. 'Don't want to be late, do we?'

Katie shook her head, harder than she needed to, in order to shake the thoughts from her mind, and followed him towards the Hall.

*   *   *

The Memorial Hall, as Ross had said, sat like a red-brick doll's house between two grey towerblocks, its arched door and Dutch tiled roof making an unexpected splash of colour in the monotone estate. *In Memory of Those Who Fought 1914–1918* was carved into a stone plaque on one side, with *First Stone Laid by Mrs Holloway, Lady Mayoress, 20 April 1922* on the other.

'Pretty!' said Katie, despite herself.

'Isn't it?' Ross pushed open the door for her.

Katie hesitated on the step. Though she cruised confidently into meetings with all kinds of people at work, she always had to give herself a sort of internal nudge; deep down, she was quite tense about meeting new people, afraid that they'd see through her hustle and bustle, or not like her.

But Ross was hovering behind her like a little boy, waiting for her to go first. He always did that. To begin with it had seemed like gallantry; now she

40

knew it was because he wanted her to take charge, so he wouldn't have to. But this wasn't the night to start on that. She took a deep breath and went in.

The Hall smelled like the old church hall her old Brownie meetings had been held in. Like all old halls smelled, she supposed—of Rich Tea biscuits and floor polish, overlaid with an all-pervasive aroma of dust. Blue plastic chairs were stacked against one wall, and crinkled finger-painted pictures marked out the corners where the playgroups congregated, alongside First Aid instructions and recruitment notices for the Samaritans.

But what Katic hadn't been able to see from the simple exterior was that the sides of the Hall were punctuated with arched stained-glass windows, and the ceiling was painted with entwining branches and leaves, flaking in places but still bright. The faded wooden floor slanted in a herringbone pattern, and though the electric light was modern, it came from three hanging clusters of dusty lamps, suspended like bunches of grapes from the beams.

Despite her bad mood, Katie felt pleased by the neatness of it all: it reminded her of an enamelled musical box, faded but ornate in an old-fashioned way. Then she realised there were already quite a few people there, and they were all looking at her and Ross.

'Hi!' she said, going onto autopilot and fixing her smilc in place. 'Hope we're not late!'

There was a young couple in their twenties, another couple about her parents' age, maybe a bit older, two women in their thirties, and a much older couple. Standing a little apart was the woman who Katie assumed, from her perfect

41

posture and neatly positioned feet, was the teacher.

'Of course not. Hello! I'm Angelica,' she said, stepping towards them so gracefully that Katie barely saw her red shoes move.

So that's what an Angelica looks like, she thought as she shook hands, because the woman fitted her name perfectly: dark hair combed back from her high forehead and pulled into a plait, coiled like a snake at the nape of her neck, sharp blue eyes lined with a quick sweep of black liner and a hint of a temper in her long nose with its flared nostrils. She had slender dancer's legs and slim, ringless hands, and a black satin skirt that rippled sinuously around her knees as she moved. She could have been any age between forty and fifty-five.

Next to her, Katie suddenly felt frumpy.

'Now then,' she said, gesturing for everyone to make a semicircle around her. 'Shall we start? Lovely! My name is Angelica Andrews, and I'm going to teach you to dance. Now, I know, from many years of teaching, that not all of you are here because you want to be, especially the chaps . . .' She shot a knowing look towards Ross, and the other younger man. '. . . but I like a challenge!'

Ross let out a nervous giggle, which grated on Katie's nerves.

'Now, I do have one or two things to mention before we begin—don't worry! Nothing too serious—but it does make a difference. So, to start with, I like my students to dress up for classes. Bring out that party dress you've been keeping for best, put on a brighter shirt. Whatever makes you feel special!'

42

Katie felt the sharp blue eyes settle on her for a second, as if Angelica was reading her mind, then they moved on, leaving her feeling oddly defensive.

So I'm wearing a trouser suit, she thought belligerently. So what? It's a very stylish trouser suit. And some of us have come straight from work.

Being the only female planner in a particularly male office meant Katie had had to develop a strategy for being taken seriously by her project development team, and her sharp-cut trouser suits started the mental shift each morning. She was never late, she never shirked the dirtiest assessment jobs, and she was called Kate at work, not Katie. Sometimes even KP. The trouble was, switching out of that tough frame of mind at the end of the day wasn't always as simple as taking off her jacket.

'I'm not saying you have to find white tie and tails and full-length frocks,' Angelica went on, 'but since dancing is all about creating a mood, I always think it gets us more in the spirit of things if you feel dressed up. It makes you stand up properly and feel more elegant, more . . .' She swept out an arm. 'More dramatic. Ladies, be as colourful as you want, but do have a practice at home if you think your skirt might swirl up a bit too high! And no garlic bread before classes.' She looked archly at them. 'That's the first rule of ballroom dancing.'

The older couple murmured agreement to that.

Angelica paused. 'Second rule is to *smile*. Enjoy yourselves. No one wants to dance with a misery-guts, and the third rule is to listen to what I'm telling you, keep your eyes on me, and pay attention.'

43

Her tone suddenly turned fierce, and Katie's attention stopped wandering around to see if she really was the only woman there in trousers, and snapped back to Angelica.

'You might think I'm a bit of a hard task mistress to begin with, but believe me, it's much better to get things right now than to try to correct sloppy technique later,' she went on, firmly. 'It's a courtesy to your partner to make the dancing as easy for them as you can. You don't want to be hauling someone else round the floor, or trying to catch up steps they've missed, or dodging their flat feet. But I'm sure you're all going to be model students!'

The fierceness was replaced by a brilliant smile, which everyone responded to with dancing smiles of their own, automatically.

'So, shall we begin with some names?' Angelica looked round the semicircle, and Katie felt the searching eyes settle on her again, raising her defensiveness like a cat being stroked the wrong way.

'I'm Katie, and this is my husband Ross,' she said, before she could be asked.

'Hey,' said Ross, raising his hand.

Why doesn't he just say hello? thought Katie irritably. He's not in some design studio now.

'I'm Lauren,' said the younger girl, and stroked the arm of the tall blond man next to her. 'And my fiancé Chris.'

They looked at each other and grinned, and Katie guessed that they probably hadn't been engaged very long. It was the half-proud, half-freaked reaction that flickered into their faces when she said the word fiancé. Plus, Lauren kept

44

fiddling with her diamond ring. Katie thought she looked the type to have been practising her married signature for some time.

'We're learning to dance for our wedding,' Lauren explained, as everyone else cooed. 'We haven't decided which style yet, because we're still planning the theme.'

'Oh, you must plan the wedding around the dance you're best at!' said Angelica. She put a finger on her chin, and Katie noted the glossy scarlet varnish with some envy. 'I see you as quite a tango man, Chris.'

His shoulders went back nervously. 'Is that one of those dances where you have to wear satin kecks?'

But Lauren was intrigued. 'Chris, tango?' she asked. 'Seriously? Wow. Can you tell that about people, like what star signs they are?'

Angelica raised an eyebrow. 'Absolutely. But it would spoil the fun if I told you all now, wouldn't it?' She turned to the older couples. 'Now, you must be the bride's parents,' she said to the small dark-haired woman and the tall fair man, standing with his hand on her back. 'I can see the likeness!'

'Yes, I'm Bridget Armstrong, my husband Frank,' she said, in a clear, confident voice.

'It's Mrs Armstrong,' whispered Ross. 'From the primary school. She has the Year Ones. You know, the class Hannah will be in next year.'

'I know what class Hannah's in!' Katie hissed back, as Mrs Armstrong spotted them across the room and gave them a little wave of recognition. Or rather, she spotted Ross. Katie hadn't had much time to go up to school since Hannah's first day, although she'd moved three meetings to be

45

there for the big drop-off at the school gates. Hannah had clung to Ross's legs. It had been left to Katie to pry her fingers away. That had made her feel *great*.

But Angelica was moving on to the next couple: the short man and his amply bosomed wife. 'Now you look like two people who know their way around a dance floor!' she said.

The woman preened modestly. In her sensible court shoes, she was a good three inches taller than her husband, but whereas she was a plain duck in her caramel twinset, he was clearly the mallard of the marriage. His dark hair shone like his black-polished shoes, and a gold watch gleamed under the sleeve of his blazer, matching its bright buttons.

'I think you could say we've had our fair share of practice,' he said, shooting his cuffs. 'I'm Baxter, and this is my good lady wife Peggy. I should say upfront that we're not beginners, but we enjoy a refresher course now and again. Don't we, Peggy? There's always something new to learn. We've been dancing here for years. Since the Ted Preston band days.'

'Well, I'm sure there's plenty you can teach us,' said Angelica.

Katie saw Peggy cast a shy look up at Angelica. 'Of course, we know all about *you*, Angelica,' she said, in a soft, uncertain voice, as if she wasn't used to speaking. 'We've followed your career for years, haven't we, Baxter?'

Angelica looked surprised, and pleased. 'Really?'

Katie was surprised too. She had no idea Angelica had had a career to follow.

46

'Oh, yes,' Peggy started to say, 'you've done the town proud with—'

But whatever else she had to say was lost as Baxter interrupted to grill Angelica about dancing shoes, and what music they'd be having, and whether she'd be 'putting them through those awful modern numbers or sticking to the proper steps'.

Katie watched as Peggy slipped into the background again, looking back and forth between her husband and the teacher. That was one thing she could say for Ross—he never talked over her.

Katie's attention was distracted by the two single women giggling about who should go first. Though they were nudging each other, their eyes kept flicking towards the door, with increasing frequency and desperation.

Office mates, she guessed, coming along to meet some new men. Not that there was any here to meet—as it was, they'd be dancing with each other.

'Now,' said Angelica. 'How about you two?'

'My name's Chloe,' said the taller one with spiralling blonde curls, pushing her round glasses up her nose as she spoke. She looked a bit like a grown-up Cabbage Patch Kid, thought Katie: snub nose, bright green eyes, and all that hair, like a mad Girl's World.

Her mate, on the other hand, looked like a bulldog with indigestion. Her small features were concentrated in the centre of her face, and she seemed liable to snap your arm off, given half a chance. Katie got the feeling she was one of those 'No offence, but . . .' women. 'And I'm Trina. And I've come with her, but I'm not *with* her, if you get my meaning. I'm not one of them. Can't speak for her, mind.'

'Trina!' said Chloe, looking scandalised, but not totally surprised as she nudged her.

'Well, not being rude, Chlo, but you never know!' Trina shoved back, then gave Angelica a direct look. 'Do you get many single blokes coming along, like?'

'I don't know,' said Angelica. 'This is the first week.'

'Bollocks,' said Trina, and Chloe gave her another admonitory nudge.

'Wonderful,' said Angelica, clapping her hands together. 'Shall we get started?' As she made her way to the centre of the room, the group followed her, like a flock of sheep. 'Now, what normally happens is that numbers go up and down according to what the weather's like and what's on television, so don't worry about having someone to dance with. I'll be mixing you all up anyway once you've got the hang of it. So!'

She spun smartly on her heel to face them, putting her hands on her hips as her skirt swung out. 'Before we get on to learning our first dance, we're just going to start with some walking up and down, to get you used to moving together. So stand opposite each other, like this, and put your arms on each other's shoulders.'

Katie turned to Ross and felt self-conscious. She always did when it came to physical activity in public. She didn't like the sense that anything could happen, that she'd have to respond immediately, and in front of other people. Those badminton sessions he'd told the counsellor about had been about as far as she could go—but in those days, she'd been willing to put up with anything to be near him. Ross might have got annoyed at her competitiveness, but focusing on being the best, and doing it properly was just her way of coping with her awkwardness.

Ross grinned, and held out his arms.

He, of course, had no such hang-ups, able to tumble and clown about with the kids, something else that made her feel inadequate.

Grimacing, Katie extended her hands, balancing them on his sloping shoulders. She could feel the warmth of his skin through the cotton of his T-shirt, and it felt strangely intimate, even though the pose was very formal. They were standing toe-to-toe, so she could hardly avoid looking him in the eye. This should feel romantic, she thought. But it's not. It's just the opposite. We're here because we don't know how to be romantic any more.

Ross jiggled his eyebrows at her. 'Is this *the* most ridiculous thing we've done?' he whispered.

'Don't,' she muttered. 'You're putting me off.'

'Oh, lighten up!' he muttered back, and she wanted to explain that she felt stupid, but there wasn't time.

'Come on, Katie, relax a little—you're going to dance, not wrestle with him!' observed Angelica, suddenly materialising behind them. 'Now, hold it everyone and just watch these two,' she said, to Katie's mortification. 'I want you to walk backwards, Katie, while Ross walks forward. And off you go. It's a trust exercise. No, no! Don't look down, don't look at each other's feet, just look at each other! Take your pace from Ross, Katie! And Ross, don't think about the step, just think about looking at Katie, and moving to the space she's in.'

Katie winced as Ross trod on her toe.

'Ow!' she said, accusingly, glaring at him.

'Now that was your fault, Katie,' said Angelica.

'How? He trod on my toe!'

'You were pulling him backwards. Carry on. Just walk . . . and walk . . . and, no, you see you're doing it again. You've got to let *him* lead *you*. Do you want me to show you?'

Without waiting for Katie's response, Angelica moved between them, put her hands on Ross's shoulders, and nodded at him to start walking forwards.

'Can you see? I'm watching him, reading his face for signals, and step, and step, and step . . .'

Katie watched as Ross and Angelica glided towards the back of the hall, their legs moving in perfect time, their eyes never leaving each other's. Ross's forehead, creased in concentration to begin with, unfurrowed and a smile spread across his face as if Angelica had just pulled off a magic trick, rather than walked ten metres backwards.

'See? Now, ladies, show me your *soles* as you walk back—it'll help get your feet out of his way . . . Lauren, point your feet! Oh dear!'

Katie couldn't help feeling a surge of relief as the big blond lad trod squarely on Lauren's foot, causing her to yelp aloud. He looked even more flustered than she did.

Angelica sashayed across to them, and took over from Lauren, her tiny neatness making him seem even more hulking.

'Come on,' said Ross, holding out his arms. 'Let's give it another go.'

Grudgingly, Katie put her arms on his.

'Watch my face,' he said. 'I'll raise my eyebrows

when I'm going to start.'

'You don't have to patronise me,' she grumbled. 'Just because you did it right once.'

But Ross was raising his eyebrows and moving his feet, and she tried her best to keep in step with him, guessing when he would step forward.

'You're pulling him, Katie!' carolled a voice from across the room. 'Just let him move into your space . . .'

'Is she picking on me?' Katie muttered. 'How come she's watching us the whole time?'

'She's watching everyone,' said Ross, 'and one, and two, and three, and four . . . Ow!'

'What?'

'You trod on my foot.'

'No, I didn't.' Katie paused. 'You left it in the wrong place.'

'And now we're going to go the other way,' announced Angelica, 'because sometimes ladies go forward and men go back! So, ladies, step forward, and aim for the place where your partner is now, and *step*, and . . . Katie, you're much better at this one, aren't you!'

'Eff off,' muttered Katie, staring at Ross's face.

'Shh!' he giggled.

'Stop giggling,' she said crossly. 'It makes you look like a girl.'

There was a screech and a clatter from the other side of the room, and when Katie looked round, she saw Lauren and her fiancé (Chris, was it?) in a heap by the stacked chairs.

'Well, that's a first!' cried Angelica. 'Normally that doesn't happen until we get on to spins! Get up, the pair of you, come on, nothing's broken!'

'Face it, Katie, we're not that bad,' said Ross.

'Only because I refuse to show myself up,' said Katie, gritting her teeth. 'Right, now you go forwards . . .'

*   *   *

It took a good fifteen minutes before Angelica was satisfied that they could all walk up and down without maiming each other, but eventually she announced that they were about to learn their first proper dance.

'Now,' she said, clapping her hands, 'let's start with a rock'n'roll step! It's a very basic, easy step to do, and if you don't want to move those feet, Christopher, you can more or less stand still and let Lauren do all the fancy stuff around you.'

'Good,' said Lauren with a sideways glare.

Things *hadn't* improved and Chris *hadn't* got the hang of it. In fact, she was totally gobsmacked by how inept Chris—king of the jinking side-step on the rugby pitch—was at something so simple even she could manage it.

'Now, rock'n'roll, or jive, is what you'd do if you were at a wedding reception and the band played "Reet Petite" or "Rock Around the Clock", or something like that,' Angelica went on. 'In fact it's the one everyone's dad does as soon as the DJ starts playing any kind of modern music,' she added to Lauren's parents, with a wink. 'Fits in with everything, doesn't it?' She stretched out a hand to Frank. 'You look like a man who's done a few of these in your time—do you mind demonstrating a rock step with me? If you don't mind, Bridget?'

Bridget's face glowed with amusement at

glamorous Angelica dancing with her Frank in his slacks. 'Not at all.'

Katie saw Lauren nudge Chris with an 'oh no!' expression on her face that didn't cover her pride.

Angelica took Frank's hands, and talked to the class over her shoulder as they began to move. 'We're just transferring our weight to the left, to the right, then onto a backstep,' she said, turning her hip out, 'and then . . . Oooh!'

Frank spun her round, sending her skirt wrapping up her legs, then spun her back the other way. Angelica laughed and took up the challenge, dancing forward, changing hands in a little spin as Frank spun behind her, then they stepped straight back into the basic step, in perfect time, and with no apparent effort.

Katie stared in amazement. It was so smooth! Frank looked like the sort of man who only got excited about lawnmower catalogues.

'Woah woah woah!' said Lauren. 'Slow down, Dad! I didn't get any of that!'

'That's a bit advanced,' said Angelica, as Frank twirled her again, this time with his hand over her head. 'Now! OK! Enough! I think we've had a preview there of what your dad'll be doing at your wedding reception,' she said, patting her chest, pretending to get her breath back, as Frank returned, pink with effort, to Bridget's side.

Katie flicked a nervous glance up at Ross, but he seemed to be hanging on Angelica's words.

'We'll do it together, to start with,' said Angelica. She shouted out the steps as they stamped painfully from one foot to the other. 'Keep it *small*. And now the lady's steps . . . Other foot, Katie!'

Thanks, thought Katie, muddling up her left and her right foot again. Draw attention to me, why don't you?

Angelica's eyes were everywhere, and her tone swooped from encouragement to gentle teasing to pretend dismay. 'Don't step *out*, Chris, you're not doing aerobics, just transfer your weight from one side to the other, and back step, that's it! That's it, Lauren—if he carries on galumphing we'll just box him in with two chairs. I usually have to box someone in till they get it, don't worry . . . Now, it'll all make sense once I put some music on. What do you fancy, Bill Haley? Some Elvis? Let's have a look . . .'

Angelica started 'Summertime Blues' on her CD player, clicking her fingers loudly to the beat.

Katie watched the two older couples enviously as they swayed with minimal effort, their actions gliding elegantly from one into the next. They made it look so easy, as if they were the teenagers, and the rest of them were the old crocks, shuffling awkwardly through the basics. She wondered why they were there at all, but if Angelica wondered that too, she didn't show it.

'Oh, Baxter, you've got a lovely action there,' she said, sashaying up behind them, mirroring Peggy's steps. 'Peggy, you're a lucky lady.'

'Thank you, I know,' said Peggy, her Hush Puppies making no sound on the parquet, as Baxter swung her out, spinning her in a step they'd probably learned twenty years before Katie was born. She kept checking his face for signs, Katie noticed, and then checking Angelica's for approval.

The other two, the Armstrongs, were much less

showy, dancing with each other as if they were just at a wedding, and the smiles they flashed occasionally were sweet 'remember this?' ones.

'It's all coming back to me now!' she heard Mrs Armstrong giggle as they passed.

Next to them, Chris swung Lauren the wrong way, nearly dislocating her arm.

'Ow!' she yelped, clutching her shoulder and glaring at him with a mixture of annoyance and surprise. 'Chris!'

'You were going the wrong way,' he explained.

'No, she wasn't!' said Angelica. 'Here, let me show you again . . .' And she took over from Chris, one hand slipping easily around Lauren's waist, even though Lauren towered over her. 'Slow, slow, and back, and slow, slow, lift-your-hand-on-the-slow-so-she-knows-you're-going-to-spin and slow and slow, and there you are.'

To Lauren's visible surprise, they'd executed a flawless turn, so neatly that her pink mouth dropped open. 'Wow!' she said. 'Chris, quick, try again before I forget how to do it.'

And she grabbed him and started counting.

If they can do it, I should be able to, thought Katie, and turned back to Ross.

'Want another go?' she asked. 'Before the music stops?'

'Yes,' said Ross, and smiled.

She could feel there was something in the rock'n'roll music that was trying to make her dance, and she wanted to—she really *wanted* to get the steps in the right order, so she and Ross could glide like Baxter and Peggy, or even Frank and Bridget, who were merrily chicken-stepping away like teenagers in slow motion.

But it wouldn't come out. Katie could see herself dancing in her head, but when she tried to match her steps to Ross's, her coordination seemed to vanish, leaving her feet hesitant as she trod on him, twisting his fingers.

'Tell me!' she snapped at him. 'You've got to tell me when you're going to spin me!'

'I'm trying,' whined Ross, 'but you won't look at me.'

'It'll come!' called Angelica as she passed, drawing attention to Katie's ineptitude. Her face burned.

How this was meant to fix their marriage, she had no idea. If anything it would prove how totally out of touch with each other they really were, in the cruellest possible way.

CHAPTER FOUR

Friday night, for the Parkinsons, was At Home Friday. Having given up all hope of ever seeing the inside of a restaurant without colouring books again, Katie and her best friend Jo took it in turns to simulate going out for dinner in each other's houses, with the kids tucked up in bed upstairs. The money they saved on babysitters was reallocated to a decent bottle or two of wine.

Katie and Jo Fielding had met at antenatal class, had an illicit cappuccino afterwards, and been good mates from then on. Hannah and Molly were both nearly five, and Jo's baby, Rowan, was a few months older than Jack. But whereas Katie had gone back to work soon after Jack arrived, Greg's

56

well-paid IT consultancy meant that Jo could afford to pack in her job at the estate agency and be a full-time mum. As it was, Ross now saw more of Jo than Katie did, with playgroups and school runs, but she looked forward to their rushed lunches and Friday nights. She always got a laugh with Jo.

Katie could have done without the hostess duties that Friday, with her new project starting to stack up overtime, but the chance to get some friendly adult company was something she'd move mountains for.

'Sorry I'm so behind with dinner,' she apologised for the third time, struggling to get the elastic band off the chicken's scaly legs so she could ram some lemon up its cavity. A hugely expensive, organic unwaxed lemon, purchased eight minutes previously from the nearest cornershop. 'Ross used the last lemon to make pancakes for madam—Hannah's a vegetarian now, apparently—but he didn't tell me until I'd got in from work and started preparing the food, *after* I'd cleaned up the pancake mess, so I had to rush out again while he was bathing them and—'

Jo put a hand on Katie's arm. 'Katie. Calm down. There's no rush.' She topped up the wine glass next to the chopping board. 'The kids are in bed, the wine's on the table, the husbands are talking about . . . something, and there's no babysitter to run home at midnight. I don't want you to get wound up about supper—I don't *care* what time it's done. You and I are going to have a glass of wine and *relax*.'

Katie gave the lemon a final cross thrust and banged the chicken in the tin.

'Or do I have to put something in your drink?' asked Jo. 'I will. I've got some Medised in my handbag, you know.'

Katie managed a wry smile. 'Sorry,' she said, running her hands under the tap. 'It's just work. I've been moved onto a big new project, town regeneration? It's going to be good for me, but every time I leave the office for ten minutes, they seem to arrange another meeting.'

'Leave the office in the office,' said Jo, firmly. 'You're at home. With your friends, and your husband.'

Katie took a large mouthful of wine. 'Oh God,' she said, staring helplessly at the chicken, lying in the tin with its legs splayed lasciviously, as if it was about to have a smear test. 'Where's the elastic band to tie it back up again? And I forgot to weigh it. How long would you give that? Roughly?'

'Here,' said Jo, handing her the bottle of wine, as she searched through the jumbled kitchen drawers for string. 'Let me.'

The string would find Jo, thought Katie. She was like that these days: a domesticity magnet. Jo was one of those women who made complete sense as a domestic goddess, but without ever making a big deal about it. She didn't need to. Everything about motherhood seemed to suit her. Jo hadn't lost her baby weight after Rowan, despite promising to come with Katie to the Yummy Mummy Bums and Tummy class at the sports centre, but she actually looked better than she had done in her skinny, suited, estate agent days. Now she wore lots of flowing skirts and soft smocks, and had the sort of hips that babies fitted onto instinctively, moulding themselves into her cosy shape. Jo exuded good sense and kindness like a chocolatey perfume, and was completely oblivious to how attractive it made her. There was something about her you just wanted to touch.

Katie's stomach was flatter but she still envied Jo. Keeping two steps ahead of Eddie Harding had helped her squeeze back into her old suits, but she knew she looked about five years older these days as a result.

'Now, you said, when you went back to work, that you weren't going to let it drive you mad,' Jo reminded her. 'Ah, there's the string, excellent!'

Katie hesitated, then sighed apologetically. 'It's not work, so much as . . .' She stopped herself, not wanting to let her negativity spoil the evening. 'I suppose it's feeling autumn starting to set in. I really felt it parking the car just now. It's bloody cold out there.'

As she spoke, a gust of wind whipped around the house, rustling leaves across the little yard and flicking the first drops of rain against the window. The long Indian summer had finally finished, and now the crispness of autumn bit into the air.

'I *love* this time of year,' said Jo, pushing back her long curly brown hair into a clip to keep it out of her round face while she ground pepper and sprinkled salt on the chicken. A few curls escaped, and she tucked them behind her ear absent-mindedly. 'You can wrap up warm, so no one can see your spare tyre, there's always an excuse for hot chocolate, and Molly's happy to play in the leaves for *hours.*'

'Yeah, but you want to try doing site inspections when it's lashing with rain,' said Katie. 'Sorry! Sorry. OK, I've stopped now. No more work.'

She took another sip of wine. With the chicken ready for the oven and still no sound from the kids upstairs, she felt softness begin to creep around her edges.

'I love your kitchen,' said Jo, unexpectedly. 'It's so homely and warm.'

'Are you insane?' Katie boggled her eyes. Ross was supposed to have blitzed the house before the Fieldings came round, but as usual he'd spent the afternoon making everything even more chaotic, dressing up with Hannah. 'Do you not *see* grime? Or bodged DIY?'

'Seriously, Katie, Greg took the kids' potato prints off the fridge. He said it would ruin the finish. Ruin the finish! With a cleaner three times a week!'

Katie didn't think that was anything to complain about, compared with Ross's constantly broken promises about housework—Greg had, after all, paid for the total refit of the kitchen—but she smiled anyway.

Jo bent down to put the chicken in the oven, and when she stood up her face was serious.

'But listen, while we're in here on our own,' she said, 'what's going on? How are things with you and Ross? I thought there was a bit of an atmosphere when we arrived.' She gave Katie a concerned look, searching her guarded expression for clues. 'It's not just about the lemon, is it?'

'Yes. And no.' Katie struggled. 'The lemon is just . . . typical.'

'Come on, tell me. I'm not stupid, I can see there's something wrong between the two of you.'

She looked up at Jo's open, caring face, and suddenly felt an overwhelming need to get rid of the guilt and misery and resentment that had built up inside her, week after week. Katie's mum wasn't the sort of woman who encouraged unburdening, to or from her daughter; Katie couldn't ring her now to confess, even if she'd wanted to. Which she didn't. More than that, telling someone there were problems would make it official.

'You're allowed not to be perfect,' Jo added. 'None of us is.'

Her tone was so close to the comforting, practical one Peter the counsellor used that something in Katie broke.

'No,' she admitted. 'Things aren't great right now. I mean, we're not actually fighting or anything, and there's no way I'd do that in front of the kids, but . . .'

'Get it off your chest,' said Jo.

So Katie told her, a thinned-down, abridged version of how Ross's martyred, asexual dependency was driving her mad. She didn't mean to go as far as telling her about the counselling sessions, but somehow, on the tide of confession, it all slipped out, and as she spoke a weight seemed to lift from her shoulders at the same time as a new depression hit her.

'. . . And I'm mean to him because I'm tired, but I'm tired because I work a full day in the office, then come home and have to put the washing on, because Ross only remembers to wash the kids' stuff, and make some supper, because he'd just have cereal if it was up to him, and make sure the phone doesn't get cut off, because the bill's not been paid on time because *he* doesn't pay bills—he doesn't have time. He doesn't care about making *me* happy, just the children. And I really, really miss the kids.' Katie topped up her own wine glass. 'I miss Jack. I miss putting him to bed. I don't get to see him do new things, I just *hear* about them. Ross gets to look after the children, and I get to look after Ross. Which wasn't the deal.'

'I know,' said Jo, sympathetically. 'You both sound under so much pressure. But you and Ross are a *great* couple. You really work with each other.'

'So everyone says.' Katie stared blankly out of the window towards the swing in the garden. *Everyone* didn't have to live with Ross—the whiny, needy, selfish husband, not the 'everyone's mate' Dad-of-Hannah-and-Jack. She shook herself. 'Anyway. We've started ballroom dancing classes— homework, by the counsellor—so never let it be said I didn't try.'

'And did you enjoy it?' asked Jo.

'If I'm honest?'

'Katie, when are you *not* brutally honest? Well, did you?'

'Not really.'

'Why?'

'Oh, I suppose I wanted Ross to sweep me off my feet, and for everything to be magically made better, but . . .' She smiled wryly, though she didn't feel there was much to smile about. 'We're rubbish at dancing, Jo. Ross kept stamping on my toes, I kept pulling him around, apparently, and the teacher's got it in for me, I swear to you. She loved Ross, of course. He gave her his "my wife pushes me about" look, and she couldn't do enough for him.'

Jo ignored that. 'But you're going again?'

'Yes, we're signed up for the full course.' Katie

62

pretended to look horrified. 'If we don't kill each other first. I mean, we weren't the worst ones there, thank God, but Ross is hopeless at leading. I don't think he really enjoyed it much.'

'No, he loved it!' insisted Jo. 'He said he had a great time, and you and he had a bit of a laugh afterwards. I think he— What?'

Katie stared at her, an unexplained feeling spreading through her stomach. Resentment that Ross now spoke to Jo more often than she did? Annoyance that Ross was lying? 'How do you know?'

'Oh, he just mentioned it when I saw him at playgroup yesterday,' said Jo. 'And before you say anything, I didn't bring it up—*he* did. Now, he wouldn't have done that if he hadn't quite enjoyed it, would he?'

'Did he say why we'd gone?'

Jo shook her head, dislodging another springy curl. 'Not at all. He just said it had been a fun evening.'

'Jo, will you do me a favour?' pleaded Katie. 'Will you and Greg come next week? For moral support?'

'Course we will!' She smiled and Katie felt a bit warmer inside. Then Jo's forehead creased. 'I'll definitely come—and I'll tell Greg, but he's working away from home a lot at the moment, so I'm not entirely sure what time he'll be back. He was away in Birmingham two nights this week.' She brightened up with an effort. 'But yes, count us in.'

Katie privately thought Greg's business success wasn't something for Jo to be getting stressy about. He supported them all, played tennis regularly, and wore proper shirts with cufflinks and ties that he could loosen sexily at the end of the day. Katie could forgive a few late nights for all that.

'Well, when there's just one of you working you never feel like you *can* stop chasing up business,' said Katie. 'It won't be because he doesn't *want* to spend time with the three of you. It'll be because he wants to make sure you can go to Disneyland again in the spring. You do have the best holidays, you lot.'

'I know. I know,' said Jo. 'Shouldn't complain! Anyway, dancing. Yes. We'll be there next week.'

'You have to wear something suitably glitzy "to get you in the mood",' said Katie. 'And be prepared for some very personal observations about the size of your feet.'

'Really?' Jo looked doubtful. 'I'm not sure I've got much that's not maternity wear. I'll have to go shopping. Want to come? How about tomorrow?'

'Can't,' said Katie, with a rueful twitch of her mouth. 'I told Hannah I'd take her to that indoor playground that's opening in Stratton tomorrow. I've promised.'

Katie made a lot of promises to Hannah, to make up for not being there for spontaneous treats. Keeping them took every spare ounce of effort and time, but she was determined.

'Sunday, then?'

'Jo, I just don't think I've got time,' she sighed. 'It's like I said, work's mad. I've got to fit in some paperwork this weekend too, along with getting the shopping in, and I get so little mum time as it is.'

Jo thought hard. 'Hmm. Well, how about we all go to the shopping village on Sunday morning—Ross can do the big shop with the kids, because I *know* Hannah loves supermarkets, and you and I can whiz off to the outlet mall? Then we can go for milkshakes while Ross gets an hour or two off to himself? Come on, we can kill three birds with one stone—you can get Hannah and Ross's birthday presents, something for you to wear, plus we can sort out their surprise at the same time?' Jo grinned. 'Multi-tasking!'

Katie put down her wine glass and squeezed her eyes. The birthday surprise: a trip to Center Parks during half-term, so Hannah could swim and Ross could . . . do something that didn't involve looking after the kids. Trail biking. Nothing, even. That's what had been at the back of her mind today. 'I haven't even thought about that yet.'

Hannah and Ross shared a birthday—October 24—which only made their 'daddy and his girl' bond even stronger. It also meant that she and Ross hadn't been able to have a romantic dinner out on his birthday since she was born. This year, of course, Katie's idea was that Jo and Greg could entertain the kids while Katie and Ross got the chance to spend some lovely grown-up time together. It would cost a fortune, but Katie's overtime would cover that. The only hard thing was making time to arrange it, since Ross did most of the domestic arrangements, and so far, work and resentment had pushed it to the bottom of her to-do list.

If Katie was being honest, right now she cared a lot more about proving to Hannah that Mummy was just as much fun as Daddy, than she did about proving to *Daddy* that she could still be fun. But you've got to try, she told herself. It's when you stop trying that you know it's over.

When she looked up, Jo's expression was

sympathetic, not disapproving, but Katie felt guilty all the same.

'Well, you've been busy, haven't you?'

'I have,' she protested. The redevelopment project was going to be massive, with new shops and new housing and if she performed well, there was every chance she'd get promoted by the end of the year. If she made it that far. Katie gazed hopelessly round the messy kitchen. Last night's clean washing was still in the dryer. That night's dirty washing would still be in a pile in front of the washing machine if she hadn't hidden it in the pull-out vegetable drawer. 'Really, I don't know where the week goes. It's not like I haven't been thinking about Hannah's birthday, it's just that I can't make personal calls at work and then . . .'

Her voice wobbled dangerously, with sheer exhaustion.

Before she knew it, Jo had swept across from the other side of the kitchen and was wrapping her in a warm hug. She smelled of babies and fabric conditioner, and Katie was overwhelmed with a desire to burst into tears, right on Jo's velvety shoulder. She didn't dare speak in case she did.

'Give yourself a break. You're under a lot of stress,' murmured Jo, patting her back. 'I know how hard you work.'

'It's not just that,' mumbled Katie.

It was the pressure, the constant pressure from everyone, to do everything, at home, at the office, with the lawyers, with the developers, with Ross . . .

But Jo was talking over her head, as if she'd forgotten she used to work twelve-hour days as a matter of course.

'Seriously, Katie, you've got to get your

66

priorities right. You and Ross. Sort it out. Sod work. There'll always be another job.'

But if I don't work, we won't have anywhere to *live*, thought Katie, wildly. If I don't work, the kids won't see the inside of a softplay centre again, let alone have birthday parties there. If I don't work, and I have to leave it to Ross to support us, it's definitely game over for our relationship. I can't even rely on him to recycle the newspapers.

The weight of responsibilities crushed her chest so hard that for a second she couldn't breathe. How could Jo possibly understand? She had unlimited credit cards, a husband who put a roof over their head and two cars in their drive, and a mother who was permanently on hand for emergency babysitting.

'Hmm?' said Jo, pushing her to arms' length so she could scrutinise her face. 'If you need some time together, tell me. I can take the kids— honestly, I don't mind.'

Katie knew she wouldn't mind, and also that Hannah would be thrilled to spend more time in Molly's pink-tastic playroom.

'It'll work out,' she said, and reminded herself horribly of her own mother, and the cover-all clichés she trotted out when she didn't want to acknowledge her unhappiness. Katie knew she was going the same way: the more stressed and desperate she got, the more she felt obliged to pretend otherwise. The only difference being that at least she knew she was doing it, and she wasn't teaching Hannah to mix her gin and tonics.

*   *   *

The chicken tasted better than normal, and Katie knew it was because Jo had discreetly done something to it while she was getting the pudding out of the freezer. She knew how to do things like that. Then again, Jo had the time to read the home sections in the back of magazines—the ones that told you what seasonings to scatter to make ready-meals taste like restaurant food. Somehow, it even looked better on the plate.

That might have been the candlelight, though. Katie gazed at her dining table, which spent more time as a newspaper-covered easel than a centre of witty dinner conversation. It had been Ross's job to run round the house tidying up while she got supper ready, and though the sitting room was still a tip, he'd done something clever with a sheet over the table, and stacks of candles down the middle and the effect was quite elegant, making the glasses sparkle and everyone's faces seem less worn-out.

'Top you up, Katie?' Greg had the bottle poised over her glass. It was a 'good bottle', one from some wine club that he belonged to. He'd explained it to her at some length while Ross and Jo were discussing car seats and the problems of getting ingrained chocolate out of same.

'Um, just a little,' she said. Two glasses made her feel relaxed, but more than that and she was liable to turn maudlin and, at the moment, who knew where that would lead.

'Sorry, Jo, you're driving tonight, aren't you?' he added, as he passed Jo's half-empty glass by.

'Or we could get a cab?' muttered Jo.

Greg didn't seem to hear her as he turned his attention back to Katie.

'Katie, I meant to ask you about office interns,' he said. 'I've been talking to my personnel officer about getting one in next year—we seem to go through temps like nobody's business. You've got them in your office, haven't you?'

'Well, yes.' She leaned back a little in her chair, gratified by Greg's attention. 'But you really need to get the selection process right—I've had some real problems with mine this year . . .'

Greg made an interested mmm noise, and loosened his tie, exposing the tanned hollow of his neck beneath the blue shirt as he pushed himself away from the table. 'Really? In what way?'

Katie dragged her gaze away from the smoothness of Greg's throat. 'Oh, it's amazing how quickly they get into office politics, specially if they're smart. Mine's made an alliance from hell with my own boss, and I think he's blind-copying him into all our email correspondence, just to catch me out . . .'

'Sneaky little bastard!' said Greg, then winked. 'Have you got evidence?'

She noticed, as they were talking, that Ross's attention was drifting away. It always did when she and Greg got on to business stuff. Jo pulled a conspiratorial face and leaned forward to talk underneath them. Ross's eyes immediately brightened.

I wish he'd look at me like that, thought Katie. I wish he saw me as someone he could gossip with. Is that my fault?

'Katie?' Greg prompted her.

'Oh, I've got my eye on Scott. He doesn't know but the security camera's trained on a spot very near his desk, so I know all about his long lunchbreaks . . .'

'Did you hear about Leigh Sinton complaining to Mrs Hodge about the snacks at playgroup?' murmured Jo, and Katie heard Ross laugh in response—a light, unfamiliar sound, not like the nervous giggles he made at dancing.

'Really?'

'Apparently she threw a real wobbler in her office because they'd used chocolate in the crispy cakes they made last week, and didn't use some fancy kind, can't remember what. Delphi's allergic to supermarket own brands.'

Ross laughed again. 'Unlike her mother, who tells me she *only* goes to Aldi for her prosciutto.'

'It's the only place to go,' agreed Jo, deadpan.

'But not on a Wednesday,' he added, and Jo giggled this time—it was obviously a running joke they had.

God, he sounds like a girl, thought Katie, crossly.

At least he was talking though. Ross had been notably quiet so far, not contributing anything to the conversation about who the reliable builders were in Longhampton and being a bit sarcastic, Katie thought, when Greg mentioned the problems he'd been having with his new car.

Ross and Greg never had much to say to each other, although clearly he and Jo were the French and Saunders of the school gates, with that in-jokey banter. There had been a time, she remembered rather sadly, when it had been she and Jo cracking jokes about leaky breasts and Kegel exercises. Well, mainly Jo.

Katie sipped her wine and tried to keep her face interested in Greg's HR problems while Ross did a silly voice that she assumed was some mother she hadn't met.

Then Jo stopped laughing, and she heard Ross say, 'Oh, here we go', and something ambiguous in his tone made her look up.

Hannah was standing in the doorway, her golden-brown hair tousled adorably around her heart-shaped face, her too-big pink Angelina Ballerina pyjamas wrinkling over her feet. She blinked in the light of the dining room, like a surprised mole, and clutched her Beanie sheep, Baalamb, once white and now grimy grey, in both small hands.

Katie's heart turned over once, with pride at the gorgeousness of her own daughter, then turned over again with frustration as she felt the final threads of a grown-up evening slip from her hands. Just an hour or two, at home, off duty, with her friends—was it so much?

'No show without Punch, eh?' said Greg, giving her a sympathetic look and topping up his wine glass. 'Molly's just getting to this stage too. Got to nip it in the bud, I reckon, otherwise you'll never get a moment to yourself.'

'Yes, well, that's easier said than done,' sighed Katie.

'Daddy!' Hannah announced when all the adult attention had turned to her. She put one hand melodramatically over her forehead. 'I just *can't* sleep!'

'I just *can't*' had become one of her favourite phrases lately. Where she'd got it from, Katie had no idea. Ross did seem to watch lots of films while she was out at work.

'*Can't* you?' said Ross, in the same

71

melodramatic tones. 'Why ever not?'

Hannah sighed. 'Bad dreams. Can I sit here with you?'

'No,' said Katie, before Ross could humour her. All the baby behaviour books said you shouldn't engage children in conversation at bedtime; she'd tried from the beginning to stick to one routine so they didn't get confused. It would help if Ross wasn't so inconsistent. Hannah hadn't had any trouble sleeping until Jack started waking up, but she was sharp enough to see the attention it got him and had started getting to be a real pest about it. Especially with an audience.

Katie looked at Ross, but he was only gazing proudly at his charming daughter, so she pushed back her chair, as a sign to Hannah that a return to bed was nigh.

Hannah's lower lip jutted and she glared at her.

Katie saw Hannah's considerable tantrum mechanisms were now semi-engaged and braced herself. 'Come on, Hannah,' she said. 'Bed.'

'Daddy, I *need* a glass of milk,' she whined, ignoring Katie. 'To sleep.'

'Oh, we know that one, don't we?' said Jo easily, glancing sideways at Greg. 'Magic sleep milk.'

Hannah widened her eyes, and brought Baalamb's ear up to her mouth to chew.

Katie looked at Ross. They'd *talked* about the chewing. He'd agreed it wasn't good. But something about it made Hannah look so much smaller, younger than her princess-y daytime self, that it was hard to be firm.

You *have* to be firm, Katie told herself. Someone has to be.

'Hannah,' she said, and leaned over to remove it

72

from her mouth. Hannah pulled away, and ran over to lean against Ross's knee. Automatically, Ross's arm went around her, making a little barrier.

Hannah and Daddy against Mummy, thought Katie, with a stab through the heart.

'Well . . .' he said, visibly weakening.

Katie could see Jo was melting too, and felt irritated. Yet again, she was going to look like the mean one.

Greg, she was pleased to see, wasn't joining in.

'Come on, Hannah,' he said, firmly. 'You'll be all tired and grumpy in the morning if you don't go up to bed now. Molly's sleeping like a good girl, isn't she?'

'Exactly. And this is grown-up time,' Katie said, getting to her feet. 'Molly and Rowan are asleep, aren't they? And Jack?'

'They're *babies*,' said Hannah, nuzzling further into her father. 'I'm a big girl.'

'Even big girls have to go to bed,' insisted Katie and held out her arms. 'Come on, I'll carry you upstairs. Say night night to everyone.'

The effect was instant.

'Daddy!' roared Hannah, bursting into heart-wrenching sobs. 'Daddy!'

'Daddy take you then,' said Ross, swinging her into his arms and getting up from the table.

'Stop it, Hannah!' said Katie, as lightly as she could. 'You're just making a show of yourself.'

Greg, she saw out of the corner of her eye, snuck a glance at his watch.

'Oh dear,' said Jo, which was worse.

CHAPTER FIVE

'Oh, Lauren, you look . . .' Bridget put her hand to her mouth as Lauren stepped out from behind the changing-room curtain, her lanky frame turned magically doll-like by a frothing cloud of pearl-strewn tulle. Her long, pale arms seemed elegant, the milky softness of her shoulders exaggerated by the stiff strapless bodice. She even held herself differently, as the corset pulled her out of her usual self-conscious slouch, making her tower like a catwalk model over the cooing shop assistant.

Bridget's throat tightened as a powerful, complicated emotion swept through her. Her little girl, her own tiny unexpected baby, standing there looking just like she'd done on her own wedding day, only taller, more beautiful, more confident. Like one of the white roses in their garden, perfect and velvety and just beginning to open up.

I'm the mother of the bride, thought Bridget, with a pang that took her by surprise. And for a second, she saw her own mum in her own wedding album, sitting with Frank's mother, May, knees clamped together, frame handbags on laps, scowling suspiciously at the camera like two owls in their C&A suits and Deirdre Barlow glasses. That's me now, she thought. I've moved up a generation.

Good God, she thought, blinking, when did that happen?

Bridget was nearly sixty, but in her own head she was nowhere near that. Somewhere along the line, the timeframe of her life had got a bit jumbled.

She'd been a young mum to Billy and David, both born before she was twenty-five, and she and Frank had taken the late nights and early mornings in their stride, barely needing much more sleep themselves. Life had settled into a routine, and her teaching had fitted in neatly around them. Then unexpectedly, just after David's first day at secondary school, she'd realised her 'funny tummy' wasn't down to garlic bread at all. It was Lauren. And then she'd met a whole new generation of mums, mostly in their thirties, like she was, and, although she'd never have admitted it to a soul, least of all Frank, having a tiny blonde angel girl after two scabby-kneed lads was like discovering a different kind of motherhood, just when she'd begun to think life's surprises had finished for her.

The kids at school, of course, had thought she was eighty-three, even when she was twenty-nine. Teaching the same class every year, always five, never aging, helped her forget time was passing, and though she was technically a granny, Billy and David lived so far away she didn't have the same constant reminders as some of the grans who picked up the Rosies and Harrys at the school gates. She and Frank were still as daft about each other as they had been, after nearly forty years, though obviously now Lauren was back at home and screeching about mental anguish every time they had a bit of a cuddle, they'd had to tone that down.

But now, seeing Lauren in her elegant white gown, a bride as she'd been, about to be a woman and have a family of her own—that made Bridget realise that time was passing. Had passed, in fact. It made her throat close up in shock.

Lauren's confident smile slipped a little, and the chunky, very unladylike toe of her biker boot peeped out from beneath the silvery hem. 'Mum?' she said. 'Say something. Do I look all right?'

Bridget gazed at Lauren, and the brief chill of sadness vanished as her heart filled up with love, just as it had the moment she'd held her extraordinary bundle in her arms at the hospital. 'Don't be daft! I just can't find the words. You look like . . .'

'She looks like a *princess*,' supplied the shop assistant, with a knowing nod to Lauren. 'If I had a pound for every mum who's been all choked up the first time they've seen their daughter in a wedding dress, I'd have enough for my own special day.'

Bridget tried not to grimace at the Special Day.

'Well, plenty of time to get used to it, Mum,' said Lauren cheerfully. 'This is just dress number one. Do you mind if she takes a quick snap, Yvette?'

Lauren seemed to be on first-name terms with every bridal shop in the county, thought Bridget, pulling herself together.

'Go ahead. Do you want me to pull you in a bit more?' asked Yvette, grabbing the silver strings of the corset. 'I've pinned it at the back. Of course, when you order your own dress, they'll make it to your own measurements.'

'I'm planning on losing a bit of weight before the wedding, though,' Lauren pointed out with a quick glance at her mother.

'I keep telling you, you don't need to, Lauren . . .'

'Ah, well, if I had another pound for every bride who said *that*, I'd be honeymooning in Barbados!'

76

Yvette gave Lauren a mighty tug. 'It falls off anyway, in the run-up . . .'

'Mum? Can you take a picture?'

Glad of the distraction, Bridget rummaged in her big handbag—past tatty packets of paper hankies, her phone, an apple, a marker pen, the swatch of satin Lauren had liked for bridesmaids' dresses, a sock—until she found Lauren's digital camera and her own notebook.

'Let's be methodical about it,' she said, opening it up at a new page. Irene wasn't the only one who could make notes.

Not, she reminded herself, that she was getting into a competition with Irene.

'Dress one is called?'

'What's this one called, Yvette?' asked Lauren, adjusting the crystal tiara stuck into her pinned-up hair as she looked at herself in the 360-degree mirror.

Those lovely shoulders, thought Bridget. Like a china milkmaid. She has no idea how lovely she is. But then does any twenty-two-year-old? Did I?

'It's Margarita, by Chanelle l'Amour. The bodice is twelve five oh, and the skirt is seven nine five. It's the detailing, you see, all that hand embroidery.'

'That's not too bad, Mum,' said Lauren, as Bridget's hand wobbled. 'Look, it's even got a little loop for the train, so I don't fall over it when we do our first dance.'

She demonstrated with a graceful step, which ended abruptly as she trod on the other side of the dress, nearly bringing down a display of table favours.

'Careful now!' said Yvette.

'So, what do you think?'

Bridget felt flattered that Lauren wanted her opinion, and tried to come up with something fashion-orientated, even though it wasn't really her thing. 'I think it's very . . . fairy-tale. Romantic. I can see you waltzing in that one. The skirt would swing beautifully when you do your big reverse turns.'

Lauren's forehead creased doubtfully. 'Reverse what?'

'I'm sure we'll get on to those,' said Bridget, hastily. 'It's very Cinderella, that one!'

'Yeah, totally. I like the way the bodice gives me a proper waist. Look!' She put her hands on her hips to demonstrate. 'Tiny!'

'Mmm. Did we decide on a budget for the dress?' Bridget asked with a discreet lowering of her voice, although she already knew the answer.

'Under two,' said Lauren. 'Dad did say if there was something really special . . .'

Under twelve hundred, thought Bridget, though it was hard to say that when Lauren was twirling and smiling at herself like she used to do when she went to her ballet classes in that pink tutu Frank's mum had made for her. Back in the days before Lauren had got all self-conscious about her height and refused to go to ballet any more.

'You can always get the skirt dyed and shortened and wear it again,' suggested Yvette. 'With a cashmere cardie, for the Grace Kelly look.'

'I love that!' nodded Lauren, as if the Grace Kelly look was something she regularly aimed for. Bridget was pretty sure Lauren had no idea who Grace Kelly was, apart from as some vague fashion style that involved big skirts.

78

'Are you OK with the camera, Mum? Do you need me to show you how it works?'

'No, no, I'm fine,' said Bridget, raising it to eye level. What was the point in spoiling Lauren's lovely trying-on session? She didn't have to get that actual one. I'll have a quiet word with her later, she told herself. Show her the budget again.

Lauren immediately adopted a serious expression, and when Bridget had taken one snap, turned ninety degrees.

'Come on, Mum,' she said, as Bridget hesitated. 'I need all the angles. And from behind too.'

'That's where your lace detailing comes in,' elaborated Yvette. 'You'll need some wow factor there for the congregation, won't you, because that's what they'll be looking at for most of the ceremony.'

Bridget mentally added 'The Wow Factor' to 'Your Special Day' on her list of irritating wedding phrases, but bit her tongue because Lauren was nodding in delighted agreement.

'Aw. Making you all nostalgic, Mum?' asked Yvette.

Lauren stopped twisting and turning in front of the mirror. 'Awwww. Did Nanna go with you to choose your dress?'

'Um, no. No, I went with Dawn, my chief bridesmaid,' said Bridget. In those days, she wanted to say, it wasn't the same three-ring circus it is now: it was about the vows, not the favours. But she held her tongue and only said, 'Took all of one hour, if I remember, from Laura Ashley, and then we went to the cinema.'

Lauren and Yvette both made an indulgent clucking sound, then Lauren said, 'Still, I suppose

79

you didn't have the same sort of choice,' as if clothes rationing had just finished.

Bridget sighed. 'No. I didn't.'

'Cool! OK, dress two!' And Lauren vanished into the changing room again, tugging the curtain so hard two of the rings pinged off.

Yvette and Bridget looked at the dislodged rings, then at each other.

'She's very excited about her wedding,' said Bridget, apologetically. 'And she's always been a little bit . . .'

Her brain scrambled for the polite adult adjective—she wanted to say 'malco' like the children at school. 'Fingers and thumbs,' she finished.

'I can tell. Shall I get you a cup of tea while she's changing, while . . .' Yvette dropped her voice, 'there's nothing for her to spill it on?'

'Good idea,' murmured Bridget.

Lauren tried on three more dresses—a tall satin column that Bridget thought made her look like Nicole Kidman, a strapless meringue that Lauren decided was 'the most gorgeous dress ever, ever, ever', and a dramatic lace flamenco-ish dress that plunged to an alarming degree at the back 'for church wow factor'.

The biggest 'wow factor' for Bridget was that real, everyday girls in Longhampton could afford to spend thousands on one dress, for one day, in the least flattering colour known to woman.

'Do you two girls mind if we have a break for lunch?' asked Yvette at one o'clock. She was clutching an armful of veils that Lauren had requested to 'complete the effect'.

'No, that's fine,' said Bridget. 'I think we could

all do with a pause.' She turned to her daughter, who had returned to normality in a pink velour tracksuit top and tight jeans. It was startling, but quite reassuring to see the normal Lauren again. 'Shall we pop round the corner to that deli place?'

'So long as you don't let me eat a whole pudding,' warned Lauren.

Bridget didn't think an armed guard could stop that happening. The chocolate biscuits at home had started disappearing at twice the usual rate since Lauren moved back in.

*   *   *

Though the precinct bore all the worst hallmarks of the 1950s love affair with concrete, and had its very own Siberian wind tunnel effect, the shops that faced on to the high street had started to smarten up in the last year; here and there were signs of new life in Longhampton, springing up like green shoots between the grey solicitors and mobile phone shops. The deli was one of the new wave of fresh, ambitious cafés, all retro glass cups and whooshing coffee machines. They reminded Bridget of the old coffee shops that had been knocked down to make room for the precinct in the first place.

'Now,' she said, looking at the menu, 'I think I need a coffee.'

'I'll get it,' said Lauren, then she leaned over and stroked Bridget's hand. 'Thanks for coming with me today! It's just how I always imagined it would be, you and me, trying on my wedding dress.'

'Really?' Bridget had to admit she loved

81

spending time with Lauren. The last time they'd done something like this, Lauren had been twelve; the last time, in fact, she let Bridget buy her clothes.

Lauren nodded, and sighed happily, tucking her long blonde hair behind one ear. 'I felt like a real princess in there! It's amazing, those corsets, and net and all that. And the head-dresses and tiaras and veils . . .'

'But you don't want the dress to be wearing you, now, do you?' said Bridget, tactfully. 'Less is more, you know.'

'Not on your wedding day, Mum,' said Lauren, looking at the menu. 'When else can you have a train? Might as well go for the dream dress.'

Bridget watched the diamond on Lauren's engagement ring—so much bigger than her own modest sapphire—glint in the sun as she raised her hand to attract the waitress. Lauren's wedding was something she and Frank had started saving for as soon as she'd begun rehearsing it with her Bridal Barbie, but even with that money set aside, Bridget wasn't sure they were going to have enough. Not when Lauren seemed to be getting most of her inspiration from *Hello!* magazine, rather than the local paper.

Still, she thought, as Lauren ordered for them, most of it's that Irene, putting stupid wedding show ideas in her head. Lauren was a sensible girl, with a job. She'd understand about being realistic, now she was over the initial thrill of it all.

No time like the present, Bridget told herself, as Lauren got out her white satin notebook.

'Laurie, love,' she said, hesitantly. 'I've been wanting to have a chat with you . . . about the

82

wedding.'

She looked up from her 'favour inspiration' list. 'Mum, don't tell me—you've promised your whole class that they can be involved. That's fine with me, honestly. You know, maybe you could get them to do a big dance with ribbons, like they did for the summer concert.'

'Well, not exactly. It's about . . .'

Lauren's phone rang on the table in front of them and her eyes turned straight to it, her fingers already reaching out.

'Mum, can I just answer this?' she asked, already answering it. 'Chris was going to get back to me about his numbers. Hello? Oh, hello, Irene.'

Bridget held her breath and tried not to think uncharitable thoughts.

'Mmm,' Lauren was saying. Her wide blue eyes were skating round the deli, trying to work out what to say. 'Yes, we are in town.'

Bridget knew Lauren was incapable of telling fibs. It was one of her most endearing traits. She also knew what Irene's questions would be on the other side of the conversation.

'Um, with Mum . . .' Lauren was saying now, her eyes falling on her mother. 'Yes, we are on a dress mission, actually . . .'

Bridget shook her head, trying to communicate 'this is us time!' without looking insane or selfish. Lauren, understanding for once, pulled a face.

'We're just having lunch . . .' Her voice changed and relaxed, obviously now off the hot topic of dresses. 'Yes, the deli opposite the bus station, have you been?' She rolled her eyes at her mother. 'You're where? You're . . . Oh, yes, I can see you,' finished Lauren dully, as a tall figure in a belted

Burberry mackintosh started waving at them from outside the window.

'Um, yes, course we can stay for another coffee,' and put the phone down. 'Sorry,' she wailed to Bridget, 'sorry, but what could I say? She was *outside*!'

'It's fine,' said Bridget, putting on her best welcoming face, the one she dragged out on parents' evenings.

Lauren rose to her feet as Irene wiggled her way between the chairs, and Bridget felt a mean-spirited disappointment, like when you finally settle down with a cup of tea and a good film, and your son rings from New Zealand for a chat.

'Hello, girls!' said Irene, arriving in a flurry of umbrella and coat and shopping bags. 'I was in the area so I thought I'd just pop into Bridal Path to see if there was anything in there that might suit Lauren and here you both are! What a coincidence! Great minds think alike! A peppermint tea for me, please,' she added over her shoulder to the hovering waitress. 'Anything else for you two?'

'Another cappuccino, please,' said Bridget. 'A strong one, if you could.'

'And, um, a peppermint tea.' Lauren looked a little shifty. 'Irene suggested I go on a detox,' she added.

'Oh,' said Bridget.

'So how did you get on?' Irene asked, settling herself down and moving their various half-finished plates out of her way. 'Don't mind me, carry on—I'm just going to have the tea.'

'Oh, I think we're just about done, aren't we? We were in there most of the morning,' said

Bridget. 'How many dresses did we look at, Lauren?'

'Four.'

'Just four?'

'It felt like twenty-four!' said Bridget, but Irene already had her notebook out, and was asking Lauren for the digital camera so she could see for herself.

She tutted as soon as she saw Bridget's handiwork. 'Oh, Lauren, why didn't you get a picture of yourself with a *veil* in that first dress? That's no use. We'll have to go back.'

Bridget closed her eyes, counted to ten in her head, and told herself that Irene didn't have a daughter, or indeed a husband, and that she should be more understanding about her interfering.

No, she corrected herself, not interfering, helping.

She opened her eyes to see Lauren's white blonde fringe hanging in a perfect curl as she bent over the camera, and she could have slid back fifteen years, seeing Lauren in that same pose of concentration: doing her homework, reading her first books, colouring-in. It was selfish to be resentful of Irene. Share and share alike as she said to her little ones.

'I meant to ask, Lauren,' said Irene, as her tea arrived. 'How did your first dancing class go?'

Lauren looked up and for a moment a shadow of a frown creased her forehead, then vanished. 'It was OK. I mean, you don't pick it up overnight, do you?'

'It's not as easy as it looks, now, is it?' Irene looked almost pleased. 'Wasn't I right to get you started early?'

'Yeah . . .' said Lauren doubtfully. 'I suppose I thought we'd just, you know, do it, like they do on telly.'

'What did you learn?'

'We sort of walked up and down together, learning not to tread on each other's feet, then we did a really basic rock'n'roll thing. The sort you do at a wedding when you can't dance.' Lauren rolled her eyes. 'We couldn't even get that right. My feet were so sore afterwards. I'm taking plasters with me next time.'

'It was a very good start,' interjected Bridget. 'They did very well, considering.'

Irene tutted sympathetically. 'Well, if you need some extra practice, Lauren, maybe we can get you some private lessons.'

'It's not *me* that needs practice, it's Chris!' Lauren objected.

Irene's smile turned somewhat tight-lipped.

'Seriously,' Lauren insisted. 'Your son doesn't know his left foot from his right. He nearly pulled my arm out of its socket when he went to spin me round.' She sipped her tea forlornly. 'I had no idea he was such a malco.'

'I can't believe that!' replied Irene. 'Christopher's an athlete, and he passed his driving test first time.'

'That doesn't mean he can steer me,' said Lauren. 'You try getting your feet out of the way of his size elevens.'

'Oh, your dad was like that to begin with—it'll come.' Bridget's eyes moved quickly from Lauren, who suddenly looked quite deflated, to Irene, whose smooth neck had turned a bright shade of pink. 'I thought you were picking it up very quickly,

Laurie!'

'Would you like me to come along and watch?' suggested Irene, ignoring her. 'Maybe I could video it, and you could see where you're going wrong later. It might help.'

'The only thing that's going to help is if you write Left and Right on Chris's shoes,' said Lauren. 'I'm telling you, it's not me.'

Irene laughed, but in a slightly grim manner. 'Oh, Lauren, I'm sure you're over-reacting. His father was an excellent dancer, and I remember when—'

'Have you ever danced with Chris?' demanded Lauren.

Irene hesitated. 'Well, not recently, no.'

'It's still early days! Plenty of time to go,' said Bridget, reaching for the pudding menu. 'Now, someone at school was telling me they do a very wicked homemade tiramisu here. Anyone want to share one with me?'

But Irene's face was suffused with nostalgic tenderness. 'I only wish *Ron and I* had the opportunity to do a lovely first dance,' she went on, wistfully. 'It would have been a very special moment to treasure.'

Bridget exchanged a look over the menu with Lauren, and was irritated to see her expression softening in sympathy, right on cue. Irene's wedding and what she would have done differently was a pretty inescapable part of Lauren's own preparations.

Bridget just hoped it wasn't going to be the deciding factor in everything.

*   *   *

Back at Bridal Path, Yvette pulled out eight more enormous dresses for Lauren to try on, and with Irene firmly in charge of the camera, Bridget was reduced to writing notes for each one, in as much detail as she could manage, not being equipped with the strange wedding-dress vocabulary that flowed from Irene and Lauren's mouths.

'Fingertip or blusher?' Irene asked Lauren, fiddling with her veil.

'Or cathedral length?' suggested Yvette.

From somewhere underneath the mass of net, Lauren said, 'Or what about all three?'

Bridget wrote, 'large skirt, sparkly top, might get dirty if it rains outside the church'. Then she remembered that the thorny matter of the venue was still under discussion, and crossed it out, in case Lauren thought she was being pointed.

She watched Yvette and Irene fussing around Lauren's skirt as she turned absent-mindedly and caught the train on a chair, nearly tipping it over. It wasn't so much that she and Frank were church-goers, but at least a church wedding would tie it all down to something—something that actually had some meaning, rather than this parade of save-the-day cards and gift lists and how many flowergirls was too many. There was something about this wedding that reminded her of the parties Lauren used to have when she was at school—the endless inviting and uninviting, and debates about the birthday cake . . .

'How much is this one, Yvette?' Irene called out.

'Two thousand seven hundred. But it's all hand-sewn and really, you can tell, can't you?'

'Oh, you can,' agreed Lauren, with a huge sigh.

Bridget wrote £2700 next to the crossed-out bit, and before she knew it, she'd added an !!. Guiltily, she crossed that out too, but it looked awful. Mean, and she wasn't mean at all. There wasn't anything she wouldn't do to make Lauren's wedding day as wonderful as Lauren wanted.

The crossings out loomed accusingly up at her.

Then she ripped out the page altogether, stuffed it in her bag, and started again.

CHAPTER SIX

Katie's week passed in an interminable series of meetings and site visits, and though she and Ross tried to follow the advice Peter had given them—talk more, explain problems, be reasonable—it didn't seem to be making much difference.

Trying to be nice didn't change anything. It just made the pair of them crabby about having to try to be nice. They were still far too close to each other, and far too tired to make any space.

And now, Katie thought, on her way home on Wednesday night, I've got to haul myself round this stupid ballroom-dancing class again.

'I'm home!' she called, hanging her car keys on the hook by the kitchen door. She checked her watch: twenty past seven. The class was at quarter to eight, so she didn't really have time to get changed out of her office suit or grab much to eat, but as long as Ross had sorted something out for the kids' supper, the leftovers would fill a hole until they got back.

Katie wasn't sure she could face an hour of Angelica's pointed remarks on an empty stomach. What she really needed was a glass of wine. Or two.

Her eye skated around the kitchen, took in the unwashed spaghetti hoop pan on the hob, and the crumbs on the work surface, then fell on the wine rack, where a lone bottle remained from Friday night. Beanie babies were stuffed in the other holes. Her hand reached out, then she stopped it. She needed her wits about her.

Where is everyone? she wondered. It wasn't as if everyone usually ran to the door when she got in but some acknowledgement would be nice.

'Hello?' she called again, but there was no response as she made her way into the sitting room, where she could hear music.

Ross was lying on the sofa, with Jack draped sleepily over his stomach, and Hannah curled into the crook of his arm, transfixed by the flashing images on the television. Ross was also transfixed by what Katie recognised as a ballroom-dancing DVD, his bare foot bouncing up and down to the music while terracotta-tanned couples spun around the dancefloor. They made a perfect picture of family bliss.

Apart from the fact that around him piles of unironed laundry were stacked precariously near half-empty cereal bowls and crumpled dollops of abandoned clothing. The Hoover was exactly where she'd left it that morning, and there were still sticky marks on the mirror from where Hannah had kissed herself while eating a jam sandwich.

Katie felt her blood pressure rise again.

Well, at least Jack was in his pyjamas already, and she could put him to bed for once, she told herself, but that didn't damp down her irritation.

'What's going on?' she asked, in as neutral a tone as she could manage, not wanting to yell in front of Hannah.

'Mummy's home!' exclaimed Ross in a stage whisper, pointing downwards at Jack. 'Shh!'

'Why isn't Jack in bed yet?' she asked, in the same tight voice.

'He wanted to watch the dancing,' said Hannah. There was glitter on her face and she was wearing her pink elasticated ballet tutu over a swimsuit and tights.

'Well, you'd both better get ready for bed, because we're going out and Gemma's going to be here in a minute. You like Gemma,' she went on, as Hannah's expression turned mutinous, her pink lip sticking out. 'She reads to you, doesn't she?'

'Ah,' said Ross. 'Change of plan with Gemma. She's split up with her boyfriend and can't babysit tonight.'

'What? At ten quid an hour? Can't she just come over here and be miserable?'

Ross gave her a meaningful look. 'I think she's . . . already getting some counselling with her friend Tia Maria. And Bailey. If you know what I mean . . .'

Katie rolled her eyes. 'Give me the phone. She's got responsibilities!'

'Don't be stupid, Katie. You want her looking after the kids in that kind of state? Anyway,' he went on, 'I rang Jo and she says she'll sort something out. Hey?' he said, cuddling Hannah a bit nearer. 'You're happy to have Jo babysit instead of Gemma, aren't you?'

'Yeah! Jo!' Hannah's face lit up, and Katie felt a twinge of resentment at her sudden mood upswing.

'Well, that's nice of her,' she said, gruffly. 'She and Greg were meant to be coming with us to dancing this week. I don't suppose she fancies babysitting the laundry basket as well, does she?' As she spoke, she started to stuff crumpled pillowcases and socks back into the laundry bag. 'This place looks more and more like a bloody jumble sale every day. Don't you *see* all this stuff lying around? Honestly, Jo's going to think we've been burgled.'

'Oh, yeah, sorry.' Ross looked around, as if noticing it all for the first time. 'I meant to do that while these two were having their nap, but we . . . got distracted.'

'We watched the DVD!' announced Hannah. 'I did the foxes trot with Daddy!'

'I wanted to show them what we were learning at dancing class,' Ross explained. 'Obviously, we concentrated on the twirling and the swinging.'

Katie lifted a pile of unmatched socks off an armchair, to reveal a crumby plate of toast crusts.

I just want to *sit down*, she thought wearily. Is this why my dad was so tetchy when he came home from work? Is it so much to ask?

But even though she hated herself, it still came out. 'All day?'

Hannah gave her mother a clear-eyed glare. 'Why don't *you* have a sparkly dress like the ladies, Mummy?'

'Because,' said Katie, piling up plates and cups with quick, cross, clunking motions.

'Because what? *I've* got a special dress for *my*

92

dancing.'

God, first Angelica, and now Hannah, thought Katie, feeling got at. It wasn't as if they were going to the classes for fun—and it definitely didn't warrant new clothes.

'Mummy?' Hannah went on. 'Why don't you have a sparkly dress? Mummy? You never wear pretty dresses. Mummy?'

'Hannah,' snapped Katie, 'that's *enough!*'

Hannah put her hands on her hips, and opened her mouth to talk back, but Katie glared back harder.

'I'll pop Jack in his bed,' said Ross, getting to his feet with Jack still cradled in his arms. 'He's about ready for it. Come on, Hannah, you can take your bowl through to the kitchen for me, can't you?'

Katie felt a terrible yearning inside for Jack, who was nuzzling into Ross's shoulder like a sleepy puppy, his eyelids twitching as he dozed. While she was at work, she could somehow switch off the part of her brain that missed him, but now she was home, the need to hold him, and smell his downy head was so powerful it actually hurt. Without realising she stretched out her hands, wanting to feel his soft weight against her chest. He was almost too heavy to carry around now, but she loved the feel of him in her arms.

'Here,' she said. 'Let me. Please? I'd love to put him to bed.'

'But you're in a rush,' countered Ross, turning his shoulder. 'Aren't you?'

'Not that much of a rush,' Katie pleaded. Jack's dark hair was growing so quickly. She hadn't noticed how long it had got at the back, curling in silky brown waves. 'Come on, Ross. You know how much I love putting him to bed! I haven't seen him all day!'

He rolled his eyes downwards and she realised too late that Hannah was listening in, taking their struggle over Jack personally, from the hurt scowl on her face.

'You spoil everything,' she said, with a rising note of pre-tantrum fury. 'We were having a lovely time till you came home. I *hate* you.'

Katie's jaw dropped, and a sudden pain, sharp and dull at the same time, spread through her chest.

'Now, Hannah!' Ross raised a warning finger.

'I *hate* her,' yelled Hannah and turned on her heel and ran out of the room.

Katie looked at him. It was easier to be mad with Ross than it was to deal with the shock in her heart. 'Is that all you can say? *Hannah*?'

'What do you expect me to do?' he demanded, nodding towards the sleeping toddler in his arms.

Still in his arms, she noted. What was she meant to do? Prise Jack away?

'I expect you to . . . To . . .' She ran out of words, unable to bear the distress in her own voice. Katie swallowed. She knew what she should be doing— hadn't she spent both pregnancies reading child-behaviour manuals?—but seeing Hannah look at her like that, with actual resentment that she'd come home, wiped every rational thought from her mind. All she was left with was the bitter sense that it was her fault.

'What am I supposed to do?' repeated Ross. 'If she's pissed off that you've come home late, then whose fault is that? What do you expect me to do? You're her mother.'

'But . . .'

'I'm not going to punish her,' he went on. 'She's upset. Maybe you should have a talk with her in the morning.'

'That's so typical of you!' Katie couldn't hold it in any more. 'Leave all the discipline to me, as well as everything else, so you can be Mr Nice Dad. Well, thanks. Thanks for that.'

'Katie, I am doing my best. What do you *want* from me?' asked Ross, and she shrugged.

She didn't know what Ross wanted. She couldn't see inside his head.

They stared at each other in painful silence.

Two words, thought Katie. I could say it now. *I'm leaving*. I could just get in the car and drive.

Then Jack stirred on Ross's shoulder, whimpering in his sleep, sending a tremor of guilt and love through her, and just as she was about to speak, the doorbell rang.

'Jo!' squealed Hannah, hurtling for the door, and Katie felt punched again.

'Sorry,' said Ross under his breath, but it was too late. Katie could hear Jo and Hannah in the hall, Hannah giggling gleefully, obviously doing spins on her toes from the audible clunks. Katie flinched, half for Hannah's feet, half for the scuffed hall wallpaper they never had spare money to redecorate.

'Careful, sweetie! Oooh, clever you! And what a lovely outfit!' she could hear Jo saying. 'Are you a ballerina, or a ballroom dancer? I love your spangles!'

Katie carried on holding Ross's gaze, willing him to say the right thing. Anything that would make her feel less like her dad and more like his wife.

95

Don't *make* me make you say something, she pleaded inside. Please just say it of your own accord.

But he didn't say anything. Instead he blinked behind his glasses, then turned to take Jack to bed, just as Hannah and Jo barrelled into the sitting room. Jo was wearing a red dress underneath her usual warm parka, and little sparkles glittered in the light.

'Hi, Ross, isn't she back yet? Sounds like you've had a grand afternoon with these two . . . Oh, hello.' Jo looked between the two of them, sensing the tension hanging noxiously in the air like burnt toast. Her friendly face suddenly became cautious. 'Everything OK?'

'Not really,' said Katie. 'But we're going to be late for *dancing*.' She glared at Ross. 'I told Ross you and Greg were going to come with us—I'm sure there are other people he could have called.'

'Like who?' Ross demanded.

'Look, don't worry about it,' said Jo, hastily. 'I talked Greg into coming to the class after all, so I was going to take my two round to my mum's for the evening. She's said she'll pop over here and sit all four of them here instead, if that's OK with you? It's nearer for her, less fuss for your two, and we'll pick ours up on the way back. Greg's just bringing them in.'

'That's sweet of her,' said Katie. Jo got her domestic goddess genes straight from her mum, Dorothy. She was the white-haired, sweetie-giving substitute granny Hannah didn't have, and Katie wasn't sure Jo knew how lucky she was.

'You don't mind Mrs Sanderson coming over to babysit, do you? Will you show her how clever you

96

are at big-girl reading now?' Katie said to Hannah, in the hope it might elicit a cuddle.

Hannah ignored her, the latest adult skill she'd learned. 'Where are you going, Daddy?' She leaned against Jo's legs and looked lovingly at Ross, her blue eyes sharp.

'Dancing!' said Ross, brightly. 'So we can do some new steps in the morning.'

'Ooh! That'll be fun, won't it?' said Jo, bending down to distract her with tickles. But Hannah looked far from convinced and Katie noticed, to her dismay, that her thumb returned to her mouth for the first time in months.

Jack stirred in Ross's arms, and Katie seized the chance to swoop him up to bed herself.

'Have you time for a coffee?' she heard Ross ask Jo, after a pause in which she was sure eyes had been rolled. But she nuzzled her nose into Jack's hair, and let herself focus on her baby for once.

$$*\qquad*\qquad*$$

The hall was chilly when they arrived, as if all the hot air had floated up off the frilled cast-iron radiators and into the rafters, but Katie couldn't help feeling her trepidation at what was to come mixed with a bit of pleasure at being somewhere different, for once.

They were the last ones to arrive, and from the way the heads swivelled when they walked in, it was clear everyone saw Greg and Jo and thought: the New People.

Already, thought Katie. After only one week.

Angelica was standing next to Lauren the Fiancée, chatting to her about something or other to do with shoes, from the way they were pointing their feet. Lauren, she noted, was wearing a pair of white satin Louis XV heels. Her wedding shoes, obviously.

Jo nudged Katie. 'That the teacher?'

'Yes,' Katie whispered back. 'Fame costs, and right here's where you start paying. In sarcastic comments about your posture.'

'So!' Angelica clapped her hands together, and everyone's attention snapped her way. 'My goodness, I can't have been mean enough to you all last week—everyone's back for lesson two! I'm so pleased that you listened to what I said about dressing up! Well, nearly all of you.'

Katie looked round the class, and instantly regretted not getting changed. There hadn't been much time after she'd put Jack to bed. Everyone was looking decidedly festive, it was true. Lauren was wearing a pink prom dress, left over from the summer, with a thick cardi on top, while her mum had stuck a feather clip in her short dark hair, and thrown on a diamanté-studded black top to jazz up her sensible red skirt. Even Chris and Frank were in brighter shirts. Of the other older couple, Peggy had swapped last week's caramel twinset for a heavily sequinned M&S one, while Baxter had added a blue silk hanky to the top pocket of his blazer. Trina was resplendent in a swirly bias-cut skirt that made her look like a gift-wrapped skittle, while Chloe had gone the whole hog with a pair of black fishnets, and put a silk flower in her curly blonde hair as well. The two of them were still looking hopefully at the door, and seemed to cheer up considerably when Greg arrived.

'And two new people!' beamed Angelica.

'Welcome to the class!'

Jo and Greg were drawing attention, and not just from Chloe and Trina, who were eyeing Greg up unashamedly. Jo's ample curves were filling out her red dress into something spectacular—the spangles made her look as if she was about to take part in some kind of professional dance competition. Greg just looked competent and at-ease, tieless and with just the right number of buttons undone. He always did look right. It was good to have them there for moral support, but at the same time, Katie felt even more conscious of her work skirt than before, and her jaw jutted defensively. At least she was wearing a skirt this week.

Trina, she saw, was glaring at her. Or she might just have been looking. She had an unfortunate face, in that respect.

'Are you a policewoman?' she asked Katie, straight out.

'No!' Katie protested.

Ross coughed, trying to disguise a giggle.

'Oh.' Trina screwed up her nose as if she didn't quite believe her. 'You look like one.'

'Come on, Katie, where's your nice dress?' said Angelica. 'Ross can hardly feel as if he's taking his favourite girl out dancing if she's dressed for a ten a.m. conference call! Everyone else has made the effort, look.'

'This isn't 1959,' she snapped. 'Women don't have to put on pretty dresses to look nice. Anyway, Ross hasn't dressed up!'

'I have!'

Too late, Katie spotted, now he'd taken his jacket off, that he'd put on a fresh shirt—his 'going-out' shirt as they used to joke. He'd never owned a suit, much less formal shirts, and this was a soft sea-island cotton one she'd bought him in London for a birthday present: a pale buttery yellow that used to make her think of spring chicks. He'd even put in the pair of silver cufflinks she'd given him to go with it.

He's trying, she thought, and felt terrible that it didn't make much difference.

'See?' said Angelica, and Katie sensed a wash of curiosity from the others, as to why they were acting so childishly.

'You'll find it much easier to move in a swingy skirt,' she went on persuasively. 'And I promise, it makes the dancing easier when you have that swish about you.' She met her eye, and Katie had the uneasy sensation that her mind was being read.

'OK,' Katie heard herself say, for a quiet life. 'Next week.'

'Wonderful!' And in an instant, Angelica was in demo mode.

'Now, you were all so good with your rock'n'roll basics last week that tonight we're going to learn something new! Then we'll go back and recap what we did so you don't forget,' she added, reassuringly, as Chris started to mumble nervously.

She gestured that they should all spread out in a horseshoe, so they could see her feet.

'So, you've got your fast dance to do at the wedding reception, but what about something a bit smoochier, for the end of the night? Hmm? This sort of music. Think about white tie and tails, and satin dresses, and big bands, and *romance*!'

'Oooh!' said Trina and Chloe.

Jo shot Katie an amused glance, and said,

'Oooh!' too, with a remarkably straight face.

Katie had to look down to stop herself giggling.

Angelica stepped back to her CD player and pressed play. The hall filled up with the big-band sound of Harry Connick Jnr, and Katie recognised the opening bars of 'It Had To Be You'.

'Now we're going to learn a very useful social dance that fits most old songs, it looks very proficient, and it's very simple. It's called the social foxtrot, or a crush dance. Now where's my volunteer?' She swooped on Frank, with her arms held open, and this time Bridget happily waved them away on to the middle of the floor.

The class watched impressed as Angelica and Frank clasped each other in the ballroom hold, then floated in curving turns from one end of the room to the other, with only a few little bumps and hesitations.

'Now, the social foxtrot is fabulous for doing when you've only got a tiny dancefloor, like at a wedding,' Angelica called over one shoulder, as they swirled back down the other side of the room. 'Watch how small we can make this,' she went on as their steps became compact, and little more than a shuffle.

'I thought the foxtrot was the quick one where the lady slides round the room backwards like she's on wheels,' said Lauren. 'That's the one they did on *Strictly Come Dancing*. The one with the dresses with floaty wings.' She spread her long arms, nearly taking Chris's eye out.

'Ah, now that's different—that's called the *slow* foxtrot,' said Angelica, while Frank twirled her round as the instrumental break took over. 'That's the one you see in Fred Astaire films. That's all about syncopation, and *gliding* round the floor as if you're not touching it, and very, very precise footwork. And it's *very* difficult, believe me.'

'We won the Longhampton District Five-Dance Cup nine times,' said Baxter. 'Slow foxtrot was our special dance, wasn't it, Peggy? And our son Ray is also an ex-champion, twice.'

Peggy nodded, her eyes sparkling.

It was hard to imagine Baxter and Peggy as a pint-sized Fred and Ginger, thought Katie, but then maybe that was the transformational power of dance Angelica kept going on about. She thought Baxter looked a bit put out, and wondered why she hadn't chosen him to demonstrate with. Frank was good, but he wasn't nearly as slick as Baxter. Baxter moved as if his soles were oiled. Maybe that was the point—maybe she didn't want to make it look even harder than it was.

'Really? How marvellous!' said Angelica.

'We were in all the papers,' added Baxter. 'Two generations of champions, if you will.'

'Everyone! If you get stuck, just have a look at what Peggy and Baxter are doing,' said Angelica, good-humouredly, as she returned Frank to Bridget with a little curtsy.

'Now,' she went on, 'that's how you do it quickly. Now let's see all that again *very* slowly, shall we?' Her sharp eyes turned to Katie, Jo, Greg and Ross.

'Great,' Katie muttered under her breath towards Jo, bracing herself. 'This is where she picks on us.'

'Not you, dear!' said Angelica. 'I've got my feet to think of. It's your husband I'm after. If you don't mind?' she added, taking Ross's hand.

Ross smiled as Angelica neatly manoeuvred him

into the centre of the hall, and beamed at the class.

'Ah!' said Jo, encouragingly. 'Doesn't he look like he knows what he's doing?'

He is such a creep, thought Katie. If he displayed that much enthusiasm at home, we wouldn't have to be here at all.

'Now I should tell you that I won't always allow you to dance with the partner you brought,' Angelica went on. 'When you're let loose onto real dance floors, you'll be expected to dance with everyone, not just your friends, so you'd better get used to swapping around.'

'Oooh!' the single girls cooed, this time with more enthusiasm, and nudging in the direction of Greg and tall, blond Chris.

'Get ready, Lauren,' said Trina, winking at Lauren, whose arms had folded automatically over her chest as her fiancé beamed in the spotlight of female attention. 'You might just get stampeded in the rush, love!'

'And then they'll get stampeded by Chris,' retorted Lauren.

Greg caught Katie's eye as the class bantered away, and he raised his eyebrows slightly, as if to say, 'Is it like this every week?' Katie adjusted her face, and returned the gesture, quite a private one, of shared amusement, and a flutter ran over her skin.

She looked down at the floor, then at Ross, who was remembering to pull his slopey shoulders back now he was dancing with Angelica, and when she glanced back at Greg again, he was murmuring something to Jo, and the amused look had vanished from his face.

Angelica explained the steps, the slows and the

quicks, while they copied her. 'Watch my feet!' she called out, over the music. 'We're going in zig-zags, like the pattern on the floor, can you see?'

To the untrained eye, it looked as if Ross was expertly propelling Angelica. Even he looked surprised.

'You're very good at this,' she added, as they turned slowly. 'I think you've got that!' She let his hands go, and gave him a little clap. 'Now, you teach Katie, and I'll have a look at . . . Careful, now, Chris! If you drag her she'll . . . you see what I mean?'

Ross came back to Katie as Angelica went to disentangle Chris and Lauren. He held out his arms in a stagey dance manner.

'Don't,' said Katie.

'Don't what?'

'Don't make me feel even more self-conscious than I already am. God, I *hate* not being able to do stuff,' Katie muttered, trying to keep her grumbling beneath Angelica's radar. 'Right, OK, which foot do we start on?' She stared at her work courts. They needed polishing. Next to her toes were Ross's Converse All-Stars, which had also seen better days.

'Stop looking at your feet,' said Ross. 'Look at me.'

Reluctantly, Katie looked at Ross. They were standing quite close together, his hand on her shoulder-blade, the other holding hers at shoulder-height, a breath apart. She'd forgotten how near they were in height, especially when she was in heels, and now they were close enough for her to smell the baby powder on him, mixed with his own end-of-the-day smell. It wasn't an unpleasant smell, and the formality of the pose did make her look at him properly.

He needs to do something about his open pores, she thought, at the same time as she realised his brown eyes actually had a ring of amber round the iris.

'Now take a slow step back,' said Ross helpfully.

'When?'

'When I decide to start. You're meant to watch my face for clues.'

'And what if I don't want to look at you?' she replied, knowing how childish she sounded. 'What if I preferred a verbal signal? And why do you have to decide when we start?'

Ross sighed. 'Fine. You tell me when you're ready, then we'll go. Now when I lead you back, I'll lean into the step and . . .'

Katie let her hands drop. 'Lead? Sorry? What?' She narrowed her eyes. 'Was that what you were watching with Hannah? A teach-yourself-dancing DVD? You were, weren't you?'

'Why not?' Ross looked surprised. 'I want to be able to do it. I don't want to let you down.'

'Well, don't! That's not on!' she spluttered. 'The whole *point* is that we're both equally crap! You can't cheat by getting ahead of me!'

Ross shook his head and stepped away from her. 'I can't believe this. Seriously, Katie. What's wrong with you?'

'Trouble in paradise?' Angelica glided up behind them.

'Oh, great,' muttered Katie.

'Now, there's nothing to it,' she said, motioning them back into the right hold. 'Clever girl like you will pick this up in no time, Katie. And . . .' She looked at Ross, who stepped forward with a nod. 'And slow, keep that long step *slow*, Katie, and slow, and together, feet together! Together! You're not Charlie Chaplin! Now *you* step forward, and . . .'

'Ow!' Katie glared accusingly at Ross as his Converse connected with her toe.

'You've got to let him lead you, Katie,' said Angelica, but sympathetically this time. 'No use shoving him around—you can't see what's behind you and he can. Here, let me show you.'

She put her hands lightly on Katie's, holding her as Ross had, and started to move so skilfully that Katie felt herself being gently eased into the right position. Her feet went to the right places without her having to tell them to, and as Angelica spoke the steps aloud, like a patient primary-school teacher, it began to fit together.

Her hands were small, perfectly manicured, no rings, and Katie barely felt their weight at all, expect for the moments when Angelica pressed her very gently to guide her in the right direction. Angelica's head was about level with her own ear, and Katie could smell her flowery perfume, and the faint cashmere smell of her fitted jumper. Even close up, Angelica's make-up was flawless: the winged flick of her black eyeliner unwavering, her arched eyebrows plucked to perfection, with only a few papery lines around her eyes betraying a few extra years more than the age Katie would have put her at.

Angelica wasn't the sort of woman Katie was used to dealing with: neither brisk and business-like, nor mumsy and frazzled. There was a sort of elegant self-possession about her that made Katie wonder, from nowhere, whether she had children. All her attention seemed focused in on herself, her precise movements, her flawless appearance—she had an old-fashioned femininity that made Katie feel even more of a failure in that department.

Angelica caught her looking and she had to glance downwards to avoid the awkwardness of meeting her eye. I wonder if she's reading me too, she pondered. Katie's senses were already jangling at the invasion of her personal bubble by this stranger, and she had the irrational sense that Angelica could hear her thoughts, and feel the coolness and desperation between her and Ross, just by putting those little hands on her tense shoulders.

'No need to get so tense,' said Angelica unexpectedly. 'You need to relax more, Katie.'

'What?' Katie panicked. She *had* been reading her mind.

'You're very wound up, in your shoulders.' She gave them a demonstrative squeeze, pulling them backwards, and Katie flinched at the touch. Maybe being a dance teacher let you grapple with people unannounced. 'Don't worry so much about what you look like. Just . . . flow.'

'That's easy for you to say,' began Katie, but she realised Angelica had just turned her round a corner.

'See? Not so hard. Now, you two,' Angelica said, stepping away. 'Let me change the music.'

Ross looked expectantly at Katie and held out his hands.

The opening brass flourishes of 'You Make Me Feel So Young' shrilled out, bringing everyone else to life, except Katie. Across the room, Frank held out his arms for Lauren to dance with him, while Bridget bravely wrangled Christopher into a starting position.

Even Jo and Greg seemed to be coping with the new steps. Jo's face was flushed and happy as she gazed up at Greg, whose broad back was to Katie.

Nice shoulders, she thought, distractedly.

'Come on, then,' said Ross and with an effort, she tried to concentrate on her steps, and not on how stupid she must look.

*   *   *

It was, as Baxter pointed out, a good night for Frank Sinatra fans. The class shuffled round the room to 'New York, New York', and 'I've Got You Under My Skin', with Angelica diving on them for spot coaching. Jo and Ross were the star turn, teasing each other loudly about their mistakes but never stopping when they fluffed a step, while Katie got the distinct impression that she kept ending up with either Trina or Chloe because she was officially the duff choice. At least Chris and his lethal two left feet gave a girl a good view while her toes were being crushed to the swinging big-band sound of Nelson Riddle and his orchestra.

But to Katie's surprise, after four or five songs, the simple steps did start to fall into place. Everyone else was moving on to simple variations, but Angelica kept her and Chris firmly on the basics, until there was a brief moment on her third lap of the room with Chris counting in her ear, during 'Night and Day', when everyone was moving around in the right time, in their own space, and the little room seemed to hum with a nostalgic glow.

She met Chris's eye, and he seemed as surprised as she was, and a boyish smile of amazement spread across his handsome face.

'Jesus,' he said. 'We're dancing!'

As he spoke, Katie trod on his foot, the brass swelled in a big finish, and when the couples disengaged with happy nods and thanks, spontaneous clapping broke out. And then Angelica called a halt to proceedings. 'Better to stop while we're all on top!' she said. 'Next week, a little bit of Latin cha-cha-cha, so bring your party feet!'

When Katie looked over to see where Ross had got to, she spotted him with Jo, talking to Lauren and her mum. He saw her looking and waved her over.

'You know Mrs Armstrong, don't you?' he said, as the older woman smiled at her warmly. 'Mrs Armstrong has . . .'

'I know, Ross!' gabbled Katie, embarrassed. 'Hello! We haven't met—I just never get time to collect Hannah, you know how it is with office hours and—'

'Oh, I do know,' said Mrs Armstrong, but Katie felt she had to go on, for Ross, not her.

'I mean, I'd love to pick her up more than I do, but I just can't leave the office that early. Hannah adores school, though, doesn't she, Ross? She's always talking about how much she loves the painting, and the trips to the park. I think she's going to be a big reader, as well, because she loves her bedtime stories, which I'm in charge of . . .'

Mrs Armstrong's smile spread into a sort of understanding look. They were really kind,

109

teacher's eyes, thought Katie, used to cheering children up, and finding something positive to say.

She scrambled herself together, conscious that everyone was staring at her. 'I love reading her bedtime stories,' she finished lamely.

'Hannah's a little star,' said Mrs Armstrong, and Katie felt the invisible pat on the head but was grateful. 'She's doing very well.'

'Everything OK?' asked Angelica, shimmering up silently behind them. 'Lauren, you were really getting that! Your arms were spot-on, very elegant. Well done!'

'Seriously? Ooh, thanks,' said Lauren, her cheeks turning pink. 'Have you taught learners worse than us before?'

'More than you can imagine,' said Angelica.

'Angelica's not just a teacher, Laurie,' said Bridget, casting a quick apologetic glance towards her. 'She used to be an international ballroom champion—she's our only proper local celebrity!'

'Really?' said Lauren—a bit too incredulously. 'Wow. You're famous?'

Angelica batted away the compliment, but again, Katie saw a brief glimmer of pride light up her face, tinged with something more bittersweet.

'Just amongst people who go dancing,' she said. 'Next week, same time?'

There was a chorus of agreement, and then Greg jingled his car keys impatiently, and before anyone could ask any more questions, suddenly they were all leaving.

CHAPTER SEVEN

It was a mild night for September, and Angelica walked home slowly from the Memorial Hall, her dancing shoes in her large bag (too large, according to her osteopath, who despaired for her knotted joints). She could have driven, but it wasn't far to Sydney Street and she liked to fit in exercise where she could. Angelica had never been one for gyms and diets. She wasn't sure she'd want to be a professional competitor these days, with all that training and nutrition and physio business.

In her day, she thought, as she walked past new-build houses that stood where the Art Deco bus station once accommodated several generations of Longhampton's bored adolescents, nerves had been what kept you thin. Nerves, and cigarettes, and not having enough money left over once you'd paid for everything else.

In that respect, Tony Canero had been one of the greatest diet aids known to woman. If they weren't dancing as if tomorrow was the last-ever competition, they were making love equally furiously in his bedsit in Vauxhall, or she was tormenting herself wondering where he was, whether his fickle, appreciative eyes would light upon a better dancer in the studio, a more experienced girl, a smarter girl who didn't come from provincial terraces like these. Angelica had worked hard on her dancing, but she'd worked even harder on herself.

She supposed, looking back now, that was something else she and Tony had in common—

their magic on the dancefloor took them miles away from the boring lives they'd been born into. But he didn't have the same need as she did, to prove something. It was always easier for men. They really *could* have it all, and for years and years; they never had to choose between their different selves, the way women did.

Angelica's brisk pace took her away from the High Street, down towards the sludgy river, and in five minutes she'd turned down Sydney Street, mentally swinging like Gene Kelly from the lamp-posts as she walked past them, as she always had.

The truth was, she didn't know where Tony was, or if he was still dancing. She'd even managed to stop wondering, for a few years now. Caring for her mother through those final days had drained her of more emotion than she thought she had left, and besides, Angelica wasn't into looking back. Looking back was for when there was nothing to look forward to.

Yet, since she'd unlocked the front door of 34 Sydney Street, she'd had the nagging sense that she'd never be happy until she'd tied up her loose ends. Maybe it had begun before then: maybe that was why she'd volunteered to come back and sort through the cupboards and wardrobes herself, just as she'd vowed to start dejunking her own life. Already she was discovering things she'd never even guessed she didn't know. Like, her father had been a Boy Scout master for a few years. Her mother had an ancient wedding dress in a bag in the attic that Angelica knew couldn't be hers because it wasn't the one she was wearing in her sombre wedding photograph. There wasn't a lot of stuff left to sort through—heartbreakingly little, in fact—but the more she looked, the more she realised the years away had made strangers of her and her parents. They didn't understand her life, but, Angelica realised, she barely knew theirs either. And now they weren't there to ask.

She knew little more now than she'd known at sixteen. Cyril Clarke was forty-nine, ten years older than his wife, Pauline, when Angelica, or Angela, as she was christened, came along. Pauline was thirty-nine, quite some age for a first child, back in 1950.

'You're the baby we longed for—our very own angel,' her mum used to tell her, her eyes filling up with happy tears, 'and that's why we called you Angela!' Then she'd hug Angelica to her bosom, which was as generous and soft as Pauline herself, and try to get her to eat up her seconds, 'for those skinny bird legs'.

Cyril was distant with his daughter, maybe, the teenage Angela surmised miserably, as a balance to Pauline's adoration. He was quite Methodist like that. He gave her a manic work ethic and that was about it. She was glad she didn't inherit his bristly moustache, or his habit of wearing trousers slightly too short, and though inheriting his parsimony might have made her hand-to-mouth early life easier, it also kept her awake at nights, worrying.

Even forty years on, Angelica still stepped quietly into the anaglypta-papered hall, as if Cyril might be disturbed in his obsessive building of crystal radios.

She used to say, without rancour, that she didn't feel particularly close to either of her parents. It was only in the last few years of her mother's life

113

that they'd reached an understanding, but prior to that, it was as if she'd gone to the moon when she moved to London, for all three of them. Or, at least, that's the front she'd maintained until she'd come across her mother's albums.

When the doctors admitted there wasn't much more they could do for Pauline's condition, five years before, Angelica had insisted Pauline move down to her airy, comfortable house in Islington. It was selfish, as much as self-sacrificing, because there was no way she was moving back to Sydney Street, but she couldn't bear the thought of her mother fading away unloved in a nursing home. She didn't have long, after all. The offer had taken both her and Pauline by surprise, but Angelica realised she meant it, and Pauline had arrived with only three bags of possessions, and once they were safely in her room, she didn't bother to unpack them. It was enough, she said, that they were there.

The months had been years, in the end, and Angelica found she was grateful for them. She only discovered the album in the bottom of the wardrobe much later, gathering her mother's things together after the funeral. It was from the year Angelica turned professional, and featured page after page of photographs, carefully cut out from *Dancing Times*, and newspapers; Pauline had painstakingly collected reports of competitions and displays she'd given with Tony, with an interview about turning pro taking pride of place on the page, with the illustrative photo opposite. There they were, she and Tony, fixed for a dramatic second in mid-spin, their fingers splayed like starfish against the darkness, the lights bouncing off their ecstatic, fake-tanned faces.

114

The cuttings were interspersed with the occasional postcards she'd sent, the odd dashed-off letter on hotel notepaper. Her mother had kept them all, sticking them in with photo corners, and adding dates in white pencil on the black paper.

It had made Angelica's breath stick in her throat, thinking of Pauline pasting each snippet into the thick pages, breathing heavily as she went, letting the journalists tell her the details about Angelica's dazzling beaded frocks and liquid footwork that she wasn't getting from Angelica herself. When she'd gone into the attic and found there were dozens of the same big, old-fashioned albums, starting with her first appearances in Mrs Trellys's display performances, and ending with her retirement, a terrible sense of guilt and love overwhelmed Angelica, and she had to sit down and cry.

Why had her mother never told her about these albums? She'd rarely come along to competitions, though Angelica frequently offered her tickets and hotels. She never asked for programmes or photographs or anything. And yet she'd made records of competitions Angelica could barely remember herself. Why had she documented her life like a fan, instead of just being there?

It was typical of Mum, she thought, never pushing herself forward in case Dad said something. Despite the fact that he and Mum still went dancing themselves, he had some hard words to say when she turned professional—it seemed to annoy him even more that she was making money out of his hobby. Angelica could picture the whole conversation now, although she knew it would be more of a terse monologue, interspersed with

115

nodding. She guessed poor Mum would rather watch from the sidelines than risk annoying him.

Ten years ago, Angelica would have snorted at her mother's weakness. Now she wasn't so harsh.

All the albums were there on the table in the front room, waiting for her to open them properly. It was something she'd put off in the few months she'd been back. Those first few weeks had been spent doing little, apart from sleeping and thinking and sorting out boxes of boring papers, listening to dance music until she fell asleep. It was like being on a retreat; alone, for once, she had collapsed into inertia as the memories washed back, powerless to do anything but remember.

Looking at the albums now, Angelica was torn, still. Part of her was curious to see what she might have forgotten, to admire her slender, proud self in her slashed finery; another part of her didn't want to be reminded of those times at all. There was something about the tension and darkness of the competition floor that felt half-nightmarish by itself, and she knew that those heart-racing moments would probably surge through her head again as soon as she went to bed. Not that the struggle showed on her face. As the photographs showed, Angelica seemed to be contemplating the love of her life in every shot.

I should go through them, she thought, taking off her coat and hanging it on a padded hanger. It's the least I can do for Mum.

Angelica made herself a strong gin and tonic and began at the first album, her first ballet recital.

'Angela Clarke, of Longhampton, gave a charming performance of the solo from Coppelia . . .*'*

116

CHAPTER EIGHT

By ten to eight, Katie was at her desk, wearing her most dynamic suit, contact lenses in and coffee on the go, and the first flickers of a headache already crimping her brain.

It wasn't totally a product of hardcore efficiency: this was the only suit that didn't require a trip to the dry cleaners, and Jack's teething had kept her up since four-thirty anyway, then Hannah had joined in with the yelling and all Ross had done was to start breakfast early. It had almost been a relief to get out of the madhouse by seven.

Just as well, though, she thought, finishing off the stale muffin she'd grabbed on the way out, because she was starting off the week in the worst possible way: a 9 a.m. progress meeting with her department boss, Eddie Harding.

The planning office buzzed with more politics than the actual council offices upstairs from them. Katie's current problem was second-guessing how Eddie was going to move her off this key, promotion-enhancing urban regeneration study and give it to his golfing buddy, Nick.

Nick Felix had three years' less experience than her, but crucially, he played golf and his father was a property developer. It was fairly obvious to everyone that Eddie was grooming him to take over quite a lot of the interesting stuff she actually enjoyed doing—finding dead areas that could be turned into something fresh and useful, working on housing and the odd renovation project—and shift her sideways into something boring like car parks.

There were lots of areas that needed renovation in Longhampton, but there were also lots of car parks.

Katie knew it made her sound a bit geeky, but she was genuinely excited about the town redevelopment plans. They'd been on the back burner for years, what with funding and developers, but finally it all seemed to be oving. There would be new shops, new flats, with substantial grants for local amenities. Longhampton was so worn out and rain stained that any new building would brighten it up. Apart from the red-brick town hall, and a few offices, there wasn't enough Victoriana left to lend the place much dignity and the best thing she could think of for the horrible post-war social housing and scuffed precinct was a wrecking ball.

She sipped her black coffee as she went systematically through the first file of paperwork. It made a change to have a quiet office to think in, and she moved swiftly through the technical jargon, stripping it back until a vivid picture emerged in her mind. Katie was good at visualising buildings and spaces. There were two sites currently proposed for the project, and her job was to co-ordinate feasibility assessment of one area, while Nick looked at the other. Katie's was, as she could have predicted, located on the scabbier side of town, including some newish housing estates, the old cider factory and the tip. That would make for some lovely site visits, she thought, skimming the leasehold reports she'd asked her intern, Scott, to sort out.

Her headache took a proper hold at the sight of Scott's jagged writing on the Post-it notes, and she reached for the super-strength ibuprofen tablets in her desk drawer.

Katie was willing to put money on the fact that Eddie Harding had deliberately allocated her the bolshiest possible trainee this year, as part of his on-going campaign to prove he was no slave to the PC brigade. Eddie's own speciality was office jargonese, but with an unpleasantly bloke-ish twist. He liked to slap desks, and bark things like, 'It's a balls/walls situation' and, 'It's your cock on the block, Kate—if you had one'. Scott might have had sloping shoulders, but he still managed to balance a chip on each one, and he had a new-wave sexist attitude to women bosses.

She blinked, and her mind slipped to the Relate session lined up for that evening. Just thinking about it made her insides crawl: they had to discuss how they met, in front of Peter's gently sympathetic gaze. Katie could remember *exactly* how they met, how exciting and dream-like it had felt to have a man like Ross want her, just as much as she wanted him, and the prospect of sitting there describing it as if it had happened to someone else felt like a betrayal.

That was the problem: she didn't hate him, he just wasn't the man she married.

I don't think I've got the energy to put this right, she thought. I can't fix my marriage, *and* support the family, *and* keep up with work, *and* do everything else . . .

She put her elbows on the desk and rested her tired eyes against her palms. Do it for Hannah and Jack, she told herself. You don't want them to grow up thinking rows and silences and tension is normal, do you?

It occurred to Katie that although she'd never actually seen her parents rowing, she'd never seen them cuddling either. Or ballroom dancing. Occasionally, her dad used to tell her mum that she looked nice if she'd just had her hair cut, but since Mum wrote that on the kitchen calendar, he didn't even have to notice of his own accord.

Katie stared out of the window, towards the ugly clock tower, and wondered if her parents had had a really happy marriage, if they'd ever gone to counselling. They certainly fit the template—Mum at home until she went to school, Dad in a suit supporting the family, church at Easter and Christmas, holidays in France, no money worries— but it wasn't as though there'd been the same snuggling in bed that Hannah and Jack enjoyed on a Sunday morning with her and Ross. Treats when she got school prizes, yes. Snuggling, no. But then these days she felt so brain-dead after a long day at work that sometimes she could forgive her dad for not being more communicative. They'd taken themselves off to Spain without so much as a backward glance once she was safely out of the nest, so maybe that was it; maybe it was having her around that put the kybosh on any parental romance. Maybe they were having their second honeymoon now, in Majorca.

They meant well, she conceded, thinking of the trusts that her dad had set up for Hannah and Jack. But they just weren't natural parents.

At least Hannah and Jack knew she and Ross loved them, she told herself, feeling very emotional all of a sudden.

Katie did something she rarely allowed herself to do during working hours: she picked up the

120

phone and dialled her home number.

As it rang, she let her gaze drift round the empty office, over the stacks of paperwork, and silent computers, the fake plants and dusty blinds, and her mind's eye pictured the scene at home.

Hannah would be stomping around now, she thought, fussing over the right shoes for school. And Jack would probably be staggering about, clamouring to get into his car seat. He loved going in the car. Her arms ached to cuddle them both.

'Hello?' Ross answered. He sounded flustered, and as soon as she heard his voice, Katie felt the spell break.

'Hi, it's me,' she said.

'Is something wrong?'

'No . . . No, I just . . .' Katie swallowed. 'I just wanted to check everything was OK.'

'Everything's *fine*,' said Ross, and there was a twinge of irritation in his voice. 'Except I'm right in the middle of getting the kids ready to take Hannah to school, and Jack's . . . Hannah! Hannah, put that down *now*! Yes, now! What was it you wanted, then? What have I forgotten now?'

Oh no, she thought, her heart sinking. He thinks I'm checking up on him.

'Nothing,' she said. 'I just wanted to say . . .'

How grateful I am that you're showing our kids how loved they are? How much I wish I could be there with you? How sorry I am for being such a cow?

A movement at the corner of her eye made Katie swivel in her chair. Someone was walking along the corridor to her office, slowing down as they passed.

Eddie Harding's fat face appeared round the door and he winked at her with his bulgy eye. His

121

expression clearly said, 'Personal call?'

As soon as she made eye contact, a gear shifted in Katie's head, and she moved into Kate work mode. It was something she'd learned to do, to shut off thoughts of home, focus on the task in hand, get the job done.

'You wanted to say what?' demanded Ross, distractedly. 'Hannah, come right away from the kettle! I've told you before about . . .'

'Listen, sorry, it's a bad time, I'll call you later,' said Katie and hung up. 'Morning, Eddie,' she said, to get in first.

'And a very good morning to you, Kate,' said Eddie. He tried to look sympathetic, but Katie wasn't fooled. 'Baby trouble?'

'No, just getting an early message in to the legal team,' she said, shuffling her papers. 'I think there may be a leasehold issue with some of the land we're looking at for the retail area of the development. And then with the council houses . . .'

'I wouldn't worry too much about that,' said Eddie, confidently. 'I've got my Compulsory Purchase Order muscles nicely warmed up, believe you me. And we're not talking peanuts with the financial backing.' He tapped his nose, which was already shiny.

Katie felt queasy, and not just on account of her too-strong coffee.

Do this project well, she promised herself, and you can get promoted right out of Eddie Harding's slimy pond.

*   *   *

Round the corner from Katie's offices, Lauren was

122

preparing the files for the morning's appointments, and trying not to worry about the fact that Mrs Carlyle was back again with her foot, first appointment, despite having just seen Dr Carthy last Friday. She made a mental note to check the front door at ten to, in case she was waiting. You didn't want to hang around in a cold wind with a bad foot.

Lauren had been working on reception at Longhampton Park Surgery for just over a year, and in that time, she'd turned it into an altogether more cheerful place to be ill.

Before lunch on her first day, she'd taken over computer duties from poor Dr Carthy, whose idea of IT skills was to turn the machine on and off when it didn't do what he wanted, and, consequently, the surgery's plague of phantom appointments vanished overnight. To the amazement of the other two part-time receptionists, Diane and Sue, Lauren's refusal to take offence had won over fearsome Kathleen, who dispensed prescriptions and also tart personal advice, usually loud enough for the rest of the surgery to hear.

She tackled the waiting room, where patients had only a dog-eared pile of Dr Bashir's steam train journals and some family planning leaflets to distract themselves from their ailments: Lauren brought in stacks of her own wedding and fashion magazines, as well as Frank's gardening monthlies and Chris's old *Top Gear*s and put flowers from their garden on the front desk. She started a book sale table in aid of the playgroup, and when mums came in with children, Lauren gave them crayons to draw pictures while they waited, then stuck them up on the wall in a special gallery.

She was, as Dr Bashir said each morning when she brought him his coffee, 'not just a little ray of sunshine—a great lanky streak of one'.

Lauren liked her job. She enjoyed the satisfying, uncomplicated arranging it involved, and she loved meeting new people—especially those sporting embarrassing injuries that proved she wasn't the clumsiest person in town. Longhampton was big enough to have an underwhelming abbey and five supermarkets, but it was small enough for her to get on chatty terms with the old folk and the nervous new mums who came in clutching their babies—Lauren was good at names and always had something nice to say about a pug-ugly toddler.

The only thing she found a strain was the whole confidentiality business. Dr Carthy had spent fifteen minutes in her interview impressing on her how essential it was to keep everyone's details absolutely, totally confidential, and she had nodded seriously and insisted that she was brilliant at keeping things quiet, and that she'd never told anyone half the things she could have done, what with her mum being a teacher and knowing half the town since they were five. As she'd told Bridget later, he'd totally softened up at that, because his grandson Jackson had been in Mrs Armstrong's class last year and why hadn't she said, yadda, yadda, yadda. Then his printer had jammed again, and she'd put the paper tray in properly for him, and the job was hers.

Anyway, it wasn't that Lauren relished gossip, not like the way Kathleen loved telling them which local councillor was back on the antibiotics and thrush cream, wink wink. It was more the strange

124

private view it gave her, once she knew little details about patients. It was like watching a soap opera, but with real people, and she couldn't help the way her imagination grabbed the scraps of their inner lives and ran away with them. For instance, Kerry Michaels had a repeat prescription for the pill, and yet she and her husband had had two appointments with the fertility counsellor. What was that about? And Mrs Herbert, who kept making appointments with Dr McKay, the new locum—several times a week, to the point where Dr McKay had to ask her to pretend he was on call. Was she ill? Did Dr McKay not know what was wrong with her? Or did she have a crush?

As she picked out the patient notes for the day's appointments, Lauren reminded herself not to be nosy—her morning mantra—but she couldn't help noticing that Mr Wrightson was in to see Dr Bashir for the third time in a fortnight.

Ooh dear, she thought, grimacing at Dr Bashir's inability to break bad news gently. I hope it's nothing serious. Poor Mr Wrightson.

Her eye scanned down the printed-out list, checking it against the files she had in the basket, until her attention was snagged by a familiar name.

Angelica Andrews.

Angelica—from class! Her file was third down; she was due in to see Dr Carthy at ten. For a ten-minute appointment.

Lauren's fingers twitched to open the file, and a stern voice in her head—which sounded a lot like her mother—nagged about patient confidentiality. There was also the small matter of Too Much Information, a problem she'd encountered when she discovered her old driving teacher had

Irritable Bowel Syndrome.

It's not like I'm going to tell anyone, she argued back. She's a new patient. I'll just check to see everything's here.

It said Angelica Andrews on the outside, but when she opened it up, the official record belonged to Miss Angela Marie Andrews.

So not Angelica after all? Lauren wasn't sure that she didn't feel a little disappointed by that.

Address, 34 Sydney Street, Longhampton.

Ooh, down by the river. They weren't big houses but they had pretty gardens, and they'd gone dead expensive in the last few years . . .

Date of birth, 31 May, 1950.

'Wow!' she said aloud, causing Sue to stop piling up her new consignment of used thrillers on the books table.

'Everything OK, Lauren?' she asked, a John Grisham poised in her hand.

'Oh, er, fine, yes.'

Fifty-seven! Lauren didn't think Angelica looked anything like as old as that. She was only three years younger than her own mother, and much as Lauren loved her mum, she definitely didn't look anywhere near as polished and youthful as Angelica.

Angela.

No, Angelica, Lauren decided. She wasn't an Angela.

It wasn't that she *meant* to carry on nosing, but there was something about Angelica's rather dramatic manner in class that made her more curious than usual to peek beneath. Hadn't her mum said she was famous, or something? Lauren's eyes travelled through the check-ups and

126

antibiotics, deciphering the doctors' scrawl easily now after so much practice, looking for . . . well, she wasn't sure what she was looking for.

'Oh dear,' said Lauren aloud, seeing a repeat prescription for the strongest painkillers and some note about knee cartilage problems.

It seemed that Angelica had moved to Sydney Street a few months ago, and her records had been transferred from a posh private surgery in Islington. That made sense, she thought, picturing Angelica swishing along a smart London street, big sunglasses on, takeaway coffee in hand. But before that, she had a couple of addresses right there in Longhampton, and her place of birth was down as the local hospital, when it was still St Mary's!

Well, thought Lauren, sitting with a thump on the nearest chair. Mum was right. She is local. I wonder why she came back?

Lauren's own version of the Angelica Andrews story began to unfold in glorious daytime-TV-scope as she stared out of the window and watched the 8.50 bus drop a load of pensioners off at the flat-roofed library opposite. A lost love, maybe. A boy she'd pined for while she was at school, and lost touch with when her dancing career whisked her away to the bright lights of a big city. She probably had to choose between them, Lauren decided: career or the love of her life. And now she was back, older and wiser, no longer Angie, but Angelica, arranging classes in the hope that he might walk in and sweep her off her feet . . .

The intercom buzzed from the nurses' rooms, and Nurse Jones's Brummie voice sliced through the soft background strings of her imagination. 'Lauren? Any sign of that tea?'

127

Lauren put the files back into Dr Carthy's basket. 'On my way,' she said, as Sue mimed a sarcastic Hitler moustache under her nose and opened the front door for the first pre-work walk-ins.

*   *   *

Angelica arrived for her appointment at ten to ten. Lauren watched through the big glass window as she walked along the street, her toes neatly pointed, back straight, but her head was bowed and she seemed preoccupied. So much that when Mr Watters, leaving after his blood-pressure check, opened the door so she could walk in first, Angelica almost forgot to thank him.

Lauren's curiosity turned a few degrees towards concern at the sight of Angelica's tired expression.

'Hello, Angelica,' she said, with a sunny smile.

It was a bit odd, seeing her in the surgery, out of her usual memorial-hall setting, a bit like seeing someone from a soap opera in the supermarket. She seemed more coloured-in than everyone else around her: her black hair was just as glossy and slicked back as it was for class, and though she wasn't wearing her full-on dancing ensemble, her clothes were chic and sort of French-looking—a creamy cashmere jumper under her red swing coat, and a neat wool skirt.

The sort of thing you'd wear for a posh lunch in London, imagined Lauren, then mentally slapped herself.

Angelica blinked in surprise to see Lauren there. But she quickly recovered, and returned Lauren's smile.

'Hello!' she said. 'How's that foxtrot coming along?'

'Oh, not bad.'

'Are you practising?'

'Er . . .' Lauren was very bad at lying.

Angelica wagged a finger. 'It only comes with practice. You just need to know the steps so you don't have to think about them. Like driving!'

'That's what my dad says,' said Lauren, glumly. 'But he's had forty years to learn. He and my mum can even do that complicated foxtrot. They were showing me the other night.'

'Oh, really?' said Angelica. 'We must get them to demonstrate.'

Kathleen sailed past behind them and snorted out loud. 'Lauren? Foxtrot? I don't think so. Cowtrot, more like. Eh? Eh? Sue? Our Big Bird, dancing?'

Sue said something Lauren didn't catch, but it ended in '. . . bless her heart', and sent Kathleen into cackles.

'Actually, Lauren's one of the best in the class,' said Angelica, as Lauren winced.

But Kathleen was cackling her way back to the dispensary.

'You're coming along very well,' said Angelica, holding Lauren's gaze with her own bright blue eyes, until Lauren felt an odd sense of belief that she was. 'You've got a lovely line. Comes with being tall. We'll have you swirling around that reception like Cinderella, just you wait.'

'Sleeping Beauty,' said Lauren, automatically, but now transfixed by a vision of herself and Chris, waltzing around in stardust.

'Whatever you want,' beamed Angelica, and

Lauren wondered if this was what it felt like at those evangelical prayer meeting things, where they convinced you that you didn't need your wheelchair. 'When that music starts, you're going to look like any princess you name.'

Lauren sighed happily, then had a more realistic thought of Chris and his two left feet, and sighed again less happily.

She shook herself. Angelica wasn't there to talk about her dancing. In fact, what was she there for? There were no notes on the computer about what she'd made the appointment for.

Lauren, she told herself, in her mother's stern voice, don't be such a *nose*.

She adopted the friendly but professional expression they were all meant to show to patients, and waved a hand towards the chairs. 'Do you want to take a seat? Dr Carthy's running a little late.'

'Thank you,' said Angelica.

It was a busy morning, with two patients over-running their appointments with 'oh, while I'm here' queries, which meant everyone else was made late, and Lauren had her work cut out keeping the waiting room from boiling over into full-on mutiny. She was helping one of the regular old dears choose a new thriller off the book stall when Angelica swept out in a mist of perfume, and for the rest of the morning, Lauren was too rushed off her feet to wonder any more about why she'd been in.

CHAPTER NINE

Angelica's ladybird-red coat made a bright splash against the drab concrete of the precinct as she walked through the middle of town. She pulled the collar up against the swirl of freezing air that barrelled between the high walls, direct from the frozen North. A couple of old ladies pushing tartan shoppers turned to peer at her as she passed, which confirmed her suspicion that bright-coloured clothing in Longhampton was still viewed with something bordering on suspicion.

Angelica was pleased that she still didn't care.

She'd always brightened herself up with red, even when she was a little girl. Looking at the first album last night had brought back a memory she could almost taste of her red summer Clarks sandals—you needed a splash of something bright growing up in the relentless grey, grey, grey of Longhampton in the sixties. The only town in the country that couldn't be bothered to raise its own Merseybeat knock-offs. Angelica had always had a bit of colour about her. A bit of something different.

Not that it had endeared her to her schoolmates. 'Olive Oyl,' they'd called her, on account of her long dark plaits, tied up with a red ribbon. And on account of her skinny legs too, probably, and her pale face. Angelica didn't care, even then. She knew she didn't fit in in Longhampton, and she knew she wasn't going to hang around to be hammered into the dull life open to girls of her age: babies, a till job, more babies, then grandchildren.

She turned the corner, where a Tesco Metro now stood instead of Dixon's the Fine Jewellers, and found herself slowing down at the old girls' entrance of her old school. It was bricked up, and a new plastic sign announced it as Longhampton Community School, rather than All Saints' Grammar, but otherwise, it was as it was back in 1961: a turreted monolith of a school, with high pointed windows, separate entrances for girls and boys, and a dominating need to shuffle everyone in line, until they were all exactly the same, trotting out of the other end like academic soldiers.

Or Tiller girls, she thought, then smiled at the memory of some of her classmates. They thought they were tough, those Evelyns and Pennys, but they wouldn't have lasted ten back-breaking minutes in a bitchy three-times-a-night chorus line.

To her surprise, Angelica realised the trickle of nostalgia breaking through was actual pleasure that the school hadn't been knocked down. It proved she'd once been here, and left, and come back her own person.

She stared up at the windows, her eyes searching out her last form room, where she'd gazed out over the terraced roofs of the town from her desk by the window, willing the days away until she could leave, and travel beyond their corrugated limits.

It had been shamefully easy to leave her mum and dad, once the offer of the job in London had come up. The pay wasn't great, but she'd be able to get some real lessons, and proper experience, more to the point. Her mum, of course, had encouraged her even with tears in her eyes; 'You have to go, Angie,' she'd insisted, proud and miserable at the

132

same time. 'You'll be able to have lessons with the best teachers, and you won't get that round here.'

It had been her mum who'd sent her to the ballet class in the Memorial Hall, and bought her the red ballet shoes she'd begged for. Pauline was one of Longhampton's mighty army of ballroom dancers, although even at twelve Angelica knew it was more enthusiasm than skill that propelled her parents round the sprung Memorial Hall floor. Her bosom, Pauline explained, got in the way, which made Angelica grateful for her own flat chest, but she was happier to have inherited her mum's small feet.

Funnily enough, though, when a friend of a dancing friend tipped her off about the audition to dance in a West End show called *Not Now, Napoleon!*, it was Angelica's dad who slipped her the train fare. He wasn't exactly a doting father, but then which dads were back then? Angelica couldn't help feeling that he wanted her to go to London, so he could have Pauline back to himself, rather than because he wanted her to embark on a glamorous life of dance. 'You've always done us proud!' her mother had sobbed on the platform, as Angelica leaned out of the train window, tearless.

Cyril Clarke always looked a bit peeved at that, and Angelica knew it was because her dancing lessons were cutting into his pools money.

Still, he got pride of place back in the house in June 1966, when Angela Clarke left All Saints' Grammar after her O-levels, too tall by an inch to be a ballerina, but just the right height to dance in the London shows with three-foot feathers on her head and sparkles on her thighs. In her free time, she followed her mum's passion, ballroom. What seemed dowdy and a little faded in Longhampton was so different in London, like taking the gauze layer away from a photo album; the costumes were brighter and more daring, the partners didn't grope you, and the music blared until her ears ached with pleasure, performed by live bands of dinner-suited musicians. And as her mother hoped, she took extra lessons whenever she could, constantly improving herself, polishing up the glamorous new Angelica.

She wrote letters home, telling her mum the dancing gossip, and sent snaps of herself in all the nightclubs, and brought her special ballroom shoes at Christmas. It was a great time to be young in London, and an even better time to be young and dancer-thin, as her Olive Oyl legs fitted Biba fashion perfectly. Her dad wasn't impressed by the kipper ties she bought him in Carnaby Street; in fact, he'd been almost offended. 'I'm not one of your nancy-boy friends!' he'd bellowed, as the highpoint of his Christmas Day 1969, and after that Angelica stopped bothering.

The bell rang for lunchtime in the school, the same shrill ring now that Angelica remembered from forty years ago, and she jumped. Teenagers started to spill out of the doors, their uniform a scruffy parody of the rigid navy and yellow she remembered, and she began walking again, before she realised how young they looked and how old she felt.

Angelica felt little jabs of nostalgia as she walked around the town centre. Her memories were like bumper cars at the fair; she could be hurrying through the precinct, with its modern shops, and then suddenly be jerked back to her childhood by a faded old chemist's sign above a modern awning, then bumped forward into more recent, sadder thoughts. She'd been reliving the past a lot recently: going through her mother's paperwork, slipping the browning photographs back into their paper corners, pulling old letters out of their envelopes and sorting out the boxes that had come from the attic. It sounded like a quick job, until you factored in the hours of suspended remembering it set in motion. Every box seemed to give her another week of broken sleep, as the new things she was learning, and the old things she thought she'd forgotten jostled their way back into her dreams.

That's why she'd called in to see Dr Carthy, for the discreet something she needed these days to help her sleep, as well as something to take the ache off her worn-out knees. She couldn't remember the last time she'd slept through a night without some help.

Angelica crossed the main road towards the abbey, where the smarter Victorian terraces started. Their white-painted and respectable fronts rose up above gardens of box-trees and honeysuckle, or, more commonly, newly concreted drives. Doctors' surgeries now, or dentists, or nursing homes. Maybe Mum would have preferred to stay here, she thought. Angelica had the uneasy feeling that her mother never really settled well in London, no matter what she said. Never got to know anyone properly and then when her hip got bad she couldn't even come along to the tea dances any more.

Angelica's brisk steps slowed as the sadness of that final year welled back up, and she had to stop, resting against the sturdy brick wall of someone's garden.

'You've been an angel,' her mum had said nearly every day, sitting in her chair by the window, growing smaller and more faint by the week. Angelica had put the CD player of big-band tunes within reach of the arthritic fingers, then turned her easy chair to face the canal, which you could see from the back of her house in Islington. Though it wasn't a river, like the one that ran through Longhampton, it was something for her to look at. There were usually some ducks. 'You're a good girl to look after your old mum like this.'

'What else would I do?' Angelica had said, every time, impatiently at first, then more sadly. 'If you hadn't sent me to ballet, I wouldn't have been a dancer, and I wouldn't have gone to America, and I wouldn't have married Jerry, and I wouldn't have this house to have you in. You looked after me, Mum. It's my turn to look after you.'

And they'd shared a look, and thoughts would pass unspoken between their eyes: Angelica never said she missed her dad, because she didn't, and Pauline never mentioned Jerry, or the woman he'd married after the divorce brought Angelica back to England, or the long months when Angelica had fallen out of touch with everyone. The loneliness she never wanted to talk about. Her mum knew what to say, and what not to—a skill she'd picked up over forty years with Cyril.

Just once, though, when Mum was a bit doped-up on her painkillers, she'd forgotten, and it slipped out like a black beetle scuttling out of a plant pot.

'Looking after me, like I looked after your little

Rosie,' she'd joked, and the pain flared up in Angelica's face. She tried to summon up her dancing expression, the wide smile that masked raw feet and an aching back, but her mother had felt her hand twitch, and sensed a sorrow that she couldn't quite make out in the bad light without her strong glasses.

'Oh, I'm sorry, love,' she'd said, contritely. 'I'm sorry.'

'Me too,' said Angelica, suddenly Angela again, plain Angela with no fake smile to hide behind.

They had sat, holding hands, not saying anything, but thinking of Pauline's cold, empty house miles away from Islington's self-conscious streets of antique shops and pavement cafés.

That was the thing about dancing, Angelica thought, shaking herself back to the present day. It gave you an escape from everyday life, but it filled up every corner until there was so little room for anything else. And your dancing life spilled into your real one, eating it up like a hungry caterpillar.

She tugged on the collar on her ladybird coat, and carried on walking, her heels clicking briskly on the pavement and her sleeping pills rattling in her handbag.

CHAPTER TEN

In Peter's sparse community centre consulting room, Katie had taken as long as she could to rearrange herself, her bag, her cup of cold water, her packet of tissues, her chair and her notebook. She'd put off the evil moment for a good six minutes, but the large clock on the wall was very visible to Ross, and, more importantly, to Peter, who was keen to get going with their session. He had the patient look of a man who'd seen a lot of desperate time-wasting, and wasn't about to start indulging it now.

'So.' He smiled patiently, but with a warmth that reached his eyes, unlike the phoney smile Katie had managed to plaster on to mask her nerves. Ross, she noted, wasn't even bothering to pretend. 'Shall we make a start? How you met. Who wants to go first?'

Ross turned his puppy-dog eyes towards Katie, expecting her to take the lead. *As usual*, she thought. Doesn't he ever think for himself?

Her incipient irritation must have showed, because Peter pounced, casually tipping his head towards Ross. 'Why don't you get the ball rolling? I've noticed you tend to let Katie take the initiative in discussions. That's not a great habit to get into, if you want to keep a healthy balance in your relationship, so why don't we turn that around now? Start us off.'

Good, thought Katie, ignoring the counsellor-speak. So I'm not the bad guy *all* the time here.

Ross cleared his throat with a dry splutter, his usual giveaway nervous tic, then said, 'OK. Well, I met Katie in a pub near where I used to work, The Horse. It was a quiz night, and she was there with some girls.'

'From the office,' added Katie. 'First time we'd been. I don't spend a lot of time in pubs.'

'Mind if I finish?' asked Ross.

'Sorry. Go on, sorry.'

'I was there with a bunch of old mates from

138

school—we went every week, but to be honest, we were there for the beer, rather than the quiz. I noticed the girls next to us were coming up with answers to everything. Well, one girl next to me.' Ross's tensed shoulders began to drop as he got into his story. He didn't even need to look at the notes Peter had asked them to make.

'They kept telling her to whisper, but Katie's got quite a carrying voice,' he went on. 'And there was something about the way she spoke that just . . . clicked with me. She sounded clever, and confident. Attractive. Anyway, the pub was packed, and the tables were really close together. She was sitting nearest us, so I kept leaning further and further back until we were almost touching, and . . .' He shrugged, a shy smile starting in the corner of his mouth. 'I pretended it was a joke for the lads, the comedy eavesdropping, but I was just looking for an excuse to start a conversation, really.'

'And you did?' prompted Peter.

'Well, yeah. She caught me eavesdropping and had a right go at me, so the least I could do was offer to buy her a drink. Then we got talking and Katie did some kind of deal where they traded some current affairs answers for our pop music round, and . . .' The smile bloomed into a full-on goofy grin. 'We swapped phone numbers too. And that's how we met.'

'Can you remember what she was wearing?'

'Yes,' said Ross immediately. 'A red V-neck jumper and a pair of black trousers that made her legs look about a mile long. And red shoes, with pointy toes.'

Peter looked genially at Katie. 'That's quite a

compliment, isn't it, that that's still so fresh in Ross's mind?'

'He's a visual person,' explained Katie, seeing where the discussion was going. 'He's meant to notice things like that.'

'Can you remember what I was wearing?' Ross demanded.

'Jeans,' she said, fairly confidently. Ross always wore jeans.

'And?'

'And . . . a band T-shirt?' she hazarded. In the old days, she'd been fascinated by all the obscure bands Ross loved but she'd never even heard of. He looked cool, with his trendy black-framed glasses, his Japanese jeans and tiny gadgets, but Ross didn't have any of the snottiness that the 'cool' people at college had had. How could he, he'd said, pushing his long fringe out of his eyes, with a name like Ross? She'd loved the way he wanted to share his discoveries, not guard them. He'd even painstakingly copied CDs for her, trying to coax her off Jamiroquai and onto scratchy, yelpy groups he'd seen in sweaty Brixton clubs.

Katie caught herself melting inside at the memory of it. But it was a memory, that someone else might have told her about. When had he stopped being so sexy?

'Which one?' he asked.

Without thinking, she answered her own question with a vivid mental image: sitting at the kitchen table, the night before their first mortgage meeting with the bank. She was three months pregnant with Hannah. When they'd argued for the first time about the household budget. And she realised that Ross had no savings, but over four hundred CDs, half of them ludicrously expensive imports.

'Which band T-shirt was I wearing?' needled Ross.

'Oh, for God's sake!' she snapped, her brain still struggling with the basic truth that she could hardly be mad at him for something that had been there all along. The sudden rush of remembered anger was as vivid as the early rush of remembered desire had been, but this time it *was* personal. That same anger was still there. Still there, and growing, and the roots of it were in an anger with herself.

'What does it matter? We're talking eight years ago! Ross, I'm so stressed out these days, I can barely remember what I'm wearing *now*!'

Ross looked wounded.

'So, how do you remember the evening, Katie?' asked Peter, turning his attention to her.

She stiffened defensively. 'Like that. More or less.'

'Do you want to describe it to me?'

'Erm . . .'

No, not now I know it's going to be marked out of ten for romantic value. And then there's the other thing, the thing Ross hasn't mentioned yet. The thing that's going to make me look like a real bitch, even though it's not relevant . . .

They were both looking at her now: Ross with an intense expectation in his eyes, Peter with a non-committal encouragement.

Concentrate, Katie told herself. Just . . . just tell them the relevant bits.

'I'd agreed to go to the pub quiz with some girls from my old office, but I had no idea they were going to be so competitive. Ross was on the table next to us, with some trendy-looking guys . . .'

Who in reality had made her feel simultaneously shy and desperate to impress.

'And, um, as Ross says . . .'

'I want to hear what *you* say,' Peter reminded her with his maddening calmness.

'OK, well, Ross kept leaning nearer and nearer me, and someone made a big deal about him copying us, so I felt I had to say something. I did wonder . . .' She paused. 'I did wonder if he was taking the mickey when he asked if I wanted a drink, because he wasn't the sort of guy who'd normally . . . I mean, I didn't think I was the sort of girl who'd . . .'

She looked up, suddenly feeling hot. 'You know what I mean.'

'No?' said Peter.

'I mean,' said Katie, gritting her teeth, 'that Ross was a trendy designer type of guy and I . . . wasn't. I'm still not. OK?'

'You thought I was taking the mickey?' said Ross. 'You've never told me that.'

'No, well, why would I?' Katie felt caught off-balance. She'd never actually let that thought slip into words before. 'Anyway, we got chatting, and he talked me into giving them some answers, in return for some help with the music round.'

'I did it so I could whisper in her ear,' added Ross, obviously buoyed by Katie's confession.

'So, you were both amazed that the other could be interested in you. That's . . . interesting,' said Peter, taking off his glasses.

Oh God, thought Katie, here comes the devastating remark.

But as far as she could see, it didn't come.

142

'So, after that, you started dating?' he went on.

Ross and Katie looked at each other, and hesitated. She saw a vulnerability in his eyes that made her feel protective—another old feeling. It was a bit weird, thought Katie, seeing Ross sitting there with her, but never being quite sure what he was going to say for once. A bit like dancing, when he danced with Jo and bothered to stand up straight, so he looked like a different man. A new man.

What if he pulls himself together, so you fancy him again, and then he decides to leave because you've been such a bitch in here? said a weaselly voice in her head, and she shook it away, speaking quickly, so the thought couldn't settle.

'Yes,' she said, at the same time as he said, 'It was complicated.'

'Katie,' Ross began, 'that's not completely . . .'

'He was wearing a Pixies T-shirt,' she gabbled. 'And Converse All-star trainers. He looked like he could be in a band, or an American sitcom, or something. His hair was so thick, and so soft I wanted to put my fingers in it—'

'She had a fiancé!' shouted Ross over the top of her. 'And she didn't tell me that until our fourth date!'

An awful silence filled the room.

Katie could feel her heart beating up in her throat, while her underarms prickled with sweat. Hot flushes of embarrassment swept through her.

That's it, she thought. I'm never going to recover from this in Peter's eyes. I'm already a cold-hearted cow, and now I'm a cheat. Well done, Ross, have another victim badge.

But it wasn't like that, wailed a voice in her

head. It wasn't . . .

She got a grip on herself, the way she did in meetings when Eddie tried to wind her up about maternity leave being women's stealth holiday. Think. It could be worse, she told herself. At least Ross didn't say that—

'You didn't tell *him* until our fourth date, either, did you?' he added, suddenly.

Oh God. Katie froze.

'Right, well, I can see how that would make the start of your relationship complicated,' said Peter in his even, non-judgemental tone. 'Tell me about that, Katie.'

Katie glared furiously at Ross. 'I don't want to talk about it. I don't see what it has to do with our marriage.'

'I think it has a lot to do with your marriage,' observed Peter.

'You can't just ignore things,' said Ross, sanctimoniously. 'Get it out in the open, Katie. Admit that's what you did. What's the worst that could happen?'

Peter turned to him. 'Of course, it must have been very flattering for you, having a woman dump her fiancé to date you. Hmm? We'll come back to that.'

Ross's mouth hung open, mid-platitude, but Peter had turned back to Katie.

'Tell me about it,' he insisted. 'I think it's important.'

Katie met his clear gaze with her own stubbornness, then, after ten seconds, realised she'd met a force even stubborner. Peter might give a good impression of a bearded muesli-eating do-gooder, but she could sense a will of iron beneath the Aran jumper.

And she was so tired. Too tired. So she closed her eyes, collected her thoughts carefully, like the sharp pieces of a broken plate, and said, 'Steve and I had been going out since our first year of university. We got engaged when we graduated— his grandmother's ring, very big deal. He had a good job in a law firm in Manchester, I'd started work, we were going to buy a house, but we hadn't set a date . . .' She bit her lip.

She hadn't told Jo this. She wasn't even sure she'd told Ross the entire story.

'To be honest, when I met Ross, things had been rocky for a while, and I suppose I just wasn't sure whether I was ready to get married. I was still very young. Steve was my first proper boyfriend and . . .' She looked up—at Peter, not Ross. 'Ross was very different. Meeting him made me realise that maybe . . . there were other options.'

'People do change a lot in those years,' agreed Peter. 'It's not a *crime* to break off an engagement.'

Katie twisted up her mouth. That wasn't how Steve had seen it. Or Steve's mum. Or her mum, come to that. Not that she said any of this aloud.

'You seem very hard on yourself, Katie. You're very worried about getting things wrong, when all you're doing is learning, like everyone else,' he went on, mildly. 'Sometimes we don't do things we'd like to imagine we could . . .'

'I didn't want to cheat,' she gabbled. 'It honestly wasn't like that. But I didn't want to throw away what I had with Steve because of some passing crush either. So, I . . .' Katie stopped, then rephrased what she was about to say. 'I didn't tell Ross about Steve until . . . Until I knew I couldn't

145

go back to Steve and be happy.'

Katie was conscious that Ross was looking intently at her but she didn't want to meet his eye.

'So, in a sense, you gave up one very different kind of life to be with Ross?' said Peter. 'You chose the man you felt would make you happier. And you did it very carefully, and thoughtfully, because you didn't want to cause unnecessary hurt.'

She looked up, surprised that he hadn't twisted the knife.

'I guess so.'

'Are you still in touch with Steve?'

'No, but my mum still is, with his mum. They do Christmas cards. He's married now, and living in London—Hampstead, I think. With three children. They always send those awful cards where the kids are on the front instead of a robin, and they're all skiing somewhere expensive and all you hear about is the new house and . . .'

This time Katie caught Ross's wince, and she stopped, mid-sentence.

Peter took off his glasses. 'Don't you think it's time you let go of Steve?'

Katie started to say, 'I don't feel guilty about . . .' but Ross interrupted her.

'Hear bloody hear!'

She looked at him crossly. 'What? I haven't spoken to Steve in years.'

'You don't have to speak to him. I see the way you look at Jo and Greg's life. You look at Greg and you think, if I'd married Steve I could have a house like that.'

'What? That's such bollocks! If you've got some kind of inferiority complex, then . . .'

Peter coughed and they stopped, like guilty

146

schoolchildren.

'I think you're *both* using this as a way of making the other one feel bad, actually. It's not as unusual as you think, letting old relationships take on a much more significant role in the current one,' he said, easily. 'Katie, you've been hanging on to the guilt, but in fact all you've done is keep an irrelevant benchmark in your life, as to where you could have been by now, if you'd stayed with Steve. You don't know how things would have turned out—he could have changed jobs, or not wanted children, anything. But you proved that Steve wasn't right for you, when you left him for Ross. And Ross, did you ever meet him?'

He shook his head.

'So how do you know what sort of life he could have given her? And does it matter? You've made a life together.'

'I don't want you to think I was measuring them against each other,' insisted Katie. 'That makes me sound really calculating, and cold.'

'I don't think that.' Peter put his glasses back on and blinked. 'You really shouldn't worry so much about what people think.'

'Yeah,' mumbled Ross.

'What?' Katie glared at him, still smarting from the Steve humiliation. 'Come on, Ross. If you're going to be personal, at least have the guts to say it to my face, instead of mumbling to yourself, the way you always do.'

He shrugged. 'You're doing it now. Spinning things to make yourself look better. I don't know why you can't just relax, instead of letting everyone else decide whether you're happy or not. It's stupid. And kind of insulting to me too, actually.

You're obsessed with what other people think but you don't give a toss about how I *feel*.' He pushed his hair back with one hand.

Still thick, thought Katie, but why can't he wash it more often?

'Can you give an example of that, Ross?' asked Peter.

'Yeah, she's constantly agreeing to work late to impress her boss at work, but she won't even consider flexible hours so she can spend time with her children. And maybe give me some time for myself.'

'That's so unfair and not true!' Katie flashed back. 'I can't win! If I leave the office on time, I get more grief than you can *imagine* for being a woman with a family, and if I leave late, I get grief from you! It's easy for you to say "come home early" when you're the one slobbing around the house all day, doing sod all, while I—'

'Doing sod all?' Ross's mouth dropped open. 'Doing sod all? I'm looking after our children!'

Katie knew she'd gone too far. 'That's not what I meant,' she said hurriedly, glancing up at Peter. 'I didn't mean that looking after the children is nothing, I meant that the laundry never gets done, the kitchen's filthy . . .' She regrouped her thoughts, trying to make it as fair as she could. 'I mean, he's never *had* to deal with the sort of office politics I have to. If I could be at home with the kids, while he went out and put the bread on the table, I would. In a flash. But I can't.'

'Yes, let's get back to you,' muttered Ross.

'But you've just told me that his creative job was one of the things you found most attractive about Ross when you met.' Peter smiled, not unkindly.

'And you liked it so much that you split up with a man who had the same kind of job as yours. Isn't that right?'

'Yes,' she admitted. 'But he was working then, and being creative. I *do* love his creativity. But now—'

Ross cut her off with a bitter look. 'Well, I'm sorry I'm so busy with childcare that I don't have time to open up Photoshop. Selfish me.'

'*Ross* . . .' Katie protested.

Peter stepped in before the row could escalate. 'Katie, Ross—I honestly feel there are a lot of positive things we can draw from where you are here,' he said. 'You might not be seeing them right now, but I want you to think about what we've discussed, mull it over, maybe try to have an honest conversation about some of the things we've touched on. It's good that you're airing some of these feelings.' He peered at them over his glasses. 'I get the impression some of this is coming out for the first time?'

Katie nodded.

'It's not about what people think,' he added. 'No one has to be in your marriage apart from you. Oh, I meant to ask!' Peter clapped his hand to his forehead. 'How's the hobby going? What is it you're doing together?'

'Ballroom dancing,' said Ross.

'And?' He looked hopefully between them.

'It's going pretty well,' said Ross. 'So far.'

Katie glared at him, but couldn't bring herself to contradict him in front of Peter.

Peter took off his glasses and cleaned them carefully. 'Good,' he said, and Katie thought he seemed to be choosing his words. 'Good.'

149

CHAPTER ELEVEN

On the other side of the river, in Chestnut Grove, Lauren's plan to cook a lovely supper, over which discussion of her new ideas for a Cinderella-themed reception might go more smoothly, was vanishing faster than the packet of chocolate digestives sitting between her parents on the coffee table. Her dad was pretending not to eat them, about as convincingly as he was pretending to be looking forward to her shepherd's pie. Lauren wasn't a great one for cooking, but this was an attempt to make up for letting her mum slave over every meal since she'd moved in.

Plus, it was Chris's favourite, and she couldn't wait to see him, and tell him about the 'guests' video memory book' Irene had told her about. Or, rather, she had been looking forward to seeing him, at six. It was nearly ten past seven now. Lauren checked her watch. Quarter past seven.

He should have phoned if he was going to be late. She frowned. Chris always let her know if he was going to be late when they were living together. It wasn't like she minded being at home with her mum and dad, but it was beginning to feel like she'd gone back to being sixteen—phoning home if she was going to miss supper, tidying her room—while Chris had rediscovered his single bloke social life, without her. It didn't seem totally fair.

'What time did Chris say he'd call?' Bridget asked, as delicately as she could. 'I'm not sure the shepherd's pie can wait much longer for him in the

150

oven. It's already looking a bit . . . parched.'

'Like me,' said Frank, holding out his mug towards Lauren for a tea refill. 'Top me up and save these creaking hips, eh, love?'

'They're not creaking,' said Lauren. 'They were looking pretty swivelly when you were doing the foxtrot with Angelica the other night.'

'That woman could make a rocking horse swivel,' sighed Frank, stretching out his long legs and turning his attention back to the new camcorder on his knee. 'Good partners do that, they make you dance better than you knew you could. Although she's not a patch on your mother,' he added with a side look at Bridget.

Bridget pretended not to be flattered. 'That won't get you extra pie,' she said.

'But I know something that might,' replied Frank, making a sort of shuffle with his feet that obviously meant something to Bridget, who dissolved into giggles.

'God! Stop! I don't want to know!' Lauren put her hands over her ears.

She didn't remember her parents being this lovey-dovey before she moved out. Had they reined it in while she was living at home? Or was it Dad's retirement and the dancing sending them into some kind of second honeymoon nostalgia phase? Or was it just the fact that she and Chris now had to compress their entire sex-life into about half an hour twice a week that made her hyper-sensitive to it in other people?

Whichever, it was great that they still got it on after, like, a million years together, but your own parents . . .

'I don't know where he's got to,' she said,

151

pushing the idea out of her mind. 'I know he's not having dinner with his mum because today's her Italian class, and he's not answering his phone.'

'Well, I'm getting peckish, Laurie . . .'

'Oh, let's eat.' She got up, unwittingly dislodging Mittens the cat from the back of the chair, where he had been sleeping peacefully for ten minutes. Bridget watched as he slunk off towards the radiator, and sat licking his paws disconsolately.

Lauren paused at the door, like the teenager she'd only just stopped being, and added melodramatically, 'It's not like Chris ever bothers to have an opinion about anything to do with this wedding. But he'd better turn up to dancing this week or else he's totally dead.' Then she stomped off towards the kitchen.

Bridget exchanged a quick glance with Frank, who shrugged in a 'don't ask me' way and pointed the camcorder at Mittens, zooming in on his ominously wagging tail.

'Woah!' he exclaimed, reeling back. 'This gadget's amazing, love. You can see dirt invisible to the naked eye.'

'It should be for what it cost,' said Bridget. She'd come back to find Frank had bought it on impulse for the wedding; it had been on special offer, he explained, and if he practised with it 'in good time', it would save money on hiring a professional videographer, which Irene was insisting they looked into, at huge expense. Plus, he'd gone on, obviously repeating verbatim whatever line they'd spun him in the shop, they'd have it to take on holiday. So it had been a bargain, spending money to save money. It would be a hobby too, he said, now he had more time on his hands.

152

Bridget suppressed a little flutter of nerves, as the cash register in her head rang up another thousand pounds. She wasn't used to spending money like this, and even less used to it being on credit cards.

Calm down, she reassured herself. It's *not* mounting up. It's all going to be paid off when the 0%-interest period finishes—and that's when you can cash in the secret savings account. It fits together perfectly. It's going to be fine.

If Bridget's mother had given her one useful piece of advice, it was that husbands never missed twenty quid here and there. And that there'd come a day when you'd be glad of those twenty quids. Over the years, Bridget had been tucking them away like a squirrel in a secret emergency-only account—and thanks to Lauren's fancy ideas, that emergency had now arrived.

Not, Bridget reminded herself, that she minded splashing out on Lauren's wedding. It was what she really, really wanted, and when you thought about what some people's children put them through, with drying-out clinics, and unexpected babies, and university fees . . .

Frank pointed the camera at her. 'Do you want to go and see what's up with Lauren, then?' he said. 'And do you know you've got hairs growing out of your—'

'Much more of that, and you'll have to watch out for your own hair,' said Bridget, and left before he could work out how to turn it off.

In the kitchen, Lauren was looking daggers at her mobile phone, but as soon as Bridget walked in, she tried to put on her usual smile. It didn't work on Bridget, who'd seen it before. She was touched, though, that Lauren bothered to pretend she wasn't furious in front of her.

'What's up, love?' she asked, as Lauren got a can of Diet Coke out of the fridge. 'Has something happened at the surgery? Have you had words with Kathleen again?'

'No.'

'Well, what? You're not yourself.' Bridget rubbed Lauren's arm affectionately. 'Tell your mum.'

Lauren bit her lip, and Bridget's heart bumped as she saw the frustrated little girl in her face. 'It's just this *dancing*. Irene called me today—she wants to talk about music for our first waltz, and whether we'll need a spotlight, and I just think . . . we're never going to be good enough!'

Oh well, if that's all it is, thought Bridget and smiled.

'You will,' she soothed. 'It just takes a bit of getting used to, dancing with someone else. Chris'll look wonderful once he's got the hang of it. Those lovely broad shoulders!'

Lauren looked unconvinced. He hadn't even really got the hang of it by the end of the class, when everyone else was well away. It was deeply unsexy, him being such a malco. 'Yeah, well, I don't even know if he's going to turn up to the class tomorrow. Kian wants him to join some five-a-side league.' She fiddled with the can. 'I bet that's where he is now, down the pub with Kian. He never used to be like this, it's just since he moved back in with him.' She looked up. 'Am I being a nag, Mum? I don't want him to think I'm a nag, but it's really annoying. Did you have to put your foot down with Dad?'

154

'No,' said Bridget. 'Well, yes. Sort of. The trick is to do it so they don't realise.'

Lauren opened her Diet Coke fiercely, as if she was snapping something off Chris.

That leech Kian, maybe.

'Now, come on,' said Bridget. 'You know he sometimes has after-work customers at the garage. Of course Chris cares about the wedding—men just don't get as into it as we do. Why don't you give him one more ring, while I put some peas on?'

Lauren looked at her watch and tutted. 'Mum, hang on with the peas a minute,' she said. 'I've got to check my auction.'

'Auction?'

'For my Snow White cake topper,' Lauren called over her shoulder, as she barged her way out of the kitchen. 'In Wyoming . . .' Her voice trailed away, drowned out by the sound of her feet clumping up the stairs.

Mittens slid into the kitchen, flicking his black tail crossly, then winding himself around Bridget's legs, begging for attention and some supper. Lauren's noisy return had thoroughly disrupted his semi-retired-cat life, and Bridget felt more than a little guilty for the loss of his peace and quiet.

'Sorry,' she said, chucking him on the white patch under his chin, and feeling the throaty purr start up at once. 'It's not for ever. She'll be married soon enough.'

Bridget made herself a cup of coffee, and took one upstairs for Lauren, in her favourite mug. She found her hunched at her computer, making nervous clicking noises as she refreshed the page over and over again. Because of all the stuff crammed into her room, Lauren had had to set up

155

her computer on her old desk, so her knees were practically round her ankles, but her eyes were gleaming with an excitement that suggested that she wasn't really noticing any incipient cramp.

'What's this, then?' asked Bridget, peering at the screen.

'eBay,' said Lauren. 'Come on, come on . . . Yes! Yes!' She clapped her hands together then punched the air. 'Look! Mum! I've won!'

'Well done!' said Bridget, automatically. 'What have you won?'

'These cake decorations.' Lauren scrolled down to the photographs of Snow White being gripped by a handsome sugarcraft prince. 'You can't get them in England. Aren't they gorgeous?'

'Mmm. Very . . . unusual. I thought you hadn't decided about your theme yet?'

'Oh, they're so cheap, it doesn't matter if I get Snow White *and* Lady and the Tramp,' Lauren replied, cheerfully. 'And Sleeping Beauty.'

'Lady and the Tramp . . . ?'

'I mean, I can always sell them on again, for at least what I paid for them.' Lauren turned round awkwardly, knocking her notebook off the desk and on to her bed as she went. 'That's the thing, Mum. It's so easy! What isn't right, you can just put back on again and someone else will have it off you. I've got rid of a whole load of stuff we didn't need from the flat . . . Look.'

With a series of clicks that Bridget didn't entirely follow, Lauren brought up a busy page of transactions.

'See? I bought the hand-dried rose petals . . .'

From New Jersey, in nine different colours, noted Bridget.

156

'. . . and the glass candle holders in the shape of swans for the table centres, and blue garters for the bridesmaids, and the banners . . .'

'It all looks very complicated,' said Bridget, uncertainly.

'Not really. Just takes a moment to work it out and you're away. People are making fortunes selling tat, you know. All you need's a digital camera and some fancy descriptions.'

An idea began to uncurl in Bridget's mind. A way of offsetting some of the outgoings that seemed to be mounting up with every passing week.

'Could you . . . could you show me how you'd go about buying something, then? Or selling something?'

Lauren looked up at her with an indulgent smile. 'Ah ha! It's those Scottish genes coming out! Are you bargain hunting, Mum?'

'Oh, you know . . .' Bridget tried not to look too interested. She didn't want Lauren thinking they couldn't afford her big day. Lauren worried about things like that; it would spoil it for her. Besides, the house was stuffed with tat, just taking up space. It would be good to declutter.

'You've got to be careful—people can get addicted to this, you know. You read about them in magazines . . .' As Lauren spoke, she was already searching for 'wedding favours Disney'. 'Still, I reckon you're pretty safe, aren't you? The world's most sensible budgeteer. The woman with just the one credit card, always paid off in time.'

'Yes, well, clever clogs, you'd be surprised how much we primary-school teachers need to know about computers these days. It's good for my morale to be one step ahead of the children,' said Bridget. 'Shift up, and let me look.' She squeezed onto the edge of the bed, so she could see the screen.

Lauren hesitated for a moment, surprised that her mum was so interested in a shopping experience that involved the scary world of the internet too, then decided she was probably doing it to make 'mother–daughter time'—without the danger of Irene dropping in.

The wedding magazines were very big on mother–daughter time. Bridget was very big on non-Irene time.

Plus, it didn't look like Chris was going to call, not now. She'd texted him four times, and that was enough.

He knew where he was meant to be. She wasn't going to go chasing after him. She suspected Kian was already brainwashing him about the evils of being under the thumb, and that, thought Lauren, wasn't something she was going to give ammunition to with shrieky phone calls. It could wait.

'OK, then,' she said, flexing her fingers. 'How about we sell . . .' She cast her eyes around the jumbled boxes of stuff piled up against the walls. 'Those satin court shoes I bought last week that don't quite fit properly.'

Before long, Lauren and Bridget had listed the shoes, along with a 'spare' veil and—just to prove you could sell absolutely anything—a knitted bride loo-roll cover Lauren's Auntie Carol had sent her. It was so much easier than Bridget had realised. And the amazing variety of wedding-related things you could buy! They had just slapped each other's hands to celebrate the successful purchase of 'One Hundred Glass Cinderella Slipper Wedding Favors' from a private seller in Toronto when a plaintive voice came wailing up the stairs, along with an acrid smell of burned pan.

'Bridget! Bridget!' yelled Frank, sounding panicked. 'What's going on with this pie? Something's burning!'

'And that,' sighed Bridget, 'is the wow factor of married life they don't tell you about in the dress shops.'

'No problem, Mum,' said Lauren, already typing. 'Non . . . stick . . . pans . . . New in box.' And she hit return.

Not such an unproductive evening after all, she thought.

CHAPTER TWELVE

Angelica sat surrounded by papers in her parents' front room, on the same scratchy brown sofa that had been re-upholstered every five years, but never replaced, and slowly turned the pages of a family photograph album. It had been at the bottom of a box marked 'Angela', right at the back of the attic under a box of Cyril's crystal radios, which, she supposed, said it all.

The album had no photos of Pauline and Cyril's life before she arrived. Angelica found it difficult to imagine what they'd been like as a young couple—she had no mental prompts to picture them picnicking in the Lakes, or laughing uproariously at a party. There were several awkward photographs of them in their ballroom-dancing finery, but only the pencilled dates on the back told her whether Cyril was 20 or 40 at the time. Pauline's comfy bosom had been there from the start, and only the size of her hair and eyeliner hinted at the fashions changing outside Longhampton.

The album began when she was a few months old, lying crossly in a Moses basket: *Angela Marie, 4 months at home*, Pauline had written carefully in chinagraph pencil. It was the first of many very similar photographs.

Is that really me, thought Angelica, who hadn't seen the photographs for years. She was a sallow little scrap of baby in a crocheted bonnet, never quite as sweet-looking as the lovingly hand-made clothes she was swaddled in. Pauline had knitted everything except the actual baby it seemed: matinee jackets, hats, all-in-ones, bootees, fancy frilled dresses.

She turned over to scenes of Pauline, already middle-aged in her twinsets, holding baby Angela at her christening, on the garden wall, playing with a bucket in the garden. Usually on her own, and well away from thorns or puddles, scowling from under a mop of dark hair, until suddenly, at a year old, Pauline had recorded, 'Her first smile for the camera!' and from then on, little Angela's eyes searched for the camera like a flower reaching up towards the sun. Pauline didn't really smile much, possibly because Cyril was usually behind the camera in shots of the two of them, barking instructions.

The album stopped when she was about five, when her mother started sending her to Miss

Trellys's, and the dancing albums started instead. That was the end of Angela the daughter, and the beginning of Angela the fulfiller of Pauline's ballroom dreams.

She turned the pages, hoping irrationally that she'd find some unseen candid shots of Cyril toasting Pauline on their anniversary, or the two of them enjoying a sweet sherry at a Friday night social. There was nothing more, apart from one or two loose pictures slipped in under the tracing-paper pages: Angela in her school uniform, toes turned out neatly in ballet position, with long black plaits; Pauline and Angela on a rare day out in Birmingham.

Then, strangely, Angelica's wedding photograph: she and Jerry holding hands, wreathed in smiles underneath a frothing American bower of flowers. The bright colours and Florida sunshine zinged out of the picture after the monochrome flatness of her black and white childhood.

It gave Angelica a start to see herself suddenly grown up, the dancing years skipped over and her life fast-forwarded to the semi-retired nearly-forty-something she'd been when she met Jerry on the cruise. He was a widower looking for shipboard romance; she was filling in some time as half of the professional couple, with that bitchy old queen, Nigel Taylor, a friend from way back. Easy money, she'd thought, and easy dancing, to heal her battle-scars after the wearing competition years with Tony. She hadn't been expecting to meet an old-fashioned gentleman like Jerry, and while the roses that turned up nightly at her cabin were charming, his relaxed, generous lead on the floor was what won her heart. He didn't want to show off; he just

161

wanted to enjoy her company. When he proposed as they docked in New York, she said yes.

The wedding had taken place in the garden of his enormous Florida home, six months later, and they'd gone on an anniversary cruise for the next seven Julys. Each time, they stopped the dancefloor when they started to quickstep, and he always smiled into her eyes as they spun, and in its own way, that meant more to Angelica than the nerve-racking tension of competing with Tony. Or at least, she told herself it did.

Angelica felt a sharp sting of hurt that Pauline had just stuffed her wedding photo into this album. She'd sent it in a special box, along with a slice of cake, and some of the lovely silk flowers that had decorated the tables. All right, so she hadn't been living in the UK at the time, and there was no chance of her popping round to Sydney Street and not seeing it on the mantelpiece, but surely the wedding of their only child warranted a photograph frame at least?

Pauline and Cyril were invited to the wedding of course, with first-class tickets, but they hadn't come, and Angelica hadn't really expected them to. She had to pretend to be disappointed, because Jerry and his family were so sad for her, but she knew Cyril wouldn't fly all the way over to Florida, and had to invent a heart murmur for him, to explain.

Angelica touched the photograph, remembering the feel of the suit against her skin. It was a real Joan Collins number: white crepe with padded shoulders and a peplum that showed off her still small waist. She'd wanted red, what with it being an outdoors blessing rather than a church ceremony, and both she and Jerry being well past that virgin bride moment, but he'd insisted on white, old romantic that he was. Men who could dance as well as he did tended to be romantics, or ladykillers. Jerry was a bit of both.

It was a lovely photograph. Jerry looked so distinguished in his tux. If she was channelling Joan Collins in her power suit, he definitely had a look of Blake Carrington with his perfectly coiffed grey hair and deep tan. Cyril should have been proud, she thought, that finally she'd achieved some sort of respectability and married a millionaire.

Angelica sighed. She knew in her head what married life in Florida had been like—she could remember the songs she'd taught those fiancés to dance to, and what sort of mineral water Jerry liked to keep poolside—but she couldn't *feel* it any more. It hadn't left an imprint on her, in the way she could still taste the fear beating in her throat while she put on her competition make-up. She'd passed through those warm, easy Florida years, and then, when they came to an end, she'd put her possessions into storage along with her tango dresses, and now it could almost have happened to someone else.

Maybe, she thought, it was because she didn't carry any bitterness in her soul about it. When she'd found out about the other woman—another dancer, not much younger than her, from their bridge club—she'd accepted it with an acquiescence that surprised the lawyer Jerry insisted she hire. Partners weren't for ever, she knew that from her career. Jerry was a good man, they'd had some good times, but Angelica was too much her own woman to be second best to anyone. She'd had enough of that with Tony, and she wasn't going to start now.

So she agreed to his generous divorce settlement, refusing to haggle over the price of her freedom, and even kept in touch, after his new baby was born. Angelica said nothing, but privately reckoned Jerry paid a high enough price for his last gasp of youth: sleepless nights and milky vomit at a time when he should have been sipping mojitos on his porch and listening to Dean Martin. Still, that was his choice.

Pauline was careful never to mention the baby, for fear of hurting Angelica, but it wasn't really the child that she was jealous of: it was the sense of belonging that the three of them would have. In the photograph Jerry sent of himself with Melissa and baby Jerrissa, they were all squashed up together in the frame, three parts of one whole. Frankly, it looked wrong to Angelica, but they were undeniably a family, and that was something she only realised she'd longed for, as her mother was dying.

You always rubbish the thing you want most, she thought sadly, looking at herself and Jerry posing expertly under the arch of gardenias. In the Tony days, it had been easier to dismiss families as a sentimental nonsense than it was to risk having that conversation that could wreck their ever-precarious balance of business and pleasure. She was never sure what was more important to Tony, Angelica the partner, or Angelica the lover, and the thought of finding out terrified her into a proud silence.

She propped the wedding photograph up on the

mantelpiece and was about to put the album back into the box when on impulse she flipped through the remaining pages, just in case there was anything else there.

Right at the back, tucked into the folded spine of the album, was an envelope.

It was addressed to her in Pauline's handwriting: *Angela—to be opened in the event of my death*, written in confident, sloping ink, which dated it to well before her mother's arthritis had set in, leaving her handwriting like a child's attempt to copy her old neat style. Pauline hadn't been as confident in person as she was in her handwriting, preferring to leave most of her opinions to Cyril until he died.

That had been one of the nicer things about having her mother living in Islington, thought Angelica, as she slit open the envelope. Free of Cyril's domineering views on everything from immigrants to white bread, and encouraged by Angelica's own disregard for anyone else's approval, Pauline had slowly started to display a healthy disapproval of cyclists who rode on the pavements, and moved on to milk cartons and folk who played their car radios so loud she could hear them in the front room.

It had been one of the little ways they'd grown closer towards the end, that shared outrage with other people's thoughtlessness. One of them would start with a cross observation over breakfast, and then they'd let their irritation spiral to furious fulmination, until one of them would crack and giggle.

I'm so glad I brought Mum down to London, thought Angelica suddenly. I couldn't bear to think

165

of her alone here now, with just these albums for company. She unfolded the letter and was surprised to see that it ran to four closely written sides. What could her mother want to write about that she couldn't just tell her? Was it legal stuff?

It can't be that important, thought Angelica, though her thumping heart suspected otherwise. Why would it be right at the back of an album I might never have found? Surely if Mum meant to tell me anything important she'd have left it in the bank, or put it in her jewellery box or something?

Dear Angelica, Pauline wrote. *I hope you will forgive me for what I am about to tell you, and understand that it is much easier for me to write this down than to explain in person. I have always been so proud of you, and what you have done with your life. You have brought me and your father so much happiness, and although perhaps it has not always seemed so, we have taken a great joy in you as our daughter.*

Angelica felt tears prick in her eyes as she heard Pauline's voice in her head. She *had* known how much pride her mum had taken in her; it was her dad who'd never shown any sort of interest in what she'd done.

But as she read on, she realised her mother's unusually careful language was inching towards something she couldn't speak aloud, and Angelica drew in a sudden, involuntary breath.

Although we could not have loved you any more if you were our own daughter, I must tell you that, in fact, we are not your birth parents.

Here the ink darkened, as if Pauline had put down her pen for a few minutes searching for the right words to start again.

We hoped and prayed for a little baby to complete our family for many years after we married, but we were disappointed. I had given up hope of ever having children, when a lady we knew from our ballroom club told us about a young friend of hers in a terrible situation. This poor girl was expecting a child that she was not able to bring up, for personal reasons, but she did not want to take it to an orphanage, as she could not bear to think of it being looked after by strangers.

I knew at once that we could give that tiny baby a loving home. We met the girl, who was happy for us to adopt you as our own, and from the moment you were placed in my arms, you were our Angela. I wish I could describe to you the joy I felt, feeling your little hand curl around my finger, and seeing your lovely face looking up at me in your cot. You had so much hair for a little baby, like a day-old chick. Angela, that was the happiest moment of my whole life, a happiness I'd given up wishing for. You made us into a proper family at last.

Perhaps you will be wondering why I am only telling you this now, so many years later. Your father and I often discussed it, and he felt you should have been told before you left home. I know your dad and yourself had a difficult relationship while you were growing up, and that you sometimes felt he was not as affectionate as you would have liked. The truth is that he knew how much you meant to me and was afraid that one day you would find out, and want to leave us to find your birth parents. I am a very selfish woman, I know, but I think it would have broken my heart.

It is very hard to love someone as much as I loved you, and to know that, at any moment, they might be

167

taken from you. My consolation was that your real mother—I find that very hard to write, Angela!—had two more children after you, and so enjoyed the same happiness your dad and I did.

Tears welled up in Angelica's eyes, and the letter blurred in front of her. She put it down, and covered her eyes with her palms, unable to put her mother's face out of her mind. She didn't feel angry, just intensely sorry for her, having to keep that secret festering away in her heart so many years. How many times must she have started this letter, and then screwed up the paper, fearing that it would break the fragile links, of care rather than blood, that held her daughter to her? How often must she have looked at her and wondered if now was the right moment to say something? Or now? Or now?

There would never have been a good moment. But worse than that, there would never be *any* moment for Angelica to take her mother's hands in her own and tell her that it didn't make a shred of difference. Pauline was the only mother she'd known—how could she love her less?

Those quiet months of looking after her mother as she slowly faded had brought them both to an understanding they'd never have had otherwise. Taking care of someone who needed your strength, and cheerfulness, and kindness had taught Angelica a patience she'd never needed before, or knew she had in her. Ironically, she supposed, it had taught her about being a mother. Angelica thought then that she was making up for the years she'd spent away from Longhampton; in fact she was doing exactly what Pauline had done for her, as an unwanted baby. Those years of trying to please her unbending father, resenting the way her overtures were rejected, vanished with the simple acts of making her mother comfortable.

And she had felt needed. That's what had moved her most.

'I'm holding you back,' her mother had murmured when she stayed in to keep her company, watching old MGM musicals on days when the sun sparkled on the canal. 'You should be out, doing things.'

'I'd rather be here with you,' Angelica had said, and by the fourth time she said it, she really meant it.

She made herself pick up the letter again, uncertain if she wanted to read to the end or not. Would it make a difference—now—to know whose family she was part of? It wasn't as if she needed to discover who she was. All her life she'd been independent, self-contained. Angelica wasn't even sure if she wanted some stranger to be able to claim her. Coming back to Longhampton had been about stripping back the versions of herself until only Angela Clarke remained, and now it seemed she wasn't even Angela; but at the same time, she was getting a clearer view of herself than she'd ever done before.

I am a changeling, after all, she thought suddenly. It wasn't me just being selfish when I couldn't see myself in Mum or Dad. Maybe they were seeing someone else they knew in me, and I never even realised.

Who was it they were seeing?

Curiosity got the better of her, and she read on to the end of the letter, past the apologies and explanations, and on to the bare facts of what other life Pauline had rescued her from. And when she turned the page, and read her real mother's story, her tears blurred Pauline's diffident handwriting, and dropped, blotting the old notepaper.

CHAPTER THIRTEEN

By the time Katie and Ross turned up for the third dancing class, it already felt like a habit. They hung up their coats on the same dolphin-shaped brass hook, exchanged the same polite smiles with Baxter and Peggy, who were already changed into their 'proper' dancing shoes, and listened to Trina's acid commentary on her latest speed-dating antics in Newtons, Longhampton's supposedly cosmopolitan wine bar.

'Ooh, that place makes my flesh crawl!' said Chloe, shaking her mass of curls so hard the velvet flower nearly fell out.

'I know,' agreed Lauren. 'The only thing cheesier than the men in there is the music they play.'

'No, I mean the *hygiene*.' Chloe's eyes widened. 'The glasses are filthy! You could catch anything in there!'

Lauren had seen what some people could catch in Newtons, direct from the nurses' mouth, but she didn't think it was wise to say, not with Trina there.

Angelica seemed distracted when they arrived, but got them straight into a vigorous cha-cha introductory session 'to get the blood flowing', demonstrating the gyrating Latin steps with Ross,

170

until they were all pink with exertion from the strutting and spinning.

'At least it's music we know,' whined Trina, as Angelica absent-mindedly put 'Lady Marmalade' on for the second time.

'What? Sorry . . .' Angelica ejected the CD. 'Social foxtrot!' Then she put her Frank Sinatra album on, pushing them through their social foxtrot steps over and over, until for the first time ever, Ross and Katie had almost managed a perfect box corner.

It wasn't a big thing, but to Katie it was like walking on water. She and Ross were moving almost as one, to 'Come Fly With Me'. OK, they were the basic steps and no fancy stuff, but it was starting to fit together. The smile of amazement was just spreading on to her face, when the parping brass solo came to an unexpected halt. The hall was left in silence, bar the shuffle of feet, and the sound of Lauren counting, 'One, two, three, noooo!' at Chris.

'Stop, stop, stop!' yelled Angelica, clapping her hands together. The sound echoed like gunshots in the high-ceilinged room.

Katie stumbled over Ross's suddenly stationary foot, and swore under her breath as she fell into him.

'We nearly *had* it then,' she hissed into his chest, resentfully. 'What does she want to stop for, the stupid cow?'

'Shh,' said Ross, knitting his brows together in a warning as he looked over her head.

Katie turned round and caught sight of Angelica's tight expression, which was a study in furious dismay. Her dark eyes were half closed and

171

she seemed to be breathing heavily, directing her gaze back and forth around the room.

Angelica's been in a funny mood since the beginning of the class, thought Katie. Distracted, and snappy. It wasn't like her to miss Chris nearly twisting Lauren's ankle, and then she'd really had a go at Greg for not turning his phone off—although Katie had to concede that it was a bit workaholic to take business calls after eight at night. And, she thought, he could have apologised to Jo, rather than just dropping her hands and rushing out.

She cast a sidelong look at Jo, who still seemed rather pained. Katie wondered if there was a reason Greg had insisted on taking the call outside. Was there some problem with the business? It was a bit late for that, but Greg did work all hours. They were both looking daggers at each other, but that might have been because Jo had had to dance with Chloe for twenty minutes during the cha-cha-cha session.

I quite like the cha-cha, thought Katie unexpectedly. It felt do-able, all shimmying shoulders and jazz hands, simple enough to make everyone feel a little better about their abilities, after the toe-squashing complications of the social foxtrot. The music helped, for a start—the party rhythms made her feet do the cha-cha-cha side-shuffle instinctively and her knees bent as if the music was telling her what to do.

For once, the younger ones had had the advantage ('It's in the knees!' as Angelica kept shouting) and Chloe's bronzed cleavage had taken on a life of its own, especially in the low-cut pink wrap dress she was wearing to comply with Angelica's dress-up code. Jo's hadn't been far

172

behind. There were, Katie thought, as Ross twirled her around and the class spun before her, six of them in that dance: Jo, Chloe and their freestyling bosoms.

Unfortunately, as soon as they moved on to the revision session on the social foxtrot, it had become apparent that everyone bar Ross and the older couples had pretty much forgotten everything they'd learned in the previous two weeks. That was when Angelica's mood had turned from absent-minded to positively dark.

'Katie!' hissed Ross, pulling her attention back to the strop unfolding on the other side of the room. 'She's looking at us!'

'Oookaay,' Katie whispered, then swallowed as she realised that the lighthouse beam of Angelica's annoyance was indeed directed at her and Ross. This probably wasn't the moment, she thought, to point out their ten seconds of flukey success.

'Katie,' said Angelica, drumming her red nails on her folded arms. 'Be honest with me here. If this was WeightWatchers, do you think you'd bother to turn up if you'd spent the week stuffing yourself with crisps?'

'No?' she replied.

'So why—*why* do you all turn up here without having *bothered* to so much as tap your *feet* from one week to the next?' Angelica demanded, her voice rising. She uncrossed her arms so she could spread them wide in a dramatic gesture of despair. 'How do you expect to get any better if you don't practise? It's not just about learning the steps, it's about feeling the music! Feeling it guide you round the floor! I mean, you look so awkward! If you weren't married,' she went on, flinging her arms

173

towards Katie and Ross, 'I'd wonder if you so much as *held* each other from one week to the next!'

Katie felt Ross flinch next to her, and she knew her own face would be turning bright pink beneath her foundation. They hadn't. Or rather, they didn't.

How come Angelica could tell that instantly, whereas Peter at the counselling sessions couldn't, she wondered. Angelica's beady blue eyes cut straight through the happy-happy image Katie tried to keep up when she and Ross were out of the house. Presumably it came from her lifetime's experience of couples faking chemistry competitively in these dances of pretend courtship and passion.

Fortunately, Angelica wasn't in the mood to linger on their shortcomings. She had already moved on to poor Lauren, standing next to them.

'And you two! Lauren! Chris!' She put her hands to her head in despair. 'What's going *on*? You're both young, you're not married yet, so presumably there's some chemistry *somewhere*? Right? So where does it go when you're dancing? It's like watching someone trying to set up a deckchair. You're never going to learn to dance like *partners* if you don't practise!'

'We try!' protested Lauren, glaring furiously at Chris. 'But *some people* are never in of an evening! Some people don't even call to say they're coming to *class*.'

'Some people have . . . commitments in the evenings,' retorted Chris, with a nervous glance at Bridget and Frank. 'I'm here, aren't I? Give me a break, Loz.'

Ross nudged Katie. 'Eh? What's going on there, eh? Sounds like a domestic to me. And in front of the in-laws!'

'Shh,' she frowned, but felt a little relief that it wasn't just her and Ross with bickering issues. She saw Bridget's expression twitch, as if she was struggling to keep her face neutral. What *was* going on there, she wondered?

'Commitments? What commitments are more important than learning to dance with this beautiful girl?' demanded Angelica, taking a step nearer Chris. He took a scared step back. 'Because if you don't start taking this seriously, she might as well do her wedding waltz with a life-sized cardboard cut-out of you! She'd stand less chance of falling over it!'

'*Thank* you!' said Lauren, crossing her own arms and glaring at Chris, who looked stunned, then sulky.

Angelica looked at Bridget and Frank and pointed between Chris and Lauren, her skinny eyebrows raised in high dudgeon. 'Am I right? Did you two dance like you do without practising?'

'I don't even remember learning . . .' began Frank, but Bridget cut in diplomatically.

'Well, we didn't have much else to do. And it's not music they're familiar with, is it? It takes a while to get the hang of it,' she said, patting his arm. 'Frank was no Gene Kelly to begin with, were you, love?'

'I bet he never nearly broke your toe, though, did he, Mum?' demanded Lauren. 'I bet he never—'

'All right, Loz! Stop going on about it!' snapped Chris, and Katie felt a flash of sympathy for his

175

discomfort.

She'd been paired with Chris for a few songs, and although she wasn't much better, she was beginning to have some sympathy for Lauren's frustrated feet. Neither she nor Chris had much sense of rhythm and the overall effect was of two people in leg-irons trying to shuffle away from a chain-gang.

'Come on!' she protested on his behalf. 'Not everyone picks physical things up so quickly!'

'And no bloke likes being compared with his father-in-law,' added Ross, but with enough of a nod to Frank to defuse the tension.

Chris smiled gratefully at her, and she gave him a twisted smile back; malcos together.

Angelica's attitude seemed to soften a little, as if Katie's outburst had brought her back from wherever her bad mood had taken her.

'Well, that's very true. But it's why you have to practise. Now, Lauren, your mum and dad dance very well. But if you want to dance like them, you've got to put the hours in,' she went on. 'All of you!' She turned her attention to Chloe and Trina. 'Enthusiasm's all very well, but if you think you're going to impress a bloke flailing around with sloppy step sequences, then . . .'

'If one ever turns up,' Trina started, belligerently, but Chloe nudged her into prudent silence.

Katie looked sideways and saw Greg looking at her. He rolled his eyes. She didn't roll hers back. For the first time ever, she was rather unimpressed by Greg. He'd been late, even before his phone call break—'stuck in traffic on the ring road'—and wasn't exactly putting his back into it now. It was disappointing, thought Katie. Not his commitment to work—that she could understand—but his obvious air of sufferance at being here. She couldn't even admire his suit with the enthusiasm that she would normally, knowing he was moving so woodenly inside it. She'd thought that he'd be as easily competent at dancing as he was at everything else, but she had to admit that Ross was picking this up faster than Greg.

In fact he'd picked up the cha-cha so fast she was beginning to wonder if it was on that teach-yourself-to-dance DVD. He even had the camp hand gestures right. Ross had danced with Jo, and Angelica asked the two of them to demonstrate a new spin step, which had made Jo's handkerchief hem float up like flower petals round her curving calves. They'd moved around each other really easily, linking and dropping hands, falling in and out of the holds, and Katie had felt a tiny stab of jealousy that Jo's relaxed swing brought out a new kind of confidence in Ross. He was leading her; she was happy to be led. Their over-the-top Latino struttings had been the performance of the evening.

Angelica's voice cut through her thoughts. 'You're never going to enjoy doing it until you're confident about where your feet are going. I want to see a bit more involvement! More passion! More instinct!' She swept a dramatic hand around the room. 'Please! Think of me here! At least get a Glenn Miller CD out of the library and listen to the rhythms.'

'But it's hard practising on my own at home,' protested Chloe. 'I don't have enough room, or a partner, and I don't know what music's right and the people below me have been complaining about the banging on my floor . . .'

'Right!' said Angelica. 'Starting this week, you're all coming to the Friday night social dance here.'

Everyone stared at her.

'Yes!' she said. 'It's a great chance to get dressed up and see what those steps look like when they're done properly! Seven-thirty till eleven, four pounds a head, free orange squash. You'll see quicksteps and waltzes and jive and foxtrots, lots of people who know what they're doing, you'll learn plenty just watching. Baxter and Peggy go sometimes already, don't you? I've seen you two there.'

Of course they go, thought Katie, as Peggy bobbed her roller-set obediently. Baxter probably rules that dancefloor like a basking shark in built-up heels.

'And can we dance with other people?' asked Trina hopefully.

'If you want to dance with Chloe all evening that's up to you,' said Angelica. 'But I think you'll find that two lovely young girls like yourselves will be in high demand. And the rest of you . . .' She paused and gave them a little wink. 'You might find that seeing your partner dancing with someone else will make you want to raise your own game a bit. Just make sure you book them in for the first and last dance. Isn't that right, Peggy?' she added with a wink.

Peggy sighed. 'Baxter's a popular man, I must say.'

Chloe and Trina didn't bother to disguise their gawps.

But Angelica's mood had changed again, for the better, and she swung back into her teaching mode. 'Now, let's stay with the social foxtrot, but this time we're going to learn a new promenade step, so concentrate, please, Christopher! I don't want you lot showing me up at the social. Ross? Would you mind demonstrating with me, please?'

She held out her arms as Ross walked into the middle of the room.

Angelica tutted and wagged her finger at him. 'Now, what did I say about smartness being the first rule of ballroom? Tuck that shirt in, you scruff! Do you think Gene Kelly left his shirt untucked? Or Bruce Forsyth? And for crying out loud, would you stand up straight? You're too young for a stoop.'

Ross grinned sheepishly as he pushed his shirt into the back of his jeans, and stood up straight, pulling his shoulders back at the same time, under Angelica's watchful eye.

'There! That's much better,' she said approvingly.

Jo nudged Katie. 'Nice arse!' she stage-whispered.

Katie was about to demur, but actually, yes, she thought, with a flicker of surprise, Ross does have quite a nice arse. She never really noticed it, what with his baggy T-shirts normally covering it up, but there it was, quite pert in his jeans, at the top of his long legs.

A warm flower of approval began to open in her chest, and bloomed as Angelica began demonstrating the new step, and Ross fell in with her, instinctively moving alongside, his back straight and his head relaxed, as if he wasn't even concentrating. His steps had a little bounce to them.

Ross looks like he knows what he's doing, thought Katie, taken aback by the sudden rush of attraction she felt towards him. He's got confidence. He's not whingeing. He's in charge.

Angelica and Ross danced the basic foxtrot steps as she talked, then turned so their hips were facing outwards.

'This is how you can talk to your partner and have a look around at who you can line up for the next song at the same time,' she said, as their feet neatly slid in unison then crossed and, for the first time, the dance started to look a little like the floating elegance of the version Katie had seen on television. Ross sailed along next to her, bemused by his own sudden shift into Fred Astaire mode.

'God,' breathed Lauren. 'That looks really pro.' She cast a glance at Chris, and Katie saw a flicker of despair in her eyes.

She wondered if Ross felt that when she muffed the new steps. Some people were just better at this than others. Jo had picked up the cha-cha in half a song.

No, she thought, determined. I'm going to master this. I'm going to make Ross look as good as that when he's dancing with me.

'Have a go?' said Ross, returning to her, with his arms outstretched.

Katie pulled a smile on her face, against the disappointment to come.

Ross began to guide her through the promenade with the same patient manner he used when he tried to teach Hannah how to tell the time, or tie her shoes. But Katie couldn't stop herself thinking

180

that he was probably wishing he could stay dancing with Jo, her heaving bosoms and her quick way with new steps.

*   *   *

In the lobby after class, Lauren plonked herself down on the plastic chairs next to Katie to change out of the wedding shoes she practised in. They were stiff oyster satin, and looked agony to Katie, but Lauren seemed determined to break them in.

'Oooh!' she said, easing the right one off with a pretend grimace. 'The things we do for fashion, eh? I can't feel my toes!'

'Doesn't stop you dancing like you do,' Katie said. 'I couldn't tell you were in agony—you look like you've been doing it for years.'

'Really?' Lauren seemed surprised, then blushed pink with pleasure. 'Thanks!'

Katie smiled back. Lauren was really easy to talk to. 'How are you picking it up so quickly? Have you done this before?'

Lauren giggled, showing her square white teeth. 'God, no! Don't be daft!'

'You're a natural, then,' said Katie. 'You look really elegant when you're dancing.'

'Aw, thank you,' she said. 'No one's ever accused me of being elegant before.'

It was a nice way of saying, how the hell did that happen, thought Katie, relieved it hadn't come out wrong. Something magical happened to Lauren when the music started; she went from lanky carthorse to graceful swan, absorbing every new instruction Angelica shouted, holding herself differently—it was incredible. In complete

181

contrast, Chris, so confident when he walked in, still flustered and stumbled, even when Angelica took pity on him and tried to guide him through the steps.

Katie wondered if Lauren realised how well she was doing. Her pretty face seemed swamped with frustration quite a lot.

'Oh my God!' Lauren said, conversationally, as she peeled off the other shoe to reveal several protective surgical plasters. 'My feet are in rags. Anyway, what did you think about that telling off? I haven't been yelled at like that since I was at school!'

'Yes, well. It's easy for her to say we should be practising—what else has she got to do? It's her job.' Katie stuffed her shoes in her bag and pulled on her coat. Half of her was pleased Lauren wanted to chat, but she also itched to get back home. Jo's mum Dorothy was round at their house looking after all the kids again, but she wanted to be there in case Jack woke up, and she wasn't there to settle him down.

She looked over towards Ross to see if he was ready, but he was talking to Jo about playgroup collecting rotas, and Greg had rushed outside to take yet another phone call. Katie wondered if Ross would be telling Jo about Hannah's strop earlier, when she'd refused to touch her tea until he agreed to put on her Angelina Ballerina DVD while they ate. Hannah had really got into dancing. Something else she and her daddy had to share.

Would Ross tell her the bit about him wimping out so she had to police the naughty step, she wondered tartly, as Jo laughed at something Ross said and batted him on the arm. Probably not.

Molly probably didn't need the naughty step.

'What was all that about, do you reckon?' Lauren went on.

'What was what about?'

Lauren nodded conspiratorially. 'The mood swings. Didn't you notice? She was fine when we came in, then suddenly went mardy. It's the change probably. I did notice she made another appointment with Dr Carthy this morning.' She stopped herself abruptly and looked pained. 'Oops, forget I said that.'

'You reckon?' said Katie, intrigued despite herself. Angelica in the surgery? It was hard to imagine her existing outside the Memorial Hall, going shopping, having a life.

'Well, she's about that age . . .' Lauren mused, then clapped a hand over her mouth. 'Oh! Sugar! Sorry, I shouldn't have said anything. So, are you two going to go to this thing on Friday?' she went on. She had a puppyish way of gossiping, as if they'd known each other for ages, rather than the three classes they'd been to. She was, Katie thought, the sort of girl who never had any trouble making friends on the first day at school. 'Pleeeease say you arc!'

'It's rather short notice,' said Katie, automatically. 'When you've got kids, you can't just make sudden plans like that . . .'

'Ycah, I think we'll go!' said Ross. 'Save you and Jo having to slave over suppcr on At Home Fridays, eh?' He and Jo had evidently finished their discussion and had wandered back to the chairs. Jo was looking pink and happy after her exertions, and she fanned herself with a plump hand, jangling hcr silver bracelets.

'Who needs aerobics, eh?' she said to Lauren. 'I can't remember the last time Greg and I worked up such a sweat! Well, not in public, anyway!'

'How old's Rowan again?' Ross enquired.

Lauren giggled.

Katie pulled a face she hoped Lauren couldn't see. 'It's the day after tomorrow, Ross. Where are you going to get a babysitter from, at short notice?'

'Oh, I'll find a babysitter,' interjected Jo, happily. 'There are some girls at the nursery who are always looking for a bit of extra pocket money.' She waved an easy hand. 'Drop yours off at ours—tell Hannah she can sleep in the princess bed.'

Katie wavered. 'If you're sure . . .'

'Course.' Jo smiled. 'It's great to get out.' She shook her shoulders, making her hair bounce. 'I'll be doing that cha-cha in my head all night now. Greg and I need to get into the habit of spending time together—you know how the kids can just eat up every second of the day! I love them, but it's good to remember what life was like when it was just us.' She nudged Katie. 'Remember that?'

'Not really.'

'I reckon the secret is to get the men into it,' said Jo. 'And if that means buying a few foxy dresses, so much the better. Eh, Lauren? Any excuse for a shop!'

'I hope you lot *are* going to come,' said Lauren, casting a baleful look towards the other end of the room, where a loud clanking of antique plumbing announced that Chris was about to emerge from the chilly loo. 'I need to persuade Chris that it's not just men like Baxter who can dance.'

'Men like Baxter meaning?' said Ross, hooking his eyebrow.

'You know, short men in pink sweaters. Men who need something else to offer a girl.' Lauren pressed her lips together. 'Men who dance with their noses level with your cleavage. If you're a decent-sized girl in high heels.'

'Have you danced with Baxter yet?' asked Jo. 'I did a turn with him tonight and, ladies, he is a revelation. He made my feet do things my legs didn't even know about.'

'Really?' demanded Katie and Lauren. Baxter had insisted on showing Jo how to 'improve' the basic cha-cha steps they'd started, leaving Greg to dance with Peggy and her twinset.

Jo winked. 'Didn't you see me wiggling around like my knees were double-jointed? Looking pretty *Strictly Come Dancing*, wasn't I? He's got a way of placing his hands just so.' And she did a little shimmy to demonstrate, twitching her rounded hips in panic as if a bee was trying to land on them.

Ross laughed and Katie had to smile at Jo's easy self-deprecation.

'Well, that's something to look forward to,' Lauren said. 'Anyway, you two were very good.' She nodded towards Jo and Ross.

'Ah, well, I should let you into a secret,' said Jo, lowering her voice. 'We've practised.'

'What?' said Lauren.

'Ross here's got a DVD,' said Jo in a dramatic whisper. 'And I've been round to his house to practise!'

'While the wife's at work!' hooted Ross, rolling his eyes stagily.

'Really?' said Katie, but Lauren obviously didn't catch the slightly steely note in her voice.

'Oh, you lot *so* have to come on Friday,' Lauren

insisted, nudging Katie happily.

'Yeah,' said Ross, 'we'll work something out, even if we just come for an hour or two. Angelica's got a point about not learning unless you go for it properly.'

'In that case, Chris and I should be doing three hours a day,' sighed Lauren.

Katie made a sympathetic face. 'Have you two got a date to aim at for your big waltz number?'

'Yeah, June the tenth,' said Lauren. 'Mum's about to book the caterers. But we need the practice. To be honest, I'm not totally sure I can persuade Chris to come, though.' Her sunny expression faded. 'Most nights he seems to be out with *Kian*.'

The way she said Kian told Katie exactly what the problem was. That was one good thing about Ross, he didn't spend every evening down the pub. *Neither* of them got to have a social life.

'Well, tell Kian to come along. Isn't that what Trina and Chloe are here for—single blokes?' she suggested.

'Exactly! I'll have to check with Greg, but count me in, definitely . . .' said Jo, as her gaze went towards the door, then returned when there was still no sign of Greg's suited figure. 'It's nice to get out and mingle with real live adults, isn't it, Ross?'

'God, yes,' agreed Ross. 'When you've had a long day pretending to be a horse, it's good to remember you're also a human being.'

'Give over! You're a sexy young dad!' exclaimed Lauren. 'And mum,' she added quickly, for Katie's benefit.

Katie gave him a look, and wished he wouldn't keep making out he was some kind of nursery slave. Didn't he ever stop to think that maybe if he could rouse himself to get some part-time work, she wouldn't have to work full time?

She bit her tongue. It sounds so petty, she told herself. But petty or not, it was all she could think at that moment. Think, but not say. Don't say anything.

'Course we'll come,' Katie heard her voice saying brightly, and the relieved expression on Lauren's open face was an unexpected bonus.

Ross too also looked rather surprised, but she wasn't looking at him, so she missed it.

CHAPTER FOURTEEN

Katie did her best to leave the office at five-thirty on Friday, but as usual, work got in the way. Her genuine intentions to look into the High Street's dress shops came to nothing as her morning meeting over-ran, and then Eddie Harding 'dropped in for a head-to-head'. When it came to creeping up to the various lawyers and architects, while leaving a discernible trace of grease and slime around the office itself, Eddie was like a de-shelled snail. But for the moment, he was her boss, and so she had to talk to him until five fifty-five, resenting every extra minute.

She rushed into the big supermarket on the way back to pick up coloured pens and other bribes to stop Hannah being difficult with the babysitter, then got a call from Ross to remind her that they were out of loo roll, so she had to rush back in, then finally Katie drove home, stabbing her finger at the radio buttons all the way, to try to find music that would put her in a sweeter mood. It was hopeless. She was wound tight with tension, and every train of thought that set off in her head reminded her of another reason to be stressed.

Inside was the usual chaos—unspecific thumping, the smell of burned toast, toy fragments scattered around—and she felt her heart sink as the front door caught on a baby trike left propped up against the hall wall.

'I'm back!' she yelled over the noise. 'Mummy's home!'

No one ran to greet her. She gave them a couple of hopeful seconds, wishing as usual that somehow Hannah and Jack would appear in spotless pyjamas and adoring expressions, followed by Ross in a Paul Smith suit and fresh haircut, but all she heard was the sound of Latin American music from the sitting room. It sounded like her Carlos Santana CD—the one Ross thought was naff.

'Hi, Mummy!' she said aloud to herself. 'Hurray! You're back! We missed you!'

Katie dumped her briefcase in the hall, and pushed open the sitting-room door. Ross was shuffling around, holding hands with Hannah, in a height pairing that made Baxter and Lauren look ideally matched. Both of them were wearing dressing-up clothes and smears of make-up, and Jack was sitting in his beanbag chair, giggling and brandishing Hannah's fairy wand.

'Hello, Mummy!' cried Ross, waving his hands at her in time with the guitar solo. 'We're practising our cha-cha! Oi! Hannah? Hello, Mummy!'

Hannah looked peeved.

'Can Mummy join in?' asked Katie with a big

188

smile. She shimmied over to the middle of the room. 'Mummy's quite good at this one. Shall we dance, Daddy?'

It was for Hannah's benefit more than anything, to show her that Mummy and Daddy still loved each other, despite the shouting, but Katie was surprised how easily she and Ross got into the dancing hold now. It felt nice. Peter was right. They'd learned something together.

His eyes twinkled at her as if they had a shared joke, while they both counted under their breath to start at the right time.

'Don't show me up in front of Hannah. She's very demanding. And, one, back rock, cha-cha-cha, forward rock, cha-cha-cha . . .' said Ross, guiding her backwards, his knees bending easily where hers were rigid with self-consciousness, even here, even in her home.

'Oh . . . I still can't get it right,' groaned Katie as she stumbled, and would have stopped right there, if Ross hadn't said, 'No, no, no, keep going, at least until the guitar solo . . .' and pushed her on.

'See, Hannah?' he said, over his shoulder. 'Isn't Mummy a good dancer?'

'No,' said Hannah. 'She's not as good as you.' She gave Katie a furious look and ran out of the room. They heard her feet scuttle up the stairs to her room.

Suddenly Katie didn't feel angry any more. She just felt weary. How did you explain to a four-year-old that the reason you weren't there to dance during the day wasn't because you didn't love her, but because you loved her so much you wanted her to have everything you could possibly get?

'It's that time of day,' sighed Ross, preparing to

pursue Hannah. 'Sorry. That was uncalled-for.'

'No, I'll go. Let me just give Jack a cuddle.' Katie went over to Jack and lifted him out of the beanbag chair, bouncing him in her arms to make him laugh. 'Hello, little man! Hello! Have you missed me? I've missed you!' She gave him a tentative sniff. 'Is Jack bathed?'

'We're dropping them at Jo's on the way. Katie?'

'What?' She turned.

Ross looked tired, and with a thick stripe of blue eyeshadow on his cheek and a string of Katie's plastic beads round his neck, rather camp. But there was something about his scrawny, long-muscled arms sticking out from under his T-shirt that stirred up an old memory in Katie. A warm one. Added to the memory of his 'nice arse' on Wednesday night, she could feel something stirring for the first time in ages.

'I want to book you for the cha-cha this evening,' he said, wagging his finger. 'Your card's marked.'

*   *   *

The blaring brass and swinging beat was audible from outside the hall: 'Moonlight Serenade', performed by a very loud big band.

Jo and Katie shivered outside as the wind cut through their thin dresses. Autumn was definitely here now, with a keen chill whipping the leaves off the trees and whisking ruthlessly through the wind tunnels made by the concrete towers around them.

'Glad I'm not the only one to have dressed up,' said Jo, her teeth chattering. A sparkly pink flowered skirt stuck out from under her jacket, and she was wearing what looked to Katie like a new

190

pair of silver satin court shoes. 'You look . . . festive.'

'Thanks,' said Katie with a wry smile.

To coax a good mood out of Hannah, Katie had put on her old faithful black dress, and let her 'decorate Mummy's outfit' with the handful of red silk flowers she'd picked up from Claire's Accessories for a wedding and never got round to doing anything with. Hannah had also graciously applied some glitter that Katie had removed with a babywipe once safely inside Greg's BMW. On her freezing feet were the only shoes that Hannah had approved—a pair of silvery sandals she'd bought for last year's office party and never worn since. Katie was already regretting it. She'd taken maybe twenty steps and already blisters were forming on her toes.

If Hannah wasn't four, Katie would have suspected her of punishment dressing.

'You look nice,' said Jo, with an encouraging nudge.

'Thanks,' said Ross, patting his hair.

Jo giggled and batted his arm with her clutch bag. 'Get away. I was talking to your lovely wife.'

'What's Greg doing with the car?' asked Katie, to put off the evil moment of going in. She wasn't even sure why she felt so nervous, but she did. She didn't know enough yet. If she couldn't cha-cha with Ross in her own living room, they were going to look like total fools in front of people who did it every week.

'He doesn't like parking it round here.' Jo rolled her eyes. 'You know what he's like. If people *look* at it too hard, he gets all nervous about scratches.'

'Well, I can understand that,' said Katie. 'I

191

wouldn't be too happy either—it's brand new, isn't it? Greg was telling me that . . .'

'Katie, it's just a car!' snapped Ross. They exchanged irritated looks.

Jo caught the exchange, and said, quickly, 'Do you reckon it'll just be, like, us?' She nodded towards the hall. 'I know it's loud, but I haven't seen anyone go in.'

'There'll be Angelica, don't forget.' Katie adopted a pretend serious expression. 'Maybe she comes here on her own every week, and this is just a sad attempt to boost the numbers.'

'You think?'

'Yes,' said Ross. 'It'll be like the class, only with louder music and twice as long. And Baxter will be able to do Gentleman's Excuse Mes, and everyone will make a beeline for Chris. While he's sitting down.'

'And you and Greg,' added Jo, as Greg's tall figure emerged from round the corner.

I hope I get to dance with Greg, thought Katie, secretly. He doesn't look that chuffed to be here either. And we were both up at the crack of dawn this morning, so that's a good excuse not to stay too long.

But if she was being honest, she was curious to see what it would be like to be in Greg's arms, so much more solid than Ross's. What he smelled of. Whether he'd bothered to shave again before coming out. What he found to talk about during the three minutes of close contact.

That was the one thing she was dreading: the conversation with complete strangers, better dancers, who might ask for a dance. What were you meant to say? Would it feel like a driving test?

192

Would they all stand out as beginners?

'Right, that's the car parked,' said Greg, jangling the keys ostentatiously. 'Didn't want to park it on the street so it's in the NCP down the road. Bit of a trek but at least it'll be there when we get back. That OK?'

Jo looked down at her feet, then at Katie's bare toes. Then up at Katie's taut face. She grinned. 'So long as you go and get it, Greg.'

'Why?' He looked confused.

'Because the ladies will have crippled themselves and probably us too,' said Ross. He pushed open the door, and a gust of thumping Glenn Miller escaped, along with a rush of warm air. 'Come on, then.'

*   *   *

Any dread Katie had about their being the centre of attention vanished before she even got her coat off. Beyond the wood-panelled entry hall, the dancefloor was packed with couples, clearly enjoying the sort of evening Katie had only seen before in old Pathé newsreels. A swinging big-band tune was blasting out of the speakers, all shrilling trumpets and urgent drums, the air was thick with the smell of cologne, hairspray and warm human bodies, and a man in the corner appeared to be doing a roaring trade in orange juice.

The dancefloor that seemed so huge when there were only ten of them clumping about now seemed intimate in the crush of couples—there were at least sixty people there, Katie reckoned. Ladies of varying ages were being swirled expertly around by confident men who definitely weren't having to

193

count aloud, their fondant-fancy coloured skirts blooming up as they floated around each other like clockwork figures, almost but never quite colliding, thanks to some mysterious sixth sense that Katie was pretty sure she and Ross would never acquire.

It wasn't just the dancing that had lifted to a new level, she marvelled: the hall itself looked completely different. Darker, more glamorous, and romantic. The overhead lights were turned down, and a huge mirrorball sprinkled diamonds of white light around the floor and over the dancers' shoulders like confetti. Chairs and small tables had been arranged around the edges, where couples and hopeful singles sat watching the dancers, sipping their juice, waiting for their turn on the floor as their toes tapped out the beat.

Standing just inside the door, also handing their coats in to the cloakroom, were Lauren and Chris. Lauren greeted Katie and Ross with enthusiastic relief, and Katie felt a little warmth uncurl in the pit of her stomach like a fern—camaraderie that they were all about to make fools of themselves together. Chris gave them a blokeish nod, his hands jammed firmly in his pockets.

'Oh my God!' exclaimed Lauren. She was wearing a tight black bustier and a flower-pattern skirt that was meant to be mid-calf, but just grazed her knee. 'Did we just, like, step back in time? Is this the same place?'

'And are they doing the same dance?' Chris looked nervously out at the floor. 'I said to Loz, that isn't what we've been learning.'

'I don't know.' Katie stared at the forest of spangly court shoes, but they were moving too quickly to tell.

'Hello, Ross! Jo!' Lauren's parents had appeared behind them, their coats already off. Her dad, in particular, seemed unusually animated by the atmosphere, nodding his head to the tune and tapping his right foot.

'Marvellous, isn't it, this music? Takes me back,' said Frank, extending a hand towards his wife. 'Bridget? May I have the pleasure?'

'You may!' Bridget beamed, and handed her bag to Lauren, who stared with the rest of them as her parents stepped onto the dancefloor and immediately began moving in tiny, intuitive steps, already smiling into each other's face as they hovered for a moment on the edge, and were then swept away in the surging merry-go-round of sports jackets and pink sequins.

'Wow,' breathed Lauren. 'Aren't the clothes great? So this is what Angelica meant about getting dressed up to get into it. I must admit,' she went on, smoothing down her skirt, 'it does make you feel a bit special.'

'You suit big skirts,' said Katie, wanting to be nice to her. 'Look at your little waist!'

'Oh, I remember when I had one of those,' sighed Jo, dramatically. 'Treasure it, Lauren. It doesn't keep.'

'Katie?' Ross held out a hand. 'Shall we?'

Katie felt the nerves clutch her. 'Can't we get a drink first, or at least get a table?'

'I'm going to the bar,' said Chris. 'Lauren, can you get a table?'

'There's one, over there! Katie, give us your bag?' And laden with three handbags, Lauren was off, inching her way around the tables to the final spare one at the back.

195

Katie turned back to Ross. 'Can't we just watch for a bit?'

'Come on,' he said. 'Take the plunge.'

'But I don't even know what sort of dance it is! It's all right for you—you know what you're doing!'

He smiled, and Katie was irritated that she was irritated by something that she knew she should be happy about: Ross taking the initiative, for once. 'Doesn't matter,' he said. 'It's got four beats. We can do that shuffly wedding dance one—it's not like there's room for much more anyway.'

Reluctantly, she let him pull her onto the floor, where they paused for a moment, to count to four, then Ross stepped forwards and they started their basic social foxtrot steps, the ones that made a slow zig-zag shape down the room. To Katie's surprise, he was right: one, it fitted to the beat, and two, there really wasn't much room for dancefloor heroics.

'Ooops, sorry! Sorry!' muttered Ross, as they bumped into a couple doing a flashy step sequence.

'Are we going the right way? What did Angelica say about directions?' panicked Katie. 'Was it clockwise or anti-clockwise?'

'Anti-clockwise. And don't stray into the fast lane round the outside,' said Angelica, spinning past out of nowhere and making them both jump. 'You'll get trampled! Hello!'

'Hello!' stammered Katie. How did Angelica just *appear* like that, when she least wanted her to?

'How lovely to see you! You must have a dance with Victor here, Katie,' she said, smiling up at her enormous partner, whose crisp white shirt strained somewhat at the shoulders. 'He has a *wonderfully* strong lead!'

'Angelica makes it so easy,' Victor explained, casually dipping Angelica so her long neck arched elegantly to the side for a slow-motion moment. He sounded Eastern European, and had a look of Rudolph Valentino. Katie had no idea such exotica existed in Longhampton. 'There is always a queue to dance with her.'

Angelica seemed more delicate than ever in Victor's manly arms. She was wearing a red satin skirt and an off-the-shoulder black top, her jet-black hair gleaming as if freshly polished. 'Very bad form that, by the way,' she added, regaining her upright stance, and nodding towards the couple who'd bumped into them. 'You're not meant to do routines on a social night.'

Victor swung her back in a neat step, then twirled her round so they overtook Ross and Katie in the fast lane.

'I'll send Victor over later!' she called, as they vanished. 'You're doing very well! But point those feet, Katie! And let Ross lead!' Her voice trailed off.

'There you go,' said Ross, as they shuffled onwards. 'We're doing very well. Are you pointing your feet? Are you trying to back-lead me?'

'Back-lead?' Katie raised an eyebrow. 'Have you been watching those DVDs again?'

'Be quiet or I'll hand you over to Baxter,' said Ross serenely, and then yelped as he tried to do a box-turn, and their feet jumbled.

'I lost the rhythm,' said Katie, then added, 'sorry.'

Ross smiled. 'Doesn't matter.'

When Katie and Ross had done a slow lap of the
room, with only three more collisions and a new
bruise on Ross's foot, they picked their way back to
the table to find Lauren in animated conversation
with Trina. Handbags and jackets were placed
territorially on the empty chairs, and their eyes
were swivelling like Wimbledon spectators as the
dancers swished by. Trina's red-lipsticked mouth
was moving even faster than her eyes in a running
fashion commentary worthy of the Grand
National.

'. . . someone should tell her pink satin isn't her
friend. It isn't anyone's friend, come to that, unless
you're a drum majorette or under three years of
age. And is he gay? Him! There, in the lime shirt.
He looks far too well turned out to be . . . Oh, hi,
Ross! Katie!'

Katie squeezed into a free chair and helped
herself to the jug of orange juice on the table. She
hadn't realised how parched she was until she saw
it. The heat and the effort of dancing were
surprisingly fierce. 'Hi, Trina. Have you been here
long?'

'Long enough to have had a foxtrot with
Mr Octopus over there in the yellow shirt,' she
said, nodding darkly at the dancefloor. 'Watch out
for him. I'd say the only thing quicker than those
flashing feet are his hands. That's where Chloe is
now. Learning a new way to get out of corners.'

'Still, at least you're meeting new people, eh?'
said Lauren, quickly. 'Katie, have you seen
Angelica?'

'Yes. She took the time to slag off my feet, then

198

sashayed away in the arms of some enormous hunk,' said Katie.

Trina giggled. 'Ooh, you are funny, Katie.'

Am I? thought Katie, but she felt flattered.

'Well, good for her—she's taken Chris off my hands for this one.' Lauren topped up her glass. 'I hope she can do something about his waltz. He's already ruined one pair of my fishnets.' Her brow creased. 'It's really unsexy, not being able to count to three. Or move your feet.'

'Your mum and dad seem to be enjoying themselves,' said Katie, as a flushed Bridget and Frank approached the table. Bridget was fanning her round face, and Frank was guiding her with a sweetly protective hand on her back.

'Yeah, it's dead sweet how good they are,' said Trina. 'You know, watching them, they obviously still—'

'Don't!' said Lauren, covering her ears. 'Whatever you were about to say, don't! I'm living at home now.'

'We were just saying,' Trina said to Bridget, 'how well you two dance together. Budge up, Ross—they'll want to sit down!'

'Sit down? Certainly not! We're just getting going!' Bridget extended her hand to Ross. 'You youngsters, no stamina! Now, Ross, I know it's not correct form, but would you care to dance?'

Ross looked quickly over to Katie.

'Go on,' said Frank. 'I'm hoping to take Katie for a spin round the floor, if you don't object?'

'Not at all!' Ross's face relaxed, and he led Bridget back into the throng of bodies as the music changed to a slower ballad, sung by a female vocalist Katie didn't recognise; like most of the songs, it was about a love affair of some kind. Happy, unhappy, it all sounded the same. Katie watched Ross's serious expression change from concentration to a gentle smile as Bridget's head bobbed in conversation, then they had turned out of sight.

'May I?'

She realised Frank was still standing there, his hand outstretched.

'I'll be coming back for you later,' he added to Trina, with a charm that Katie would never have guessed at from his quiet, brown-jumpered appearance in class. There was something about stepping onto a dancefloor that seemed to do something to people—well, Katie corrected herself, some people. Not her.

Awkwardly, she got up from her seat and took Frank's hand, very conscious of the unfamiliar contact. It was warm and dry, with little ridges of hardened skin. Gardening, she wondered? Or DIY? Katie knew she was over-analysing to take her mind off the nerves that still plagued her when she had to dance with someone other than Ross. It was intimate but formal at the same time; they were almost hugging, thighs nearly touching, hips brushing, hands moulding together, but all so they could move in ordered, formal steps.

It felt different from class. Like the first time she set off in a car after passing her test.

'All set?' Frank said, with a kind smile. 'I think this one's a waltz, isn't it?'

'It is,' she said. He knew it was. He was just being nice, to make her feel less of a complete beginner.

'Now then,' he said, as his hand settled on her

shoulder-blade and, with a tiny pressure from his fingers and a bend in the knee, let her know they were setting off.

Katie felt acutely self-conscious, and wasn't sure where to look. At his face? Over his shoulder? Come on, she told herself. People have been doing this for hundreds of years without getting into a tizz about it.

Frank turned her round into a simple waltz step and she lost sight of the dance-class table.

So if they can all do it so easily, why can't I? thought Katie as she trod on Frank's polished toes and stumbled in her high heels. I'm never going to be any good at this.

'No need to look so worried!' he said, steering her effortlessly out of trouble. 'You're doing very nicely. Just relax.'

'Sorry.' Katie looked instead at the faces of the dancers passing around her. They were chatting, smiling, flirting, singing along to the music, having a wonderful time. Not concentrating hard on the basic waltz steps they knew.

They were nearly at the end of the room. Katie was gripped with panic as the edge of the floor loomed up, the music pressed relentlessly on and her mind went blank. How were you meant to turn round? She didn't want to mess things up.

She looked up at Frank apologetically. 'We've only had one waltz lesson. And I'm not very good in corners!'

'Not to worry, love, I've done a few waltzes in my time. You know,' he went on, moving them slightly to the side to let another couple pass, 'it might be easier if you let me take charge of the directions. What with being a bit taller, I've got a

201

better view of the on-coming traffic, you see.'

'Oh God, am I leading? Sorry,' stammered Katie, flushing. 'Angelica's always on my case about that, but you get into habits, you know . . .'

'Don't worry.' With a very subtle pressure on her back and a little extra angle in his foot, Frank eased them round the corner, turning her so neatly that her skirt twirled out, although Katie was concentrating too hard to notice. 'You'll get used to it—I know it took Bridget a while to believe that a bloke knew what he was about, and that was forty-odd years ago!'

'Did we just do a corner?'

'We did indeed.' Frank twitched his eyebrows and smiled, and the bags under his eyes deepened. He had a comforting, dad-like smile, and she felt some of the tension in her arms melt away. 'Rather neatly too, if you ask me.'

'We haven't done waltz corners,' marvelled Katie.

'Well, you have now. And you didn't feel a thing, did you?'

Her brow creased, trying to work out how it had happened so she could practise it. 'How did we do it? What were the steps?'

'I'll show you later,' he said, as she forgot to change feet. 'Let's not get tangled up in details now, shall we?'

They danced on, and Frank let her concentrate, giving her an encouraging smile now and again.

Lauren was so lucky, having nice Frank to practise with, thought Katie. If only Dad had taught me to dance, I wouldn't have to be here having lessons now.

She couldn't imagine her father dancing. He

didn't have time for that sort of thing. He barely had time to play golf at the weekends, which would definitely have taken priority over waltzing.

'Sorry, sorry!' she said, as her brain suddenly froze as Frank tried to turn her into a spin of some kind.

'My fault, I should have let you know that was coming,' he said easily. 'Ba dah, pah, pom, pom, pom . . . When I was learning all this, about a hundred years ago,' Frank went on, conversationally, 'my mother told me that *her* mother had told her that the trick was to listen to the music, not the voice in your head counting. I reckon that's the secret. Enjoy the music, and forget about where you're meant to be putting your feet. That's not your problem—that's the man's! Leave the tricky stuff to him, eh?'

'Things have moved on a bit since then,' Katie said, automatically.

'At work, maybe, but not on the dancefloor, love.' Frank nudged her into another corner, deftly slipping between two twirling couples who passed in a ' 'scuse me, 'scuse me' flurry of hot breath and Magie Noir.

One of them, Katie noticed, was Ross, holding Bridget's little hand up high, as if he'd been doing it for years. When had he learned to turn around like that? They were chatting away, Bridget nodding and laughing as Ross's eyebrows moved, obviously in the middle of some story. They looked like proper dancers.

'Ross seems to have picked this up much faster than me,' she heard herself say, and hated how petulant it sounded.

Frank gave her a funny smile. 'Well, Bridget's

been making me look like Fred Astaire for years. Good partners can do that.'

And suddenly the music came to a close in a flourish, and around them couples separated in gracious curtsies and bows.

'Thank you, I very much enjoyed that,' said Frank, nodding his head. A few beads of perspiration had appeared on his bald spot, but he looked flushed in a happy way.

'No, thank you,' said Katie, as they squeezed their way back to the table. 'Sorry about your poor feet. I just can't get mine to do what's in my head.'

'Oh, it'll come,' he said. 'Penny'll drop and we won't be able to keep you off the floor!'

Katie smiled politely. That was hardly likely. Prisoners who learned basket-weaving in prison didn't usually end up master furniture-makers.

'Lauren? May I have this quickstep?' he said, as the band on the sound system struck up a brisk forties rhythm.

'We haven't done the quickstep.'

'Nothing to it, love. Just follow me.'

She saw Frank offer his hand to his daughter, who pretended to pull a face of sheer embarrassment at her mother, but then took it with a half-hidden smile of genuine love that made Katie want to sigh inside. Lauren and Frank stepped onto the floor, about the same height, with Lauren in her wedding heels and they sailed off.

That's a lovely relationship, she thought. I hope Hannah and Ross will be like that one day.

If we haven't screwed up the kids by getting a divorce by then.

We're not going to split up, Katie told herself. We're going to fix it. Somehow.

204

She sat the next few dances out, preferring to watch as Angelica came back for Ross, and then for Greg, then sailed off with Baxter, at which point swathes of dancefloor cleared so everyone could admire their fancy linked steps and trailing arms. Ross was in demand, from Chloe and Trina, and every so often she would catch sight of him.

'Katie?'

She turned. Ross had led Bridget back to her seat, and was standing very close to her, so close that she could smell his deodorant and the more intimate musky smell of his warm skin. 'I'm reliably informed that this is a cha-cha,' he said, seriously. 'And I think that's the one we can do, isn't it?'

His hair had turned darker and flopped into his eyes with the exertion of dancing in a crush of bodies, and he'd undone another button on his shirt. Ross wasn't unattractive, she thought with despairing objectivity, trying to fan her earlier flickers of attraction into something more—so why can't I feel it any more? Why don't I respond to him as a man, the way I used to? What's wrong with me?

'I've been waiting to dance with you, but it's so hard to say no when people ask and you feel a bit sorry for them,' he added. 'Come on.' He led her into a little space. 'There isn't so much moving around in this. We can just stand here, near the table . . .' His expression was mildly ironic. 'Nice and safe.'

Ross took her hand, slipping the other one around her shoulder-blade and she put hers on his arm.

Come on, Katie told herself. Feel his hand

touching you through the dress! Feel his hip brushing against yours! Fancy him! But there was nothing. She looked at the shirt and was reminded that unlike Greg's, Ross's wardrobe depended on what she decided to get for him. That wasn't sexy. That was being his mother.

'Katie,' said Ross, warningly. 'Don't lead.'

She was about to protest when Greg and Jo came rushing up. Jo's hair, carefully piled into a chic updo when they entered, was escaping in messy spirals, and her shiny face was creased with concern.

'I'm so sorry, but we have to go,' said Jo, putting her hands on both their shoulders. 'There's a problem at home.'

'Oh God, what?' Katie's head filled with a slideshow of disasters, the ones that sometimes tormented her in long meetings when her phone was turned off. 'Is it Hannah? Are they OK?'

'Honestly, Jo, don't be melodramatic,' snorted Greg. 'We don't all have to go. The babysitter called,' he said to Katie. 'Apparently Hannah's complaining of a tummy ache, and so Molly is as well. You know what they're like at that age. No puking or anything, but she's worried. Didn't want to leave it till we got back.'

'Just when we were having so much fun!' said Jo, apologetically. 'Listen, if you want to stay, Greg's right—I can look after her and Jack, if you want. Stay. Call a cab.'

Ross looked at Katie, without taking his hand off her shoulder. His face was asking the question, but he obviously didn't have the courage to come out and say it.

'Of course we can't stay,' said Katie, already

reaching for her bag.

CHAPTER FIFTEEN

'In terms of dessert, I've had a brainwave—how about a cake of cheese?' suggested Irene brightly. She moved the plate of Duchy Original Shortbread towards Chris. 'Have a biscuit, Christopher. You look peckish.'

'A cheesecake?' repeated Bridget, taking one herself. She knew they were Duchy Originals, because Irene had made sure she'd seen the packet before she arranged them on the plate. 'Are they fashionable again then?'

'No,' explained Lauren, 'a cake of cheese. You know, a whole Cheddar with a whole Stilton, with a whole Roquefort then a whole . . .' She racked her brains for the right size cheese.

'Chevre,' Irene supplied, helpfully. 'It's very continental.'

Chris helped himself to a couple of biscuits, and said, 'Sounds better than profiteroles.'

It was the first comment he'd made in the hour they'd spent around Irene's dining table, which was now cluttered with papers and files. Bridget thought he looked about as interested in proceedings as Lauren's celebrated sugarcraft Prince cake topper, taking pride of place in the middle of the table. Possibly less so. Maybe Lauren could find a couple of wedding mice to go on top of the cake of cheese. There was probably someone in Texas who specialised in making them, for fifty pounds a go, not including P&P.

207

Amazing how amounts just lost all relative monetary value once a cake cost four hundred quid.

She shook herself.

'Your dad would like that, Laurie,' she agreed, trying to think of a nice way to say no. 'You know how he is with his Stilton at Christmas. But how about a proper pudding, for those that don't . . . like cheese?'

'Well, of course,' said Irene. 'We were planning on a selection of four, weren't we, Lauren? *Plus* the cheese cake. That'd be on a separate buffet table.'

Lauren looked uncertainly between the two women, torn between wanting four puddings and sensing her mother's unspoken tension. 'Um, yeah. Mum, did I give you the new catering quote? Here . . .' She passed her a set of papers, stapled together at the corner.

'No, you didn't.' Bridget braced herself as she flipped through to the end, but even so, she couldn't stop herself flinching as she read the figure.

I have to say something, she thought. This is now officially out of control. It's all very well Irene suggesting these things, but she isn't the one who's just about to put fifteen hundred pounds down to secure 'peak time' caterers.

'Does this include the plate hire and so on?' she asked hopefully.

Lauren shook her head. 'Well, no, because we wanted those special gold plates Irene saw at the bridal show, remember? For the banquet theme?'

'It's a bit more than the budget, love,' Bridget pointed out. 'I mean, what would you rather have, gold plates or that special punch fountain?'

'Oh, Bridget! We can't expect Lauren to *choose*!' exclaimed Irene. 'It's a very special day! There's absolutely no point cutting corners—I've been to too many weddings where it's all been spoiled for the sake of a few pennies here and there. That's not going to happen to Christopher. And Lauren.'

'No, no, *of course* we want it to be lovely,' protested Bridget, stung by the idea that she was about to spoil Lauren's wedding out of meanness. 'I just think we need to make some decisions . . .'

She could see Lauren's forehead wrinkle between her eyebrows, and her round blue eyes tilt down at the edges: she had such a sunny face that the first signs of distress had always been easy to spot. Bridget knew Lauren hated conflict more than anything, apart from not getting her own way. Her dad was the same.

Irene spotted it too, and immediately patted Lauren's hand: a tiny gesture that annoyed Bridget.

It wasn't Lauren's fault, Bridget told herself. She'd just had so little of either in her life— conflict *or* the word no. She and Frank were equally to blame for that. Blame. That wasn't the right word. It wasn't like there was anything *wrong*.

Irene looked over at her. 'Hear me out, Bridget, before you say no. Now, I've said it before, but if you'd like me to pay for the reception, you know I'd be more than happy to do so,' she said, grandly. 'It's what Ron would have wanted to do, were he still with us, bless him. He'd have wanted Christopher to have the very best wedding . . .'

'No,' said Bridget. There was something about

Irene's attitude that made her stubborn where she'd normally be happy to give in graciously. 'No, we agreed. You're going to pay for the cars and the flowers, and we'll stand the rest. It's what *Frank* wants,' she added. 'You know what proud fathers are like. Especially old-fashioned Northern ones like Frank.'

Lauren shot a quick smile at her mother and Bridget felt a mixture of pride and panic.

'Mum, can I put some washing on?' said Chris, unexpectedly.

'You brought washing home?' demanded Lauren. 'To your mum's?'

'Yeah? Kian's machine doesn't work. And he doesn't have an iron.'

'You've been there months!' exclaimed Lauren. 'Have you only just noticed?'

'Of course,' said Irene, already getting up from the table. 'Where is it? No, don't get up, I'll put it in for you. Make sure it's on the right setting . . .'

'In the hall.' Chris leaned back in his chair, until Lauren dug him in the ribs.

'You pig!' she hissed. 'You knew she'd do it for you! What are you like?'

'Oh, come on, she enjoys looking after me,' he hissed back, trying not to look at Bridget. 'Makes her feel she's still my mum.'

'Well, I hope you don't expect *me* to do all the washing when we're married.' Lauren glared at him. 'I haven't been brought up to run around after my husband. Have I, Mum?'

'There!' said Irene, returning with an overflowing sports bag of dirty laundry. 'I'll just pop this on—anyone want more coffee while I'm up?'

'Yes, please,' said Chris. 'And more biscuits.'

'Now, Lauren,' said Irene gaily, pointing her finger. 'Are you sure you're feeding him enough?'

'He feeds himself,' Lauren replied, tartly. 'If he and Kian aren't eating anything apart from pizzas that's his look-out.'

'You can *never* feed lads enough,' said Bridget pouring oil on troubled water as Irene's heels clicked away across her kitchen tiles. 'And I should know. Your brothers used to have that fridge emptied before I'd even unpacked the shopping. Anyway,' she went on, racking her brains for something that would break up the simmering mood. 'I thought you were looking very smooth on the dancefloor the other night, Chris! Don't you feel you're starting to get the hang of it?'

The stormclouds left Lauren's face. At least she was easy to cheer up, thought Bridget.

'Sort of,' Chris grunted.

'You just need a bit more practice,' said Bridget, encouragingly. 'It'll fall into place soon enough. Your dad said you were really coming along when he took you for that spin round the floor.'

'Did he?' Lauren looked pleased. 'It felt much easier dancing with Dad. Even though he sang all the words right into my ear. Didn't you ever tell him not to do that, Mum?'

'Frequently,' said Bridget. 'You learn to tune it out.'

Lauren cut a sidelong look at Chris, and asked, with an air of disinterest that didn't fool Bridget for a second, 'Is Kian around tonight, Chris?'

Chris was too distracted by the arrival of Irene and a plate of biscuits to think two steps ahead of what Lauren was saying. 'No, he's out with some

211

bird he met last weekend.'

'Good. Forget the pub. We can go back and have a practice.' Lauren helped herself to another biscuit. 'Before we forget what we learned.'

'Ah, Loz!'

'Practise what?' Irene's sharp eyes turned immediately to Bridget. 'Their waltz?'

'Yes,' said Bridget. 'Turns out Lauren's quite the Ginger Rogers. Her granny was a keen ballroom dancer, and of course that's where Frank and I met—it must run in the family!'

Lauren beamed shyly.

'Really?' Irene didn't need to put into words what her doubtful expression said so much better.

'Really,' said Lauren. 'It's like . . . when I know what I've got to do, my feet just do it. I don't need to worry about knocking stuff over or treading on things.' Her smile increased. 'Dad said I didn't tread on his toes *once* on Friday.'

'I've given Christopher some DVDs,' Irene told Bridget. 'Instructional ones—very helpful.'

'I know,' said Lauren. 'We've watched them.'

Chris grunted.

'Well, I've watched them,' she added, unable to lie confidently with Bridget there. 'Chris has been really . . . busy. But we've watched my *Dirty Dancing* DVD again, haven't we, Chris? And *Strictly Come Dancing*? It's not exactly what we're doing yet, but . . .'

'Maybe I *should* come with you to the class,' mused Irene. 'I don't know how experienced this teacher is. I might be able to give her some pointers.'

'No!' said Bridget and Lauren at the same time.

Bridget's eyes met Lauren's, and she widened

212

them in pretend shock as Lauren suppressed a giggle. The idea of Angelica taking pointers from Irene was unthinkable. Almost.

Chris glanced at Lauren and rolled his eyes. 'I don't think Angelica needs any help, Mum,' he said, firmly.

Irene pursed her lips. 'We'll see about that.'

*　　　*　　　*

'We're never going to get any better if we don't practise,' said Lauren, as Chris accelerated out of Irene's smart cul-de-sac. There was a bag of M&S ready-meals in the boot, while the sports bag of laundry was still in Irene's tumble dryer, and would, Lauren knew, be ironed before it was returned. Even his jersey boxers.

Chris turned to her, letting his hand slide further along her thigh. 'I can think of a few things we're not getting much practice at right now.'

'I mean, dancing.' Lauren tried to ignore Chris's fingers wriggling up her leg. He always drove too fast, probably even faster when his mates were in the car. She replaced his hand on the steering wheel. 'Your mum's right—you don't just pick it up overnight, and I don't want everyone watching when we fall over each other's feet, do I?'

'Who says we're going to fall over each other's feet? Anyway, it's a long time off . . .'

Lauren bit back a snotty reply about him needing every minute between now and then. It wasn't like her to get annoyed with Chris, but there was something weirdly annoying about the fact that he couldn't pick up even the basic steps. Normally it was she who had trouble getting it

213

together, but he didn't even seem to care that they were way behind everyone else, and even the dim giggly one from the tax office didn't mess up the waltz box now.

'Seriously, Chris—it's going to be a big— Get off, will you?' She glared at the hand that had returned to her upper thigh. 'Will you concentrate on the road?'

'Woah!' He raised his hands. 'What's wrong with you?'

'Both hands on the wheel!' she yelled.

They'd come to a halt at the traffic lights at the top of Kian's road.

Lauren collected herself. For some reason, the more she thought about Chris's inept shuffling the more it bugged her. What was that about?

'Sorry. Sorry, it's just been a busy week at the surgery, you know, with me setting up the new computer, and there's still so much to decide about the reception. I mean, I should have told my mum about the horses only after she said about the catering quote . . .'

'The horses?'

Lauren remembered too late that she hadn't told Chris about the horses yet either.

'Do you not think it would be nice to stop thinking about the wedding for one evening, and think about me instead?' he grumbled. 'While Kian's out?'

She tilted her head towards him. 'You're sure Kian's out?'

Since Chris had moved in with Kian, he'd been out precisely twice. Actually, he'd been out far more than twice, but on those occasions, Chris had been out with him.

'Definitely. He told me he wasn't planning on being back tonight at all,' he added. 'And if we push the sofa back, there might even be enough room to practise that box junction thing?'

Lauren put her hand on his knee, and stroked the long muscle of his thigh. He was still in his suit, having gone round to Irene's straight after work. 'Thanks, Chris.'

'And once we've got that sorted, then we'll move on to more horizontal dancing,' he finished, with a cheeky grin. 'Deal?'

Chris was seriously hot in a suit, thought Lauren. Maybe I should pop round to the dealership in my lunchbreak. Investigate the romantic possibilities of a test drive, like we used to.

'Fair enough,' she said.

*   *   *

Kian's flat was the exact opposite of what Lauren wanted their first home to be: messy and under-furnished, the doormat littered with junk mail addressed to previous tenants, and smelling of curry and mildewy washing that had gone dry in the machine. She was clinging to the hope that living in such blokeish squalor after the six months of relative grown-up living they'd enjoyed together would make Chris realise just how nice it was to sink into a freshly made bed, and know that the bathroom wasn't harbouring more suspicious bacteria than the surgery fridge.

Unfortunately, Chris seemed to be settling in a bit too much.

'Go through,' said Chris, waving her through to

the sitting room then abruptly added, 'Actually, hang on, let me just . . .' before rushing past to do some emergency tidying up.

Lauren followed him slowly, to give him a chance to hide whatever horrors were lurking.

The only furniture in the sitting room, bar an old table and a 'No Parking' sign, were two large sofas, one each for Chris and Kian to watch football on the enormous plasma TV. Kian earned a decent wage now he was a manager at the power station down the road, and he believed in 'putting it back into the local economy', hence the vast television, Bose sound system and various black boxes Lauren didn't recognise. She wasn't sold on Kian's financial planning. He was always on at Chris to get a top-of-the-range car, 'to promote the dealership', and she had a sinking feeling the stag night was going to cost more than the reception.

Chris saw her looking at the sofas, and he threw a cushion over the largest stain, then shoved them back against the wall to make room for a few steps.

'Thought about telling Kian to get a cleaner, but then I reckoned it was better to save the money for our deposit,' he explained. 'If you want, I can run a Hoover around later?'

Lauren melted as Chris's earnest eyes searched her face for signs of approval. When he smiled like that she reckoned he had a look of a young David Beckham. And it wasn't just her who thought so: it was every woman under fifty in Longhampton. He's just getting it out of his system, she told herself, as he took her hands and moved her into the space he'd cleared. Teenage years in Irene's house probably hadn't allowed for a lot of stains. Better now than later.

Then she remembered about Chris taking his laundry back home, and kicked herself for even thinking he'd do housework.

Maybe I'll drop hints to Irene about the state of the flat, she thought mischievously, as he slipped an arm around her back in a waltz hold. It might distract her from coming to dancing class.

Lauren looked up happily at Chris and put her hand on his strong shoulder, feeling the rounded muscle under his fine cotton shirt. He took her hand in his and raised it to the height decreed by Angelica.

'So, you want to practise that dip thing your mum was doing at the social night?' Chris tightened his grip, pressing his fingertips against her shoulder-blade. 'You bending over backwards—carefully, like.'

'No, that's boring—what about that fancy lift from *Dirty Dancing*?' she said. 'You have to lift me right up, and turn round slowly.' She looked around the room. Fortunately there wasn't a lot to knock over.

He jiggled his eyebrows. 'OK. It'd give them something to talk about in the next class.'

'Just don't drop me,' said Lauren, as visions of a show-stopping wedding routine floated through her head. They didn't *have* to do a waltz for their first dance, after all. What was the point of going out with an amateur rugby player if you didn't make use of his strength training? 'You're the only one there that could do it without putting his back out.'

Before she could prepare herself, Chris grabbed Lauren round her hips and hoisted her off her feet with a skilfulness more suited to a line-out than the dancefloor.

Lauren squealed and tried to stretch out her arm, as he swung her round in a rough attempt at what Patrick Swayze made look so easy, but when she lifted her leg into a better pose, Chris lost his balance and went stumbling backwards into the sofa. Wriggling, Lauren hit the cushions first and brought Chris down on top of her. A bit hastily, she thought.

Still, she wasn't complaining. And the flat was empty for once. She tried not to think about the stains as Chris's warm weight bore down on her body and sent hot rushes of arousal through her.

'Mmm,' he said, sliding his hand up her shirt and burying his lips in the crook of her neck, finding the exact point that made Lauren's skin tingle in a delicious line of silvery electricity all the way down. 'It's been *ages* since we had some time on our own.'

'Mmm,' agreed Lauren, twisting her fingers into his thick hair and scratching his scalp until he groaned. One of her legs was still hooked over one arm of the sofa, where she'd fallen, and Chris's other hand slid up it, stroking from her knee up her thigh. 'Ages . . .'

He kissed further round her neck, dipping down her chest into her hot cleavage, while his fingers tickled and pressed under the thin wire of her bra. 'Mmm, Lauren . . .'

The sudden note of urgency in Chris's voice made her shiver and she found herself reaching round to his trousers, to find the buckle, then the zip.

'Mmm, Lauren,' Chris groaned again, and she had just shifted to allow him better access to her own buttons when the front door banged.

218

'Aye, aye, aye!'

Lauren and Chris sprang apart, and she struggled to pull her skirt down to a decent level while Chris let rip with a string of unappreciative greetings.

Kian Matthews stood in the doorway, blocking half the light with his stocky frame. From the pungent waft of aftershave, stale smoke and beer, he'd come straight from their local, but unusually he seemed to be returning alone, apart from a can of Stella.

'Hello, police?' he said, into an imaginary mobile. 'My flat's been broken into by a pair of horny teenagers . . . oh no! It's just my flatmate and his girlfriend.'

'Fiancée,' said Lauren. 'I thought you were out tonight.'

Kian and Chris had been mates since school, though Lauren hadn't taken that much notice of Kian, not until she started going out with Chris in the sixth form. Then she'd got to know Kian well enough. He was, by his own definition, the 'funny one' to Chris's Golden Boy Wonder.

'Kian, you knob,' said Chris. 'I thought you were *stopping* out?' He pulled his shirt back into his trousers. 'Dead cert, you told me.'

'Yeah, well, had to call in the video ref on that Becky,' said Kian, opening his can of lager. 'Turns out I was beer-goggled up when I got her number. Action replay revealed her to be Mrs Moose of Moose County.' He took a deep slurp, then gasped out a loud, 'Aaaah! Had to leave her in the Rose and Crown while I did a runner. Still, plenty more where she came from.'

'And you didn't think about staying out to give

219

the rest of the lucky ladies a chance?' asked Lauren, sarcastically. 'It's only half nine. The night is young.'

'No, no,' said Kian. 'It's no fun without my wingman.' He gave Chris a matey slap on the shoulder. 'They see the good looks first, then they're hooked in by my charm. Carry on, like. Pretend I'm not here.' And he bent down to turn on the new PlayStation, setting up his steering wheel and pedals set.

Lauren looked at Chris and her narrowed eyes said, Wingman? Hello?

'He's taking the piss. Take no notice.' Chris rearranged himself awkwardly. 'Kian, have you eaten yet?'

'No,' said Kian. 'Have you? Eh? Eh?' he added, with a lascivious wink at Lauren. 'Eh?' he said again, in case she hadn't got his meaning.

'Oh my God,' said Lauren. Any vaguely sexy feelings she might have had were out of the window now. Kian sucked any romance out of the atmosphere like a Dyson on full power. How he managed to pull such Russell Brand-worthy numbers of women was beyond her—and yet he did, according to Chris, anyway.

'Do you want to get a takeaway?' Chris turned to Lauren with a placatory expression. 'How about it? You can choose, Loz.'

'I'm not really hungry,' said Lauren.

The sounds of a Formula One Racing game began to roar from the speakers positioned around the room as Kian settled himself down on the beanbag that doubled as a racecar. Lauren had heard the familiar 'set-up selection' chimes so often now that they set off a Pavlovian reaction in her: one of intense irritation. In the beginning she'd tried to be interested, asked to have a go, but it was just one of those things that blokes were more into. Even now she could practically feel Chris's need to take over the other steering wheel. And Kian knew it.

This happened nearly every time she went round. Him and Kian, laughing about people she didn't know, cracking open the beers, talking about Formula One until she wondered if she'd gone invisible. It was like trying to share her boyfriend with another woman, and to make it worse, Lauren knew she'd made the whole thing happen because she'd insisted on them saving up for the flat deposit—it hadn't been like this before.

Lauren glared openly at Chris, who was edging nearer the television. Finally he couldn't help himself.

'You need slicks on that circuit, Kian, you tool!' he blurted out, then looked guiltily at Lauren.

She didn't want to say it because she'd vowed she'd never say it again once she stopped being a teenager, but Kian was leaving her no choice—and he knew it, the manipulative sod.

'Come on, Chris,' said Lauren, trying not to sound like a nag. 'Let's go to your room.' She pulled herself off the sofa, grabbing her handbag, and hauled him after her.

Chris threw a final longing gaze at Kian's new pedals, then followed.

*   *   *

Lauren missed her old any-time access to Chris's lovely toned six-pack, and it was fair to say that

221

absence was making the heart, not to mention the rest of her body, fonder for both of them, but any lingering romantic atmosphere soon evaporated as the squealing sounds of Kian's attack on Le Mans cut through the seduction music Chris had hastily put on in his room.

'That's it. I'm going home,' Lauren announced, pushing Chris off her with an effort, and struggling up to a sitting position on his single bed.

Chris slumped face down on the pillows with a frustrated moan. 'Why?'

'Because . . .' In the sitting room, Kian crashed, swore, and burped. 'Because the walls in this place are too thin. And Kian is too . . . *here.*'

Chris turned his face upwards. 'What are you saying? It is his flat.'

'Then maybe we need to think about houses again.' Lauren paused. 'Or maybe I need to get my mum and dad to go away on holiday for a week.'

'Or *we* could go on holiday?'

'We're saving up for the flat, remember?'

'Oh, yeah,' said Chris, without much enthusiasm. 'Fair enough.'

They lay in silence for a few minutes, as Kian roared away next door.

'You know what I really miss?' sighed Lauren.

'Doing it in the shower?' asked Chris, hopefully.

'No. Just . . . being together. Not talking. Not doing anything.'

'Mmm.'

'Chris? You don't sound very enthusiastic.'

'I am. It's a girl thing, that, isn't it? That whole "being together" business. We're good as we are, aren't we?'

'No, it's not, it's a . . .' Lauren stopped. 'I'm

going home.'

Chris didn't try very hard to stop her, and as she was leaving, she distinctly heard Kian say, 'Don't get under the thumb, mate!' as he threw Chris the other controller.

*   *   *

The lights were off in the sitting room when Lauren let herself in, and she guessed that her mum and dad had turned in for the night. They were both early risers, even at weekends.

She closed the door softly behind her. The cat wound itself round her legs and she bent down to stroke it, nearly knocking it over as her handbag swung round. Mittens knew Lauren well, though, and skipped neatly out of the way, like a footballer swerving a tackle, curling round her other ankle.

In the kitchen, Lauren made herself a hot chocolate, and, after a cursory inspection of the fridge, added a slice of ham and egg pie and a piece of toast and jam. Unlike Kian's smelly excuse for a fridge, there was always more than beer in theirs, especially if her mum had just done a big shop. Chocolate mousses, crème fraîche, low-fat dips . . . all her favourites.

I really *must* do a shop for Mum soon, she told herself.

The toast popped up and she opened the cupboard to find the jam. It wasn't there. She reached her hand into the depths, in case it had been pushed back, but instead of jam jars, her fingers closed on something else: letters.

Bridget and Frank had lived in the same house virtually all their married life, and during that time, nearly every spare corner had silted up with old birthday cards, postcards, and dog-eared paintings scrawled in playgroups over thirty years ago. It wasn't mess, Bridget always said; she had a very specific mental impression of where everything was, and tidying up would spoil that. There was The Official Box, Lauren knew, where all the important documents were kept, in case of emergency, and another one where all the bank statements and bills were filed—Bridget was very organised about her budgeting. Apart from that, you never knew what school report or newspaper cutting you might come across. It was like having *This Is Your Life* in your own cupboards.

Without telling her mum—who would have told her she should look after her things more carefully—Lauren had been on the hunt for the premium bond certificate she'd been given for her eighteenth birthday since she'd been home. Thinking she might finally have struck gold, she eagerly drew out the clutch of envelopes. There were some promising official ones in there, but apart from a TV licence reminder, they were mostly credit-card statements.

Oh God, thought Lauren, they must be mine. I'd better get them filed before I get the lecture. But when she looked more closely, she realised they were for cards she didn't have: First Direct, and Barclays. Lauren pulled out the statement, and saw her mother's name on the top: Mrs Bridget Armstrong. The pay-by date was last month. Hastily she pushed it back in, feeling guilty.

She stood for a moment in the quiet kitchen, wondering what on earth her mother was doing filing bank statements in the jam and coffee cupboard. It was the kind of thing old people did when they were starting to lose it. How old was her mum? Sixty? Lauren saw a lot of old people at the surgery with senile dementia, their faces slack, eyes wandering helplessly at people they should love. It wasn't something she could associate with her bright, neat mother, and a cold hand gripped at her heart.

She shook herself. Mum's not senile, she thought. Probably Dad's put them there while he was looking for the coffee.

She tucked them in her pocket and headed for the staircase, slipping off her shoes and treading quietly in case her parents had had an early night. But as her head drew level with the top floor she saw a thin sliver of light underneath her own bedroom door.

Curiously, she padded up the remaining stairs and pushed open the door with her elbow, trying not to spill her hot chocolate on her toast.

To Lauren's surprise, Bridget was sitting hunched awkwardly at her computer, fiddling with a digital camera, trying to work out which port it slotted into. An array of knick-knacks were spread out on the bed—tea cups, belts, butter dishes, Lilliput Lane houses . . .

Honestly, thought Lauren, I've only shown her this a thousand times. Maybe she is losing her marbles.

'Here,' she said, leaning over to get the lead. 'Let me.'

Bridget jumped, banging her knees against the desk. 'Ooh!' she said, clapping a hand to her chest. 'You gave me a shock. I thought you were staying over at Chris's tonight?'

'Yeah,' said Lauren. 'So did I. Look, it goes in here.'

'Oh, never mind that. Do you want some supper?' Bridget turned round, half hiding the screen.

'No, I've got some toast. Mum, are you eBaying this stuff?' Lauren looked impressed.

'Well, I thought I'd get rid of some junk, save going to a car boot and having people pick over your things.' Bridget swept the bits and pieces into a fold-down laundry crate.

'What's your seller name?' asked Lauren curiously.

'MrsArmstrong47,' said Bridget. She looked flustered. 'Listen, we'll be waking your dad. I'll get out of your way. You'll want to get to bed . . .'

'It's OK, Mum,' said Lauren. 'I don't mind helping.' She put her hot chocolate down on the bedside table and uploaded the photographs Bridget had been trying to add to her eBay listing.

'Wow!' she exclaimed. 'Are these all the things you're flogging?'

'Erm, yes.'

'You're going to make a packet, with this lot. Have you been doing this all evening? Does Dad know? Won't he wonder where his old power drill's gone?'

'He's gone and got himself a new one, hasn't he? Without telling me. Besides, we need a clear-out.' Bridget gave Lauren a warning glare. 'Don't tell him, though. You know what he's like—trying to buy back his old trousers from the firemen's jumble sale.'

'Fair enough. But, Mum, you haven't put a reserve on this . . . set of fish knives. Are you sure?'

226

Lauren added, clicking on the pictures of the fancy presentation case. 'They look dead old. Were they a wedding present?'

'Yes, from my auntie Doris.' Bridget sighed and stroked the leather case on the bed. 'Never used. Never likely to. But they're silver, so they're worth a bob or two. Mother-of-pearl handles.'

Lauren turned to look at her mother properly. 'But you *love* stuff like this.' Her gaze fell on something else she recognised. 'Are you flogging your silver coffee spoons? No! Not the ones with the little silver beans on the ends?'

Bridget fiddled with her watch. 'It's a lot of clutter,' she said, in a tone that didn't quite ring true with Lauren, somehow. 'You know what the house is like—full of stuff.'

'Hmm,' said Lauren, but inside she thought, maybe Mum's been watching those daytime antiques programmes. And they were about to retire, after all. What was the point of hanging on to fish knives when you could be using the money to fly to New Zealand to see your grandchildren?

'Don't tell your dad,' Bridget insisted again, her cheeks flushed. 'He's still not convinced about the internet.'

'OK. But you need to fix a reserve. See, that's why modern wedding lists are a *much* better idea,' said Lauren, typing. 'You get what you want, and you can always swap what you don't want for things that you do. Which reminds me, you can do lists on the internet now, save you going round the shops. Do you want to see? I've already registered with a couple.'

'Yes,' said Bridget, as if she had a choice. 'Let's do that.'

'Oh,' added Lauren, remembering the bills. 'These are yours.'

She was too busy logging into her M&S list to notice the look of panic that went across her mother's face when she saw the statements, or the guilty way she slipped them into her pocket.

Lauren was also too busy showing her carefully selected bathroom accessories, to notice the nervous way her mother was twisting her eternity ring round and round on her right hand.

Bridget thought the ring had been a lovely idea of Frank's: 'To thank you for the life we've had, and for the life we're going to have when we're *both* retired,' he'd said, a smile splitting his face, as she opened the little box and gasped at the diamonds that sparkled inside.

She had started to remind him they couldn't afford it, but Frank—the old romantic—insisted. 'We've both worked so hard, and you deserve something beautiful. I've taken it out of my golden handshake, love. It'd only get spent on bills otherwise.'

He'd slipped it on her finger as he spoke and once it was on, Bridget hadn't wanted to take it off. Ever. She knew he wanted to make a gesture, and it was the last chance they'd have of that sort of lump sum. But Bridget wished Frank would remember they just had the one full income now— he still went to M&S for the groceries, and splashed out on new hobbies like his camcorder. Somehow the overdraft had crept up to five thousand pounds; the bank had extended it twice already this year.

Then she thought of the bills in her pocket and for the first time in her life, Bridget didn't think she had the nerve to open them.

She looked down at her finger.

How much did she really need this ring?

How much would it hurt Frank if she sold it?

It's just money, thought Bridget, shoving her niggles away just like she'd hidden the credit-card bills. But that was the trouble.

CHAPTER SIXTEEN

Later on, sitting paralysed with misery in the darkness, Katie worked out that the bitter row that finally derailed her marriage could be traced back to Eddie Harding. Not directly—it wasn't as though he had sat there between her and Ross and goaded them on—but via tight little links in a nasty chain that she couldn't have undone, starting on Monday morning, when Eddie knocked and walked straight into her office.

'Can I have a quick word, Kate?'

Katie gritted her teeth, and closed the Monsoon website. Jo was still nagging her to frock up for dancing, and was now sending her internet links to appropriate ruffly confections, since Katie had no time for real shopping. Katie had to admit she was softening to the idea: after the last class, Lauren had been raving on about how much easier it was to strike elegant poses when you were wearing something pretty—and Katie wanted to believe that perhaps it was just beading that transformed lanky Lauren into Ginger Rogers.

The parade of pretty dresses vanished and she looked up at Eddie. He had his 'you're going to do me a favour' face on. It was impossible to imagine Angelica's fantasy world of graceful women and chivalrous men while breathing the same air as Eddie Harding.

'It's about the town project,' he said, still without bothering to wait for her response. 'You've made such a cracking job of getting your research team underway that I've decided it's only fair to let you take credit for the whole thing. Move you up to team leader at this stage. And you know what that means . . .' He tapped his nose, winked, then rubbed his fingers together.

'Great!' smiled Kate, interpreting his pantomime as something to do with promotion, then added, as it dawned on her, 'But what about . . . ?'

'Nick? I'm moving him sideways onto liaising with the various contractors, playing to his contact strengths there, so you'll be taking over his site analysis—shouldn't be too hard, now you've got everything set up, eh?'

Katie's mouth opened and shut. So Nick was now in charge of a punishing schedule of lunches and a few rounds of golf, while her paperwork nightmare had doubled. Tripled.

Eddie sensed her panic and added, condescendingly, 'I mean, if you don't think you're really ready for more responsibility . . .'

She set her jaw, and focused on the extra money, and the added days of holiday and the chance to go for flexitime.

'No,' she said. 'I don't mind. But I'll need all the documents he's been working on so far. And I'll be putting in for overtime.'

'Good girl, Kate. Just as you like,' Eddie had

said, and slimed out of her office, a bit too quickly, which should have triggered alarm bells.

When she got the files from Nick's intern after lunch, Katie realised why he'd been so keen to pass the buck: the other site was right in the middle of the town centre, centred on the precinct and the slab-sided tower blocks behind it. It would be a nightmare of leaseholds, freeholds, Compulsory Purchase Orders, commercial versus residential allocations . . .

And the deadline was the same as for the site she was already working on. There was an initial appraisal meeting at the end of that week.

Katie made herself take deep, calming breaths as the enormity of it set in and her heart quickened with panic, but even as she did so, her professional pride began to rise inside her.

I can *do* this, she told herself. And he'll owe me so many favours it'll be worth it. And I'm definitely booking us a three-week summer holiday next year.

She had just started making notes of the contacts she needed to call when the phone rang, and she grabbed it automatically, thinking it might be Nick Felix wanting to apologise.

'Katie, it's Jo. Listen, sorry to phone you at work, but I wanted to check while I'm in Asda—do you and the kids need anything for our magical mystery tour?'

Katie stared out of the window, where a steady drizzle had set in. Now her brain was in hyper-work mode, it took a second to flick it back to home matters. 'Er, one or two bits and pieces, but I was going to get them at the weekend.'

Jo laughed on the other end of the phone. 'Bit

late then!'

'Late?'

'Well, yeah, since we'll already *be* there! We're going on Thursday, dumbo. Three days.'

Katie looked at her desk diary, the days already blocked out with morning meetings and afternoon site visits with tenants associations and local business people, with her new dates for the second site pencilled in around them. Was she going mad? She flipped over the pages. Nothing.

Katie's stomach turned as she flipped back and forth in her diary.

A cold sweat broke out on her forehead.

How had that happened? She'd definitely written it down somewhere.

She scrabbled in her handbag for her own diary, the one with dancing classes and counselling appointments, and there it was, clearly marked— Hannah/Ross birthday.

You forgot your own daughter's birthday, goaded the horrible voice in her head. *You are a careless, selfish mother.*

I didn't forget, she protested, trying to drown it out. I *didn't*! I just . . .

She'd asked Scott to sort out her holiday allocation. And he'd made a big deal about not doing her personal chores and she'd left it with him, and now—she checked frantically through her email inbox—there was no confirming email from Personnel about the days off.

'Oh God,' she groaned. 'You're not going to believe what I've done.'

'Try me. I found the kettle in the fridge this morning.'

Katie sank her head in her hands and a lead

232

weight settled on her shoulders. 'Look, give me ten minutes, I'll call you back.'

Scott was nowhere to be found; fortunately for him, he was off on a site inspection. Katie knew she'd have to call in a favour from Eddie to get out of the meeting, and that gave her a headache already.

He wasn't alone when she knocked on his office door; he was ensconced with two men in suits.

'Ah, Kate,' he said, 'I was just talking about you. Have you met Councillor York? And Clive Jenkins, our head of regional development?'

Katie's stomach knotted. This wasn't the best time, but she had no alternative. 'Hello!' She forced out a smile. 'Eddie, this meeting on Friday . . .'

Eddie beamed at the two other men. 'Kate will be presenting initial findings for the proposed regeneration sites.'

'Ah, wonderful!' said Councillor York.

'Yes, er, Eddie, I've been looking over those documents Nick sent over.' Katie bit her lip. There was no point pretending she had prior commitments, since she'd known about that meeting even when she was only presenting one site. If she could move the meeting, then pulled an unheard-of sickie, she might just be able to make it. 'I was wondering if it would be possible to move the meeting into next week? I don't want to skim over what he's done, and not do justice to that hard work.'

But Eddie was already shaking his head and sucking his teeth. 'I hear what you're saying, but I'm afraid not.'

'We have a findings deadline too,' added Clive

Jenkins. 'For capital investment applications.'

'It's a big ask, but if anyone can step up to the plate it's Kate!' Eddie slapped his desk, and she knew the twinkle in his eye was more of a glint of warning. 'You'll hit this one out of the park for us, won't you?'

'Do I have a choice, Eddie?' she asked, with a metallic laugh.

Eddie's face turned serious. 'No.'

She shook her head and left.

You've brought this on yourself, Katie told herself as she flung herself back in her chair and called Jo.

'I know what you're going to tell me,' said Jo when she picked up.

'What?'

'That you can't come because of work.'

Katie squirmed. 'Look, I had it down in my home diary, not my office one, and I've been moved onto this huge project at work, literally about an hour ago, and there's no way I can take two days off now.'

'Get someone else to do it.'

'I can't!'

'Can't you?' Katie thought she could detect a chill in Jo's tone. 'That's the kind of thing Greg would say. And I would say, what's the point of being in charge of a team if you can't delegate? Come on, Katie, you deserve a break as much as Hannah and Ross do! Just tell them!'

'It's not like I don't want to go!' she protested. And it wasn't the break so much as the chance to be there with the kids, doing things with them, with no pressures or phones ringing. 'I'm desperate to go, but this is the big regeneration project we've

234

won, and I've only just been landed with the files for a meeting on Friday morning . . .'

There was a telling pause at the other end of the line.

'Well, I suppose it's not like you've already promised Hannah you'll be there,' said Jo, and Katie could tell the implication was, 'so you're just disappointing her, not letting her down'. If she was trying to make Katie feel better, she didn't succeed.

'Is Greg going?' she asked.

Jo hesitated. 'Probably.'

That did make Katie feel slightly better, but not much, since Greg was the least hands-on parent since Darth Vader.

'I can try to get there for Friday night,' she suggested, scanning her diary for any meeting she could move. 'I mean, the traffic will be awful and . . .'

'Do you want me to tell Ross?' Jo interrupted her. 'I mean, I know it ruins the surprise, but if he's going to be bringing the kids on his own, he ought to know.'

Katie rubbed her temples, as she saw in her stupid diary that she and Ross also had their fourth marriage counselling session on Tuesday evening, and it was 'talk about your family experience of married life' time. No doubt Ross would get maximum mileage out of this with Peter.

Katie's mind raced, trying to see what she might still be able to salvage. Maybe there was still a way she could make it into a treat for him and Hannah: pack their bags in secret, with extra little presents in, or something?

'No,' she said. 'I'll tell him.'

* * *

Hannah took the news better than Ross did. But then as far as Hannah was concerned, Katie's bright-eyed travel-agent descriptions of pony-riding and indoor pool with slides outweighed the disappointment of Mummy's absence, which was hastily glossed over, to the point where Katie wasn't entirely sure it had sunk in. Ross noticed though. To give him his due, he did back her up with slightly fake excitement until Hannah had rushed off upstairs to try on her swimsuit.

As soon as she was out of the room, his eyes turned cold and tired, and he went back to picking up the Lego scattered liberally over the rug as if she hadn't said anything.

'Thanks,' he said. 'Really thoughtful of you.'

'What?'

'Another four days' solo childcare but with waterslides. Are you sure you've got something on at work? Four days at home on your own sounds like a holiday to me.'

'Ross, don't start,' she said, sinking wearily into a chair. 'Of course I'm working. You can't feel more angry with me than I am already, honestly.'

'I don't feel angry,' he said. 'It's not like I expected you to be there. But next year? I'd like an afternoon off for my birthday present. Cheaper, and you don't have to be there for that, either.'

'Don't!' Katie looked up at him. 'We'll do something at the weekend, I promise. I didn't mean this to happen, but it's the biggest project I've ever run, and I couldn't say no. But I really did want us all to go away together and have fun. Ask

236

Jo—I've been planning this for ages.'

'Jo's coming?'

'Yes,' said Katie, seeing a ray of light. 'So you will get some time off—Jo's happy to look after the kids and there are crèche facilities so, you know, you can have a birthday drink.'

Ross's face seemed to lose some of its tension, and Katie felt relief, followed almost immediately by a prickle of jealousy.

'Well, if Jo's going . . .' he said.

'If Jo's going what?' she demanded.

Ross stared at her, and there was something in his face she didn't recognise. 'If Jo's going, I might at least get a laugh. We all might.'

Katie felt stung. 'And if I were there, you wouldn't?'

Ross shrugged theatrically. 'How would I know? You never are.'

'Don't be glib,' snapped Katie, because she knew he meant it, and at that moment she hated herself more than she'd ever done in her life.

He said nothing, but dumped the Lego in his hands into the tub, and started on the half-finished jigsaws, his mouth a thin, tight line.

Katie watched him, unable to find words to break through the tangible sulk. That was Ross's most hurtful tactic, she thought: that withdrawal of himself. Putting barriers of silence between them.

I suppose that's what he thinks I do with work, she thought, miserably. Something that comes between us that he can't understand or be part of. It's all he's got, his silence, and he knows how much it hurts me to feel excluded. We're going to suffocate each other. Like putting a cushion over our marriage and smothering it to death.

In his beanbag chair, Jack's round brown eyes moved from Katie to Ross and back to Katie.

'I can take some time off next month,' she bargained. 'We could do something then?'

'Oh great,' said Ross. 'We'll move Hannah's birthday. And mine. Doesn't make much difference. I'll still be a grown man who spends his days scraping play-doh off the sofa.'

Hannah's feet came thundering down the stairs, and Katie pulled herself together with her very last shred of energy, just as Hannah burst through the door, her chubby arms and legs peachy-soft in her frilly red swimsuit, and her silky hair flowing round her shoulders.

'Mumm-ee-ee!' she yelled. 'Look at me! I'm a mermaid!'

She did look like a mermaid, thought Katie, with a pang. Fragile and perfect and that hair—shimmering with golden light in a way hers never had as a child. And she wasn't going to see her screaming with laughter as she splashed in the pool—how could Ross believe she *wanted* to put work first?

She's forgotten I'm not coming, she thought, painfully. I'll have to tell her again.

'You look lovely!' she said. 'Now, are you going to help Mummy put Jack to bed while Daddy puts his feet up? I need a big girl to help me with his bath . . .'

Katie lifted Jack out of his chair, and the sleepy heaviness of his body as he clung to her made her want to curl up with him and Hannah, just feeling them near her. She wasn't sure she'd ever get out of bed if she did.

'Yaaaaaay!' said Hannah, still giddy with

excitement. 'Tell me about the pool again, Mummy!'

'Is Greg coming?' asked Ross, as she shuffled to the door, with Jack in her arms and Hannah clinging to her leg.

Katie turned back with some effort. 'Jo doesn't know. Work's busy. He's going to try. It's not that easy, Ross. We can't always do what we want to do.'

Ross turned away, so she couldn't see his face. 'Yeah, yeah,' he said.

*   *   *

Ross's sulk continued throughout the evening, while they watched television in silence, and through the night when his back, protected in the T-shirt he always wore to sleep in now, was turned to her even before she got into bed.

He kept it up through breakfast, where Katie had to field Hannah's new questions about the pony-riding (names of ponies, colours of ponies, magical powers of ponies) and had subsided into a sullen antipathy by the time she came home the following evening, her brain numb after a day of disentangling lawyers' letters about freeholds on the scabby, unloved precinct. She had tried to start conversations, about the new shops that were coming, or the phone call she'd had from Lauren, about whether the council hired out London buses for transporting wedding guests, but Ross was determined to punish her with disinterested grunts and dead eyes.

The thought of the counselling session on top of that was, Katie thought, like finishing a marathon and seeing there was an assault course at the end.

Peter looked particularly happy when they shuffled into the counselling room—not, Katie assumed, because he was pleased to see them. His eyes had a sparkle left over from a nice day, his beard was freshly trimmed, and he was wearing what looked like a hand-knitted Aran jumper.

'New jumper?' asked Ross, as he sat down.

'Absolutely! Anniversary present from my wife!' beamed Peter, smoothing it over his chest. 'She made it for me herself.'

From the size of it, thought Katie, his wife must have been knitting it since they got married.

'Congratulations. How many years?' she asked, politely. Really, if relationship counsellors were going to pass judgement on other people's stuttering marriages, they ought to post their own marriage certificate on the door by way of authorisation, like cabbies or beauticians.

'Ten years,' said Peter proudly, then added, seeing the expression on Katie's face, 'second time round for both of us. Which goes to show, it's perfectly possible to find happiness more than once in your life. Now, let's get started on you two, shall we?'

Katie wasn't sure whether she felt consoled that if things weren't going to work out with Ross, Peter would vouch for her desire to get out and start again, or faintly cheated that clearly he hadn't followed his own advice and 'worked on the good parts'.

'Ross, why don't you tell us about your parents' relationship?' Peter began, and Katie half listened as Ross described his dad, Julian, the local newspaper journalist, and his mum, Lynn, who'd

240

done 'all sorts—helped out in a school, run a café, whatever she could fit in around us really'.

'And did they argue?' asked Peter.

'No more than usual,' said Ross. 'You know, the odd squabble.'

'What did they argue about?'

'Does that matter?' demanded Katie.

'Well, yes,' Peter replied. 'Sometimes it can show you what sort of arguing style you learned, what sort of issues trigger conflict . . . Ross?'

'Money, normally—my dad freelanced quite a lot, so Mum had to find part-time work to make up the difference. But we got by. I suppose it's because of that that I've always known that you can manage, that things come and go.'

Katie realised Ross hadn't really ever told her that. She thought his dad had always been full-time on the paper. As he talked, revealing flashes of his past she hadn't seen before, a little of the old interest flickered, reminding her of the days when they hadn't heard each other's best anecdotes three million times.

'But you had a happy childhood?'

'Oh, yeah. I loved having Dad around,' he went on, 'because we used to go off for walks and adventures and stuff with him so I didn't associate him being at home with money pressure for Mum . . . I don't know. Maybe that's why I didn't mind the idea of Katie going back to work and me staying at home.' He paused and his open face darkened defensively. 'One thing I don't like about our arrangement is having to ask Katie for cash. It makes me feel . . . like a beggar.'

'What?' demanded Katie. 'You've never *ever* said that in all the time I've been working.' She

241

looked at Peter. 'He's never said that before,' she repeated.

Peter shrugged non-committally. 'That's the point of counselling,' he said. 'People often feel able to say things here that are too hard to say at home. Can you explain that for Katie, Ross?'

Ross's ears turned pink with effort. 'It makes me feel like I have to account for everything I spend, and then you give me a hard time about a fiver here for a birthday present, or why do I need more money for swimming . . . I hate having to ask you for money, Katie,' he said, turning to her, his eyes full of hurt pride. 'As if I haven't earned it.'

'It's *our* money,' she said. 'In our joint account! For us!'

'Is it? When you go through the statement with a fine-tooth comb every month, querying every cash withdrawal?'

'I just worry,' she said. 'I worry about where it all goes!'

'We're getting a little off-topic here,' said Peter, 'but we can come back to this, it's very relevant. Katie, how about your mum and dad? Did they argue?'

'Never,' she said at once.

Peter's bushy eyebrows shot up. 'Never?'

'Not once.' Katie felt quite proud about that. Her mum had been too: 'not one cross word in forty years', as she used to tell people.

'And how did that make you feel?'

Katie's brow furrowed. 'What do you mean, how did it make me feel? Secure, of course, like my parents loved each other. They had a great marriage.'

'Right,' said Peter. 'And did they show you they

loved each other in other ways? Were they openly affectionate? Lots of cuddling?'

Her confident manner faltered. 'Well, no. They're not . . . touchy-feely. Not everyone is. It's not the only way of showing love.'

'Are you still close now?'

Ross couldn't resist. 'They emigrated to Spain just after she qualified,' he pointed out. 'So, no, not really.'

Katie glared at him. 'Don't try and make that an issue. They're entitled to their own life. But,' she turned to Peter, 'they never argued in front of me, and they always supported one another unconditionally. I make a point of never arguing with Ross in front of Hannah—if we're having problems, that's not something she needs to worry about.'

Ross gave her a funny look. Sort of sad.

'Of course, as Ross says, we don't always get the real story of our parents' relationship.' Peter took off his glasses, and looked absently for his hanky. 'It's wonderful, of course, if you don't *have* anything to row about, but it's perfectly natural for adults to disagree. And it's quite healthy for children to see that parents can fall out and resolve those conflicts and still love each other.' He looked at Katie. 'Children do pick up on far more than we'd like to think when it comes to tension. They're like little radio sets, they tune in. They might not understand words, but they're very good at body language.'

Stop talking like a magazine article, thought Katie, but didn't say anything. What was the point?

'Mmm,' said Ross. 'That's really true. I mean Jack's not talking much yet, but he can tell when

Hannah's cross or I'm tired.'

Katie's irritation started to build, like a quick flame starting to lick dry twigs into a bonfire. So Ross was some kind of child psychologist now. She turned her annoyance on Peter. 'So you're saying we *should* be yelling in front of the kids?'

'No, not at all,' he insisted. 'I just get the impression, Katie, that even *admitting* you have problems is something you're reluctant to do. There's absolutely nothing wrong with renegotiating now and again. All Ross is saying is that because he spends more time with the children—being their primary carer—he's noticed things that perhaps you don't get quite so much time to—'

'OK, OK,' snapped Katie, as Ross's face took on a new mix of smugness and martyrdom.

Where is this going, she asked herself. So far, I've been made to feel bad about forgetting the colour of Ross's T-shirt when I met him, for working hard to support my family, now for having parents who didn't squabble. Angry, exhausted tears prickled at her eyes, as she thought of how she might have been able to put it right on this surprise holiday, but would end up looking evil.

'Katie?' asked Peter, reaching for the paper-hanky box. 'Are you all right? There's really no need to bottle your emotions up in front of me, you know. Better out than in, as I tell my kids!'

No way, thought Katie. There's no way I'm going to break down in front of you. Crying in public was something she didn't do. Ever.

'I'm sorry,' she said, fighting back the tears with deep breaths. 'I've just had a hard day at work, and I'm really tired, and—'

'Katie's feeling guilty because she planned a surprise getaway for me and Hannah, for our birthdays,' said Ross, as she turned, open-mouthed, to him. 'But she can't leave the office to join us—that's not the surprise, by the way, it's totally predictable. Personally, I'm sick of her thinking she can buy her way out of our children's lives when all they want is her time.'

'Stop making this about the children!' protested Katie, twisting inside as Ross jabbed right on her sorest, weakest spot. 'That's totally underhand! I *love* our children! It's only because of them that I'm still *in* this marriage!'

There was a hideous pause.

It took Katie a moment to realise what she'd actually said.

'Oh, right,' said Ross. 'I see.'

'Do you mean that, Katie?' said Peter quietly. 'It's a very strong statement.'

The silence stretched out like a swimming pool in front of her, flat and blue and still.

I just have to say the words, thought Katie, her blood pulsing with an awful recklessness. All the words I've been biting back for the last few years, trying to keep things together. I can't keep it up for the next forty years. Why put Ross through this too?

'Yes,' she said before she quite knew what she was saying. It was like being drunk, this unsettling permission to speak her mind. 'It's only the thought of hurting the children that stops me from leaving.'

'And me?' said Ross. 'You don't feel . . .' His voice cracked. 'You don't feel anything for me any more?'

245

Katie shook her head, very slowly, from one side to the other, as the words tumbled out. 'I love you . . . like a brother? Or a son. I care what happens to you. I don't want you to be unhappy. But I don't love you . . . The way I used to. That's all gone, with the rows and the stress. We're not lovers any more. Just parents, and you won't even let me be a proper parent. You want that all to yourself. It's only because I loved loving you *once* that I can't stand not feeling that way. I don't think it's enough.' She couldn't bear to meet his eyes.

'And that's it?' said Ross, bitterly. 'That's it?'

'You know, it's not unusual to feel a bit emotional at this stage in counselling, Katie,' said Peter. 'You're facing up to a lot of realities that you've both been ignoring—but that doesn't mean it's the end. Don't you feel that, in some ways, you've learned something new about each other from being so honest? Look at Ross.'

She couldn't.

'Look at Ross,' said Peter, more sternly. 'You've just said something very hard for him to hear. You can't just ignore his reaction.'

'That's one of the things I like about dancing,' said Ross, quietly, 'you have to look at me when I hold you.' His voice wobbled. 'But even then you stare over my shoulder. Like you'd rather be dancing with someone else.'

Katie suddenly realised she didn't have the energy any more. Her and Ross—ballroom dancing? They thought ballroom dancing would save their marriage? It was embarrassing to think she'd ever thought it might help. What good were silly clothes? Prancing around with strangers? All that fake romance?

246

She made herself look at Ross, and immediately saw how distressed he was. His brown eyes were filling with glassy tears, thickening his long lashes as he tried to blink them away. He lifted his sleeve, like a teenager, and wiped pathetically at his eyes.

'Ross?' said Peter, with absolute kindness.

Feel something, Katie yelled at herself. Feel something for this poor well-meaning man sitting here crying because you've hurt him! But she couldn't feel anything beyond pity. If Ross had chopped off her arm with an axe, she wasn't sure she'd feel anything.

Is this what it feels like when you're going mad, she wondered. Or depressed? Wasn't that a sign of depression, when you couldn't feel happy or sad or anything any more?

'If that's what she thinks, then what's the point in anything I can say?' he managed. 'I don't want to make her stay, if she doesn't love me.'

And that was it, thought Katie. He'd rather let someone else make the decision for him, and . . . I need someone who's tough enough to help me carry this family.

'For once in your life, Ross, stop being so fucking *nice*,' she said, and got up and walked out.

CHAPTER SEVENTEEN

Katie didn't know where she was walking, but she found herself on the precinct, and when she saw the warm bright lights still on in the new deli, welcoming in the gloomy concrete, she pushed open the door. The checked tablecloths suggested the owners had tried to turn it into a pizza parlour in the evenings, but she was the only customer, bar a few teenagers making a milkshake last as long as possible.

Katie slumped at a table and tried to get her thoughts in order, but couldn't. All she could think was that she wanted to close her eyes and wake up somewhere else.

So, what are you going to do? Now you've told Ross your marriage is over and stormed out like you're in Coronation Street?

It was all right in soap operas. They just cut to a different scene with different people. But in real life, Katie knew she'd have to deal with the messy aftermath with Ross. She had to go home and deal with what happened next.

But what *would* happen? Part of her was electric with the prospect of having finally stirred them out of their miserable rut; maybe now he'd yell and have an opinion she could respect him for. But maybe he wouldn't, and she'd have to drag it out of him, and be responsible for this too.

She stared out at the drizzle-slicked high street, but her brain stayed sullenly empty, like the abandoned electrical shop opposite, its windows smeared out with white paint. The council's going to knock all this down, she thought, as her thoughts ran back onto the research/check/confirm track of her in-tray. The architects who designed this horrible, sterile precinct thought they'd made something that would be here as long as the abbey, something modern and fresh. And now we know better, we're going to flatten it and replace it with a Waitrose and outdoor coffee retail units and eco-friendly light.

248

Ross walked in an hour later and she still hadn't got any further.

'There you are,' he said. 'You know they're sweeping up around you?'

'Yes,' said Katie. She hadn't even taken off her coat.

'I thought I might as well stay to the end of the session,' he went on. 'Seemed pointless not to, after what you said. I needed the counselling after that.'

'And what did Peter say? Called me a selfish bitch, probably.'

'No, we talked about me, actually,' said Ross. He rubbed his chin. 'He gave me a hard time about how I let you shoulder all the decisions and transfer my frustrations on to you, rather than dealing with them.'

Katie stared at Ross, amazed he was being so calm. Was he in shock or something? Why was he acting so normal? As if she hadn't just said their marriage was over?

He frowned. 'Shall we go home?'

'Home?' Katie repeated. 'You want to go home?'

'Where else is there to go? We're about to be late for Gemma—she's got revision to be getting on with, and I need to make sure the kids have got clean clothes if we're going away.'

He must be in shock, thought Katie. Delayed reaction.

*   *   *

Ross drove home in silence, and out of guilt, Katie gave Gemma a tenner on top of her usual money

249

for the extra half-hour. She looked thrilled.

'Thanks, Mrs Parkinson,' she said. 'That's really sweet of you!'

Normally Katie would have been pleased to have got such a positive reaction out of Gemma, who was always a bit off with her, since unlike the other mothers, she didn't have time to gossip about the current scandal on the babysitting circuit. Tonight, though, she forced out a smile and hurried Gemma on her way, so she and Ross could talk. His silence was starting to unnerve her.

He wasn't in the sitting room or the kitchen when she closed the door on Gemma. Nerves started to flutter in Katie's stomach, as she tiptoed round the house.

She found him in the spare room, getting Hannah's pink suitcase down from the top of the wardrobe.

'Ross?'

He looked at her blankly, then reached up for his own weekend bag, the battered old Head squash bag he'd had since they'd first moved in together.

'Ross, we have to talk,' she said in an urgent whisper. Hannah's room was right next door and it didn't take much to wake her up if she thought something interesting was going on.

'Not yet,' he said, and he sounded like a stranger. 'I haven't finished thinking.'

An odd sensation prickled at Katie's throat and she found herself thinking: this isn't going how I thought it would.

She realised that in all her fantasising about yelling out some home truths, she'd never really thought what she wanted to happen next. Now she'd set the wheels in motion with no idea of where the conversation was going, or how she could get it to stop, she wasn't even honestly sure how she felt, underneath the anger. An icy-coldness spread through her veins.

'Didn't you listen to anything he said? We have to talk . . .' Katie stopped and swallowed. This wasn't coming out right. 'You can't just ignore it! We need to discuss it. It's not as simple as . . .'

Ross turned, and her words trailed away. His eyes were guarded, but she could see an ocean of hurt in them.

He spoke very quietly, but with a precision that told her he was exerting massive self-control. 'You've just told me you don't love me any more. That you're only here because of the children I look after for you. That's a lot to take in.' He unzipped his bag, and picked up some unironed laundry from the pile, stuffing it inside. 'You've obviously been thinking about this a lot. I had no idea. I mean, I knew things weren't great, but I thought they were improving. With the dancing . . . I thought we were starting to have fun again. Stupid me.'

'Are you moving out?' she demanded, panicking. That would make it real. That would leave her to explain it to Hannah, and Jack. Leaving the mean stuff to Mummy, as usual.

'No. I'm not moving out,' he said, then paused, biting his lip.

For the first time in years, literally, Katie had no idea what Ross was going to say next.

He hadn't burst into tears, as she'd expected, or raged, or vanished to lick his wounds. He was still here, suddenly a much more masculine presence in her house, and he was angry in an adult, controlled way. She was the one who was quivering with nerves and fighting the urge to bawl her eyes out.

'I'll be sleeping in here tonight, obviously,' he added.

'No, no, you have our bed,' she insisted, wanting to give something, anything. 'It's only fair, since it's my . . .' She trailed off.

'Your fault?' Something like anger flashed in Ross's dark eyes. 'Your fault you've brought this to a head? Or your fault for making this marriage unbearable? I don't *want* to sleep in our bed any more. It's not *our* bed. Just leave me alone.'

'We can't go to bed like this,' protested Katie, 'not with everything just hanging. Surely Peter said we should talk this through . . .'

'Oh, that's right—check what the *rules* are for screwing up someone's life,' said Ross, sarcastically. 'Don't you think it's a bit late for you to start following Peter's advice now?' He started rolling Hannah's favourite frilly white socks into tiny balls, and clamped his mouth shut in a tight line.

A car came and went in the street outside, and he said nothing.

Katie didn't want to leave the room. It would move everything on, somehow.

'Well, what?' she demanded, unable to bear it. 'Didn't Peter say *anything* about what we should do?'

'If you must know he told me to work out what *I* wanted, before I just bent to your wishes, like normal.'

'And what do you want?' Katie held her breath, as Ross stared at Hannah's socks, like baby mice in

252

his hands.

The silence stretched and tightened between them.

Eventually, he said, 'I don't know. But there's no point upsetting the kids until I do, so I'll go away on this trip you've so thoughtfully planned with Jack and Hannah.' His voice cracked, as he returned to his packing. 'Then you can give your undivided attention to *work*, and when I come back, we'll talk about how we're going to sort things out. Now, can you please just fuck off and leave me alone?'

He looked up, and Katie could see tears in Ross's eyes, although he was struggling to keep his composure and his jaw was rigid with the effort. There was a sort of distance around him, as if he'd withdrawn something from her that she'd never realised was there until it had gone.

She stepped forward to hug him, but he stepped back. 'Don't touch me,' he whispered, almost inaudibly.

The sight of him standing there with Hannah's tiny socks in his hands was too much for Katie to bear. She backed away, closed the door and went downstairs to pour herself a glass of wine.

I should feel relieved, she thought, sitting on her velvet couch and running her hand mechanically along its soft pile. The old numbness had been replaced with a new, heavier weight in her heart. I've taken the first step, and that's the hardest. I've got things moving.

But when she went to bed, she couldn't sleep, despite the second and third glass of wine. In the darkness, while her subconscious usually listened out for Jack's baby squawks of distress, she strained her ears for sounds of Ross crying,

CHAPTER EIGHTEEN

Angelica was sorting through her music collection, trying to find songs that would make the waltz come more easily to Chris and Lauren. Some music did, in her experience. If the rhythm was right, and the lyrics chimed in with your own mood, putting into words what you were hunting around to express, then your feet did the hard work by themselves while your mind was swept away by the song.

She didn't like teaching engaged couples, as a rule, not even wealthy American ones whose parents had come to her waving wads of cash and begging for private coaching. There was simply too much riding on that one dance. Every secret doubt and tension went into the hour's lesson, and every stumble was An Omen. More than one couple had come for three lessons, then mysteriously never reappeared for the final ones. Tears, accusations, unflattering comparisons with mothers/fathers— Angelica had heard them all, and there was only so much she felt able to advise.

Her own romantic history was so closely bound up in her dancing partnerships that they were impossible to untangle—which was, she now thought, where she'd gone wrong.

She looked at the CD in her hand: Victor Silvester. That took her back. Right back to the beginning with starchy old Bernard, and his white tie and tails. Where would I be if I'd stuck with

Bernard, she wondered. A semi in Bromley, probably, with grandchildren, and terrible feet.

Angelica got up and went to open the second of her mother's albums, now stacked on the sitting-room bookshelf: the amateur years in London, while she and Bernard worked their way up the competition ladder.

He was a nice chap, Bernard, she thought, as she turned the stiff black pages. Jug ears, poor lamb, but a lovely line. She'd been paired up with him by her first London teacher, Jarvis Carmichael, because Bernard 'came from the provinces too'. Jarvis was snotty, but they'd worked really hard to show him that hometowns didn't mean anything.

Angelica smiled sadly at the photographs. Bernard was a very old-school ballroom dancer. Waltz was their best dance, closely followed by the quickstep and foxtrot—the dances where Bernard could imagine he was Vernon Castle, basically. He was a bit of an obsessive about Vernon Castle. You couldn't see in the black and white photographs where the collar gave him a rash, but his hair gleamed with Brylcreem. So did hers for that matter.

In those days, Angelica had been quite old-school too, not to mention baby faced. Her dresses were stiff-petticoated, spangled confections with tiny nipped-in waists, and her make-up would have put Diana Ross to shame: thick winged eyeliner and pale shell-pink lips that made her look like Cleopatra in a fuchsia tulle evening gown. Of course, you had to wear make-up that could be seen from the seats for competition, but it helped that, back then, Angelica was trowelling on just the same amount of eyeliner to go to the shops.

They made a stylish couple, she and Bernard, and they certainly won their fair share of competitions, but something wasn't there. Looking at the photographs now—photos she hadn't seen in thirty years or more—Angelica could see it quite clearly: Bernard had a sort of restrained stillness, the dignified poise that made a great ballroom dancer, but there was a restless movement about her, even when they were standing, feet neatly positioned, for formal portraits. She needed to move. And move on her own, not be guided around.

It wasn't such a great surprise then, when she met Tony Canero and he swept her off her feet. Literally, in fact, in her first cha-cha lesson, in a Soho studio recommended to her by one of her new London friends, in a lift that she later found out was illegal in competitions but sent all the blood rushing round her body in a way she'd never thought possible. Tony and his amazing sense of rhythm were already getting talked about in the circles she moved in—and not just on the dancefloor, either. When he and Angelica touched their hands together, the steps weren't play-acting flirtation any more. Each brush, and glance, and flick of the hip was a silent conversation.

From that one lesson, Angelica was hooked. On Latin and on Tony.

Bernard 'didn't care for Latin'. It was too wild, and required too much 'hip action'. The closest they got was the Ballroom Tango: a stiff, stalking affair, in which he whipped her from side to side while she glared furiously over his shoulder. By this stage, she and Bernard weren't getting on too well, so the tango became one of their better dances, since it revolved around avoiding each other's gaze, holding one another so there was very little body contact and generally looking piqued.

It finally fell apart when Angelica announced she wanted to do the ten-dance competitions, dancing all ten of the ballroom and Latin styles. Not just waltz, foxtrot, quickstep, tango and the spinning, dizzying Viennese waltz, but the hot, party rhythms of cha-cha-cha, sexy rumba and samba, paso doble and swinging, finger-snapping jive. Not just new steps to learn, but new costumes, and new attitudes—new people for Angelica to be on the dancefloor. That, she'd realised, was her great talent: she could change like a chameleon with the music, always searching for a different, more exotic skin to slip into.

'Why?' Bernard had demanded, in shock. 'What's the point of doing ten dances not very well when you could do five properly?'

'Because I want to learn new things,' insisted Angelica, which was really her way of saying, 'Because I want to learn new things with Tony.'

It upset a lot of people, she and Bernard splitting, not least their teacher who she suspected had some kind of accumulator bet on the European Amateur Championships.

It upset her parents, who didn't really think Latin dancing was something nice girls did. Nice girls didn't live on their own above a gay nightclub in the middle of London either, but they didn't know she was doing that.

'The dresses, Angie!' her mother had pleaded, rolling her eyes in shock. 'There's nothing to them! Just fringe!'

Worse still, Tony was a professional, and if she

danced with him, Angelica would have to turn professional too. 'And we know what that means,' said Cyril, even though Angelica was pretty sure he had absolutely no idea what it meant at all.

It also upset Bernard, who threw his final cards on the table, at their last waltz lesson.

'I'll marry you!' he said, as if that would solve everything. 'How about that?'

Angelica just smiled, not wanting to hurt his feelings, and as she left, she quietly gave the teacher the names of two girls she knew who were looking for a nice starter partner, no hanky panky or unorthodox step sequences.

Within a couple of hours of leaving Bernard and his stiff-backed world behind, she and Tony were having their first Paso Doble lesson, and she could make as many huge, dramatic shapes as she liked, without worrying about Bernard's dodgy neck. Rather than keeping her face in a glacial expression of mild surprise, Tony goaded her to use it as part of the dance.

'You're the bull!' he kept saying, his Spanish accent even more pronounced as he yelled over the furious accordion music. 'Scare me! Be angry! Want me!'

Angelica did want him, with a passion that made her ache, even though she suspected he said this to every girl who came into his father's tapas restaurant in Clapham, let alone into his arms on the dancefloor. But she knew at once how to get what she wanted: she prowled and flicked her skirt in the Flamenco style, and when he threw her over his arm in the chasse cape, she stretched her long neck back, feeling his strong arm holding her, and thought she'd never been so alive. There was no way now she was going back to just ballroom.

Tapas or not, Tony made a very convincing proud matador and she made an excellent Latin student, arching her supple back and flashing her long, slim legs as if she'd been born in Buenos Aires, not Longhampton. They were both dark, and dramatic, and when Tony touched Angelica, she felt every hair on her skin rise to meet his warm fingers. He had a slightly cruel mouth that could smile with lazy seduction, or close tight and hard with annoyance: he was, in short, a London version of all the Spanish bastards her friends had their hearts broken by on the Costa del Sol, but the difference with Tony was that he was a brilliant dancer. For that, Angelica could forgive him anything.

When the music started, the waiter and the part-time model vanished, and Tony and Angelica stepped onto the floor as if an imaginary spotlight was always trained on them, even in practice. Their inventive, natural style made every single eye follow them on a crowded competition floor, but beneath the flamboyance, their technique was flawless. And, clearly, they couldn't keep their hands off each other.

Over the next six months, Angelica cut her long hair into a short crop (the better for dancing and showing off her cheekbones), lost ten pounds (the dresses made you very paranoid), developed muscles she never knew existed in her legs with all the lifts and poses, and, at Tony's insistence, changed her name to Angelica and left Angela Clarke behind for ever. She chose Andrews as her new surname, out of proud independence, and a lurking suspicion that Angelica Canero might be a while in coming.

Angelica knew the really exciting years of her life had started, and it was impossible to separate the dancing from Tony, and Tony from the dancing. They practised late into the night until her feet bled and her arms ached, then went back to his bedsit to rip off each other's practice clothes and make love until they were exhausted. At weekends, they travelled up and down the country to get their professional ranking up. The battered Mini was swapped for a smarter Rover, as money came in from exhibition evenings and lessons, and then they were flying abroad to compete. Motels became hotels, and the rooms grew bigger for practising, and fighting, and making up, and the costumes got smaller and sometimes Angelica had to put body make-up on bruises, but afterwards she couldn't tell if they'd got there in the practice, or the fighting or the making up. It hardly mattered; it was all the same.

The CD fell from Angelica's dreamy grip and she shook herself, realising she was nearly asleep.

Victor Silvester, she thought, looking at the cover. Bernard would approve of that for Chris and Lauren. Something nice and traditional. Something the lady could dance with a massive skirt safely protecting her from any untoward interference from her partner.

She'd been fibbing a bit when she told Lauren she saw Chris as a tango man; what she actually meant was that with a back as stiff as that, tango was the best thing for him. Lauren, though, was perfect for the waltz. Most girls loved the waltz, imagining they were at some fairy-tale ball as they rose and fell, and the music swelled with all its romantic associations. Most of them never really grasped the calf-burning work that had to go on underneath that swan-like appearance, but Lauren had strong legs, and her height gave her an elegant line. Angelica could tell she loved the romance of it, the costume and performance.

Was that why Lauren was getting married, she wondered. For the costume and performance? She, out of all the class, was the only one who treated each dance like a chance to escape, a chance to be someone else. Angelica could see that, because she'd been just the same.

She tapped the CD case against her hand and smiled. Much cheaper, surely, to take up waltzing, where you could wear your big dress every week and change your partner when you grew out of him.

Or he grew out of you.

The smile slowly faded from Angelica's face.

CHAPTER NINETEEN

On Wednesday morning, Katie got up half an hour earlier, just in case one of the children tried to come into their bed and found only her there. It wasn't hard—she'd barcly slept anyway, turning things over and over in her head.

Ross had clearly had the same idea because when she went into the kitchen he was already up, sorting out laundry and making breakfast for the children at the same time. He didn't respond to her attempts at starting conversation about fabulous birthday treats when they all got back, so she shouldered her bag with a heavy, self-hating heart and drove off to work, her whole body filled with fog.

The site meeting took far longer than it was meant to, because it was raining, and when she got back, she was soaked and irritable.

'You've got messages,' said Scott, the second she walked in. He waved a string of Post-it notes at her. Since she'd bawled him out about messing up her holiday allocation, he'd adopted a bolshie work-to-rule attitude that was bringing out the worst in both of them.

'Can you read them to me, please?' Katie dumped her bag on the desk and started searching the drawers for her super-strength Tylenol. She was dying for the loo, and her head ached from the constant arguments and counter-arguments running through it.

'Phone Jan in HR about your *new* holiday allowance, phone Paul Bailey about the maintenance contract on the sports centre, your car's been clamped in the car park because your permit ran out yesterday . . .'

Katie swallowed two tablets with a mouthful of cold coffee and with a superhuman effort summoned up a beady look. 'Scott, as my assistant . . . you're meant to keep an eye on things like parking permits.'

'I'm a graduate trainee,' said Scott, huffily. 'Like we established, I don't have to do personal stuff.'

'*Like we established*, that's not personal stuff. It's a company car.' Katie took a deep breath and gave Scott her scary, level glare, the one that reduced wolf-whistling builders to meek apology. 'Someone must have called up here to tell you my car had been ticketed. Before it was clamped.'

He waved further notes. 'Yeah, if you'd let me finish—can you ring security about your car, can you ring security about your car again, and can you phone home?'

He said 'phone home' in exactly the same way that Eddie Harding said 'phone home'.

Katie counted to ten in her head, pretended to be looking at something important on her emails, then when she was sure she could speak without hissing, said, 'Thank you, Scott. Leave me the messages and I'll get right on to them.'

It was ten past five. God alone knew how she'd made it through that far. Anyone else would have taken a day off to rescue their marriage, she told herself. Instead Katie was almost ashamed of what a relief the rhythms of work had been. There's no point, she told herself. No point until Ross gets back and we talk.

Scott was hovering by the door, looking as if he was hoping to sneak off home early. He can forget that, thought Katie, spikily.

'What?' she snapped.

'There was a personal call.'

Her heart thumped. Ross. Surely.

'Can you ring your friend Jo,' he added, as he sloped out of the door.

Once he was out of sight, Katie slipped her shoes off under her desk and rubbed her eyes. Jo. She'd have to tell her what had happened with Ross, if he was planning to mooch around 'thinking' while Jo looked after Hannah, Jack, Rowan and Molly, trying to pretend nothing was wrong. Maybe she should call it off, keep the kids at home with her. It was typical of Ross to think

263

that *her* friend wouldn't mind going away with him, in these circumstances. Poor Jo.

The answering machine cut in at Jo's end, and Katie frowned, then dialled her mobile. Answering machine again.

It would be something about the surprise, she thought. A present for Hannah or what Ross might like. She squeezed her eyes shut against the pain. Or ballroom dancing. Katie was acutely aware of her diary commitments now. Probably something about a bloody dress. Well, it's too late for that.

She pressed redial and got the answering machine again.

She can't want to talk to me that much, she thought, turning back to the forty-three emails that had appeared while she'd left her desk.

It wasn't a conversation she was looking forward to having in any case. It could wait another ten minutes.

*   *   *

Katie tried to leave the office as soon as she could, to get back home so she and Ross could at least start to talk before he went away, but it took her half an hour to despatch Scott's letters, which were riddled with grammatical errors and worryingly casual promises about forthcoming service provisions.

Finally, when the cleaners arrived, she forced herself to drive home. Jo still wasn't answering her phone, and Katie left a short message, just saying she and Ross wouldn't be coming to the ballroom class that evening and could she apologise to Angelica.

264

The lights were on downstairs as she let herself in, and the sound of Girls Aloud and excited children's voices twanged her tense mood.

For Christ's sake, she grimaced, how can we talk about our future with that racket going on?

She reined in the thought at once. Don't be mean, Katie, she told herself. Look on the bright side, the kids are still up. I can spend some time with Hannah before she goes!

It was even more important now to be good to the kids. They weren't to blame for what was going on, and they mustn't think they were.

But what came out of her mouth when she went into the kitchen and discovered some kind of small-scale flapjack factory, complete with sticky, syrupy spoons, loose oats covering the floor, chocolate and margarine everywhere, including Hannah's hair, was, 'For God's sake, Ross! What's going on? This is meant to be wind-down time! Why are you filling them with *sugar*?'

Katie hated herself as soon as she said it.

Ross gave her a broad, obviously fake smile, but his eyes were dark and warning. He turned down the CD player just a little bit. 'Oh, we're just having fun! With Molly and Rowan!'

Now Katie looked, Jo's older daughter, Molly, was stirring up bowls along with Hannah while Rowan was sucking her fingers happily, squashed into the beanbag chair with Jack. Rowan and Jack didn't look remotely sleepy, and had chocolatey mouths, while Hannah was in her element, standing on a stool, cooking and bossing in her dancing tutu. Katie already knew something was afoot: Hannah loved making cakes, and Ross only had to show her the scales to get her to behave.

'We're making cakes!' Hannah announced.

'I can see! They look delicious!' said Katie automatically. 'But it's nearly bath-time, isn't it?'

'Daddy! Help me with the tin!'

'Let me have a quick word with Mummy and I will, sweetie,' said Ross as he pulled Katie to one side. 'Where've you *been*?' he muttered urgently.

'Site meetings,' said Katie. 'Is something up with Jo? I got a message from her, but she wasn't picking up her phone, so—'

'Greg's walked out.' Ross shot a quick sideways glance at Molly, who had almost as good a nose for trouble as Hannah, but she was happily sticking her fingers in the syrup tin. 'He turned up out of the blue this afternoon, said they "needed to talk". She was in a total state, so I brought the girls round here, and Jo and Greg have been talking at home ever since.'

Katie's mouth dropped open, then, thinking of Molly and Hannah's sharp eyes, she closed it at once. Remorse swept through her at the unanswered messages. 'Oh my God. Really? Greg—he's *walked out*? I can't believe that. Is there someone else?'

'I don't know.' She felt an uncomfortable reprimand in Ross's expression. 'Jo didn't really go into details. I think she'd prefer to talk to you about it. But I thought the best thing to do was to keep Molly and Rowan busy here so Greg and Jo could . . . I don't know. Do whatever it is they're doing.'

Katie tried to process it, but couldn't. It didn't make sense. Greg—responsible, hard-working, family man Greg—walking out? On Jo? The beautiful, home-making mother of his kids? It couldn't be right: their marriage was fantastic. There had to be a reason. Maybe Ross hadn't understood it properly. Maybe Greg had to move them away for work, or something, and Jo had refused. Or there was a problem with the business. Something like that.

Damn, she thought, helplessly. Why didn't I ring again? Why didn't I have my phone on?

Because you were at work, she reminded herself, but it didn't make her feel any better.

'I've had the girls here most of the afternoon,' Ross went on. 'We've run out of everything else to do, so in the circumstances, flapjacks seemed like the only . . .'

'Forget it, I didn't realise, I'm sorry.' Katie squeezed her eyes shut, then opened them, as her mind began running, sorting the problem into boxes. If it had happened this afternoon, then Greg might have gone. Jo would need someone there. She was probably going to pieces. 'Well, is he still there? Did she say what's happening? I mean, I assume he's packing his bags—he'll have to be the one to move out, not her, with the kids.' She pushed her hair behind her ears, trying to remember what you were meant to do in the event of a huge bust-up. 'I mean, if he has decided it's over, she'll need to get the locks changed as soon as possible.'

'I don't know the ins and outs,' said Ross. 'But I don't know if she's up to thinking about locks at the moment.' He glanced back into the kitchen and frowned. 'Hannah? No! Put that down. Wait for Daddy to do that, OK?'

Katie reached into her bag and pulled out her mobile, which she'd had on silent driving home.

She had twelve missed calls, and it was already buzzing again.

Jo Home.

'Jo?' asked Ross.

'Yes. Hello!' she said, keeping one eye on his reaction.

He didn't say anything; he only pointed towards the sitting room and turned his attention back to the chaos in the kitchen.

'Wow! Molly! Those are the *best* flapjacks I've *ever* seen!' she heard him marvel in a voice that bore no trace of the anxiety he'd shown a second ago. He didn't want to upset the children. It was sensitive, and kind. It was typical of Ross, she realised, suddenly.

As he carried on talking over the excited gabbling, a bittersweet little wave of affection for him washed over Katie's heavy heart. He was good at being a dad. 'Are you going to let me taste one? No? Oh, please?' The girls squealed with delight.

He's kind, she thought, staring at his long back, bending over to cuddle Hannah so the T-shirt pulled out of his jeans. He's gentle.

'Katie?' said Jo. She sounded far away.

'Jo, I've just got back in, what's happened?' she gabbled into the phone. 'Do you want me to come over?'

'Um, yes, please.' Jo's voice was high, and hoarse, as if she was trying hard to sound normal after hours of talking and yelling. 'Are the girls all right? Are they upset?'

'They're fine, honestly. Making cakes with Ross.'

'Oh, Katie, he was so sweet this afternoon. I don't know what I was thinking . . .' Jo's voice wobbled. 'Greg's such a thoughtless bastard, he met us outside playgroup of all places, and Rowan thought he'd come to pick us up and she was so excited, but he hadn't, and Ross just . . .' She swallowed. 'Ross just took the kids and I knew at least they'd be all right with him.'

Katie heard a terrible in-drawn breath and then, away from the phone, guttural choking noises that were too raw to call sobs.

'Is he still there?' she asked, trying to sound calm, though she raged inside at Greg's cruelty. 'Are you on your own?'

'Yes. He's gone.'

'Jo, listen, Molly and Rowan can sleep here tonight if you want,' said Katie, firmly. 'You can too, come to that. I'm coming over now, OK? Is there anything you need?'

'Oh God, how am I going to tell *Molly*?'

Her heart broke at the sound of Jo's gasps. I should have done this hours ago, she thought. God, I'm a rubbish friend as well as a terrible mother.

'I'll be there in five minutes,' said Katie, so Jo didn't have to reply, and hung up.

Hannah nearly bowled her over, rushing out of the kitchen with something sticky.

'Mummy, Mummy, have some flapjack!'

Out of habit, Katie was about to swerve to avoid getting Hannah's syrupy hands on her best suit, but she stopped herself, dropping to her knees so she could wrap her arms around her daughter's small frame instead, breathing in the little girl smell of her oat-strewn hair. Her arms went round Hannah and back on her own, and she had to stop herself squeezing her right into her chest.

269

'I love you, Hannah,' she said. 'I really do.'

'I love you, Mummy,' said Hannah, rather muffled. 'More than flapjack.'

*   *   *

Katie drove the two miles to the new estate where the Fieldings lived, trying to think of practical positive things she could do so Jo wouldn't have to think too much. That was how she coped with major upsets in her life: channel all that energy into doing things, then at least when you fell apart, you didn't have to worry about the locks being changed, or the post being redirected because it was already done.

She pulled up on the three-car drive, where deep grooves in the gravel suggested that Greg's BMW had left in a hurry. It was a big house, with large Georgian-style windows and a conservatory, but only one sad little light was on: downstairs, in the children's playroom. It glowed pink, through the princess curtains.

Katie got out, and crunched her way over to the door, ringing the bell, then stooping to call through the letter box. 'Jo? Jo, it's me.'

She drummed her fingers and the door swung open to reveal Jo, her curly hair mad and Medusa-like around her head, her eyes red and swollen with tears.

Quickly, Katie stepped in front of her, so any nosy neighbours wouldn't see her looking so upset, and guided her indoors.

The hall was exactly as it always was—uncluttered, airy, but the gold-framed family photograph that usually stood on the telephone

270

table had gone, and there were blank, brighter spaces on the wall where the glossy wedding photos had greeted visitors. Katie's quick surveyor's eye spotted a dustpan and brush just inside the kitchen, full of broken glass.

'Oh, Jo, I'm so sorry,' she said, putting her arms around her friend and hugging her with a sympathy she didn't trust herself to put into words. Katie felt Jo's chest shudder up and down as the tears started again beneath her, and held on tighter, resting her chin on her shoulder until they'd subsided.

Dealing with Jo's pain meant she could ignore her own for another hour, as Jo wept and went silent by turns while Katie made contingency plans.

'Now, then. Can I make you a cup of tea?' she said, with brisk kindness. 'Hot sweet tea. That's what you need. I could definitely do with some. Come on, come through to the kitchen. Have you had anything to eat?'

'I don't want anything.' Jo slumped, stunned, onto a high stool.

'A biscuit?' Katie opened up the fitted cupboards, to find teabags and mugs. Her hand closed on an 'I love you daddy' mug, with a baby handprint, and she pushed it to the back.

'He's leaving us,' said Jo, before Katie even had time to work out how to ask. 'Our marriage has been over for ages, apparently, only I've been too wrapped up in family stuff to notice. He's been trying to drop hints, he says, but you know, stupid me, too tied up with raising his kids.' She looked at Katie through watery, angry eyes and counted off her fingers. Her hands were wobbling with so much emotion that she had to grab each finger firmly. 'I'm not the woman he married, he's fed up with

271

our boring life, I've let myself go, I don't talk to him, I put the kids before him every time, it's never going to work, and he wants to get out now so he can start again. So *both* of us can start again, sorry,' she added, bitterly. 'He's thinking of me too.'

'Jo, I'm so sorry.' Katie poured boiling water onto the tea bags. That sounded really final. Why hadn't she noticed? What signs had she missed that things were so bad?

Jo had no idea we were going to counselling until I told her, Katie reminded herself. It's amazing how much you can hide if you don't want people to know.

'I didn't realise you were so unhappy. I wish I'd known.' Katie bit her lip.

'Well, neither did I,' said Jo, bitterly. 'I'm still . . . shocked! I mean, Greg was always obsessed with work, even when he had all this, so how he's got the nerve to tell me now that I wasn't putting him first, when he's put his business before everything else . . .'

That hit a sore spot in Katie, and she reacted automatically. 'I'm sure he was doing it for you and the kids, Jo.'

'He didn't have to tell me I'd turned into a flabby, boring housewife, though!' she spat, and Katie put the kettle down and hugged her fiercely.

'You're not! Of course you're not! What have you done since he left?'

Jo deflated. 'Nothing.'

'Nothing? Well, you have to do *something*. Let's get the locks changed, for a start, and call your solicitor about where you stand financially. He hasn't closed any bank accounts, has he?'

She shook her head. 'He knows I need money

for the girls. He wouldn't do that.'

'Wouldn't he?' Katie grabbed Jo's shopping notepad and started making a list. 'Right—solicitor. Locksmith. You drink your tea and I'll pack up his clothes. In bin bags.' She tried a smile. 'I won't even bother to fold them neatly, either.'

'Katie, I'm so grateful to you and Ross.' Jo stood up, wobbled, then sank back down, defeated. 'You know, you're so lucky. Ross is the sweetest man I know. Look after him.'

Jo spotted her flinching and pounced at once. 'What? What's happened?'

Katie considered not telling her—this was Jo's hour of need, after all—but she and Ross were going away, he'd tell her anyway.

'We . . .' It stuck in her throat but she made herself say it. 'We're having a rough patch. I think it might be a make or break one.' Katie's stomach plummeted as she heard the words coming out of her mouth. 'Last night at counselling—I, I told him we were only still together because of Jack and Hannah.'

Jo covered her mouth with her hand, and above it, her brown eyes were round with surprise and horror. 'Katie!' Her hair bounced as she shook her head in disbelief. 'I mean, I know you were having counselling, but I thought things were better, Ross seemed so much *happier* at dancing and he told me that . . .'

She paused, as if aware she'd said too much, and Katie looked more closely at her, suddenly angry that Ross had been discussing their problems with her.

'He told you what?'

Jo pressed her lips together. 'Katie, I'm not

273

taking sides between you and Ross. You know that.'

'I'm not asking you to! What's he said?' Katie resisted the temptation to add, 'You're meant to be my friend,' but only just.

Jo seemed to be struggling with herself, but suddenly it burst out of her with an emotion that took Katie aback. 'He hasn't said *anything*, because he's incredibly loyal to you, but don't you realise how hard it is for him sometimes? Looking after children is *exhausting*, and *difficult*, and you never feel like you're doing it right, even when you are! I know how he feels! And then you come home and give him a hard time about stuff that doesn't really matter, when what he deserves is a bloody medal. He's the only dad at the playgroup and he's managed very well, but he's lonely! He feels like you're only interested in your career, and the house, and the kids—not him. You make him feel as if he's let you down.'

I *make him feel*—he must have said all that, thought Katie, picturing the sad 'poor me' look on Ross's face as he moaned about his rotten stay-at-home life. How else would Jo know? The betrayal felt like a punch.

She's just getting how Greg made her feel out of her system, Katie told herself, don't take it personally. But she couldn't stop herself snapping back.

'And he's whined about that, has he? Don't you think you're just getting one side of the story?'

'Oh, for God's sake, get some perspective!' Jo retorted. 'Greg has screwed up our whole family by acting like a selfish bastard, never thinking about talking to me first. And I'm trying to stop you

274

doing the same bloody thing.'

Katie's mouth dropped open. 'Stop!' she hissed. 'You have no idea what Ross is like at home!'

'I know he's a good man!'

'And you think I don't know that?'

'Obviously not.'

There was a weird atmosphere in the kitchen, as if the room was filling up with misery and panic and change, like poison gas swirling around.

Jo said nothing, but just shook her head, and the passionate, angry words that had tumbled out of her moments before hung in the air between them.

It's your fault. You pushed him away. You took him for granted.

Someone else would appreciate him, would look after him.

Someone . . . like Jo?

No, thought Katie. *No.*

'If I'm being honest with you, Katie,' Jo said, 'I've never *ever* seen this drippy, selfish, victim Ross that you're always moaning about. He's practical, and positive, and one of the best parents I know. All the mums love him. It is *hard* being the one stuck at home with the kids, losing your own personality while you do nothing but heat things up and change shitty nappies! It's like you're determined to see such negative things in him!'

'Let's not talk about me and Ross now, OK?' said Katie. She was trying hard to not yell at Jo, not right now, but she was definitely going too far now. 'Let's focus on you.'

'Oh . . . God.' Jo sank back onto her chair, drained of all energy. With a last effort, she said, 'Look, it's not for me to get involved. I care about you both, I love the kids. But if you could just take

275

a step back. If you don't love him any more, then fine. Just don't try to make out it's all his fault. It's not fair.'

Jo just doesn't understand, thought Katie, and suddenly she felt very, very lonely. And then she felt mean, because everything Jo had just said was probably what she'd wanted to say to Greg, if she hadn't been in shock.

To block it out, her brain shifted into practical, coping mode. 'Do you still want to go to Center Parcs?' she asked. 'I mean, I'd understand if you didn't feel up to it.'

'No, it'll be good for the children,' said Jo. 'And me. If Ross is going, I'll get some time on my own, to think.' She looked up at Katie, and Katie could see how much of an effort she was making to hold herself together. 'Should give you chance to think as well.'

'I'll clear Greg's stuff out while you're gone if you want.' Katie wanted to be helpful. She was too weary to be angry at Jo, even if she was missing the point. What good would it do to repeat all the stuff about work pressure? She'd only sound like Greg. 'He is moving out, isn't he?'

'Yes,' said Jo. 'He didn't say where, some hotel I should think.' She paused. 'What about Ross? Does he want to leave?'

There was something about the way Jo said it that made the situation begin to seem sharper-edged to Katie: Ross packing his jeans and T-shirts away, taking his CDs, emptying the bookshelves of his design books, explaining to the children where Daddy was going, and why . . .

'I don't know,' she said. 'We haven't got that far yet.'

276

The phone rang in the hall, making them both freeze.

'I don't want to speak to Greg right now,' said Jo quietly.

'OK.'

'You really do have a good marriage, Katie,' she went on, awkwardly. 'Don't mistake a rough patch for the end. I'm not being a bitch for fun. I mean,' she twisted her mouth up wryly, 'if I were a real bitch I'd be encouraging you to walk out, so we could all be bloody miserable together.'

She hugged herself, squeezing her own soft arms as if she'd never feel comforted again.

'I know,' said Katie, getting up off her stool. 'Come here.'

She buried her head into Jo's shoulder and they stayed like that, in Jo's spotless show kitchen, as the reality of what had happened slowly sank in. In both cases, it was easier to comfort the other than face the darkness of their own next steps.

CHAPTER TWENTY

Meanwhile, in the Memorial Hall, the rest of the class were standing around, watching Lauren ring first Katie, then Jo. The class looked very sparse, without the Fieldings and the Parkinsons.

'No one's answering at Jo's house,' said Lauren, hanging up the call and looking to Angelica for further instruction. 'Do you want me to try Katie's mobile again?'

'Can't we just start?' moaned Chloe, rubbing her ample upper arms until her whole body wobbled

277

like a pale jelly inside her silky summer frock. 'I'm freezing to death here. If I don't get moving soon I'll start chilblains.'

'I have a spare cardigan if you'd like to borrow it,' offered Peggy, shyly. 'This hall's never had much in the way of heating, you know. Especially since the council took the boiler out last year for being unsafe, and never replaced it.'

'I'll . . . er, I'll be fine as soon as we get going, I'm sure,' said Chloe. 'Thanks all the same.'

Trina winked. 'You'll have to take her for a spin, Baxter,' she said. 'That'll put some colour in her cheeks!'

Chloe gasped, but Baxter winked good-humouredly and jiggled his dark Poirot-ish eyebrows.

'Well, we'll just have to carry on without them,' said Angelica. 'At least we've got even numbers.' She smiled. 'And with four fewer people, you'll all get the benefit of more individual attention!'

Next to Lauren, Chris groaned, and she gave him a shove with her hip.

Lauren wasn't best pleased with Chris. He'd left her a series of crap excuses about not coming along tonight—first Kian needed someone to stay in and wait for a delivery, then he was working late—and she'd had to resort to the ultimate weapon and call Irene to 'check Chris wasn't going to miss his dancing lesson'.

She shot him a sideways look, and he glowered back. It had been all the pair of them could do to stop Irene coming along with him.

He might be here, but Lauren wasn't one hundred per cent sure she hadn't stored up some trouble for herself later.

278

'Now, the reason I wanted to wait for Jo and Greg, and Katie and Ross, was that I've a couple of announcements to make,' said Angelica, clasping her hands together. 'The first is that I've decided you're going to do a little demonstration at the Christmas social dance! Unless,' she added, 'you really, really, *really* don't want to. Or, for the sake of my reputation, if I don't think you should.' She gave them her dark look for a moment, then beamed. 'You're all coming along nicely for the four-week stage, and you've covered the basics in four dances now, so that's a good start. So far, I don't think there's anyone I'd *actively* hobble.'

'Even me and Lauren?' asked Chris, glumly.

'Especially you and Lauren!' exclaimed Angelica. 'Good God, yes! Haven't you noticed that Lauren is one of the stars of the class?'

Bridget beamed with mother-hen pride and Frank nodded proudly at her.

'Along with her mum and dad,' added Angelica, generously.

'Don't take this the wrong way,' said Trina, 'but—no offence, Chloe—do I have to dance with her?' She nodded towards her friend, but then her face brightened hopefully. 'Could you not find me some bloke to dance with instead? I mean, you must know some, like.'

Chloe tightened her folded arms, shoving her bosom up around her neck. 'Well, thank you, Trina. Thanks a bunch.'

'Be honest, it's what you're thinking,' protested Trina. 'Don't ask doesn't get, that's what I say.'

'Very true,' agreed Angelica. 'But I'm not a dating agency. If you want to dance with a man you'll have to get recruiting at the Friday night social, won't you? Hold your own auditions.'

'Like Dance Idol,' mused Trina. 'I get where you're coming from.'

'So what exactly do we have to do?' asked Lauren. 'I'm not very good at . . . demonstrations.' Which was a polite way of saying she'd bottled every exam she'd taken, tied up in knots just with wanting to do well. She looked at Chris, who had gone a bit white around the lips. Chris, of course, had been one of those jammy types who did no revision whatsoever and still fluked Bs. Although Lauren wasn't so sure he'd be able to fluke a social foxtrot on no revision, not unless Angelica could hypnotise a sense of rhythm into him. Could you get tapes? Like those 'Think Yourself Thin' ones?

Irene would know.

'It's not a test! Just a chance for you all to show off what you've learned! Think of it as practice for your big day,' suggested Angelica. 'You'll be fine! It'll be fun!'

'I don't see why . . .' Chris started, but stopped when Angelica's finger pointed straight at him.

'Christopher, you have the best partner here. She deserves a chance to shine. And you will be Fred Astaire to Lauren's Ginger Rogers by December fourteenth, even if I have to glue the toes of your shoes together and let her drag you round like a puppet.'

'Is that when it is?' gasped Lauren. 'We're nearly at the end of October now! That's only . . . six more Wednesdays!'

'Plenty of time,' said Angelica. 'Now, with that in mind, and the fact that some of you seem to be allergic to practising, I've got a revision present for you.' She bent down and opened up her big leather

Kelly bag.

'Loz, can we talk about—' Chris began, but Lauren shushed him.

'I've made special CDs for you to listen to. One each.' Angelica began handing out the CDs, labelled in her flowing copperplate handwriting. 'It's got every type of music for the dances you know about, plus a couple you don't yet but you will by next month. You can choose what you want your special dance to be. Now, I've written down the type of each song, and I want you to put them in your cars or on your Walkmen or whatever you have, and imagine yourselves dancing along with the music.'

She paused when she got to Baxter and Peggy. 'I've made a CD for you two, although I expect you've got plenty of music for inspiration at home?'

Peggy simpered nervously, as she always did when Angelica spoke directly to her.

'We have a selection of our own competition preferences, music-wise,' Baxter said, with a modest smoothing of his hair. 'Although we don't like to make a big show about it.'

'Of course not,' said Angelica.

'But we're happy to give a little extra coaching to the others,' he added. He inclined his shiny black head graciously. 'Not that we want to take over your role, but, you know, if anyone in particular needed a little extra coaching . . .'

'Christopher, you have your own dance coach,' announced Angelica. 'That's really very generous of you, Baxter. And brave.'

'Shall I take one for Ross and Katie?' asked Bridget, as Angelica handed her a CD.

'You know where they live?'

'Well, I know roughly,' said Bridget. 'It's on our way home, in Willoughby Road. And I can get the house number from school—I'm sure they'll want to get practising. If you give me two CDs, Ross can pass one to Jo. Their two oldest are in the same class.'

'Where do you reckon they are?' asked Lauren, curiously. 'It's a bit weird, the four of them not being here.'

'Maybe they're on a wife-swapping holiday,' suggested Trina. 'They look the type.'

'Trine!' snapped Chloe. 'That's . . . gross.'

'It's probably something to do with the kids,' Bridget explained. 'It's half-term—maybe they've gone away together.'

'They might have let us know last week, then,' sniffed Trina. 'Makes a big difference being two men down.'

Lauren was surprised to find herself agreeing inside. It was amazing how quickly they'd all gone from being an awkward group who didn't like dancing too close to each other, to noticing when people were missing. Well, not amazing, really, she conceded, when they were all cuddling up and treading on each other's toes for hours at a time. She liked dancing with Ross, if not Greg so much. Greg didn't like to talk, and tended to hold her hands a bit too tight, whereas Ross always made her feel better than she really was.

'That's kind of you, Bridget,' said Angelica, and waved the one remaining CD like a tambourine as she swept back to her CD player. 'And now, let's start, shall we? First song on the CD is "Are You Lonesome Tonight", a lovely old-fashioned waltz, especially for you, Lauren! I want to see you floating up on the balls of your feet, light as air, and *imagine* this is the last dance you're doing before going off to a war! Everyone swap partners, please, and start in a big space, there's plenty of room, so no excuse for crashing tonight . . .'

'Here, Laurie, give your old dad a spin,' said Frank, holding out his hands to Lauren. 'Saves my bad back, having a nice tall girl to hold, 'stead of bending down to talk to your mother.'

'I heard that, Frank,' said Bridget, as she accepted Baxter's hand with a smile.

Elvis's massed choir with their introductory chorus of oohs echoed off the rafters.

'Ready? And one, two, three, and . . .' Frank and Lauren set off with a gentle push, like a boat being launched from the bank, and stepped gracefully across the floor, their feet finding the spaces easily.

'Bend your knees, Lauren!' shouted Angelica. 'Imagine that big wedding skirt swaying as you *swing up* on that step! That's it! Beautiful!'

Frank beamed as Lauren's cheeks turned pink with pleasure and effort. 'It's nice to see you smiling, love,' he said. 'You've been really quiet tonight. Is something up?'

'Not really.' Lauren bit her lip.

'Not really?' He tilted his head, trying to see under her downcast eyes, so she had to look at him. He'd always done this, ever since she was tiny; he knew it made her laugh. Lauren was only a few inches shorter than her dad in her wedding shoes, and she couldn't avoid his gaze.

'Now,' he said, 'is that "not really—I need some money for a new dress" or "not really—Chris and I are emigrating to Canada and I don't know how to

283

tell Irene we don't need a wedding cake"?'

Lauren's lips curved into a smile, despite herself.

'Tell me,' said Frank, steering her expertly round a corner, narrowly avoiding Chris and Angelica as they stumbled past in a mess of elbows and feet. Or rather Chris was a mess; Angelica was firmly holding him together. He saw Lauren's eyes follow Chris as he shambled past, and he knew her funny mood had something to do with him.

That made Frank even more determined to put the smile back on Lauren's face.

Lauren saw his expression change and she knew she had to come clean.

'You know how Chris and I are meant to be saving up for a house,' she began slowly, 'and that's why we can't live together, while we save up?'

'Oh! And I thought you'd come home to spend more time with us,' said Frank.

'No,' said Lauren, 'don't be daft. Although obviously it's dead nice to be able to come home to you both but . . .' She hesitated. Dad didn't need to know about Chris's bachelor behaviour; it would only make him storm round there and give him a lecture and a thick ear. 'I miss him. Like you'd miss Mum if you had to live apart, you know, we're both . . . grown-ups, and . . .'

'I know what you mean, love,' said Frank. 'We're not so old that we don't still like our private time together.'

Lauren squirmed. This wasn't the direction she'd wanted this to go, and she hauled it back as fast as she could. 'Anyway, you know those new houses they're building, down where the old cattle market was?'

'And now I want you all to do your reverse turns!' yelled Angelica, over the chorus. 'Men, face the corner of the room, and *big turn* to face the other corner, and feet together, and a bridging step and, now, ladies, the other way!'

Frank and Lauren swung round breathlessly, their feet stepping inside each other, as Lauren's skirt twirled out with the exaggerated spin.

The reverse turns, with their wide, swift swing always made Lauren feel she was dancing 'properly' and, for a moment, she did imagine herself in her huge wedding dress, with the stiff Disney-style petticoats underneath. In her mind's eye, she was looking down on herself, a vision of white and crystal elegance, with her blonde hair piled in high frosted curls, floating on her reverse turns like a dandelion clock blown in the wind, and she felt elated at what she'd learned to do.

I love dancing, she thought, her heart beating faster as her body spun and her feet moved to the music, fitting like clockwork together. It's the closest I'll ever get to being a princess, even when I'm dancing with my dad.

And then she remembered how she'd be dancing with Chris, and she sank a little. Still, she thought, rallying herself, just think how gorgeous he'll look in the silver brocade cravat.

'I know the houses,' Frank said, getting them back on an even keel with a few sets of basic steps. 'Titchy things, like dolls' houses, aren't they?'

Lauren's attention snapped back to the money situation.

'Well, yeah, but we're never going to afford anything much bigger, and if you put your deposit down now, they're about twenty per cent cheaper

285

than they will be if the estate agents get their hands on them once they're finished, Dr Carthy says. Anyway, the thing is, his daughter Charlotte was buying one, but she's had to pull out—she's got a new job in Glasgow—and he wondered if Chris and I were in a position to take her place. She's got a few days to think about it, and after that, it'll go to the next person on the list, and there's already a waiting list to get *on* the list.'

'But they're not even built yet! I've been past there in the car—they've only got two finished.'

'I know. She's down for the next house but two—it should be ready to move into by spring, they reckon. In time for the wedding.'

And if I don't get Chris out of Kian's party-time clutches, there might not even be a wedding, she thought, dropping her eyes in case her dad's x-ray vision spotted something was up. Now they weren't living together, every conversation had to be 'about' something; they never seemed to chill out, just talking about nothing any more. More worryingly, he often seemed miles away when she got talking about the wedding, and he'd started on about going back to college to do some management course—and not necessarily in Longhampton, either. It wasn't that she didn't *want* him to make plans, but there wasn't much 'us' in them.

If they could move in together, she thought, it would start their life properly. They could start making plans for the future, *together*.

Lauren's eyes had dropped again and Frank peered underneath them. 'So . . . ?'

'We'd need to pay the fee this week to keep her place on the list,' she blurted out. 'Then we'd need to have the mortgage all ready to go. We've only got eighteen hundred pounds saved up! Chris reckons Irene will loan us the whole deposit, but I don't want her to pay for it all. She's talked about getting a mortgage herself, and renting the place out to us, but I don't really want to do that.'

'Absolutely not,' agreed Frank, horrified. Much as he thought Irene was a decent sort, he could hear her tea-party voice in his head, complaining to Lauren about keeping the place clean, interfering with their furniture . . . 'No, you don't want to start off with your mother-in-law as your landlord. That's a terrible idea.'

'Well, yeah. I want me and Chris to get our own mortgage, you know, and equally.' Her lip set firm. 'Right from the start.'

'How much is this deposit?' said Frank, but he already knew however much it was, he was going to get Lauren that money.

She looked up and his protective-father instinct kicked in even harder at Lauren's furrowed brow. 'About fifteen thousand pounds. I've been on the internet all day, working out what we could afford a month, and I think we could just about make it, if I get some overtime, Chris meets his bonuses and we cut back on treats.'

Frank whistled through his teeth. 'You know how much our house cost?'

'Eight pounds and a shilling?'

'Something like that.'

Frank tried to keep his face serious, but inside, he was marvelling at how things turned out. Only that morning, he'd been in the bank, paying in the jar of loose change they kept by the front door, and the cashier had asked him if they had any plans for this savings account they'd have withdrawal access to this week. Eight thousand pounds it came to. Did he want to talk about it with someone?

Now he was retired, Frank's mornings seemed to comprise a long list of errands, nothing very pressing, so even though Bridget was the one who dealt with the family finances, he'd happily chatted for forty minutes with the new young customer advisor about tax allowances and so on, and left with a print-out of their bank accounts.

Bridget hadn't mentioned this account before, but Frank reckoned it had to be some ancient policy they'd taken out that had come to fruition on his retirement. He knew she'd set up a separate savings account for Lauren's wedding; that was the one with a couple of thousand in, and if she knew about this other money, doubtless she'd have pooled it with the wedding budget. But surely this was more important, Lauren set up in her own little house?

They'd miss having her around, he thought, guiding Lauren past Trina and Chloe, arguing as usual about who was going backwards. Lauren made Bridget laugh and seeing her sprawled out in front of the telly, skinny legs ending in thick socks, made them both feel young again, as if they'd slipped back to when Lauren was a teenager. But deep down, Frank had got used to having his Bridget back to himself, and his house quiet of an evening, and the fridge full, and the phone bill under fifty quid a month. The way property was going up and up in Longhampton, Chris might end up moving into Lauren's old room too, after the wedding. You read all those horror stories in the Sunday papers about children moving back in and staying until they were thirty . . .

Life begins at sixty, wasn't that what all those magazines said these days? Bridget would be retired next year too, and it would be nice to have some time on their own, enjoying themselves—before Lauren had them babysitting.

The decision made itself, really.

'We'll lend you the money, love,' he said. 'You can pay us back when the house is worth half a million.'

Lauren's face lit up with relief and happiness. 'Dad? Really? Oh, that would so cool of you! Thank you! You're the best dad in the world!'

Frank felt his heart swell with love, as it always did when Lauren looked at him like that. It was reassuring, still, to feel he could do something for his little girl. Maybe the last thing he could do for her, before she was all grown-up and married to Chris. And if he was honest, it was nice to think he wasn't completely useless, now he was an OAP. Senior citizen. What have you.

To celebrate, they finished off with a set of reverse turns right down the centre of the room, so neat and smart that when they finished, Angelica applauded.

*   *   *

On the other side of Longhampton, Katie put the phone down in Jo's hall and clicked her Biro shut.

'Right, the locksmith should be round in an hour to do the locks. They're all twenty-four-hour these days—makes you wonder what kind of town we're living in, eh?'

Jo managed a smile.

289

'Now, can I make you another pot of tea?' Katie bustled through into the kitchen and started opening and shutting cupboards.

'Um, yes, please. Listen, Katie, shouldn't you be getting back to Ross?'

Katie paused, tea bags in her hand. 'I think I'm more help to you here. In case Greg comes back?'

'You have to talk to him,' said Jo, firmly.

'Jo, I told you, he doesn't *want* to.'

The phone rang and they stared at each other.

Jo broke the stare first, and picked it up. 'Hello?'

'If it's Greg, give the phone to me—I'll give him a piece of my mind,' hissed Katie.

But from the relief that broke through the tension lines on Jo's face, it obviously wasn't Greg. 'Oh, hello!' she said, happily, then her eyes darted towards Katie, and turned more watchful. 'How are you?' she began, awkwardly, then, before the person on the other end had time to respond, she added, 'She's here, yes, do you want a word?'

Katie stepped forward to take the call. It was Ross.

But Jo lifted a hand to stop her coming over, and shook her head. 'Oh, OK. No, good idea—that's sensible. I'll tell her.' She paused, and her round eyes went bright with tears. 'That's kind of you. Thanks. Yes. Right, fine. Fifteen minutes. See you then.' And she hung up, blinking hard.

'Ross?'

'Yes. He's bringing Molly and Rowan back—finally got them worn out, thank God. We've got an early start in the morning, to miss the worst of the traffic, so he suggested your two sleep over here, since we're taking the people carrier.' Jo hesitated, as if she wasn't sure she should say more. 'And he thought it might help if someone were here—in case Greg came back.'

'But *I'd* be happy to stay!' protested Katie. 'You know that!' She felt hurt that Jo would prefer Ross's company over hers, until a new, horrible thought occurred to her. 'In case Greg came back'—what did that mean? 'Jo—Ross didn't mean that Greg might do . . . he wouldn't try to hurt you, would he?'

Was this a secret only Ross knew about? If Greg had been violent why hadn't Jo *told* her? She felt a flicker of anger: it was one thing Ross taking over as Jo's school-gate sidekick, but this was something she needed to know!

Jo shook her head, bouncing her wild curls. 'No! No, I don't think so! Nothing like that, honestly! It's just . . .'

'Just what?'

Her lips curled into a half-smile, half-grimace, and she rubbed her forehead wearily with the back of one hand. 'Look, I know you like Greg. I know Ross *doesn't*. If Greg comes back tonight, for whatever reason, I just . . . I just want him to *go*. I don't want him to start negotiating till I've got my head round this. I've been trying to keep myself together, for the girls, but it's so much to come to terms with, overnight. I know what he's like. If you were here, he'd try to persuade you to get involved, and . . . Well. You know.'

Katie pressed her lips together. 'Jo, I'm on your side. I'm . . .'

'Greg's obviously been thinking about this for weeks,' said Jo, quietly. 'It all came out a bit too easily. Like it was some business decision? I think he expected me to roll over and take it.' She sank her elbows onto the table, and snorted. 'He said babies made my brain soft. Like childcare's the *easy* option. He wouldn't last half a day. If I wanted to leave Greg I wouldn't get one full minute to think about it, much less plan my announcement.'

This is going to change everything, thought Katie, unhappiness seeping through her whole body. I'm going to lose Jo as a friend now, because she's going to side with Ross and even though I hate Greg for hurting her, I can totally see how they've ended up like that: his frustration, her hoarding of the kids, their lack of conversation about anything other than money or childcare.

'I'm really sorry,' she blurted out, and she didn't need to say what for, because she was just sorry for everything.

Jo let out a long breath through her nose and Katie wondered if she was going to unleash another torrent of relationship therapy.

But she didn't. 'Let's leave it,' she said. 'The kids'll be here soon and I don't want to be in floods of tears when they arrive. Can we talk about something normal?'

'Like what?' asked Katie, miserably. Nothing was normal any more now.

Jo racked her brains. 'Like . . . you know we should be at ballroom-dancing class tonight?'

She knew as soon as she said it that it was exactly the wrong topic. The artificial glamour, the easy couples' co-ordination they'd failed to learn, the suspicion that everyone would be discussing their absence . . .

Katie felt as if she'd been slapped in the face, and from Jo's stricken expression, she clearly felt

292

the same.

'I'll make that tea,' said Katie, instead.

*   *   *

Ross arrived soon after with the children.

'They're shattered,' he said, carrying a grizzly, half-asleep Hannah in over his shoulder, with Rowan asleep in her carry seat. 'At bloody last.'

Glad of something practical to do, Katie rushed out and unpacked Jack from his car seat while Jo led a grumbling Molly into the house. Jack was snoring breathily, a cotton-soft deadweight in her arms, and she carried him in as if he was the most precious thing in the world. Which he was.

She leaned against the hall wall, while Jo and Ross talked in the kitchen, just pressing her nose against Jack's silky head, unable to move as waves of love and misery crashed over her at the thought of upsetting her baby's home, of having to share him over weekends, of having to explain to Hannah what was happening.

It hurt so much that everything went white in front of her eyes and hot tears dropped on to Jack's hair.

He snuffled in his sleep, aware in some dream of the dampness, and nuzzled further into her neck. Katie's arms ached with the weight of him, but she welcomed the pain.

What are you doing? What the hell are you doing?

For a second, she wanted to walk into the kitchen and tell Ross she'd made a terrible mistake, that she hadn't meant what she'd said, but, deep down, she knew it was too late. He'd never be able to forget what she'd said—the pain

293

had been so obvious in his eyes. She'd done it now. She'd set it all in motion and the responsibility of hurting everyone rested on her.

Katie tried to rally. One of us had to make the first move, she told herself. We couldn't have gone on as we were much longer. And this will pass. Couples separate all the time, and this is the hardest part, but after it's over, then you'll know it was the right thing to do. You can't let the fear of this pain keep you married to a man you don't love any more. That's just insane. It's a waste of both your lives.

In the kitchen, she could hear Ross's low voice, rising and falling with sympathy, like a woman's, as Jo's lighter voice ran on and on, filling him in. He was good at sympathy, at comforting.

But so am I! thought Katie angrily. And I never get the chance to do anything like that any more, because that's Ross's thing!

But it was herself she was so furiously disappointed with, and she couldn't pinpoint why.

Jack wriggled in her arms, balling his tiny fists against some imaginary nightmare, and Katie put one hand over his hot scalp, murmuring soothing noises.

Now you've got children, it's not about you, said a cold, clear voice in her head, and she closed her eyes.

There was a cough.

Ross was standing in front of her. 'We'll be back on Saturday night,' he said. 'I've left contact numbers on the fridge.'

Katie heard the dismissal in his voice and realised she didn't want to say goodbye to Hannah yet. 'Shall I try to come on Friday afternoon? I could—'

'No. It's better if you don't.' He cleared his throat quietly, so as not to wake Jack. 'We can talk on Sunday. Jo says Dorothy can babysit for a few hours so we can get things thrashed out.'

'Jo says?' Katie's eyes narrowed, as a voice she didn't recognise slipped out of her mouth. 'Didn't take you long to start discussing our private business with Jo.'

'Don't be ridiculous. You mean you haven't mentioned it since you've been here?' Ross sounded tired, but terse. 'She's doing her best not to take sides—you should be grateful. I'll put Jack to bed. You get off home.' And he held out his arms.

Katie couldn't let him go. 'I want to put him down,' she said. 'Since I won't be seeing him for a few days.'

Ross looked as if he was about to argue but then didn't. 'Whatever,' he said and turned away.

Katie took Jack to the nursery, which had been decorated like a princess's castle to distract Molly from Rowan's arrival. Jo had put up the travel cot in a corner. Beneath the pink, ruffled curtains were proper black-out ones, as per Jo's various baby instruction manuals, and her eyes took a moment to adjust to the pitch darkness. She worried for a moment that Jack would panic, waking up in a strange room, but told herself that Hannah was there. Hannah would calm him, and Ross would be next door. She stood in the baby-scented darkness for a while, unable to bring herself to put him down. Hannah was fast asleep in the spare princess bed, next to Molly's, her thumb stuck fast in her mouth, the fingers of her other hand curled round her ear.

Katie's heart sank at the sight of it. She'd almost got Hannah to stop thumb-sucking. Now she only did it when something was bothering her. Kids knew, Peter had said. Did Hannah already know?

She jogged Jack in her tired arms. He was such a weight. It didn't seem like any time since he'd been a tiny baby. Like just a few minutes ago. And Ross had been so thrilled, so proud, so amazed by his family, promising to do everything in his human power to keep them happy and safe. He'd held them all in the hospital bed, her and Hannah, and Jack in the middle, and Katie had felt absolutely free from pressure for the first time in years, with Ross's arms around her.

When did I grow up, thought Katie, silent tears spilling down her face. When did I go from being a twenty-something dating a fit designer, to suddenly being a worn-out absentee mother? And when do I get that book of mother answers, the one I'll need when Hannah comes back on Saturday and asks me what's going on with Daddy? And where Molly's daddy has gone?

There's no book, she thought. Mum never had that book. She just banked on me never asking the questions. And that's not the way I've brought Hannah up. Hannah never shirked, as Katie had done, from asking the questions that made the grown-ups exchange nervous looks.

The room felt darker than ever.

CHAPTER TWENTY-ONE

Frank Armstrong was the sort of husband who still got up first thing on a cold, dark October morning to bring his wife a cup of tea in bed, even though he no longer had to be in the bath by half-seven and be at his desk in the post office at half-eight.

The habits of two-thirds of a lifetime were hard to break overnight, and besides, it was much easier to drag yourself downstairs when you knew you could go back and doze for as long as you wanted afterwards while the rain lashed down outside and your wife went to work.

'Thanks, Frank,' said Bridget sleepily, reaching a hand out from under the cosy duvet to take the mug from him.

'There's not much milk,' he warned her. 'Madam's just about finished the last pint, with that cereal she had when we got in last night.'

'Oh . . . damn.' Bridget sipped at her tea and willed her brain to get going. She had an early meeting at school, about the nativity play. It got more and more complicated every year, with the trendy variations these new teaching students liked to put in, hence having to go in at half-term. Christmas would be here before they knew it; November always seemed to speed by once the play rehearsals started.

This'll be my last nativity, she thought, suddenly, and wasn't sure which emotion won out: the sadness or the thrill of freedom on the horizon. By the time Lauren's wedding came round in June, she'd be right about to retire.

Lauren's wedding triggered less welcome thoughts. The credit-card bills. Another round had arrived yesterday and if she hadn't whipped them out of Frank's sight, he'd probably have opened them—and probably had some kind of cardiac arrest. Just the other day, Frank had 'guessed' that a wedding cake, a really fancy one, mind, might cost, what, fifty quid? No idea. Absolutely no idea.

You're starting to sound like Lauren and Irene, Bridget thought, and her mind slid back to the overdraft. She didn't want to, but she couldn't help it; it was like having a hole in a tooth that you couldn't stop poking at. They were dangerously close to their limit on that too now, thanks to that camcorder.

Bridget's skin felt chilled beneath the duvet as she chided herself again for not reading small print properly. Her, of all people! That's why those cards were 0% interest to begin with, obviously; they made up for it once they did start charging you. Still, she'd got the timing right; it was just what she'd spent up until now—Bridget tried not to think how much that actually was—and then it'd all be paid off in one fell swoop. That savings account had at least eight grand in it, which should clear the worst of the credit cards and even make a little dent in the overdraft as well, and she still had her eternity ring to sell, if need be . . .

'Ooh!' she exclaimed, as Frank's freezing toes came back into contact with hers. 'You've got feet like ice!'

'But warm hands. Give us a cuddle.'

Frank was a good man, thought Bridget, as the familiar arms closed around her waist, as they had done virtually every morning since she was twenty two-years old. There's no price you can put on love like his.

She put her tea down on the bedside table, and turned to curl into him, breathing in the morning smell of his warm body and clean cotton pyjamas. He'd even bothered to brush his teeth on the way back to bed.

Then, just as he began to pull her closer into his hairy chest, greying like a grizzly bear, she thought of the debts in their name, and felt ashamed. They'd never had secrets. Not her and Frank.

I'll sort it out this week, she thought. Get it out of the way and done. And I'll tell Lauren she'll have to start choosing *between* things, instead of having both, plus a spare.

Deep down she knew that'd be easier said than done, and the stiffness in her body gave her away.

'Bridge?' said Frank, hurt. 'No time for a cuddle?'

'I've got to get up,' she said, throwing back the duvet. 'Christmas play meeting.'

*   *   *

In her old bed next door, Lauren stared happily at the ceiling, imagining how she was going to decorate her new house. Every little thing about it was going to be so new, and fresh, with no one else's old Blu-tack on the walls, or grime in the shower grouting, and, according to the brochure Dr Carthy had passed on, you could specify right down to your carpets and wall colours and everything, before you even moved in.

White with accents of turquoise and silver, decided Lauren, picturing herself swishing through

299

the house in a red checked apron, carrying plates of cupcakes to Chris in the living room.

Where he'd be sprawled across the floor with Kian, playing some nasty shoot-'em-up. Lauren's fantasy screeched to a halt.

That's not going to happen, she reminded herself. That is the whole point of doing this.

Lovely Dad to the rescue. Like always.

Lauren decided she'd do a special display dance with him at the reception, as a thank you.

Then her alarm went off, and she leaped out of bed before her mum could get to the bathroom but, to her surprise, the door was already locked and the shower was running.

*   *   *

Katie was lying awake before her 7 a.m. alarm too, half listening to the rain lashing down against the window. She hadn't slept all night, apart from one weary half-hour when her sore eyes had shut from sheer exhaustion. She'd woken too soon with a start, as if someone had shaken her, and for a blissful moment, she couldn't remember why she was so upset. Then it all came back in painful flashes, and she wanted to be asleep again.

She got out of bed, unable to lie still, even though it was barely six o'clock. By the time Lauren was hammering on the bathroom door, reminding Bridget not to take all the hot water, Katie was on her way to the one place she knew would stop her mind going round and round: the office.

*   *   *

Outside Angelica's bedroom window, early-morning ducks cruised silently by on the river while she slept on, unconscious beneath her satin eye mask. She never woke before ten in the old days: all those years spent dancing into the small hours, and training her brain to be most alive after eleven at night. The sleeping pills helped now, but while they gave her aching body some rest, they didn't stop her dreams.

Angelica was dreaming now, of the Tower Ballroom, Blackpool, the drum-beating heart of British ballroom, where rococo banks of arched gold boxes overlooked the sprung floor, a patterned masterpiece of glowing wood. It was a dream she had at least once a month, more often since she'd opened her mother's albums. The ballroom was massive, high ceilinged and imperious, with room for hundreds of couples beneath the crystal chandeliers, but there were only five: her competitors, already standing there, frozen in the opening pose. It was the final dance. They were waiting for her and Tony.

Angelica was standing just off the dancefloor, her hands nervously smoothing down the sequins on her foxtrot dress. She never lost a competition in this one, a glittery creation of thousands of hand-sewn sequins and red feathers that floated like powderpuffs around her calves when she paused, mid-step, as if she had all the time in the world. That was their ballroom trademark, she and Tony. They could stop, and it was as though the whole room stopped with them, holding their breath until they carried on.

Angelica's ebony hair was slicked back in an

exotic bun stuffed with unexotic hairgrips, and her feet were flexing, ready for action, in her gold shoes. She was poised on the edge, all her concentration and fear built up to a peak and if she didn't start the routine soon, it would tip over, and be lost in the nerves that were always so close behind. When Angelica was dancing she never felt the nerves, but if she stopped, they swamped her.

Where was Tony? He'd been right by her side a moment ago. She turned and searched the crowd for that familiar foxy face with its teasing, flashing eyes, and eyebrows that checked her steps without words, but saw only blank faces, expectant faces, hostile faces.

'And the final competitors dancing the Foxtrot, Angelica Andrews and Tony Canero!' called the announcer.

Tony wasn't there.

Husky drumbeats sounded, the introduction to 'Night and Day'—the ones that were meant to accompany their shimmy out to the spotlight. The singer waited at the microphone, her sympathetic eyes joining everyone else's, boring into Angelica's mind until she felt pierced, like a pincushion.

Where was Tony?

'Angelica Andrews and Tony Canero!' This time more impatient.

Hot dream fear crawled through her, and she was rooted to the spot as the band launched into the introduction to 'Night and Day', as their spotlight moved round the floor without them inside it.

This was the foxtrot! Her favourite song! The lyrics, brimming with passion and addiction, were all about them—their night and day existence.

Where was Tony?

Her eyes skittered round the room, the scary blank faces, the gold fittings, the red velvet swags, the strangers, the spotlight moving on without her. And then, as she always did, she saw her father, sitting with the stuffed-shirt judges on the centre table.

'He's not coming,' he said, in his flat Midlands tone. 'You're not good enough for him.'

Then Angelica woke up, slick with sweat, and as the rain pummelled the windows, she counted her breaths until they were back to normal.

CHAPTER TWENTY-TWO

The autumn rain carried on lashing the windscreen as Katie drove to work, unable to stop imagining the scene in Jo's Zafira.

Ross hadn't taken her birthday presents. They were still hidden in the wardrobe. Hannah would be upset, she thought. She'd think Mummy had forgotten, when in fact Mummy hadn't forgotten, Mummy had got her a really nice present, the thing she really wanted even though Daddy hadn't . . .

Stop, she told herself. There's nothing you can do now. Worry about work instead for one day—there's enough of it.

Katie found a pile of thick folders on her desk when she arrived, her feet soaked in her court shoes, and, for once, she was glad of the mountain of paperwork. There'd be absolutely no chance to think about anything other than planning permission and Compulsory Purchase Orders until lunchtime at the earliest.

She hung up her wet coat, put down her coffee, and laid her mobile in her in-tray, turned to silent, where she could see it. Just in case Ross rang with some emergency. Then she opened her first file.

*   *   *

After three hours' solid reading, Katie knew most of the town centre land had belonged to local landowners, the Memorial Hall-building Cartwright family, whose line ended with Lady Eliza's three daughters. Little Ada died of flu, and Clementine and Felicity never married. The smart family villa became part of the hospital while most of the land was sold off to pay death duties, some to the council for the housing development and some to a consortium for the shops. Katie knew that when the flats were thrown up in 1954, they'd been the first council housing locally to have fitted kitchens but there had been well-disguised mumblings about the state of the foundations. When she opened the tenth file, her heart stopped in her chest.

The Memorial Hall was right on the edge of the proposed development site, and a Post-it note in Nick Felix's handwriting had been slapped carelessly on top. He'd scrawled: 'in recorded disrepair—roof decayed, unsafe heating'. Which was as near to flattening it as if he'd gone round with a bulldozer and driven through the porch with its dusty aspidistras.

An unconscious breath whistled out of her. Could they do that? Surely it was listed. Those stained-glass windows alone were rare enough in

Longhampton to warrant protection, and as a subscription building, erected in the memory of Longhampton's war dead, it had historic importance, surely? It was beautiful!

Katie flicked through the file: there was still so much paperwork—the deeds, notes about ownership, notes about what that area would be used for in the regeneration, but nothing about listed status. The land for the hall had been a personal gift from Lady Cartwright to the Memorial Hall Building Committee, and that was it.

She sat back in her chair and picked up her mug, barely registering how cold the coffee now was. Katie was the last person to get sentimental about buildings, but something about the casual way Nick had just condemned the hall outraged her. He clearly hadn't been there. He couldn't have seen the hand-painted friezes, or that incredible old glitterball—and he definitely couldn't have seen the way it went from simple community hall to a time-machine on the social nights, when those enthusiastic jivers and quicksteppers in all their once-a-week finery transformed the place back to whatever glory it had had in 1955. People *loved* that place. It wasn't as if it was some manky old prefab scout hut. Even the clanky, freezing loos with that hard toilet paper were like a trip to another age.

Her chest ached as the dancing class flashed in front of her eyes: images of Ross sliding expertly into the steps while she stumbled, of Angelica making her feel hopeless, and of Jo cha-cha-cha-ing, so happily, with her curls bouncing, before Greg ruined everything for her. Katie pushed it all

305

away, and made herself look at the hard facts in front of her.

The developers were planning to build houses around that area. New first-time buyer flats, neat 2-bed units, with rock-solid foundations this time. Shops would be one thing, but houses? How could she, in all fairness, claim a memorial hall that maybe two hundred people used, was more important than council housing? It just wasn't.

But if they preserved the hall, and built *around* it, she argued, pressing her fingers to her temples, trying to think professionally, it would be right in the middle of a community again. With some upgrading, it could be an arts centre or a performance space—weren't the Community Arts Committee always going on about how few venues the council made available?

The phone rang and she jumped in her skin, grabbing the receiver and hoping for the first time ever that it was a personal call.

It wasn't. It was Eddie. 'Just checking you got those files from Nick?'

'Yes. Yes, I did.'

'Still all right for tomorrow? Because,' Eddie coughed his irritating phlegmy cough, 'I thought I should check, before the meeting . . . There aren't going to be any wrinkles on that town centre site?'

'Eddie, I can't tell that yet.' Katie felt the weight return to her shoulders. 'I mean, I've got some queries, but it's only meant to be a preliminary meeting, isn't it?'

'Well, technically, yes, the main meeting's Friday next. That's the one all the do-gooders'll be at, but this is the real inner circle one, if you like. What I mean is . . .' Katie recognised that tone. It was

Eddie's 'don't make any problems' tone. 'We really want to get this green lit early-doors so the deal can go ahead for this quarter, don't we?'

We, thought Katie? Who exactly is the we here?

Eddie had some interesting connections when it came to golfing partners. Katie didn't think she'd be surprised at all if it turned out that he had something to do with the developers buying the land off the council. Properly hidden, of course.

'If I run into anything I'll bring it up as soon as I can,' she said. After all these years, she'd got pretty adept at covering her back, at the same time as being totally non-committal. The trouble was, so had everyone else.

'That's my girl,' said Eddie. 'I've got a good feeling about this for you.' And he hung up.

Katie narrowed her eyes at the phone, and dialled Ross's mobile number again, so she could say hello to the kids.

It was turned off. And Jo wasn't answering hers.

*   *   *

Outside the Abbey building society, with the money transferred and the mortgage set up, Lauren flung her arms round her father, and nearly knocked him over with the force of her gratitude.

'Thanks, Dad!' she said, her blue eyes sparkling just like they had on Christmas mornings when she'd been surrounded with parcels bigger than she was. 'You are so the best dad ever!'

'Don't forget your mum,' Frank reminded her, taking the umbrella so she didn't have anyone's eye out with it, waving it around like that. 'It's her money too, you know.'

'I know! Course I'm grateful to Mum too. I'm grateful to both of you—I'm dead lucky.'

But Frank could tell Lauren was already thinking about curtains and carpets—and he couldn't blame her. It was a bit of a thrill, getting your foot on the ladder. He remembered how he and Bridget had felt, moving into their own first little flat, when they weren't that much older than Lauren was now.

Twenty-two. It had seemed very old then. Now, of course, Frank thought twenty-two sounded barely out of nappies.

They'd set off walking back to the surgery, so Lauren wouldn't run over her lunchbreak, when she paused and looked at him. 'Mum does know, doesn't she? I mean, you have had a chance to talk to her about this?'

'Sort of,' hedged Frank. 'I told her this morning that you and Chris had the chance to get on this scheme and she thought it was a great idea. A good investment, she said. And I know she wouldn't like the idea of Irene putting up the whole deposit.'

If Frank was being honest, he hadn't said much more than that. Bridget had been in a mad rush about her Christmas play meeting, and he wasn't sure she'd been listening anyway. But it wasn't like he couldn't make financial decisions on his own. She had enough on her plate as it was.

'Your mother and I don't need each other's permission to do things!' he said, and realised he was only half joking. Retirement had put him in the totally new position of being the one without somewhere to go during the day, and it didn't sit easily.

308

'Oh, I don't mean *that*—I mean I don't want her thinking I'm moving out in a rush because I don't like living at home,' Lauren went on, widening her eyes. 'I don't want her getting upset, and taking it personally. Should I get her some chocs or something?'

'She won't think that. It's been lovely having you back, but your mother and I quite enjoy each other's company, you know. Anyway,' he said, squeezing Lauren's arm, 'it's only fair to let your old dad sort out the boring stuff for you, what with your mum rushed off her feet with bridesmaids' dresses and what-have-you. Eh?'

Lauren stopped, and gave him a hug. 'Aw! Don't feel left out!' she said. 'You're my dance coach!' She paused. 'Come to think of it, maybe that's what Chris needs. Mum as his dance coach. I don't think he likes Baxter much, not since he made those remarks about men with earrings. Do you think she would?'

'I'll have a word,' said Frank.

* * *

Maybe it was delaying tactics to avoid going back to work, but Katie found herself heading towards the library on her way back from the deli at lunchtime.

Longhampton's Local History section wasn't large, but she called up whatever documents they had about the Memorial Hall. There was, it turned out, a whole archive box. And under the harsh yellow strip light, the faded documents and crinkled old silver-plate photographs started to tell a more colourful story to Katie, as gradually, letter

309

by letter, the Memorial Hall sprang to human life in her imagination.

Rather than the building, though, it was the people who'd proposed, designed and built it who emerged. First, Lady Cartwright, white haired despite her young face, dignified and smart in her widow's weeds, as she chaired the committee of equally firm-jawed, bolster-bosomed Longhampton ladies. Katie read through the minuted discussions about balancing the serious commemoration with a celebration of life; how local materials, and local craftsmen would be used wherever possible. She imagined the labour it would have generated in the shell-shocked town, and the social buzz there must have been on its opening day, the main hall smelling of new wood and fresh paint and polish. Fresh flowers, she read in a note, had come specially from Mrs Clarence Bonnington's own hothouse, and each stained-glass window had a neatly tabulated copper subscription plaque.

Then there were photographs: a posed row of little girls from the 1930s in sailor suits; a ballet class of skinny post-war youngsters; a black and white snap of Longhampton's formation ballroom dancers from the 1960s, the men in awkward black tie, and the ladies' puffball fruit-crème-coloured dresses water coloured in by some enthusiastic hand. More snaps of visiting big bands, a Gilbert & Sullivan operetta from 1948, some teddy boys from 1960, a dark-haired prima ballerina, *en pointe*, her skinny legs tense with effort, but her face shining, no date.

Katie sat back in the library chair with watery eyes—she was getting that proud-to-be-British brass band, male voice choir-inspired wobble. It

310

wasn't just a building, it was Longhampton's dusty social heart. There were shreds of that still there in the building—they should be restoring it, not knocking it down!

She signed out what she could, photocopied the rest, then stuffed the thick files into her shoulder bag, and walked back to the office. As she typed and checked leases for the rest of the day, half her mind stayed on the Memorial Hall, and what she could do to save it. What she *should* do, if it was right to save it.

Katie was normally very good at using work to push all other thoughts out of her head, but despite her clandestine scurry of Hall activity, as the clock ticked nearer to hometime, it was impossible. All she could think of, apart from a wrecking ball smashing into the stained glass and it all being her fault, was Jack's soft face, and Hannah's almost-a-little-girl attitudes, and at five-thirty on the dot, she scooted out of the office, to be by the phone.

*   *   *

When she got in and saw Jack's yellow snuggler that Ross had left in the tumble dryer, she had to fight back the desire to get in the car and drive straight there with it.

She stood by the phone with it in her hands.

What would they be doing now? Why hadn't they phoned? Had Ross remembered to pack Hannah's Baalamb too?

Stop it, she thought, pushing her hands into her hair. Calm down. There's no point phoning him in a state and getting into a row.

311

Katie took off her coat, and poured herself a glass of wine—which she could, as much as she liked, since there was no one else here to look after—and dumped her bag on the table.

Ten to six. Jack's bedtime, nearly. She couldn't fight it any more, and rang Ross's mobile.

When he didn't answer, she made an effort to sound light and cheerful. 'Hi, it's me. Just ringing to check everything's OK. You left Jack's snuggler in the dryer, and I know he can't get to sleep without it, so call me back if you want me to drive over with it.'

That's stupid, she thought. How could I possibly drive over with it now?

And it sounded bossy.

'Um, I hope you're having a lovely time, all of you . . .'

How could they be, what with both Jo and Ross reeling? The kids would be picking up on it too. Hannah could sense Katie's PMT like whales picked up earthquakes—she usually played up, just to join in the shouting.

'And that the rooms are as nice as they looked in the brochure . . .'

That's right, Katie, remind him who paid for it—well done.

'And, er . . .' She was close to tears now. 'And maybe if the kids aren't in bed, they could ring me to say they're all right?'

As she hung up, the front doorbell rang.

A quick, bright hope sprang up inside Katie's chest. Maybe they've come back, she thought, hating herself for her selfishness. Maybe the children missed me so much they wanted to come home! And maybe Ross will be standing there too,

312

and he'll have sorted himself out, and grown a backbone, and we won't have to break up after all . . .

At the door was Mrs Armstrong, from Hannah's school.

Bridget, Katie corrected herself, as she rearranged her face into a friendly expression.

'Hello!' she said, and at once her brain diverted into new panic: had something happened at school?

'Hello!' said Bridget, and her sharp brown eyes softened at the sight of Katie's smudged eyeliner. 'Oh dear, have I called at a bad time?'

'No, no!' That sounded a bit too emphatic, thought Katie. She tried to smile, to soften the effect, but it didn't feel right on her face, and from Bridget's concerned expression, it obviously only made things worse.

'You're sure? Oh, it's not about Hannah!' She put a hand on Katie's forearm. 'Don't worry! That's the awful thing about being a teacher—it's like being a policeman. People expect the worst when you turn up at the house!'

'Right, no, good,' said Katie, running a hand through her fine hair. 'Sorry, it's been a long day. The kids have gone off for a little holiday with Ross, and I . . . I'm working late.'

'Oh, well, I won't keep you—I just popped round to bring you this, since you weren't at class last night,' said Bridget, reaching into her battered shoulder bag, and pulling out a CD. 'Angelica handed these compact discs out—they're for the display. One for you two, one for Jo and Greg.'

'Display?' Katie couldn't care less, and yet at the same time, something in her rallied.

Bridget smiled sympathetically. 'I know. As if we don't have enough on our plates! She wants us to do a display, at the Christmas social dance—get our moment in the spotlight. I'm sure she'll explain it to you properly at the next class, but she told us all to put these on in our cars and imagine we're dancing while we're driving to Tesco.' Bridget did a wickedly accurate impression of Angelica's London vowels at that point and Katie smiled.

'I'd love to see you and Frank dancing a solo,' she said, glad of something nice to say, and meaning it. 'You're far better than the rest of us.'

'Well, after all these years we ought to be,' sighed Bridget. 'And of course my mother—and Frank's mother, come to that—used to spend most of her weekends at the Memorial Hall. It's the only reason Frank's any good,' she added, with a confiding half-wink. 'His mum told him how easy it would be to find girls if he could dance, so he learned pretty quickly. I think he tried to tell Chris something similar, in a pep talk, you know, but I don't reckon it's the same these days.'

'You used to go to the Memorial Hall in the old days?' asked Katie, suddenly interested.

'Oh, yes. Well, on and off. Everyone did, right up until . . . ooh, the late seventies, I suppose. There wasn't much else to do round here. Everyone danced.'

'Bridget, have you got time to come in for a quick cup of tea?' Katie opened the front door a little wider. 'There's something I'd love your opinion on.'

*   *   *

314

'Ah, I remember this!' Bridget's eyes widened over the photographs. 'Look, that's my mum's friend Jean. There, with the beehive. She was one of the best girls on the sequence-dancing team. Oh . . . look at those dresses. They really were good, you know. They used to do a marvellous Viennese waltz, where they'd be spinning round and round and their big net underskirts would swirl up to here, and then suddenly they'd all stop, like clockwork, and set off in the opposite direction. Like spinning tops. They went to Blackpool, you know—won all sorts of prizes.' She sighed. 'You wouldn't think it was punk rock and what-have-you in London then. Time moves slowly round here.'

She checked her watch as Katie handed her another photo, and she gave her a remorseful look over the top. 'Speaking of which, I should be getting back, really. Leaving Frank to get his own supper. He'd live off ham and chips if he could, that man. Not like your husband—men today are so much more self-sufficient, aren't they?'

Katie flinched and she knew Bridget's sharp eyes had spotted it.

'Can't Lauren make supper?' she asked, before Bridget could say anything. Katie passed her another photograph of some ballerinas, and she cooed with nostalgia.

'Look! Those radiators haven't changed! No, she's out with Chris tonight—said she had something important to discuss with him.' Bridget pulled a wry face. 'It'll probably be about bridesmaids again, bless her. The only time she's not thinking about this wedding is when she's asleep. Not that she's much better than Frank in the kitchen—if it doesn't come in a sealed packet,

315

our Lauren's not interested. Frank'll just have to fend for himself. Anyway,' she patted Katie's arm, 'this is a lovely unexpected trip down memory lane.'

Lucky Lauren, thought Katie, wistful for a second, having Bridget for a mum. They'd only been sitting at her kitchen table for half an hour, and already Bridget had told her about how she and Frank met at a dance she'd gone to with his best friend, Martin. She'd spotted Hannah's paintings on the fridge door, and warmed Katie's heart by telling her how many friends Hannah had in her class.

'Are you doing a research project, then?' asked Bridget, gesturing at the papers.

'Not exactly. Listen, I probably shouldn't be telling you this, but there's a chance the hall might be demolished,' Katie blurted out.

'What? No!' Bridget let the photographs drop from her fingers.

' 'Fraid so. It's for work—I'm analysing a couple of sites for a new regeneration development, and the hall's right inside the boundary line of the town centre proposal. To be honest, there's a lot of . . .' Katie searched for the right, non-slanderous word, although the more she thought about it, the dodgier Eddie's interests seemed to get. 'A lot of *enthusiasm* for the town site, and I can see the benefits of doing it that way, but what's the point in regenerating the town if you have to flatten everything that makes it distinctive?' She shrugged, seeing Bridget's horrified expression. 'That's the way it goes, I'm sorry to say—developers are very black and white when it comes down to cash.'

'But surely it's a listed building?' She picked up

a photograph of the exterior. 'I mean, just look at that brickwork!'

Katie shook her head. 'No, I thought it would be too, but it's not. But if there's some kind of listing assessment in *progress*, you know, due to public interest,' she added, slowly, 'then obviously that would make a difference to the feasibility study. And I thought maybe . . .'

'Ah,' said Bridget, catching on. 'Maybe if some letters were written? By interested supporters and keen users of the hall?'

Katie nodded, encouraged by Bridget's keen expression. If the objections came from independent sources, Eddie could hardly brush them away, as she knew he'd try to if she raised them. He had an answer for anything, and a manner that didn't encourage argument, but would the council risk looking like Philistines, with local elections coming up next spring? It was worth a try.

'It's quite tricky because there's really only so much I can say in my report, especially since the building's been allowed to get quite run-down. But if there was a lot of local support for restoring it, or giving it some kind of heritage status . . .'

Bridget's brown eyes sparkled. 'I'll get right on to it. I used to teach the deputy editor of the *Longhampton News*—I bet he'd be very interested in setting up a campaign to save it. And then we can do some kind of project on it at school, and—'

'Bridget, we have to be quite discreet about this,' warned Katie. 'It's quite political—if my boss found out I'd been trying to derail his plans, he could, well, make things really difficult for me.' She clamped her mouth shut, realising she'd said a bit too much.

That was because of Bridget and the soothing, comforting atmosphere she created around her. Katie felt temporarily sheltered from all the stress whirling around in the back of her mind, just by seeing Bridget on the other side of the table— warm, and capable, and kindly. She gave off that reassuring confidence that things could be fixed.

'Leave it with me,' said Bridget, tidying the photographs into a pile. 'It'll give me something else to think about other than this blessed wedding of Lauren's. Honestly, they never really leave, children! You must be missing your two little ones,' she added. 'Although, it's nice to get a few nights of peace, isn't it?' She leaned over the table conspiratorially. 'I don't know a mum who doesn't, secretly!'

Now the conversation had moved off the distracting topic of the Hall, the nervous misery she'd been keeping at bay crashed back over Katie, swamping all other thoughts. Her heart turned too light in her chest as she thought of Jack, without his snuggler.

Ross still hasn't returned my call, she thought.

'Something up?' asked Bridget, innocently.

Don't, Katie told herself, fiercely. Hannah's future teacher is *not* the person to unburden yourself to.

But who was? Ross was her best friend. He still was, really. He was the person she'd have gone to in the past when she felt hurt and lost, and now she'd never have that again. The loss of it made her feel sick.

'Are you all right, love?' asked Bridget. 'Have I put my foot in it?'

Katie pulled herself together.

318

'Actually,' she managed, 'I'm feeling terrible. It's Hannah and Ross's birthday tomorrow, and I should be there with them, but I have to be at work. For this meeting. They'll be back on Saturday, but . . . I feel like I've let them down.' Katie bit her lip.

'Drive over after work tomorrow and have the party then!' said Bridget at once. 'I'm sure one late bedtime won't hurt!'

'No,' said Katie, looking down at the photographs. 'It's . . . I can't.'

Bridget paused, in case she wanted to elaborate. *Don't! Keep it in!*

'I can't,' she said.

'Then I'm sure Hannah won't mind having another treat on Saturday,' replied Bridget, sensing that Katie wanted to glide over something. 'Lucky her. Will you be coming along to the social dance tomorrow night, in that case? We can drop some hints to the others about the letter writing!'

Katie smiled, gratefully. 'Yes. Yes, we can.'

'Do you need a lift there?'

'No,' said Katie, getting up from the table. She didn't have much time before her composure went to pieces again, and kind as Bridget was, she had some pride left. Somehow, not breaking down in front of Bridget gave her enough focus to pull herself together. 'No, I'll make my own way there.'

Bridget turned back at the door, her eyes full of concern, as if she wanted to give Katie a final chance to confess whatever it was that was upsetting her, but Katie had a grip of herself.

She smiled firmly and Bridget's heart ached at the tension in Katie's tired eyes.

Something was obviously wrong there, but

Bridget knew better than to ask. She'd seen so many weary, wound-up mothers over the years and longed to tell Katie that it would pass, but she sensed that wasn't what Katie wanted to hear. She looked, to Bridget anyway, like someone who would feel bad whatever she did.

'Thanks for bringing the CD round,' said Katie. 'I'll listen to it in the car.'

'Thank you for the tea,' said Bridget. 'And the nostalgia! See you tomorrow.'

Katie closed the door, and suddenly she was alone in her house again. It was only when Bridget's car had driven away that Katie realised she'd been too discreet to ask where the four of them had got to last night.

It's like being on pause, she thought. I can't think about anything or take any steps until Ross gets back. Even *now* he's being totally passive aggressive.

The text alert bleeped on her phone and she scrambled to read it.

It was from Ross. 'Kids asleep—worn out. Will get them to call in the morning. Snuggler in tumble dryer is old.'

It was the last part that drove a shard of glass into Katie's heart.

CHAPTER TWENTY-THREE

'I reckon that went well, considering,' said Eddie, yanking off his tie as he waddled out of the committee room.

'Considering what?' Katie demanded.

She was still reeling from the presentation. Not the presentation itself—she'd done loads of them over the years—but by the unsettling way Eddie kept interrupting on key points, hustling her over details, and then putting her right on the spot about other aspects, that he *knew* she wouldn't have had time to research.

Like that business with the environmental assessment of the out-of-town site—a process he'd been perfectly fine with just last week.

But curiously, she couldn't get as upset as she normally would, not when at least half her brain was constantly thinking about Ross and Hannah's birthdays, and whether they were having a good time and missing her.

'We'd need more time to prepare findings, yes,' she'd said, and added, before Eddie could speak again, 'but I think there are listed-building issues regarding certain areas within the town centre site.'

Eddie had spun round at that, and fixed her with a froggy glare. 'Nick never mentioned that.'

'Well, like you say, Eddie, there are always new shoots in the information garden,' Katie had said, and moved on to the problems of long-lease residential tenants.

Eddie stopped now, in front of the chocolate machine, and fed in a handful of small change from his pocket. 'It went well, considering your nonsense about listed buildings. I don't think you understand how much is on the line here, Kate. We're talking millions.'

'I said in the meeting,' said Katie, levelly, 'I haven't had time to co-ordinate comprehensive reports. I'm just covering all bases.'

Eddie leaned forward, dropped his voice to an unpleasantly intimate croak, and said, 'I thought you were a smart lass, Kate.'

'I am.' Katie took a step back. She could smell Eddie's brown-sauced breakfast roll on his breath.

'Then have another look at those leases. Think of the lovely new development and how much nicer the town centre will look with an eco-mall. Sometimes, sadly –' his lips drooped down at the corners to indicate deep regret—'eggs must be broken to make sexy retail/residential omelettes.' He turned back to the machine and selected a king-sized Mars bar, and a king-sized Twix, and, while the mechanisms clunked, he went on, 'It's not our job to break the eggs, love, just to pick 'em out. And I think the developers, and the architects, and the local government redevelopment funding bods and I would prefer to get on with this project while the frying pan's sizzling, so to speak.'

He bent down in anticipation of his Mars bar and Twix, keeping one meaningful eye on Katie's face as he did so.

God almighty, thought Katie, irritated, he really does think he's in his own sleazy cop drama.

There was an anticlimactic pause when Eddie's hand flapped around in vain as nothing appeared in the slot.

With an annoyed tut, he turned his attention to the machine, gave it a hefty wallop on the side, at which point two Mars bars, a packet of Revels and a sesame seed bar fell out.

The sesame seed bars were only in there as part of a council healthy-eating initiative. No one ever selected them.

A broad smile cracked across his face. 'There we

go,' he said, handing it to Katie, while pocketing the rest. 'Everyone's a winner.'

And if Katie hadn't got it, he added a huge wink, and waddled off towards the executive car park. 'If anyone wants me after two, I'm in the office. On the fourteenth hole!' he bellowed over his shoulder.

Katie refused to give him the satisfaction of seeing how enraged she was by his attitude, and stormed back to her office to work out what she could do next.

*　　　*　　　*

At exactly the same time, Bridget was having an unsettling moment in the bank, and not, for once, because she couldn't quite remember if she'd taught the cashier.

'No, that can't be right,' she said, smiling politely at 'Sean' (Sean Barnes? Sean Thornton?). 'I think there must be a computer error. I know there's at least eight thousand pounds in that account. Can you check again, please?'

She flashed an apologetic grimace at the man behind her. A queue was building up. Maybe lunchtime wasn't the best time to sort out bank arrangements, but she hadn't been able to sleep properly last night, thinking about that great big balance on the card. Yvette from the bridal shop had phoned, all coos about how show-stopping Lauren's dress was going to be, but she 'needed card details for the deposit so the dressmakers can get started on it'—as if royal dressmakers were standing by, waiting for Lauren's nod. Bridget had to admit, what with all the compliments and deference, she'd felt an intoxicating little flicker of Lauren's wedding fever as she'd read out the magic numbers: it wasn't even like spending money. When Bridget thought about it, she realised Yvette had barely mentioned a figure. She glided over it so discreetly that if Bridget hadn't jotted down £850 deposit in her wedding notebook, it wouldn't even have lodged in her brain. That was the problem with weddings. Eventually the actual cost of things just turned into a series of meaningless numbers.

But when Bridget had made a few calculations, she'd realised that that £850 took her dangerously close to the limit on that card, with her other secret one also nearly maxed out with catering deposits and band-booking fees, and suddenly she'd lost her nerve about her clever credit arrangement altogether. The total amount loomed over her subconscious like a loose mountain of bricks just waiting to flatten her.

So she'd decided to get it paid off, and damn the two interest-free weeks remaining. She'd probably lose a pound or two in interest by withdrawing the money and paying it off before she absolutely had to, but it was worth it just to get her peace of mind back.

You'd make a terrible gambler, Bridget told herself, wryly. No matter how good Frank thinks you are with money.

The cashier frowned at the screen. 'Won't keep you a moment, Mrs Armstrong.'

'Is there a problem?' she asked, nervously.

The cashier printed off a slip. 'No, I don't think so. The money was transferred into your current account yesterday by your husband? Here are the details.'

'Oh, fine.' Relief flooded through Bridget's chest. 'Fine. In that case . . .'

'But then he withdrew the whole lot.' The cashier looked embarrassed. 'He did have ID, Mrs Armstrong. Perhaps he's planning a surprise for you?'

Bridget stared in horror, then plastered a smile on her face. 'Perhaps he is.'

'While you're here, would you like to talk to someone about extending your overdraft again?' he asked, but she was already sweeping her bag off the counter. She just had time to get home before she had to get back to school for yet another meeting.

*   *   *

'I've given it to Lauren, so she and Chris can get a mortgage and get on the housing ladder,' said Frank, smiling with a paternal pride that normally Bridget would have found adorable but now made her want to scream.

'But why didn't you tell me?' she asked, trying not to let her panic show through. She relaxed her grip on the edge of the kitchen table, but her fingers still itched to fasten onto something. Frank's neck, perhaps.

'I did try, love, but you were in a rush,' he said, easily, as if she was checking on the recycling collection. 'We had an appointment with the building society yesterday about the mortgage, me and Lauren. They had to act fast, or else they'd have lost the place—ask her. She's very full of it.' He laid his knife and fork on the plate. Bridget had interrupted his lunch of sliced ham and chips. She was too distracted even to worry about his cholesterol.

'She didn't mention it to me,' she said.

'I think she only found out a day or two ago herself. But that's the way with houses these days, isn't it?' he added, knowledgeably. 'Why? Is there a problem?' His forehead creased. 'I reckoned if we hadn't known about the money till now we wouldn't miss it. Better that Lauren has it, to help her get set up. I mean, even I know property's a prudent investment.'

Prudent investment. Honestly, thought Bridget, breathing hard through her nose. Frank had so much time on his hands these days he even read the Money sections.

Don't panic, she told herself, as the lists and lists of the money she owed flashed in front of her eyes. Get all the facts first.

'It's an excellent investment,' said Bridget, tightly. 'So, in terms of the actual cash . . .' No, that was the wrong way to approach it. That would set off alarm bells. What she wanted to know was whether Frank had given Lauren a *theoretical* deposit, in which case she might be able to get it back, or whether her nest-egg was now a real-life, non-refundable deposit.

But Bridget knew that snatching the house-deposit money from Lauren, even if things weren't already in motion, would be more than she could bring herself to do.

'Is she . . . is she moving out soon?' she said instead.

Frank's face softened. 'That's what she thought you'd be worried about! No, she's got to get the

326

money paid up front with Chris's share, and the mortgage arranged, but the house won't be finished until spring. So you've got your chick at home till then, don't worry!'

'Good,' said Bridget, faintly.

'Have you got time for a chip?' Frank pushed his chair back from the table. 'I can put the deep-fat fryer on again.' He regarded it lovingly; it was his new favourite toy—again, bought from his new favourite electrical shop in town. 'We should have treated ourselves to one of these beauties years ago . . .'

Bridget looked at the kitchen clock. Twelve minutes to two. There wasn't time to have a meltdown right now. It would have to wait.

She pushed away the dread starting to envelop her, but it was like trying to fight back fog.

'I've got to get back to school,' said Bridget faintly.

*   *   *

Katie had wanted to phone Hannah to wish her happy birthday as soon as she woke up, but she had made herself wait until they'd all be up and having breakfast—pancakes, she knew. She and Ross, and now Hannah and Jack, had pancakes for birthday breakfasts.

Ross had answered on the fifth ring, and passed the phone over with minimum acknowledgement of her 'Happy birthday!'—he claimed he had to change Jack, but she could tell her didn't want to talk to her.

That had been hard, knowing she'd killed the easy way they'd always had of talking.

She heard him say, 'It's Mummy!' with an enthusiasm he clearly didn't feel—Ross was too decent to start manipulating Hannah's loyalties—and suddenly there she was on the other end, the familiar deep breaths, a bit snuffly from a cold.

'Happy birthday, Hannah!' said Katie, and tried not to let her misery show through.

She listened in the empty kitchen to Hannah's breathless giggles about how she and Molly had got hair braids and there were tropical pools and Jack's swim nappy had come off and he'd run around *nude*, and she wished desperately that she was there too. Her heart skipped at the excitement in Hannah's voice. It didn't sound as if her absence was holding up the fun much.

'. . . and Jo took me to get my face painted and I was a fairy queen!' finished Hannah. 'Jo gave me a dressing-up box and it's full of tiaras and wings and wands!'

'Well, I've got a lovely present for you here for when you come back tomorrow,' said Katie. 'I can't wait to see you, darling! Won't be long now!'

There was an ominous pause at the other end.

Stupid, Katie chided herself, seeing Hannah's face crumple in her mind's eye, you shouldn't have said that.

She knew it was selfish, but she couldn't help it—it only slipped out to make herself feel better.

'Hannah? Hannah?'

Ross was back on the phone, and in the background, Katie could hear grizzling. Her stomach dropped.

'Thanks for that,' said Ross.

'Well, it sounds like you're having a great time,' retorted Katie, defensively.

'We were. Look, I'll get her to call you later, OK?'

And he'd hung up, before she could ask him how Jo was, or how he was, or whether Jack had been happy to sleep in a strange cot.

*   *   *

Katie rushed home from the office to see if there were any messages from Hannah and Jack. She'd been ringing Ross's mobile on and off all day, but he hadn't answered.

By now, nearly six, she knew the kids would be having supper, or getting ready for bed, so she tried Ross's mobile again before she even took off her coat.

He answered his phone on the second ring.

'Hi, Ross!' Katie made herself sound cheerful. 'Can I talk to Hannah? Is she in the bath?'

'Katie, I don't think it's a good idea for you to talk to her,' he said. 'She's dressing up with Molly for supper and Jo and I want to try to get them into bed for seven, so we can get something ourselves. We'll be setting off tomorrow morning before lunch—why don't you ring then so there's no tantrum about leaving?'

'But . . .'

'Katie, I'm thinking of her, not you.' Ross sounded less wimpy than usual. 'She was upset after you called this morning. It took Jo ages to distract her.'

Jo. Of course. SuperJo the SuperMum.

Don't be a bitch, Katie told herself, rubbing her tired eyes.

'Well, if she . . .'

329

'If she asks, we'll phone. But I don't think she will.' He softened. 'That's not because she doesn't love you, it's because she's having a good time. Be happy about it.'

And he rang off.

Katie sat back and stared into the silent, tidy sitting room where her lavishly wrapped presents (pink bike for Hannah, new shirt and aftershave for Ross) sat accusingly by the sideboard. The house felt empty. It smelled wrong. The longer she sat still, the more doubt and guilt about what she'd set in motion attacked her from every shelf and discarded toy, and then her eye fell on the CD of dance music that Bridget had brought round for her.

I could go to the social dance, she thought. Bridget's expecting me. She even asked if I was going.

The little act of thoughtfulness touched Katie's battered heart so much that she found herself heading for the stairs, to change out of her work suit.

Katie showered quickly, one ear listening out for the phone all the time, and then changed into the first dress that fell to hand—a plain black thing that never needed ironing. At least at the social, all she'd have to think about would be her feet, and it would fill in three of the twenty-six hours until they were back.

She tried not to look at the big brass bed in the bedroom as she pulled on a fresh pair of tights. Ross had chosen it, and she paid for it with her first Christmas bonus money. It was going to be their heirloom, he'd said. A bed for lying in on Sundays, for letting kids pile on between them. He

330

used to wrap tinsel round the frame at Christmas, and paper flowers on her birthday. Well, before the children came along and they were both too knackered to bother.

Now she couldn't bear its reproachful pile of pillows—firm for her, supersoft on Ross's side.

Katie made herself think about the Hall instead as she hunted through her wardrobe.

Which shoes? Which jacket went best with this dress? She could hear Angelica's energetic voice in her head, urging her to dress up, feel glamorous, get into the spirit. Earrings, how about earrings? Make an effort, that's half the fun. She didn't think about going there on her own; she made herself look for something to stick in her hair.

It was like putting on armour, thought Katie, clipping back her thick fringe with a diamanté clip. It disguises how rubbish you feel underneath. She looked in the mirror, and focused on her own reflection: the woman staring back at her seemed older than she remembered, but her back was straight and her clothes looked ready for a night out, even if the face didn't.

Unexpectedly, the beehived, eye-linered dance team came into her head—how fierce and glamorous the girls looked, even with their spotty, awkward partners lined up behind.

'Come on, Katie,' she told herself. 'You're not the first woman who's gone to that hall to forget things. And you won't be the only one there without a partner either.'

She wasn't sure whether that cheered her up or not, but when the phone still hadn't rung by eight, she put her mobile in an impractical evening bag, and left for the Memorial Hall.

CHAPTER TWENTY-FOUR

Katie put Angelica's CD into the car stereo on the way, and such was the relentlessly cheerful nature of the songs Angelica had picked that by the time she parked outside the Memorial Hall, she was almost in the mood herself, albeit an artificially enhanced one.

Lights shone through the stained glass, and a big-band beat thumped away inside. Katie stood for a moment outside, hugging her coat to herself and looking properly at the simple but solid red brickwork for the first time. It seemed different, somehow. It was as if she was suddenly seeing the people who'd built it, not just the building itself.

The commemorative plaque was illuminated by the street light, and, knowing what she now knew, Katie pictured the Lady Mayor in her fur tippet and veiled hat, cutting the thick ribbon in front of a crowd of hats where men were scarce, shadowy figures. The people leaped out of her imagination: an architect from Dayton Graham Hollister, still there off the high street, had sketched the graceful arches of the generous windows; some local craftsmen had chiselled the bunches of ivy that curled around the door, and glazed the windows, and laid each strip of the wooden floor. And the ballroom dancers had come here on Friday evenings, during the thirties, the forties, the fifties, searching the crowds in case this was the night they'd meet the love of their lives, and to let the bursting, shiny music sweep away the working week, for a few hours.

Katie felt a sharp tug of protective emotion. No building had ever made her feel protective before. Deep down, in her super-rational mind, she knew it wasn't the Memorial Hall. But she wanted *something* to stay the same, to feel that she was protecting something, instead of just breaking things up.

And I can do that, she thought, bravely. At least I can do that.

She pushed open the red door and a blast of warm air and loud music rushed into her face, along with fragments of chatter, and the smell of warm bodies, and cologne. It still amazed her that the little hall could suddenly seem so big, so alive, on these nights.

Through the glass in the main hall doors, Katie could make out the swirling movement of Friday-night dresses, and for a second, she felt as if the green-tiled vestibule was a doorway into the past, where there would always be foxtrots and quicksteps and gentlemen's excuse mes, and it would always be Friday night, and the glitterball would always start turning at 9.30 p.m. whether the Hall was full or empty.

Then she saw a very modern granny, shiny-faced and happy in a gold lamé vest, pop out to the ladies, fanning herself so hard with her hands that her bingo wings wobbled, and the mysterious feeling vanished. But not in a bad way.

'It's so hot I thought I was back on the flushes!' she gasped, with a how-we-girls-suffer! wink, and Katie managed a smile in reply, and got out her purse, ready to pay the four-pound entrance fee (squash included) just inside the main door.

The dancefloor was crowded, and as she walked

in 'In the Mood' drew to a close, setting all the ladies off into their 'big finish' twirls and there was the usual ripple of thank yous and nods, before 'Pennsylvania 6-5000' started and the dancers sprang back into their close holds. Nearly all the tables were empty, bar a few wistful single girls and flushed men talking about the football with their ties undone.

Katie edged her way round the dancefloor, until she saw some familiar faces: the ballroom class had pulled two small round tables together and the empty plastic glasses were already piled up.

Lauren, in a rose-print prom dress that showed off her model-long arms, was wedged between Trina and Chloe, who were obviously marking the outfits out of ten as they twirled past. Trina was actually pointing as her mouth moved nineteen to the dozen, which Katie didn't think was very tactful, and the look on Chloe's face was a mixture of profound embarrassment and secret agreement.

Chloe, ever exacting about hygiene, had brought her own plastic cup, Katie noted.

When Lauren spotted her, she nudged the other two, and they all smiled with genuine pleasure to see her. It was just a tiny thing, but it made Katie feel better.

It turned a little sour when they looked over her shoulder to see where Ross and Jo and Greg were, but she forged on and sat down in the spare seat next to Trina.

'Hi, Katie!' said Lauren, warmly. 'It's nice to see you!'

'You on your own?' asked Trina, getting straight to the point as usual.

'Um, yes.' Katie scanned the dancefloor

hopefully for Bridget. Bridget was the sort of mum who knew when certain topics needed skipping over. But there was no sign of her.

'Why?' Trina went on. 'I always had your Ross down as the keen dancer. Didn't think you were really into it.'

Chloe glared at Trina, then smiled apologetically at Katie. 'Are you having a night off on your own? Good for you!' She nudged her. 'Hey! Girls' night! Great!'

'Yeah,' deadpanned Trina. 'Get the orange squash in for the lasses.'

'Ross and Jo have taken the kids away to Center Parcs for a few nights.' Katie met Trina's inquisitive gaze dead straight. 'It's half-term. I couldn't get away from work, so they've gone on their own. And I'm here, because the house feels really empty without the kids running around.'

'Aw, poor you,' sympathised Lauren. 'I bet it docs. Still, we'll take your mind off it. Have a nice dance tonight.'

'Ross and Jo, eh? Gone off on their own, have they?' said Trina, arching one eyebrow. 'Is that good-looking husband of hers with them? Or is he stopping at home with you?'

'No,' she protested, 'Greg's not . . .' Then she realised it wasn't really up to her to let Jo's problems out of the bag, but as her mouth snapped shut, she realised Trina had taken that as meaningful, and wished she hadn't said anything.

'Will you give it a rest, Trine?' demanded Chloe, embarrassed by the loud cackling Trina let out. 'Sorry about her—she's peed off because we still haven't found partners for this dance thing. Plus, Baxter told her she had heavy arms when he took her out for a foxtrot.'

Trina's wrath was distracted at once. 'What would he know, the oily little shortarse? I don't know how Peggy puts up with it. I know he's good, like, but he's like a bloody driving instructor, never shuts up. And as for that polyester ruffled shirt he's got on tonight . . .'

Chloe ignored her. 'Anyway, you've picked a good evening—this is the first chance we've had to sit down since we got here! Even Chris has got a dance!'

'With his mum,' said Lauren, leaning over. 'My future mother-in-law, Irene, has graced us with her presence. But be nice to her, because she's giving us her old suite for our new house!' She raised her thumbs and grinned wildly. 'Me and Chris! Homeowners-to-be!'

'You're buying a house? Congratulations!' said Katie, grateful for the change of topic. 'When are you moving?'

Lauren's grin faded slightly. In the excitement of getting her deposit, and Chris wrangling his share out of Irene, it was easy to forget they'd not be moving for a while. 'Yeah, well, it hasn't actually been finished yet, but in the spring hopefully. Before the wedding anyway!'

'Is it one of those ones on the old cattle market site?' Katie had seen the plans for that estate; the builders were the same ones Eddie was pushing for the regeneration project. They seemed to get pretty much every contract going, and completed with a speed that would stun Six-Day Creation theorists.

Lauren nodded. 'Do you know them?' Her hand went over her mouth. 'Oh God, don't tell me

336

they're built on an old graveyard or something?'

'No, no. They're fine. There's going to be a new bus route and everything. But you need to get new houses checked for snags—little problems the builders leave for you to deal with? Here.' Katie reached in her purse and fished out a business card. She scribbled her mobile number on the back and passed it over. 'Give me a ring and I'll get it checked over for you—someone I know's a specialist. If you mention me, they'll do you a deal.'

Lauren's face lit up with her easy, open smile and Katie felt her tense mood thaw. 'Aw, thanks, Katie,' she said, 'that's really kind of you!'

'Your mum and dad must be pleased you've found somewhere,' she said, spotting Frank leading Bridget back through the crowds.

'Yeah,' said Lauren, doubtfully. 'I thought she'd be more pleased, but she seems a bit . . . off tonight. I think she's just sad I'm moving out.'

'Hello, Katie!' beamed Frank, as they got nearer. 'Can you put me down for a foxtrot, once I've got my breath back?'

'Of course!' said Katie. She smiled at Bridget, who was, as Lauren had said, looking a bit distracted, not as smiley as normal. 'Hello!'

'Hello,' murmured Bridget, but before Katie could think of something nice to say about Lauren's house, a tall skinny woman in a champagne bias-cut dress swept over, hauling a mortified Chris behind her. Her silvery-blonde hair bounced for emphasis as she spoke.

'Just remember that everyone'll be looking at you,' she was reminding him in an undertone that coincided unfortunately with a lull in the music. 'Your father would turn in his grave if he could see the way you—'

'Katie!' said Chris, seizing her hand. 'Do you want to dance? Great! Come on!'

There wasn't much Katie could do but allow Chris to drag her onto the floor, and as the music changed to 'Fly Me to the Moon', they found themselves swept up into the crush of dancers, and away from the table.

Chris's brow furrowed in concentration as they went into their social foxtrot basic in the limited space they had. It wasn't easy when you were worried about treading on other people, let alone your partner, and Katie could hear him counting under his breath as he guided her round, his big hand pressing on her back.

Counting was a real social no-no, according to Angelica's etiquette lessons. Counting (and not smiling) at your partner was tantamount to telling them they had two left feet and a tin ear. But Katie didn't take offence. She'd danced with Chris before, and sometimes it was reassuring to know your partner would only ever do the basics and not try to swing you into some fancy new step, just to prove he could, as Baxter was wont to do.

After half a lap of the floor and a series of awkward smiles and nods, they hit a traffic jam, and were forced to do little boxes backwards and forwards on the spot until it cleared. Suddenly Chris looked panicked and said, 'Is it me, or are we doing a different dance to everyone else?'

'Does it matter? So long as we're moving in roughly the same time.'

Chris didn't look convinced. 'Try telling my mother that.'

'You're not dancing with your mother, you're

338

dancing with someone who can't tell a foxtrot from a merengue,' said Katie. 'We're doing fine. Congratulations about your new house, by the way!'

His face tensed even further, and Katie felt sorry for him.

'It's a good thing to do,' she added, encouragingly. 'Sensible.'

'Can I ask you a personal question?'

Katie raised her eyebrows. 'Depends how personal. No, go on.'

'Did you . . . ?' he began, then stopped.

'Did I what?' said Katie. 'Go on, Chris, I was only joking.'

Chris seemed to struggle with himself, then blurted out, 'Did it freak you out, when you signed your mortgage?'

'What, the amount of money? Yes, absolutely,' she said. 'I still get freaked out by it—what would happen if I lost my job, what'll happen if the rates go up again . . . But you just have to get on with it. Get insurance!'

'Yeah, but . . . No. What I mean is . . .' He looked at her and Katie realised he was genuinely spooked. There was a complicated emotion in his pretty blue eyes that she'd never seen before— she'd rather dismissed Chris as one of the popular lads, a 'beer and a curry and the cutest sixth-former' type. Now she had to look at him properly, and she saw he was desperate to get something off his chest.

'Tell me,' she said, gently. 'I won't tell Lauren, or Bridget, if that's what you're worried about.'

'God, no, don't!' He looked horrified and then Katie knew it had to be something to do with the wedding.

Like she was in a position to advise on *that*.

'Promise,' she said, in what she hoped was a big-sisterly way.

'Did you look at the twenty-five-year-term thing, and think, God, when this is paid off, we'll be forty-eight! And we'll have been together longer than I've been alive now?' The words poured out of him as tiny beads of sweat formed on his forehead. 'And we'll probably have kids? Twenty-five years! I mean, it's a hell of a long time! Like, 2032! I don't even know what I'll be doing in *five* years from now!'

'Um, well, I was a little bit older than you,' said Katie, taken aback by the force of Chris's panic. 'You're still quite young to be taking on a mortgage, but . . .' She looked him firmly in the eye. 'Chris, have you and Lauren been to pre-marriage counselling? To discuss the vows and everything?'

He nodded, a bit wildly. 'Yeah, but to be honest, it was just the usual guff about listening and compromising, but this mortgage business kind of brought it home . . .' His eyes skated nervously over her head towards the class table where Lauren was chatting animatedly to Bridget, who was in turn staring out into space. 'I've had a ton of emotional stuff from my mum about what my dad would have wanted, and then Lauren's dad had to match the deposit money, because I don't think he thinks I can look after his little princess, and Kian reckons . . .' Chris dragged a smile up from somewhere but it didn't reach his eyes. 'It's getting out of hand. And the only thing anyone ever tells me about the wedding is how my crap dancing is

340

going to spoil the whole reception.'

'Marriages aren't just about the wedding,' said Katie, wearily. 'It's what comes after that that you need some proper advice on. No one ever tells you about that.'

They'd come to a sort of halt now, doing boxes in a corner while the more proficient dancers swirled and sashayed past them. Katie found she was able to do boxes and talk at the same time, which came as a pleasant surprise. Although they were holding each other with an intimacy that would lead to kissing anywhere other than a dancefloor, there was a matter-of-factness about their steps, danced so many times in practice with Angelica yelling at them about heartbeats and knee-flexing, that made frank conversation quite easy.

It was a bit like being in a confessional, thought Katie. You felt you could say things within the privacy of one song, while it was just the two of you, experiencing that particular song and dance together.

'I . . . I had to call off an engagement,' she heard herself say. 'It was the hardest thing I've ever had to do, because it was a gut feeling, not a rational one. It wasn't like me. But now I know it was the right thing to do, because I'd have married the wrong man.'

She looked up and met Chris's eyes, not feeling as awkward as she'd expected. He looked surprised, but curious.

'That must have been . . .' He pulled a face. 'Tricky.'

'Listen, I'm not saying you should. But don't ignore your instincts. You're agreeing to share your

341

life with someone,' she went on. 'Through everything—good and bad. That's a big promise.'

'But Lauren . . .' he began, his shoulders slumping.

'Lauren loves you, she'll want to sort this out. *Now*. Chris, this is the happiest time,' she added, trying to smile so it wouldn't sound so depressing. 'When you add children and money worries and everything else to the mix it gets even tougher.'

'I know,' said Chris, and chewed his lip.

Katie didn't want to drag anything else out of him if he didn't want to talk but the poor lad looked about as stricken as a blond rugby player ever got.

'I'm no expert, but talk to Lauren,' she said, gently. 'Forget about in-laws and mates and other people's advice. She's the one you'll be waking up with for . . .' She was about to say 'for the next fifty years' but realised that would probably make him sprint for the door. 'But talk to her *now*, so you've got time to work things through. The longer you leave it, the harder it'll get.'

'I'm not having *doubts*,' Chris protested rather too emphatically. 'I just feel . . . like it's going a bit quick. It's not about me and Lauren, it's about her getting a dress out of Cinderella, and my mum making a big deal about a stupid cake.' His eyes hooded. 'But if I say anything I'm going to look like a real bastard, like I don't want to get married.'

'Do you want to get married?' asked Katie, with a directness that surprised even her.

Come on, she thought, it's not like he can tell anyone else. And it had been Peter's direct questions that had brought her own true feelings out from under a rock.

Chris looked stricken; clearly the ambush tactic was having similar effects. 'I think I do . . . And then . . . I don't. But no, I do. I do.'

'If I asked Lauren the same thing and she gave me that reply, would you be happy with it?' asked Katie.

'Nnnnno?' He stumbled in his step and they had to stop. It broke the tension that had built up between them and they had to look each other in the face so Chris could start them off again.

'And two, three, four, and . . .' said Katie, stepping back.

'You're leading,' said Chris.

'That's what marriage does to you,' she replied without thinking. 'Sorry,' she added, smiling wryly.

Chris gave her a more confident look from under his thick row of dark eyelashes, and suddenly Katie felt ancient: she could see exactly why he was a heartbreaker—and just out of his teens.

'You're very young to be settling down with a mortgage at your age, Chris,' she said, as non-patronisingly as she could. 'Don't you want to travel? Work abroad?'

'That's what Kian says.' Then his glum expression switched into one of panic, as the music changed to a slower song that Katie didn't recognise, and Frank's broad figure loomed up behind them as the singer (Ella Fitzgerald? Julie London?) started warbling about her broken heart.

'Gentleman's excuse me!' said Frank, cheerily. 'I think Katie's seen about enough of that corner, Christopher! Katie? May I?'

Chris looked crestfallen as Frank swept her back

out into the main current of dancers, and she watched as his beady-eyed mother swooped down on him like a seagull on a sprat, her French-manicured nails just missing his eye as she grabbed him in a close hold and started counting aloud, her mouth exaggerating each word.

'He's a nice lad,' said Katie, feeling a sudden need to defend Chris.

'Nice enough,' said Frank, turning her capably, his knee moving inside hers to guide her around. Frank's hold was more reassuring than Chris's had been. He would, Katie thought, make a good Santa Claus. 'Bit of growing up to do, I reckon, though, between you and me.'

'He is only twenty-three.'

'When I was twenty-three I'd a wife and baby. But things were different in those days.' Frank spun Katie in a series of reverse turns, swinging her as if she was light as the feathers on a ballgown. The lights glittered in front of her eyes, and she caught sight of a pair of old dears in fabulous peppermint-green dresses, sitting the dance out. When had those dresses first seen the mirrorball? The sixties? Earlier? Were they part of Longhampton's formation team, still wearing their gowns out?

He smiled down at her. 'That's the trouble about being a dad—you know what twenty-three-year-old lads are like, because you were one yourself once. You wait! Ross'll be the same with your little girl when the time comes. Where's he tonight, then? We all missed you on Wednesday.' He winked. 'It's much harder work without you and Jo to partner! Don't tell Trina, but it's not the same.'

344

If he hadn't said it so kindly, his words wouldn't have cut through Katie so sharply, and she pleaded the need to concentrate on her steps to avoid any more explanations.

*   *   *

The hands on the big Hall clock swept round the hour in a whirl of Cole Porter and Frank Sinatra, as the Hall got hotter and hotter, and the chatter rose above the slow dances, then stopped as the quicksteps filled the floor and left everyone gasping for breath. The orange-squash cups piled up on the tables as, one by one, each of the ballroom-class dancers were whisked off, sometimes with each other, sometimes with friendly strangers.

Even Trina was kept busy, although each time she flopped back into her seat it was with a fresh critique of some poor bloke's personal hygiene or a devastating remark about the need for support tights.

'I should tell her—as a friend to fashion,' she kept saying, and Chloe kept squeaking in panic, and flapping her to quiet down. Before long, Katie and Lauren had joined in the ringside judging, awarding marks to 'Mr and Mrs Jive Bunny' or 'Mr Action Man Gripping-Hands', and passing on key information about the smartly turned-out men who paid the charming old-fashioned courtesy of asking for dances.

'Oooh, watch out for Mr Sunbed, girls,' observed Lauren, as she sank back gratefully between Katie and Chloe, wriggling a finger in her left ear. 'He's a Singer-Along. Mrs Sunbed must be deaf, or if she isn't, I bet she wishes she was.'

In the odd moment when she wasn't besieged with dance partners, Angelica would drop by the table, glorious in her lipstick-red dress and shining jet chignon. She seemed to come alive even more when the music was loud and catchy, and no part of her was still. She rippled around the floor like a flame, illuminating whoever was leading her until they seemed to be dancing in their own spotlight. Even Chris.

'I never know whether to be inspired by Angelica, or whether just to give up now,' sighed Chloe enviously, as Angelica and Baxter shimmered past in a flawless pattern of complicated turns and locksteps, their feet moving with swift precision, punctuated by pauses that seemed to hang, suspended in the air. The fact that Angelica's pale forehead was clearly visible above Baxter's own Brylcreemed head didn't stop them looking like the only proper dancers in the room; he led and she followed with a skill that made it look like the most natural thing in the world.

'Mum says she was a professional for years,' said Lauren.

'She was a world champion,' said Peggy, gazing out at them. 'Best dancer I've ever seen.' They turned, surprised to hear her speak without Baxter. Katie had almost forgotten Peggy was sitting there with them.

'Her mum and dad were in the formation team, weren't they?' she asked, thinking of the archive pictures. That would explain where she got it from.

Lauren nudged her, nodding at Peggy's unwavering eyes, following Baxter's effortless motion across the floor. 'Sweet, isn't it? After all

346

this time, she still can't take her eyes off him.'

'Peggy?' Katie repeated. 'Were Angelica's parents on the formation team?'

Peggy's attention seemed to snap back. 'Yes,' she said, nodding. 'They were, yes. Very good.'

*　　　*　　　*

Katie felt her energy dive at about ten, when she'd normally be slumped in front of the telly, and for a few songs in succession, she waved away a couple of offers, pleading sore feet and exhaustion.

Surreptitiously, she checked her phone, in case Ross had called. She didn't think she wanted him to, but at the same time . . . she sort of did.

'Care for the next dance?'

Katie glanced up and realised a man had been standing there waiting for her to finish with her phone. The slinky introduction to 'Fever' was almost through, and Lauren and Trina had both been whisked away by partners, leaving her and Chloe guarding the handbags.

She tried to arrange her face into a polite putting-off smile, so the man wouldn't feel too offended. He wasn't bad looking—dark hair, clean-shaven, thirties. Some distant part of her brain registered surprise that young guys like that went to evenings like this.

He's probably here to meet women, she thought. Divorced, probably. And if you divorce Ross, you'll have to start meeting men somewhere. You'll be on the dating scene, like Trina and Chloe are.

And so will Ross. Finding someone new. Finding someone who loves him more than you do.

A sudden plunging dread took Katie's breath

347

away.

'I'm sorry, I'm . . . sitting this one out,' she stammered. 'Blisters!'

He angled his head regretfully. 'Maybe later, then?'

'Um, yes, yes,' said Katie. 'Maybe later.'

'How about me, then?' asked Chloe, with a boldness that surprised Katie. She was on her feet before he could reply. 'I'm trying out partners for an exhibition!'

He smiled, nervously, and nodded.

'Don't tell Trina,' Chloe mouthed, as she followed him to the floor.

'Now then, Miss Picky, I hope you've got a good excuse for turning Rod Coward away—he's an excellent lead,' said Angelica, materialising next to Katie. 'You can't just turn men down because you don't like the look of them—it's the height of bad dancing manners! Word gets round, you know.'

Katie shoved her phone back in her bag with trembling fingers. Did Angelica know *everyone*? And see *everything*?

'Will you let me do this?' she went on, reaching into her own bag and pulling out a big red silk flower. 'I've been wanting to do this all night, put some pizzazz on that black dress of yours. I know you're not a girlie girl,' she went on, pinning it deftly to Katie's shoulder strap, 'but you have to think of the dancefloor as a *stage*, where you can play a *role* for the evening. Imagine yourself as Scarlett O'Hara on the floor, or Liz Taylor. Let yourself go! Be someone else!'

'But I'm not sure I . . .' murmured Katie.

'And,' Angelica went on, not seeing her stricken face, 'I hope you appreciate Ross's footwork a

348

little more after tonight! Hmm? It's a shame he's not here. I hope your foursome hasn't given up on us?'

'No,' said Katie, and blinked.

'Because you and Ross have got the makings of a good ballroom couple,' said Angelica. 'If you stopped being so self-conscious and let him lead you more. But that'll come, once you stop thinking so much. And your friend Jo's a natural Latin dancer . . . Katie? Are you all right?'

'Yes, I'm fine. Fine.' Katie didn't feel fine: she didn't want to think about Ross. She didn't want to think about Jo.

Particularly after what Trina had said about them going off together with the kids. It had niggled away, mainly because it had never even occurred to her, but if it was so obvious to everyone else, was she being stupid?

Don't be so ridiculous, Katie told herself, but the uncomfortable creeping sensation wouldn't go away that easily. Hannah worshipped Jo. How much time was Jo spending with them?

'Katie?' Angelica said again, and this time Katie made herself meet Angelica's eyes.

'I'm fine,' she said, pulling on her unreadable business face, the one she'd developed to hide her inner feelings during years and years of meetings with patronising surveyors and accountants. It was a tough face.

There was a flicker of acknowledgement in Angelica's face: she seemed to recognise the mask for what it was, and changed the subject.

'Bridget was telling me she wants to start a campaign to get the hall listed.' Angelica's feet tapped as the introduction to 'Moon River' picked up.

'Yes,' said Katie. 'Will you write a letter?'

'I'd love to,' Angelica said, with a little smile. 'The happy hours I've had in here . . .'

She was going to say more, but they were interrupted. 'Would you care for a waltz?'

Katie looked up and saw Baxter's neat figure in front of her, his hand outstretched in a formal gesture of invitation.

'Go on, we can talk later,' said Angelica. 'I don't teach wallflowers.'

'Thank you,' said Katie, and stood up. Dancing with Baxter required total concentration, what with one thing or another, and she was glad of the chance to empty her mind.

*   *   *

There were only five more dances for Katie to fill, and between Frank, Baxter, Mr Sunbed (not just a Singer-Along, but a very flat one with clammy hands), a skinny Polish man whose close hold Katie made a note to warn the others about, and a subdued Chris, she didn't have time to think much beyond getting out of the corners.

But at ten to eleven, the lights went up, chasing the moonlight and vintage romance out of the spangled dancefloor and turning it back into a community hall filled with plastic chairs. The dancers, so elegant and polished in the flattering dusk of the final slow waltzes, were transformed like frog princes and princesses back into grandmothers and postmen, hairdressers and accountants, glowing and fanning themselves as they kissed and shook hands, and pulled off

350

'crippling' shoes in the cloakroom outside.

Trina was busy swapping mobile numbers with a bloke she'd had 'six dances' with, according to Chloe. Chloe herself was wiping out her plastic cup, and peering anxiously at her coat, which she'd only reluctantly handed into the cloakroom.

'Oooh, see you on Wednesday, then!' said Lauren, wrapping her scarf round her neck and nearly knocking the remaining cup of orange squash to the floor.

The poised Lauren only lasted as long as the music, thought Katie with a wry smile, as Lauren grabbed Chris round the middle and hugged him. 'Come on, Fred Astaire, it's time for bed.'

Chris caught Katie's eye and looked away, embarrassed.

'Not now, eh, Loz?' he muttered.

'You won't be able to say that when I'm your *wife*!' she replied, still under the spell of the dancing. 'Grrr! Are you giving me a lift home?'

Katie bit her tongue. Lauren looked so happy she couldn't even see the cloud over Chris. Maybe it wasn't a cloud, she argued; maybe it was a sign that he was thinking about what marriage really meant. He'd made her realise something too; when she'd told him she'd broken it off with Steve, to marry the right man, it had been her heart speaking. They'd both been honest.

'Can I give you a lift?' Frank asked her. 'We go your way, don't we, Bridget?'

'Um, we do,' she said. 'Yes, and we can have a chat about . . . you know what,' she added, casting her eyes meaningfully around the painted walls.

'That's kind of you but it's fine, I drove here,' said Katie, and suddenly the effort of the dancing

351

and the strain of keeping her face calm and her emotions at bay crushed her last remaining defences. Lauren was cooing something about how romantic the songs were, and whether all the couples could dance at her wedding in a display team.

I want to go home, thought Katie. Even if it's silent and empty.

'We're off, or we'll never get a cab. Bye, Katie!' said Chloe. 'See you next week!'

'Wednesday?' said Bridget. Her sharp eyes missed nothing, thought Katie. 'The four of you?'

'We'll see,' said Katie. 'Bye, Frank, thanks for the lovely dances.'

'You drive carefully now,' said Frank, kindly.

Katie managed to keep herself together till she was safely in the car, and then she put on the radio to distract herself, but tears still slid down her face all the way home.

But when she stepped into the silent house, somehow she couldn't cry any more. She just had to wait, and that filled her with a very sobering dread.

Ross and Hannah and Jack would be home in twelve hours.

CHAPTER TWENTY-FIVE

Katie took two Nytols but she still couldn't sleep. The swinging quickstep rhythms of the social kept going through her head, with snatches of the hopeful, romantic lyrics repeating over and over in a mocking loop: *'You do something to me . . . You made me love you . . . You'd be so nice to come home to . . .'*

How come romance was so much easier in those days, Katie wondered, staring bleakly at the ceiling. Even the heartbreaks? Was it because they only expected to find perfect harmony and romance in four-minute bursts on the dancefloor? The rest of your married life never had to live up to that magical courtship, what with you doing your bit in the kitchen and him dutifully providing. Lots of rules to follow, but if you followed them you were safe. Not like now.

No wonder the stupid ballroom lessons were doomed for her and Ross. They were doing it the wrong way round: trying to put some sparkle into their marriage by faking the courtship, when they both knew the happy-ever-after wasn't that happy.

Katie threw back the covers, and got up, even though it was barely five-thirty in the morning, and still pitch black outside. Her toes hurt where people had trodden on them, and by the door, her dress hung like a shed skin over a chair, with Angelica's big red flower still pinned to the strap.

I don't even make the grade when it comes to *dressing* like a ballroom dancer, let alone being the perfect partner, thought Katie, miserably, as she ran the shower.

*   *   *

At half-nine, she wiped her hands on a tea towel and drew breath. The house actually looked OK when it wasn't covered in toast crumbs and Lego. Ross never cleaned. He just didn't seem to see dirt, something that annoyed Katie, who did, but who

353

rarely had time to do much about it. As she was Hoovering and wiping and stacking magazines, all she allowed herself to think about was how she could help Bridget organise a letter-writing campaign for the Hall, and, underneath that, a steady hum of how satisfying it was to see order reappearing in the rooms.

Katie pulled off the Marigolds as she looked round for something else to take her mind off things.

Jo. You could go and put some flowers in Jo's house. Tidy round. Make it nice for her coming back too.

What if the kids haven't *missed you? What if Hannah* hasn't *been wishing you were there?*

What if Trina was right about Ross and Jo?

No, thought Katie. That is one thing I'm sure of: Ross isn't unfaithful. That's just not him. Greg, the competitive, ambitious alpha male, probably; Ross, no.

She took a deep breath and went back upstairs for another shower. Tidying seemed to have worked up a sweat.

*   *   *

Katie let herself in at the Fieldings' with her new spare key, and couldn't stop her habitual rush of envy at Jo's show-perfect house sweeping over her. Today it only lasted a split second before her sympathy for Jo's horrible situation surfaced, and she went into the kitchen, looking for a vase in which to put the roses she'd picked up at the supermarket on the way, along with some milk and fresh bread. Jo's massive American fridge was

354

bursting, but Katie needed to feel she was doing something helpful.

'Right, a vase,' she said, putting the flowers on the kitchen table, still in their Cellophane. They were forced foreign roses, raspberry-ripple pink with no smell, but something about them reminded Katie of the dancers last night: they had an old-fashioned corsage-y feel to their frilled petals.

She opened and shut cupboard after cupboard until she found where Jo kept her vases.

'Nice flowers,' said a dry voice behind her. 'Very thoughtful.'

Katie jumped, and spun round, her heart banging as everything she'd been told about self-defence vanished from her mind.

But it wasn't an intruder. It was Greg.

She clapped a hand to her chest as her blood carried on spiking in her veins. 'Jesus, you gave me a shock.'

'So did you,' he replied. 'I wasn't expecting anyone to be here. Least of all you—shouldn't you be in Center Parcs?'

Katie registered that he was carrying an empty overnight bag, with two bulging Hamleys bags and a giant fluffy Tweenie.

Bribes, she thought, nastily, then hated herself for jumping to take sides.

'I couldn't go—work. They're not coming back until later,' she said, quickly. 'I just thought I'd pop over and . . .' Katie trailed off. There was an awkward atmosphere building up between them, and she didn't like it. He knew she knew. But not how much.

Greg raised his eyebrows. For a man who'd just left his wife and kids, he didn't exactly look

355

haggard, thought Katie. His angular jaw was clean-shaven, his brown hair was tousled, and he was wearing the complete Boden weekend kit, as rejected out-of-hand by a scornful Ross every time she'd waved the catalogue at him: artfully washed-out polo shirt, dark jeans, suede trainers, smug expression.

In fact, thought Katie, her mind racing ahead, he looked suspiciously like someone making an effort. Someone whose clothes were now being chosen by a different person . . .

'I thought I'd leave these,' he raised the bags, 'and pick up some more of my stuff.' The studied casualness slipped, as his face tensed. 'I suppose Jo's filled you in on my evil home-wrecking ways, has she?'

'She told me you felt your marriage was over, yes,' said Katie, evenly.

How can I feel so disgusted and furious with him when I'm doing exactly the same thing to Ross, she thought. But at least I'm *upset*. At least I can't sleep.

'Hmm.' Greg looked cynical. 'And that's all?'

'Yes, that's all. She's pretty loyal. She didn't go into details, just that you wanted to leave.'

'Right,' said Greg, and pushed his lower lip out, nodding.

'Greg, I'm sorry, but I can't understand how you can be standing there looking so calm!' Katie burst out.

'Well, when it's over, it's over,' he said, matter-of-factly. 'There's no point dragging it out, is there?'

Katie stared at him, unable to believe how dispassionate he was being. This wasn't the Greg she'd secretly fancied in the past. Or if it was, she had no idea that business-like exterior went all the way down to where his inner sensitivity was meant to be.

'Jo's *devastated.*' She didn't want to lay into him, but they were standing only feet away from where Jo had slumped, her natural cheeriness crushed by misery, only days ago. Suddenly Katie couldn't stop her anger breaking through. 'You know how she feels about her family. She's a *great* mother! A great wife! I hope you know what you're losing, Greg, because you're bloody lucky to have someone like her.'

Greg dumped his bags and ran a hand through his hair. He looked bitter, and it didn't suit him. 'Yeah, well. Maybe that's the problem.'

'What?'

'That's all she does these days—be a mother. It's her only topic of conversation. What they did today. What they ate. Where we should send them to school. Whether we can afford another one.'

'*And?*' Katie glared at him. 'That's important stuff. She's trying to *include* you. You miss out on a lot, with the hours you spend at work, and she's trying to keep you in touch!'

'Oh, and I should be grateful for that, should I?' Greg raised his arms sarcastically. 'What about our marriage? What about *us*? All right, I know it's selfish, but it's like I don't exist in this family, except as a cash machine! She's not my *wife* any more, she's Molly and Rowan's *mother*! We had five fantastic years together before . . .' He bit his lip, as if he was trying to stop himself saying too much, then shook his head. 'It's not that I don't love the girls. I'd do anything for them. But the

357

stuff that held me and Jo together, it's getting pushed out. I thought you'd understand. You, of all people.'

Katie didn't feel inclined to help him out, especially when a tiny, controversial voice in her head was reminding her that, yes, she did understand what it felt like to come second all the time. To see her children turn to Ross before her, to feel she was failing them for being out at work, which was, in turn, her own choice for marrying someone who'd never support them . . . It was like a knot that kept tightening.

'Why?' she demanded, to push that voice away. She didn't want to agree with Greg, not when he was acting so self-righteous. 'Why would I understand?'

Greg looked surprised at her question and a touch of vulnerability crept into his face, making him more like the charming Greg she knew. 'Well, because you work so hard, and take on so much that Ross ought to be doing for you.'

Katie stared at him and softened. No one ever said that to her. A sense that maybe she was doing the right thing began to spread through her chest. She didn't *ask* for sympathy, but it didn't mean she didn't need it. 'Well, yes, I suppose . . .'

'There's no suppose about it,' Greg went on. 'It must be even harder for you. You've got all the pressure of keeping the money coming in, plus most of the housework, because—don't take this the wrong way—I know Ross isn't much of a domestic god. But then what man is? It's not a natural instinct. I don't know how you put up with it.'

'No,' agreed Katie, 'it is hard, sometimes.'

358

They looked, long-sufferingly, at each other.

Then Katie remembered that she wasn't meant to be agreeing with him.

'Are you sure it's not just a blip?' she said. 'Something that can be worked through?'

Greg shook his head. 'No. It's been over for a while. There's no spark any more. You know what it's like,' he added, ruefully, 'it's pretty hard to get aroused when someone you used to fancy the pants off turns into a slob with nothing to talk about except what happened at nursery. Meanwhile you're working every hour God sends, slogging your guts out and getting guilt trips about how you don't spend enough time with the kids—which, in my considered opinion, stems from guilt because they feel bad, deep down, about how much they've let themselves go.'

They. He means Jo *and* Ross.

Katie felt a flicker of defensiveness. Greg didn't really have the right to be so dismissive—about either of them.

'I mean, you've had two kids and you're still the size you were before they were born.' Greg's smile turned a little too flattering. 'You were back in your jeans in weeks, weren't you? Size ten, right?'

Katie bridled. 'That was stress, not a diet. Everyone's different, Greg. Jo looks better now than she's ever done! I can't believe you don't think that.'

'Maybe she needs to get back to work too then,' he said.

'Looking after children is a full-time job,' snapped Katie.

Greg rolled his eyes and fiddled angrily with the pile of post on the table. 'Oh, don't give me that bullshit. I've heard that so many times, and we both know it doesn't compare to a full day of crap at the office.'

'It is. And that's the deal, Greg. Jo gave up her career to look after the children. Do you have any idea how hard that is for a woman these days? She gave up her independence, as well as her income—and she's doing a great job.' Katie's eyes flashed angrily. 'You can't say she isn't because you have two perfect daughters. If there's a problem with your *marriage* then . . .'

'We don't have a marriage any more. At least, not the one I signed up to.' He waved the bills at her for emphasis. 'And don't tell me you planned to marry a whining house-husband with long hair and a degree in the Tellytubbies?'

Katie's jaw tightened and she opened her mouth to defend Ross—and by extrapolation, herself—but he hadn't finished. Resentment was boiling out of him, and an unpleasant bully she'd never even been aware of began to emerge from the smart weekend Greg. It wasn't nice.

His eyes narrowed as he spoke, and Katie noticed a vein on the side of his head, throbbing.

'I mean, to be frank with you, it was embarrassing, seeing Jo at that dancing class, bulging out of that red dress,' he went on. 'I know she was wearing it to remind me of a holiday we had, before the children. She used to look amazing in it. Now?' He shrugged. 'She just doesn't care any more. She doesn't see herself as a woman, just a mother. But I didn't marry some obese housewife, I married a gorgeous, smart woman, with a great figure. But oh no, I'm not allowed to say anything, because that's sexist and

360

unsupportive.'

Katie's heart shrivelled in sympathy with Jo: she could see her putting on the dress, trying to rekindle some bedroom excitement, thinking it would stir up some sexy memory of a hot night, knowing it didn't quite fit, hoping Greg wouldn't notice—then sensing his revulsion and feeling even worse about her body than she did already.

But Jo was beautiful: soft and generous and velvety and yielding. She'd been pinched before, thought Katie, always halving her cakes and scraping off dressing—now she knew why, if Greg had been such a body fascist. Poor Jo, she thought. Ross had never ever made a big deal about her weight; he'd told her she was beautiful even when she was ten days over her due date with Jack and she couldn't see her own legs.

'Jo is stunning,' she insisted. But Greg wasn't listening now he was on a roll.

'She's a milk cow. And the worst thing is she doesn't seem to care. I've tried to get her to go to the gym, but she makes pathetic excuses. It's not a turn on. That and the constant babybabybaby conversation—God knows how she thinks this third baby's going to get made.'

'Greg,' said Katie, warningly. They were getting into Too Much Information territory now.

'It's what happens. No man wants to shag his mother. And don't tell me things are still sizzling in the bedroom with you and Ross.' He rolled his eyes. 'I've seen the way you two dance at those classes—just like me and Jo. Zero physical spark. And he used to be a good-looking guy! What's with the saggy polo shirts and the pot belly, eh? It's like they don't care about anything other than the kids.'

361

'That is enough!' yelled Katie.

Greg arched his eyebrow. 'Ah. So you do know what I mean. I've thought for a while that you didn't look that . . . well, satisfied, shall we say?'

There's no point denying it, Katie told herself. Don't be a hypocrite. She struggled with herself, while Greg leaped on her hesitation as a mute agreement.

'I knew you'd understand,' he crowed. 'It's not pretty, and it's not very PC, but it's bloody hard when you've got all the stress and they've got the moral high ground.'

Ross would never do this, she thought. He'd never rip our relationship apart in front of Jo. He's a better man than Greg in so many ways.

Slowly an unpleasant truth started to take on a solid shape in Katie's mind: I've made a mistake. I just needed to say those things aloud, so Ross would see how serious I am about fixing them. But I don't want him to leave. I want *us* to fix them.

There was another thing: Greg wasn't actually the man she'd always fondly assumed he was. How much of that idle crush had just been projection— imagining the sort of suited, salaried man she thought she should be with? How much—Katie shuddered at her own shallowness—had been about Greg's suits, and wine knowledge?

Jo didn't deserve this self-centred bully.

'I thought you were making a big mistake, but now I'm not sure you are,' she said, slowly.

'I know.' Greg beamed smugly. 'Sometimes you just have to be realistic. I don't think they get that.'

They, thought Katie. *They*?

'Do you? I don't think you're being that realistic at all. You clearly have no idea how lucky you are

362

to have Jo. So maybe it's better that you don't have her. Let her find someone who appreciates her. God, she was *so* right to change the locks!'

Greg stared, speechless.

'After all,' Katie went on, her cheeks reddening as she raged half at herself and half at him, 'you'll be paying alimony and seeing the children at weekends, so no change there. You just won't have to suffer the unbearable humiliation of having a wife who enjoys herself. You can find some skinny twenty-year-old instead. If, of course, you haven't already.'

Greg snorted. 'Now, Katie, that's . . .'

'What?' she demanded.

But his face gave him away. His eyes dropped guiltily and when he raised his gaze from the roses on the kitchen table to her face, she could tell he was guarding himself. Then he looked surprised.

'What?' she yelled.

Greg said nothing but stared over her shoulder.

Katie spun round, and Jo was standing there, clutching her housekeys in her fist.

'Jo! I thought you weren't coming back till this afternoon!' said Katie. 'Are the kids OK?'

Jo nodded mutely. She was wearing a green wrap dress that stretched over her curves; Katie couldn't help looking, after Greg's outburst, and, as usual, she felt jealous of Jo's creamy cleavage.

Stupid Greg.

Jo still hadn't said anything, and Katie started to wonder who she was staring at with such intensity: her or Greg.

Shit, thought Katie. This'll be the first time they've seen each other since Greg dropped that bombshell on her and walked out. No wonder she looks ready to explode.

Was that only three days ago? It felt like weeks.

'Listen, is Ross in the car?' she asked, feeling in the way. 'If you two want to, um, have a chat I'll look after Molly and Rowan for a few hours, give you some time on your own?' She tried a smile, but Jo's face was stony.

The kitchen was deathly quiet and thick with unspoken tension. Katie could hear the chirping of birds outside.

She itched to rush out and see the children, probably hug them a bit too hard, but she wasn't sure it was a good idea to run off until she was sure Jo didn't want her to stay.

Finally Jo spoke. 'How long has this been going on?' she demanded, coolly, and Katie couldn't tell which one of them she was speaking to.

Katie furrowed her brow. 'How long's what been going on?'

Jo directed her scary hard gaze to Greg. 'Greg? How long? When were you going to tell me?'

'I don't know what you're talking about!'

'Yes, you do! You know exactly what I'm talking about! Was it going to give you some kind of cheap thrill, doing it in our bed because you knew I wouldn't be back till later? You're sick! The pair of you are sick!'

Katie looked between Greg and Jo, and realised Jo had jumped to a bizarre conclusion. For a second she was glad the kitchen table was between them because Jo looked ready to kill.

'God, no, Jo. It's nothing like that!' she protested, horrified that Jo could even think it.

'Did you *plan* for me and Ross to be out of the way, is that it? I mean, it all makes sense now—you needing to go to Manchester for work, and you . . .' She stared at Katie, pain and rage mingling in her face. 'You, telling Ross you had to be here for work. Such an easy excuse for the pair of you, wasn't it? And we even took the kids out of your hair too. That's *appalling*. And yet so absolutely *typical* of the pair of you!'

Her voice was high and breathy, barely under control.

'Jo, no . . .' Katie looked at the flowers on the table, and Greg's bag, and her own dishevelled appearance, and she could see it didn't look good, especially after Jo's three days away, trying to work out how her world had fallen apart.

Jo laughed, mirthlessly. 'Ross wondered if there was someone else, and I said, no, no, Katie's not that type. Greg, yeah—I assume you've got someone else, but you . . .' Her eyes burned through Katie. 'I thought you were my friend. I've been telling Ross you're better than that, that you'd never look elsewhere, but Jesus, you weren't even looking very far!'

Katie's blood chilled. Ross. Was he going to walk in next and hear all this? What about the kids?

'Honestly, Jo, I swear to you there's nothing going on!' she protested, trying to keep her voice level. 'I came round to freshen up the house, and Greg walked in. I had no idea he was going to turn up—I wouldn't have come if I'd known. I've been here ten minutes, if that.'

'You didn't mention anything about you and Ross splitting up,' said Greg.

Katie turned to him furiously. 'No, because it's none of your business, and anyway, you've just been talking about yourself, non stop. Now tell her! Tell Jo there is absolutely nothing going on between you and me.'

For a clawing instant, Katie saw a mean reticence in Greg's face, as though he was toying with the idea of dropping her in it, just because he could.

'Tell her!' Katie screeched.

I don't want Ross to think I've been cheating on him, was the thought that seared through her, and the strength of the fear took her by surprise, then dropped her back into despair, that everything was going wrong faster than she'd be able to stop it.

'There's nothing going on,' said Greg at last, pushing a hand through his hair. 'It's like she says, Katie was here when I arrived. I only came round to leave some things for the girls and pick up some more clothes. In fact,' he added, nastily, 'it's just as well she was because if she hadn't left the door open, I wouldn't have been able to get in.'

'Yes,' said Jo, 'that's because the locks have been changed.'

'I don't think you've got the right to do that,' he began. 'And if I find you've done anything stupid to my stuff, then don't think—'

'Just get your clothes and go.' Jo shook her head and turned away, reaching for the thick rail of the Aga to hold on to.

'They're in the spare room,' added Katie. 'I put them in bin bags.'

Greg picked up his bag: a large Mulberry overnight bag. Katie noticed, dully, that the airline tags from some recent trip were still hanging off it.

Not exciting and globe-trotting any more; just ostentatious. It was probably only a flight up to

366

Glasgow.

She looked up to see if Jo was OK and saw that the intensity had drained out of her as quickly as it had come. Her shoulders had dropped again in a submissive, defeated slump, and her hair was starting to frizz. They must have had an early start to get back, and she probably hadn't had time to tame her curls in the rush to get all four children ready. Katie instinctively moved around the table to stand at her side.

Greg was looking at Jo too, but not with the same sympathy that Katie was. He turned his gaze to her, and raised his eyebrow ironically, and Katie knew he was nudging her to think about what he'd said.

'Let me know if I missed anything in the bin bags,' she snapped.

Greg opened his mouth to say something, but Katie's fierce glare put him off, and he strolled out of the kitchen.

'I'm sorry,' whispered Jo, without looking up. 'I . . . I'm really sorry.'

'Forget it,' said Katie, hugging her.

'I know he's been seeing someone—I've suspected it for ages.' Jo bit her lips. 'You're his type, you know—successful, ambitious.' There was a painful pause. 'Thin.'

Katie winced. Jo'd never even hinted that she had a problem about her body before. She held her at arms' length. 'Shut up. You're gorgeous. You know that. Please tell me you didn't really think that I'd ever try it on with Greg. Please tell me that.'

Jo sighed. 'No. Not really. I'm sorry. I guess I just wanted an explanation . . . something concrete to be angry with, instead of this . . .' She made a despairing gesture. 'This . . . *mess*.'

'I know what you mean,' said Katie, quietly, and hugged Jo back to her shoulder.

Upstairs, they could hear Greg stomping about, opening cupboards, slamming doors.

'We came back early because Hannah and Jack were missing you,' said Jo, quietly. 'We all missed you.'

Katie didn't know what to say. So she said nothing, but squeezed harder.

'I should tell Ross what's going on,' said Jo, suddenly, springing out of Katie's embrace. 'He'll be wondering what's happening.'

*   *   *

Ross was in the car, gamely singing the theme tune to *Big Cook Little Cook*, with Hannah and Molly, while Jack and Rowan garbled the occasional word. Katie recognised it at once as the malevolently catchy CBeebies CD that drove her so insane she pretended it wouldn't work in her car. It still sounded horrific, but Katie thought she'd never seen anything sweeter: Ross had two thin braids in his hair, as did Hannah and Molly, and the back seat was piled with things they'd made from straws and pine-cones.

'Mummy! Mummy!' As soon as Hannah and Jack saw her, their faces shone with delight, and Katie thought her own heart would break, so fierce was the need to hold them.

'Hello! Hello!' she cried, leaning into the car to hug them. 'Hello, Molly! Hello, Rowan!'

Molly looked somewhat startled to be hugged by

368

Hannah's mummy, who didn't normally go in for such dramatic displays of affection.

'Mummy, you're crying,' observed Hannah.

'Happy tears!' Katie wiped her face with her hand. 'Happy tears to see my lovely babies!'

'Is everything OK?' asked Ross in a low tone.

'Yes!' Jo had dragged on her cheerful face, in front of the children. It didn't fool Katie: the smile was too wide and the pink cheeks were due to hastily applied blusher. 'Yes, I think Greg and I are going to have a chat, and then . . . yes, we'll be fine.'

Katie looked at Ross, then Jo. 'If you want to stay, Ross, I'll take everyone back to ours.'

'No!' said Jo, brightly. 'Everyone's settled in this one—why don't you all pop out for some lunch and leave your car here? Swap over when you come back.'

'If you're sure . . . ?'

'I am.'

Katie turned back to the car full of children. Molly was starting to look a little teary, and Hannah was fidgeting in her seat. 'Right, then! Who wants to go for a drive-through belated birthday doughnut?'

'Yay!' said Ross, making thumbs-up signs to the back seat.

'Yay!' replied Molly and Hannah at once, in an adoring echo.

Katie couldn't tell whether the enthusiasm was for doughnuts or Ross. She suspected equal amounts of both.

'Doughnuts?' said Ross, as he reversed off the drive.

His tone was level but Katie knew what he really

369

meant was: you don't allow doughnuts, you're clearly trying to curry favour, I know what you're up to.

She thought of Greg's hopelessly inappropriate presents, and thought fiercely, at least I know what my children like.

'I need something sweet,' she said, and turned up the theme tune to *Balamory*.

CHAPTER TWENTY-SIX

For Lauren and Chris's mates—and for anyone under forty, and a few who pretended they still were—Saturday night in Longhampton traditionally started at the far end of the high street, at the Jolly Fox Inn, the dog-eared pub opposite the town hall, but tonight Lauren was feeling neither Jolly nor Foxy, unlike the heaving crowd of under-dressed, under-age drinkers around her.

'Another orange and soda, Lauren?' asked Kian, but he wasn't looking at her. He was looking at the well-built redhead serving on at the bar, who was trying not to meet his eye.

Not even looking, thought Lauren, crossly. Leering.

They'd been wedged in a booth for over an hour, and so far all they'd done was drink and listen to Kian rate the various girls in there, one of whom Lauren had seen very recently in the surgery with a funny sprain she didn't get playing netball. Lauren hadn't even been drinking, what with Irene phoning her daily now to 'encourage' her about

370

sticking to the detox plan. If she so much as looked at a Bacardi Breezer, she could hear Irene's disappointed sighing in her ear.

What with one thing and another, she was beginning to wonder why she'd bothered coming out at all.

To see Chris, she reminded herself, shooting him a sidelong look. But then Chris was acting rather weird, trying to divide his behaviour between a night out with the lads and a romantic evening with his fiancée: drinking, encouraging Kian and occasionally asking her if she wanted a proper drink.

'She is an eight point three, and she is *feeling* me,' said Kian, still giving the barmaid the eye. 'Go on, look up, look up, you know you want to . . . Yes!'

On cue, the barmaid peeked up from under her eyelashes at Kian, rewarding him with a cheeky grin, and what was either a wink or some kind of unfortunate squint—difficult to tell with all that mascara. Lauren could see that even from a distance of fifteen metres the legendary Matthews charm bait had worked again.

She turned to Chris to roll her eyes, but Chris just shrugged indulgently, then when he saw her glowering, said, 'What?' under his breath.

'Who does he think he is, Calum Best?' she hissed, but Kian was too engrossed in winking and flashing his watch.

'Watch and learn, my man!' gloated Kian. 'Watch and learn—oh, sorry, Chris. I keep forgetting you don't need to know this stuff any more.'

Lauren glared at him, but Chris was too busy

giving Kian a bloke-ish shove.

'Anyway, drink?' said Kian, smoothing down his hair. 'I'm going to the bar. And I may be some time.'

'Pint for me, mate,' said Chris, cheerily. He banged his empty glass down on the table where four empty glasses already jostled for space with the crisp packets, and leaned back in the velvet booth, his arm around Lauren, a happy man.

'I'll have a Smirnoff Ice,' said Lauren, abandoning all attempts to stay off the booze, seeing Chris and Kian definitely weren't. 'And get someone to come and clean this table,' she added, as Kian swaggered off towards the crowded bar.

As soon as he was gone, Chris took the opportunity to pull Lauren closer for a beery snog, but she wriggled out of his grasp, annoyed.

'Not here! Not in front of the whole pub!' she snapped.

'What is up with you tonight?' Chris demanded. 'You've been acting up ever since we got here.'

'Acting up? Well, maybe it's because I didn't expect Kian to come along this evening! I thought it was just going to be you and me. To celebrate the house! A drink—one drink—then something to eat somewhere, and then some time on our own. At your flat. Without Kian hanging around like a bad smell.' Lauren heard how crabby she sounded, and tried to pull on a more seductive face. 'Actually, if he's going to hang around here chatting up barmaids, maybe we should take advantage of the empty flat right now?'

Chris fiddled with a beermat. 'Ah, well, Kian's already told me he's got plans for himself tonight . . . back home. So that might not be the best idea.'

'What?' wailed Lauren. 'You are joking, aren't you?'

'Lauren, it's his flat! I can hardly hang a sock on the door, can I?'

Lauren struggled to keep her frustration under control. 'So if you knew that, why didn't we just stay in this evening, then? Or we could go back now?'

I can't believe I'm suggesting that, she thought. I'm scheduling sex like some kind of teenager and I'm twenty-two and engaged!

She stroked Chris's thigh under the table. Chris had great thighs: long and lean and really hard from years of rugby training. 'The only thing getting me through the last hour has been the thought of getting you, on your own, at home, out of those sexy jeans,' she murmured. 'Come on, Chris, let's go. Now. Kian's happy enough here, and I haven't . . .' Lauren jiggled her eyebrows meaningfully. '. . . *been alone* with you for days . . .'

Some hot and steamy sex, she reckoned, might just blow away the niggles at the back of her mind. That's probably what was up, not enough tenderness and intimacy and appreciation of Chris's gorgeous thighs.

But he didn't move. Instead his square jaw jutted even more.

'What if I wanted to go out, with my mate, and my girlfriend, into town? Where I might see my other mates?'

'Other mates?'

'Yeah, well, Kian phoned Mark and Rich, and they're on their way . . .'

'Chris!' protested Lauren. 'Saturday night was meant to be for us!' How obvious did she have to make it?

Chris looked properly pissed off. 'For God's sake, Lauren, I've given up Wednesday nights to make a dick of myself at ballroom-dancing lessons with you, and I was out with you and your parents and *my mother* last night at that social whatever. I've had her on the phone already today, giving me earache about my bloody waltzing! Can't I have one night out with my mates?'

Lauren turned so she was facing him in the booth. 'It's not just one night, though, is it?' she heard herself say. 'You never used to spend so much time out drinking when we were living together. I don't know where you *are* half the time. I hope it's not going to be like this when we've got our own house.'

'What are you saying?'

They both knew exactly what she was saying, but neither wanted to put it into words. Words that would lead to a really big bust-up. Instead, they glared at each other mutinously.

Chris cracked first. 'It's not that I don't want to . . . go home with you, but . . . I want some time out with the lads. They're already saying I'm under the thumb cos I'm engaged, and what's it going to look like if you're dragging me off halfway through the night?'

'Like, you're the only one with a girlfriend?'

'It's not about that, it's about male bonding,' whined Chris, and that was the final straw for Lauren, because right up until they'd moved out of their houseshare, Chris and the lads had had maybe three big nights out a month, and that was as much bonding as they'd been able to deal with. Even then, he'd have binned it for one flash of her hold-ups. He didn't need his 'boys' time' *that* much.

'Oh, well, fine,' she said, grabbing her bag. 'If spending time with me is making you feel *under the thumb*, then go ahead. You know where you can stick your thumb.'

'Lauren!'

She got to her feet clumsily, jolting the table so Kian's last pint glass tipped over and spilled beer dregs on the table. 'Don't bother.'

'If you're asking me to choose between my mates and you . . .' began Chris, but Lauren wasn't having any of that.

She pointed a finger at him. 'I didn't say that. *You* did. And you were meant to be spending tonight with *me*.'

Before he could protest any more, she turned and marched out of the bar, her heels stomping on the wooden floorboards as her blonde hair swung well above the general mass of heads. On her way out, she nearly knocked over Kian coming back from the bar with two pint glasses and a bottle of Smirnoff Ice.

'Aye aye,' he said to Chris, who was staring helplessly after her retreating back.

Bollocks, he thought. Bollocks. Lauren didn't lose her temper often, because she hated upsetting people, but when she did, God, did he know about it. Besides, Chris knew, deep down, that this time she had the right to be mad.

But sometimes you had to say things, didn't you?

'She'll be back, mate,' said Kian, dumping the drinks on the table. 'Probably just the wrong time of the month. Simple as that.'

Chris took a thoughtful draw on his pint, and Kian made a happy clicking noise with his tongue, meaning a new phone number had just been entered on his phone.

The trouble was, thought Chris, his life wasn't as simple as Kian's, because his life wasn't just his any more. It was Lauren's too. For twenty-five years, like the mortgage said. And the rest after that.

*   *   *

Bridget slipped into the spare room, and shut the door carefully behind her. Frank was dozing in his chair downstairs, and Lauren was having a night out with Chris, staying over at his afterwards. That gave Bridget at least an hour uninterrupted to sort things out, longer if Frank decided to make his own cup of tea when he woke up.

She blinked hard. If things could be sorted out in an hour.

No, she told herself, briskly, just as she told the children at school, when something's wrong, you've got to face up to it. There's no point ignoring what isn't going to go away.

And before she could chicken out again, she opened the plastic folder with all the red bills and bank statements in, and spread them across the bed.

Bridget swallowed as the reality of her situation sank in.

Four credit cards, thousands of pounds of overdraft, one wedding, half of which was still to pay for. And no secret stash of cash to save her bacon.

Bridget and Frank had never used credit cards

much during their marriage—'If we can't pay for it straight off, we can't afford it', had been Frank's motto, inherited from his own dad who'd only stopped keeping money under his mattress in 1985, when he'd gone into hospital and the nurses had refused to be responsible for it. Frank wouldn't have understood the smartness of playing one card off against another. But he did like the novelty of having things now, instead of waiting.

So she hadn't told him that the new lawnmower she'd treated him to had gone on her Capital One card, or that she'd also popped their Easter holiday on the card too, so she could use the cash in her account to pay for the hand-engraved 'Save the Day' cards Lauren had ordered without telling her, as well as putting a deposit on the band.

Bridget bit her lip as she surveyed the statements, each innocuous purchase looming up at her. None of them seemed so expensive on their own, but together . . .

She'd managed to fit everything into her budget perfectly to begin with. But then Frank's pension had turned out to be nearly a third less a month than he'd been expecting, and they'd had to spend fifteen hundred pounds putting the car right after the clutch went; that had gone on the overdraft. Then there were the household bills, so much higher than usual with Lauren back, on the phone and on the internet and in the fridge all the time, and Frank 'enjoying his retirement' with M&S luxury ready-meals, and buying her that eternity ring. Bridget didn't want to alert Frank to the amount of money owing on the cards by writing massive monthly cheques to clear them, so she'd only been paying off the minimum balance, but the amounts splashed out at Bridal Path and Wedding Belles seemed to be double what she remembered spending.

And now she had no idea where she was going to find fifteen thousand, nine hundred and eighty-three pounds, seventeen pence—not counting the rest of the money the wedding was going to cost.

Bridget sat back and stared at the statements, and felt sick.

She knew she should come clean and tell Frank. She should have said something before now, before he even gave Lauren the money, but how could she now, seeing Lauren so sparkly eyed with excitement and love, hugging her dad and telling her what a lifesaver he was and how she had the best parents in the world? And him, all thrilled to be helping her. She'd have had to have a heart of stone.

She rested her elbows on the table and tried to think. They could try to get a second mortgage on the house, although where were they going to find an extra three or four hundred a month? They could cut back. (But on what?) She'd have to tell Frank.

Even as she thought it, something in her recoiled in shame. For their entire marriage, Frank had boasted to their friends about how his Bridget was so pennywise that they'd never had a moment's worry over money in their lives. He was so proud of her for her common sense, and he trusted her to keep them right, financially. And now she'd let him down over something so stupid.

They'd been looking forward to retiring for years, knowing they hadn't a fortune, but they had 'enough to see us out', as he liked to say. It was the time of their lives for relaxing. Enjoying themselves. Not scrimping and panicking about mortgage rates. Bridget's heart ached as she thought about the times they'd slumped in front of the telly, after long days at work, and joked wanly about how it'd all be worth it once they were retired. 'I can't wait to do nothing with you, Mrs Armstrong,' he'd said. 'We'll have enough for chocolate digestives then, eh?'

Frank's blood pressure was only just coming down now after years of strain, and if he found out she was going to have to work longer to pay off a credit-card debt . . .

A sudden, sharp image flashed in front of her eyes, of the two of them dancing at the social night, smooching round the crowded dancefloor, held tightly in each other's arms despite their height difference, moving with the practice of thousands of songs and hundreds of nights. Frank had leaned down to whisper in her ear. 'I don't think I've been this happy since we first met,' he'd said with that gentle smile that had been for her alone since she was seventeen years old.

No, thought Bridget, struggling to keep calm. I'm just going to have to work out a way of dealing with it. Frank needn't know. Lauren definitely mustn't know; if her special day was going to cost this much, there was absolutely no way she was going to allow it to be spoiled by worry.

Special day, thought Bridget. They've got you at last.

She picked up a sheet of paper, with her neat figures running down the right-hand side. So far, she'd managed to drum up nearly four hundred pounds eBaying bits and pieces from around the house, without touching the two or three items that would raise the most money, but had far more sentimental value—her charm bracelet, a painting her mother had given her. Frank hadn't noticed a few china dolls vanishing from the sideboard, but he'd notice if she suddenly wasn't wearing her eternity ring.

The letter from the newest credit-card company sat unopened in the file, and she had to force herself to open it.

When she did, an involuntary gasp escaped from Bridget's throat. There was a note about how much the calculated interest would be next month, when the 0% period expired, if she didn't pay it off in full. When Bridget had been banking on making her smart transfer, that sum had seemed fairly outrageous. Now, along with the minimum payment that she didn't have, it seemed terrifying.

She scrumpled up the letter in fear, then made herself unscrumple it, smoothing it out with shaking fingers.

Bridget sat on the bed, surrounded by the overspill of stuff from Lauren's room—her boxes of wedding shoes, and Save the Day cards, and stacks of glossy magazines full of ideas for spending money on white things—and for the first time in her entire life, she felt scared.

*   *   *

The lights were on when Lauren pulled up outside her parents' house and she sat in the car for a few minutes, to calm herself down. She took two or three deep breaths through her nose, like a horse, rehearsing how much she'd tell her mum, so she'd get the whingeing off her chest, but without making her worry that the wedding was off.

But bloody hell, it wasn't on, all that 'don't make me choose between my mates and you!' business. Who said there had to be a choice? That sounded to Lauren like a previous conversation *someone else* had had with Chris. That someone being a friend who had a vested interest in keeping him available for pub-crawling.

Lauren ran a hand through her hair, smoothing down her blonde fringe as she'd done since she was little. She felt like storming round to that building site and telling them to get a move on with her house, because the sooner Chris was away from Kian Matthews, the better.

She tried to ignore the voice at the back of her head reminding her that Kian wasn't exactly handcuffing Chris to the bar stools, and that he was a big enough boy to say no if he really wanted to.

It was starting to drizzle again, and Lauren hopped from foot to foot on the step as she let herself in. She spotted Dad of the Year asleep in front of the television, a book about ballroom dancing rising and falling on his chest. He looked old, Lauren thought with surprise. When he was asleep, the bags under his eyes seemed pouchier, and his skin slacker, yet when he was awake and bantering away, he looked the same as he'd done all her childhood.

But then her parents *were* old—in their sixties. Her mum was filing credit-card statements with the coffee, and her dad actually wanted slippers for Christmas. Would Chris look like that, snoring in front of the fire with her in forty years' time?

Lauren couldn't picture it.

There was no sign of life in the kitchen, so she made a cup of tea for herself, and one for her mum, then headed upstairs, thinking Bridget might be eBaying more junk on her computer. Good for Mum, she thought, taking care not to tread on Mittens, sprawled out deliciously under the landing radiator. She might be getting on a bit, but she's embracing the internet.

The light was off in her room, but there was a thin strip of light under the spare-bedroom door, the one her mother used as a study.

'Mum?'

As Lauren pushed her way in, there was a flurry of activity, much more than if her mother had just been doing the monthly bills.

'What are you doing?' Lauren crossed the room in one step, and put the mugs down on the paper-strewn desk. Too late, Bridget swept away the papers, but even Lauren could see they were red bills. Very red bills. And when she looked at her mum more closely, she could see Bridget's eyes were red too, as if she'd been crying.

'Mum?' she asked, her heart quickening.

Bridget wiped her eyes with the back of her hand and tried to look normal. Her mouth twisted in a crooked, unconvincing smile.

Mothers should never cry in front of their children, she told herself. Never, never. Not until you were so old they were looking after you and not the other way round.

'I'm fine, love. I thought you were meant to be round at Chris's tonight?'

'I came home early . . . Oh my God, Mum, are you all right?' exclaimed Lauren, dropping to her knees and wrapping her arms around her mother where she sat in the chair. 'Have you been crying?'

To her horror, she felt her mum's shoulders start to shake under her, and for a moment, Lauren was swamped with panic. This was all wrong; her mum was meant to comfort *her* after her crap night with Chris, not the other way round. And if her mum was crying, her capable, sensible mum, then it had to be something *really* bad.

Her mind raced. What could it be? Dad ill? He looked OK downstairs. Billy ill? Something wrong with her granny, in the nursing home?

How can it be to do with those bills? wondered Lauren. Mum's great with her budget. Maybe these are Gran's bills. That must be it, she thought, her imagination filling in the gaps with lurid images as usual—she's had her identity hi-jacked and someone's run up store cards in her name and now Mum's having to sort it out.

Lauren made soothing noises and stroked her mother's thick hair. She felt so small and fragile in her arms. 'Don't cry, Mum,' she said. 'There's nothing we can't sort out. Don't cry.'

She felt Bridget make a gargantuan effort to stop sobbing and pull herself together, and was quite relieved when she sat up, wiping her bright eyes.

'It's fine,' Lauren went on. 'Isn't it? Tell me what's wrong.'

Bridget took a couple of deep breaths, but while she was composing herself, Lauren caught a glimpse of a bill that had slipped onto the floor while Bridget was trying to hide them. The name on the top was definitely Bridget Armstrong and the outstanding amount was thousands. Thousands that they wanted repaying really, really soon.

She looked up, shocked. 'Mum? Are those your credit-card bills?'

Bridget nodded, miserably.

Lauren's mouth dropped open as all the daytime TV shows she'd ever watched about stupid people who'd run up thousands of pounds of debt played in her head. People who'd lost their houses, and broken up their marriages. Chavvy people, greedy people, not like her parents. There had to be a mistake!

'Seriously?' Lauren struggled to make sense of it. 'Is it a computer error? We can go to Watchdog, Mum, these things happen all the time. I was reading about it the other day in *Cosmo*, about some girl who'd—'

Bridget grabbed her wrists. 'Shh!' she hissed urgently. 'I don't want your dad to hear!'

That was even worse to hear. 'Dad doesn't know?'

'Of course he doesn't!'

Lauren stared at her mother, now really freaked out. She'd never seen her like this: wild, worried, keeping secrets from her father. It felt as though the ground was moving beneath her. It was like she'd walked back into her own home, but with a strange, new Mum in it.

Bridget drew in a deep breath, and edited the truth as she went along. 'It's nothing for you to worry about, but . . . I've been a bit foolish with my credit cards.'

'It's for my wedding, isn't it?' said Lauren, realising. 'You've gone into debt over my wedding.'

'Well, no, not exactly, love.' When she saw the troubled expression on Lauren's face Bridget's

384

automatic mother reaction kicked in over her panic. 'Don't start worrying about—'

'How much?' demanded Lauren.

Bridget looked down.

Lauren felt her hands shake. She didn't want to know any of this, but she had to. A childish part of her wanted to walk out of the room, out of the house, get back in the car, and start again, in the hope that when she came in this time, there would be no debts, no panicking Mum, no uncomfortable sense it was all her fault.

Lauren steeled herself. She wasn't a little girl any more. She was about to sign a twenty-five-year mortgage for thousands and thousands of pounds.

'How much?' she asked.

'Quite a lot,' admitted Bridget. 'But it's not something for you to . . .'

Lauren's eyes widened. 'Mum! Just tell me!'

'Fine! You want to know? Including our overdraft, it's nearly sixteen grand!' snapped Bridget.

Lauren's mouth formed the words, sixteen thousand pounds, and she sank onto the bed.

'And that doesn't include the other bits of the wedding we haven't paid for,' Bridget added out of fear rather than anything else, then felt terrible for adding to Lauren's guilt.

They sat in silence, each trying to think of something helpful to say.

Nothing sprang easily to mind.

'Well, according to the bridal magazines, that *is* what the average wedding costs . . .' Lauren began, then stopped, chastened. 'I sound like Irene, don't I?'

'A bit.'

Lauren looked at Bridget, and knew she was being as diplomatic as she could about Chris's mother. Normally, Irene's name would have raised a laugh but it wasn't funny now.

Lauren sighed. 'I can't believe it's that much. I did a budget. I added it all up!'

'Yes, but, Laurie, your budget keeps moving!' Bridget tried not to sound too frustrated. 'You budget for one thing, then get something else, and Irene doesn't help with all her suggestions, I know, but . . .' She raked her fingers through her hair. 'It's not just the wedding. I think there've been some impulse buys on there too.'

Lauren looked up at Bridget and her blue eyes were confused. 'But, Mum, I thought you'd set some money aside for my wedding! Dad told me you had a wedding savings fund. I didn't realise you were putting it all on *credit*.'

'We're not! There *is* a wedding account, but your father . . .' Bridget stopped herself in the nick of time.

What was the point of making Lauren feel even worse? There was nothing they could do about that money now, not without ruining Lauren *and* Chris's chance to get started in their own home. Bridget's own married life had got off to a significantly better start than her sister's, largely because she and Frank had had their own living room to argue in, instead of being trapped with their in-laws.

'That's for the reception, love,' she said. 'That's covered. I must admit, I hadn't realised it was going to be quite so . . . elaborate, but we'll manage,' she said, even though she didn't believe it herself. She patted Lauren's hand. 'It'll sort itself out.'

Lauren looked at her mother. Did she think she was stupid or something? You didn't just *manage* when you owed sixteen grand on your cards!

'No, it *won't*,' she said. Her lip jutted out. 'Mum, I've seen what happens to people on television, getting into debt! It can ruin your life!'

'I'm not going to go to some loan shark! Don't think that!'

'So what can you do?'

'Well . . .' There was a long pause, that didn't reassure Lauren at all. 'We can remortgage the house.'

Though that would mean telling Frank, of course, thought Bridget. And it didn't answer the question of how they'd be able to afford higher mortgage payments, on their pensions.

'Mum,' said Lauren, slowly, then hesitated.

'What, love?' Bridget tried to look cheerful.

'Mum, you know that money Dad lent me and Chris for the house? If I can get that back from the bank . . .' She paused, trying not to let the disappointment show in her eyes, despite her words. 'Maybe Irene can lend us the whole deposit, and then I'll pay her back.'

'No,' said Bridget at once. 'You're not doing that.'

'I'd rather do that than see you and Dad be made homeless!' she wailed. 'How can I be happy in that house, knowing you're going bankrupt?'

'Laurie, you're over-reacting,' said Bridget, tightly. 'We'll just have to cut back a bit, and I'll go and talk to the bank next week. I'm sure they'll have some solution.' She squeezed Lauren's hand, still clutching hers. 'It's not going to spoil your wedding, love. I promise.'

Lauren said nothing, because she was too busy hating herself for thinking, yes, it's going to totally spoil my wedding. Totally. How could it not? The individual silver roses on each plate and the fairy lights in the outdoors-indoors box trees shrivelled before her eyes. Between cutting back on all her gorgeous plans, and feeling personally responsible for bringing unholy stress on her mum and dad, how on earth could she be happy?

And that was without Chris behaving less like a fiancé and more like a lad about town.

Lauren twisted her hair round her finger, something she hadn't done for years.

Bridget saw Lauren's distress and wished she could wind the clock back to that first stupid credit-card application. Better yet, to years and years back, to when she could fix things easily for Lauren, when all it took to make her smile was a strawberry Mivvi.

Unbeknownst to her, Lauren was thinking pretty much the same thing.

'Come on,' said Bridget, hugging Lauren. 'It'll come right.'

Lauren leaned in and hugged her mother, but even though she really wanted to, she didn't believe her.

CHAPTER TWENTY-SEVEN

The conversation Katie was dreading having with Ross didn't happen immediately; instead, it hung between them like a thunderstorm all day, the air heavy with tension as they went through all the normal Saturday motions with the children. Only now, Katie felt, every tiny thing had taken on massive significance: who paid for the doughnuts, who changed Jack, who told Hannah to use her indoors voice when her yelling attracted disapproving attention. It felt as if they were acting out the roles of Mum and Dad, instead of their usual natural parenting. She tried to distract herself by worrying about Jo and Greg, but even that led straight back to her and Ross.

A sugar-crazed half-hour or so at the drive-through doughnut shop was followed by another two sugar-crazed hours of Hannah and Molly running around in the princess-y dressing-up clothes Jo had bought Hannah for her birthday. Katie knew she was letting Hannah get away with some equally princess-y behaviour—ordering Molly off her new bike, for a start—but she couldn't bring herself to tell her off, and that wasn't a good sign.

At half-three, Ross murmured, 'Do you think that's long enough? For Greg and Jo?'

'I don't know.' Katie kept one eye on Molly and Hannah, now enacting a Disney coronation. 'How long's too long?'

'I'll take the girls home,' he said, getting up from the baby jigsaw he was doing with Rowan. 'It's time for their tea. Do them good to get back into a routine.'

Katie kept up a bright stream of chat as she made some tea for Hannah and Jack, but inside she was worried about Jo. Really worried. A corner of Jo's bubbly confidence had been peeled back, and Katie was shocked at the vulnerable woman underneath. Was she really so paranoid that she'd believe she and Greg were having an affair? Had he really undermined her self-confidence so much? And, she berated herself, what sort of a self-absorbed friend had she been not to notice?

Unless Jo was speaking from a guilty conscience, wheedled an insinuating voice in her head. Unless she only suspects you because she's up to something herself with Ross . . .

No, Katie told herself firmly. No. Not Ross. Not Jo.

She was in the middle of bathing Jack when Ross came home, and heard Hannah's surprised 'Daddy!' from downstairs.

Jack splashed his starfish hands at her, and giggled, but Katie held him still. There was something odd in Hannah's voice.

'I'm fine, sweetie!' she heard Ross call, as his feet jogged upstairs. 'Silly Daddy! Bumped his head!'

Katie froze, the baby sponge in her hand, and suddenly Ross was in the bathroom behind her, shutting the door.

'Don't say anything,' he warned her, running some water in the basin.

But she turned round anyway and let out a gasp of surprise.

An angry red mark had swollen up on Ross's cheekbone and his lip was split. He stood by the mirror, looking hangdog as he tentatively touched the swelling, but still with the last flickers of anger in his eyes.

'Oh my God!' Without thinking, Katie leaped up and took his face in her hands. His skin was cold, from being outside, and smooth. 'Ross! What

390

happened?'

He grimaced with pain. 'It's nothing.'

Katie's chest swelled protectively. 'Don't be ridiculous! What is it? Did you have an accident?'

'Sort of. I punched Greg. But he goes to the gym and does tai-bo so he made a better job of punching me back.'

Katie stared. Ross punching someone? That was beyond out of character; it went all the way to surreal. Ross wouldn't even cook mussels because he felt cruel knowing they were boiling to death.

'Why?' she managed.

Ross pulled a face, and moved out of her hands, so he could soak a flannel in the cold water. 'He . . . said some things that made me lose my rag.'

'What things?' Katie turned back to Jack, frightened he'd slip while she wasn't watching, but he was playing happily with his fishes. To be on the safe side, she pulled him out of the water anyway and wrapped him, wailing, in a towel. 'What did he say that you had to punch him?' she went on, drying Jack off as distractingly as she could.

'He was . . . vile. About Jo. And he made some insinuations about me and you. I don't know . . . I just couldn't let him stand there, and be so smug and offensive. Ow!' Ross touched his lip. 'I'm crap at the big hero stuff. But it made me feel better at the time.'

Katie stopped towelling. 'The kids didn't see, did they?'

'No.' He shook his head. 'Jo was with them in the kitchen. She didn't hear what he said either. It was just me and him.' He snorted. 'Makes it sound like a Western, doesn't it?'

'You hit him . . . out of *honour*?'

391

Ross turned to her, and even with a flannel pressed to his cheekbone, he looked different somehow. Less soft. More sharply focused. There was still some anger in his eyes, and it made them flinty, not amused and gentle, as they normally were. 'Partly. And partly, if I'm honest, because I wanted to hit something. Greg was an arsehole, and he got in the way. Now I feel a bit stupid, all right? I don't like hitting people. I won't be doing it again. But Greg . . .' He pressed his tongue against his lip and winced. 'I know you like the guy, but if you'd been there and heard some of the things he said about Jo, and about us . . .'

'I don't like the guy,' Katie interrupted him. 'I spoke to him this morning. He's a total prick.'

Ross raised his eyebrows, but said nothing.

'I was so wrong about him,' Katie went on. 'I thought he was better than that, but I bet he's got some new woman on the side, probably thinks he's invincible right now. Jo's better off without him, if he can't see how lucky he is.'

As she spoke, her throat tightened; if she couldn't appreciate Ross, did that mean he was better off without *her*?

I'm not as bad as Greg, she thought fiercely. I can still make this work out.

'That's what I told Jo,' said Ross, cutting into her thoughts. 'She deserves someone who'll appreciate her.'

'Yes,' said Katie, 'she does.'

'Talc!' said Jack. 'Daddy, talc!'

Jack liked talcum powder, for some reason; given half a chance, he'd have the bathroom snow-drifted.

Katie reached for the powder but Jack whined,

'No. *Daddy*, talc.'

She would have insisted normally, but tonight, Katie had no fight left, so she handed it to Ross, who proceeded to puff and squirt talcum powder all over the bathroom, to Jack's happy giggles.

'Mummy join in!' commanded Jack, and she did, putting the Hoovering-up out of her mind, as she clapped her hands, as Ross giggled with him, pulling faces. For a moment, all three of them were laughing at the same time, and Katie felt a sudden flash of hope that they might still be able to get through this, because they both loved the children, and the children were part of their marriage too.

'We need to talk,' said Ross, after he'd talced Jack to his specifications, and the sudden gravity in his voice cut that little hope dead.

'I know. But let's get the children to bed first?' said Katie, pulling Jack's pyjamas over his downy head. 'Later.'

She knew she was delaying, but there was something new in Ross that was making her think this might not be as easy to fix as she'd hoped. It was a Ross she didn't think she knew.

*   *   *

They got through the rest of Saturday night with Ross making up some hilarious story about walking into a naughty slapping tree that he acted out so amusingly Hannah bought it wholesale, and even demanded action replays. They ate supper, and Hannah went to bed with only the usual demands for extra stories from Mummy, which Katie was happy to give her, and then fell asleep quickly, worn out with the past few days.

Katie sat for ten minutes outside her door, not wanting to go downstairs, but knowing she had to.

The conversation she'd had with Jo, and the almost identical one she'd then had with Greg went round and round in her mind like water circling a plughole. It was weird how a matter of hours could turn the way you saw something completely upside-down.

The thought of Ross moving out made her sick. But at the same time, she still couldn't dredge up any feelings more passionate than concern and affection for him.

And nothing was going to change; she'd still have to work, he'd still coast along, being great with the kids, but like a brother to her.

Was that enough?

Ross was loading the dishwasher in the kitchen, with the martyr-like demeanour of someone who rarely remembered to do it normally.

'So,' said Katie, 'are you ready for us to talk?'

Ross put the last dish in, and stood up slowly, then turned to face her. His expression was calm, but Katie sensed a distance between them, a separation of mental space that she hadn't felt for years. She had no idea what he was going to say and her skin went cold.

'No, I need to talk,' said Ross. 'I'd like you to listen, and I don't want you to interrupt like you always do until I've said everything. Otherwise it'll turn into a row and I'm past that, after today.'

Katie opened her mouth, then made herself close it. She nodded.

'Right.' Ross gestured to the table. 'Should we sit down?'

It seemed ridiculous to make it even more

394

formal, but Katie sat down anyway.

'I've been thinking over the last few days,' said Ross. 'About what you said. About not loving me any more. I don't think I've ever felt so humiliated or hurt in my life. I gave things up for you, and because I thought it would make you happy, and now you're telling me that, basically, I'm not a man to you any more. And how is that my fault?'

Katie flinched.

'I'm not going to lie to you, I was . . . gutted, and I wanted to pack my stuff and leave, but I can't do that, not now we've got the children to put first. We've got to think of what's best for them. So I need you to give me some straight yes or no answers. Nothing else. Just yes or no.'

'OK,' said Katie, cautiously. 'If I can.'

'Are you going to move out?'

'No!' she said, startled.

Ross mocked her startled expression. 'Well, do you expect me to move out?'

Katie blinked. 'No! I mean, not unless you want to. I don't know.'

'You don't know.' He looked sarcastic. 'I thought you'd have planned this a bit better. Done a spreadsheet agenda or something.'

'Ross, I haven't planned anything. I kept telling you.' This is the moment, thought Katie. *Take it back. Tell him you're not sure.* 'It's not definite, I mean, I'm not saying I don't . . .'

'It doesn't work like that,' said Ross, his voice suddenly quite tough. 'You can't just say, "Oh, I only wanted to get it off my chest! I didn't really mean it!" and expect me to *forget*. You've said it now.'

'No,' said Katie, startled by his bitterness. He

395

was right. She had to take responsibility for what she'd started.

'I'm the one who looks after the children,' he went on, 'so I can't move out. And anyway, I can't afford to pay rent—and you can't afford to stop working or get a nanny. So we might as well just stay as we are. But . . .' Ross spoke briskly, as if he was trying not to feel what he was saying. 'If you're going to treat me like an au pair, then I need two days a week off, when you can sort out childcare. I want an evening off during the week, too. And I don't want to share a bed with you any more, so I'll move into the spare room. That's my space. I'll move my computer in there, so the kids don't think it's such a big deal, and hopefully they won't notice. It's about time we stopped them coming into our bed at night anyway.' He corrected himself painfully. 'Your bed.'

'Fine,' said Katie, though she was beginning to feel nauseous. 'If that's what you want to do, then fine.'

'Don't put it back on to me,' he said. 'This is what you want. You don't love me any more. You can't bear to touch me.'

'I haven't said that,' Katie began but Ross glared with a hurt pride in his eyes. It cut through her like acid.

'You don't need to say it. When was the last time we made love?'

Her eyes dropped to the table; to the pine-cones Hannah had brought her, to Jack's dummy that he wasn't supposed to have these days.

'Don't *you* put it all on me—when was the last time you touched me?' she said. 'It's not like you ever want to.'

Ross let out a frustrated groan. 'I'm not an *animal*, Katie. I'm not going to force myself on you when you get into bed and turn your back on me. I mean, I could understand, after Jack was born . . . but I thought eventually, you'd want me to touch you again, not just hold you while you fall asleep. But you haven't, and you make me feel like some kind of sex pest if I do try to start anything.'

Katie stared at him, trying to overlay the sexy designer she'd fancied so much in the pub with this cold, weary man. She was tired, constantly, but that wasn't the only reason her desire had died. She longed to point out that the only reason Jack was conceived in the first place was because of a brief phase of freelance work Ross had taken on for the local paper; the thrill of him showing some creative spark, of taking some of the burden off her, of getting properly dressed in the morning, had led to a little holiday for the three of them—and then to Jack.

But that would sound too cruel, and too materialistic, so she said nothing.

'I miss it,' he said softly. 'I miss making love to you.'

Katie gulped, unable to bear the humbled longing in Ross's voice. 'I do too.'

She ached with nostalgia for a time that seemed like someone else's memory, and for a moment, she thought Ross would put his hands over hers on the table, linking his fingers with hers, the way he used to in the days when they went out for dinner: their little sign at the table that he couldn't wait to get her home and into bed. Sometimes not even into bed, sometimes on the stairs or the sofa, her slim legs entwined around his.

He didn't. He folded his hands, waiting for her to say something, but Katie didn't know what to say. It was as if someone was desperately ill; there was so much she wanted to say, but she was too scared of using the wrong words that she couldn't speak at all.

Well, something is ill, she reminded herself. Your marriage, and those holding-hands-at-seventy dreams you had. It's never going to happen, but instead, you're going to have to live in the shell of what you thought would work, for years and years and years.

Katie looked at Ross over the table, the pink braid still in his hair where Hannah had twisted it, his cheek swollen from Greg's punch. The same old Ross, but different. A Ross who didn't love her enough to argue with her any more.

'I don't want you to leave,' she blurted out.

'I'm not going to,' he replied, and pushed his chair back from the table. 'I'll move my stuff.'

Katie felt tears force their way up her throat, choking her. She wanted so hard to say the right thing, to stop all this, but her mind was blank.

'Ross,' she called out, when he was at the door. 'Ross?'

He turned back.

Katie had to force herself to say it. 'Do you still love me?'

He paused for an agonising few seconds, then said, 'Don't make me answer that,' and walked out.

CHAPTER TWENTY-EIGHT

Angelica stood in her mother's small back garden, breathing in the cool November air, trying to put her finger on what had changed. It wasn't just the weather turning nippier. It was something inside herself, sharpening up as her old lives, the different Angelicas jostled for space, challenging her to decide what was real, and what was a myth she'd forgotten she'd made up.

Underneath. She'd never liked to peer underneath before, but now . . . Now, she realised she was almost curious to see what would be there.

The light had nearly gone but she could make out the pale white stone that marked where Rosie was buried, appropriately enough, under a rose bush by the back wall. Full of guilt for being poolside in Florida when she finally died ('I'm so sorry, Angie, she just stopped eating . . .'), Angelica had sent ten rose bushes for her mother to plant in Rosie's memory, but only three had survived, and were now all gnarled up, leafless and hunched against the coming frosts.

Rosie had been her constant companion until she moved to Florida, and Jerry. Angelica had always claimed to hate pets, but on a whim she'd picked up the little Yorkshire terrier at the dogs' home the first time she and Tony fell out, and Rosie, unlike the men in Angelica's life, had never looked at her with anything less than devotion in her liquid-brown eyes.

All Angelica's unconditional love had been lavished on Rosie. Safer than lavishing it on a man, and more likely to come back to her.

Selfish, she thought now. I've been a selfish cow. I should never have left Rosie, even if she did remind me of Tony. Maybe it was a blessing we never had children.

Maybe.

With a heavy sigh, she turned back into the house, and steeled herself to face the box.

It had been delivered that morning, but Angelica hadn't been able to bring herself to open it straight away. But now, she knew it had to be done, and mixed herself a gin and tonic to work up the courage to slit the brown tape and pull back the layers and layers of frothy bubblewrap.

It was a huge, heavy box, that two men had carried into the sitting room for her, and it still had the markings on it from the storage unit it had been stored in for over ten years.

'What's in here, love? A body?' one of the young men had joked, pretending to hold his back.

Angelica had laughed because, in a way, there was a body in there: the old Angelica, and the multi-coloured, bejewelled and bedazzled skins she'd danced in. She tipped them each twenty quid, before her judgement could get the better of her, and she insisted they took the box away again.

Most of Angelica's life was in storage, and she hadn't really missed it. Memento shelves weren't her style. Until she moved into Jerry's sprawling mansion, she'd lived in a succession of tiny Soho studios and one-bed flats that barely had a cupboard, let alone an attic. Every time one phase ended, she'd pack what she didn't want hanging around as reminders, and lock it up in her storage unit. Her first years dancing in London, her life with Tony, her competition days, her marriage—all in boxes. She didn't want to be reminded of the past, but she couldn't quite bring herself to sever her connection to it either. It meant it belonged to her, which was different, Angelica thought, to her belonging to it.

For the first time, though, she felt ready to start shedding these skins for good, and accepting the one she'd had all along. Besides which, there was something in this box that she wanted.

Angelica took the final gulp of gin and tonic, put down the heavy glass, and pulled aside the last layer of old bubblewrap.

A pungent, familiar smell of dry-cleaning fluid, and perfume hit her nose as she lifted the first dress out: her red ballroom dress, from her first years on the professional circuit. It was delicate but extraordinarily heavy, with hundreds of ruby-red stones set like curling flames up the bodice, and long floating chiffon sleeves that trailed behind her like angel wings as Tony swept her round the floor in the smooth, elegant patterns of the waltz and the foxtrot. Angelica held it high, to let the long skirt hang; it was fluted and cut to rise up in a cloud when they spun, moving as one, revealing her finely turned ankles in the matching crimson satin court shoes.

They were stoned too, she remembered: tiny roses on the toe.

Just holding the dress again made her feet ache to dance as she had done then, when she was twenty-five and had no idea about anything.

This isn't what you're looking for, she reminded herself sternly, and laid the ballroom gown carefully over the small sofa.

The next dress was from the same time, but it was for Latin, and cut tighter and higher to show off the quick, flirtatious leg movements. Angelica murmured adoringly as she stroked the shimmering scarlet satin, fringed along the slanted hem with long jet beads. It finished right up, almost on her hip, and instead of sleeves, it had scarlet armlets that emphasised her slender arms when she wound them round Tony's neck, or flexed them in the showy Latin poses.

Everyone said she and Tony were made for Latin; both dark, and stormy, with long limbs and snaky hips. Not that they were bad at the ballroom dances—she had the necessary grace to make the formal European dances look effortless—but the fiery Latin rhythms inspired a kind of magical lustre to their steps, as though their shoes were singeing the floor as they passed.

Then again, the Latin dances were all about sex, she thought. And she and Tony were all about sex. None of those dirty glances and seductive stroking were faked with them, not like some of their competitors. At first Angelica had pitied the girls who had to feign grand passion with partners who were more Liberace than Valentino off the floor, but in the end, she had to admit that, like the deep tans everyone sported, keeping things artificial was by far the safest way.

She lifted out another short, thigh-skimming samba confection: gold, this time, with silvery flowers appliquèd on the bodice, and virtually no back to it at all, just silvery chains. Tony had a silver shirt to match it, peacock that he was. They'd won a national title when she'd worn this dress—or 'what little there was of it', as her father had apparently commented when she'd sent the photos home. She'd only found that out last year, when her mother had been rambling in her memories, and Angelica had relived those years again, at her side.

Angelica's breath stopped in her chest as she held it in her shaking hands. Feeling the fabric, instead of looking at flat photographs, made it all vivid, as if the emotions were soaked into the material along with the old sweat and smoke and body oil and the smell of the Empress Ballroom, Blackpool. She felt the agony in her calves and toes, and the exhilaration and the triumph of that final, flexed pose that said, 'we've won'.

If she'd known then it was going to be her final dance with Tony, she would never have sent it to the cleaners. She'd have kept it, just as it was, with his fingerprints and aftershave and quick breaths still on it.

She carried on delving into the box, and laid out one dress after another over the sofa, until it was piled with net and sequins and trailing chiffon floats, most in glowing shades of red—tomato, scarlet, lipstick crimson. The box was huge, but still held only seven of her sumptuous, complicated dresses. Angelica knew there were at least ten more in storage, thousands of pounds' worth. She always had more dresses than anyone else, and they were always more twinkling, more beaded, more unusual. Then again, she'd always eaten less than anyone else, gone out less than anyone else, and spent virtually every penny she made on her gowns and shoes.

Everything else, she knew, someone would buy for her. But Angelica made it a rule that she, and only she, paid for the gorgeous clothes she danced in.

The dress at the bottom of the box was the one she was looking for: her favourite tango dress.

Well, she corrected herself, stroking the sequins on the thin shoulder straps, her second favourite, *competition tango* dress.

Her favourite tango dress was the one she wore to dance the Argentine tango with Tony, and that was their own dance, their private dance that wasn't for judging, that they danced in the milongas, the hot tango salons. It was more like foreplay, and fighting, than a dance. And that dress was the one he loved: simple and tight and sexy, with none of the gaudy embellishments you needed to shine under the unforgiving spotlights and the judges' critical eyes.

This, though, was the formal dress she'd worn for the exhibition tangos they danced in ballrooms round the country, as well as for one or two smaller competitions. It wasn't very forgiving, to put it mildly, and even back then, when she could count each velvety rib, any sign of PMS-bloat meant Angelica didn't bother trying to squeeze into the tight, back-laced bodice. It was cut on the bias, from coal-black satin, with a long, narrow skirt, slit up the thigh to allow for the sinuous strides that characterised the ballroom tango. Angelica had insisted that her dressmaker—a patient woman who lived in Tooting and was used to the feverish demands of half-starved dancers—lined it with blood-red satin, so it would flash as she slid and twisted her body into the dramatic turns.

That red lining was her way of bringing a little of the teasing, hot-breathed Argentine tango she and

Tony danced in private to the rigid formality of the competition style: the Europeans in their dinner suits and polite tea dances might have smoothed the raw edges, formalising the steps until it was a sleek, polite parody of Latin seduction, but the secret crimson splashes were her sign to Tony that she knew what was beating at the heart of their ricochet head-turns and straight armholds.

She sighed, feeling the mesh against her palm. She half wanted to try them on, knowing she wasn't so much bigger now than she was in her best dancing days, but she was scared to, of seeing how much had changed in her face.

The right dress made such a difference. Not just to the dance, but to everything. The magic of those sequins and stones and cleverly cut skirts: they bestowed a fairy-godmother touch of glamour, a VIP pass into a Technicolor world where everyone's eyes were on you. You couldn't be your normal everyday self in a tiny scrap of satin, held on by flesh-toned angelskin fabric so it seemed, from the audience, that only air and the speed of your steps was keeping it up. You couldn't shuffle, or stoop, when hundred of sequins glittered with every move you made, and yards of chiffon swirled around your feet. You weren't just Cyd Charisse or Ginger Rogers in your mind, you actually looked like Ginger Rogers, and the music playing for you was just the same as was played for her. The dress and the dance and the music, all together, meant you could turn a daydream into something real, for those three minutes on the floor, his hands holding yours, your knees brushing his thigh. You could be a dream woman, and your partner could be the man of your most romantic fantasies.

Angelica's plan was to lend Katie one of her ballroom dresses to try on. She knew it would make the world of difference to the way Katie saw herself, and she hoped it would help her understand that dancing the woman's steps didn't mean the end of feminism as she knew it.

Angelica felt sorry for Katie. She was the only woman she'd ever taught who hadn't turned up for the second class in her most gorgeous party dress, just for the chance to wear it out. Every week, the same plain black dress, the same awkward posture.

Katie could be a much better dancer than she realised—Angelica knew it, even if Katie didn't. She was athletic, and though she wasn't the quickest at picking up steps, she didn't forget them, or get confused when the music changed. What was really holding Katie back, thought Angelica, picturing her self-conscious cha-cha, was her inability to let herself go, and to trust her partner to lead her properly. She wouldn't even relax with experienced leads like Frank or Baxter; Angelica watched her resisting them until they gave up. She was so focused on being Katie, that she just couldn't relax enough to play the waltzing princess, or the unbridled hot-to-trot Latina.

Lauren, on the other hand . . . Angelica smiled, just thinking about her. She was a natural because dressing up and playing was something she actively enjoyed. When Angelica watched Lauren in class, she saw her blue eyes were miles away, and she knew Lauren was letting her own imaginary love scene play out in her mind, sweeping round the floor with her lovely long arms and legs in perfect instinctive lines.

And Jo was good too, because she knew how to

hold herself. It was a curious thing, a dancing cliché that Angelica had learned over time was true, but bigger girls really did have much more grace on the floor than their skinnier friends. Being constantly aware of their bodies meant they carried themselves carefully and lightly. Jo had hips that moved, and she danced like someone whose inhibitions had long gone from romping around with kids; she wasn't afraid to get things wrong, or look silly, and Angelica could tell from watching Frank's face, or Ross's, that she was a pleasure to dance with because of that.

She looked down at the tango dress in her hands. Its old sequins glimmered in the soft light of the table lamp, as if they longed to be spangled by a glitterball again, shimmering like serpent's scales as the dress whisked about.

Angelica had a moment's doubt. Was it interfering to give it to Katie? Something was wrong between Katie and Ross, though Katie seemed to think no one could tell. She was better at disguising her unhappiness than he was. But years of scrutinising couples who were hiding furious quarrels behind the rictus grin of their show faces had given Angelica x-ray eyes for tension. Tony always said she could predict couples splitting even before they knew themselves.

Well, you had to, didn't you? Angelica had reasoned. It wasn't prurience, it was smart business sense. Good partners didn't come on the market often, and when they did, it was all change for everyone.

No, something was definitely wrong between Ross and Katie and it made her sad, because they were a nice pair. Decent, she felt, unlike Jo's Greg, whom she didn't trust an inch. He was good looking, but a pushy lead, too forceful, refusing to slow down a little for Peggy, tutting when Trina messed up her steps in front of her, so Angelica would know it was Trina who'd messed up, not him.

Worry about one couple at a time, she told herself. And that's if you've got the nerve to tell them how to fix their marriage—in this dress of all dresses?

She hugged the fabric to her chest, releasing another memory-tingling noseful of ballrooms and starch and hairspray. She closed her eyes to smell it better, and when she opened them, she realised there was one more dress in the box, screwed up in a ball so small it had got lost in the packing.

Angelica leaned forward and pulled it out: it was Tony's favourite—the slinky black jersey practice dress, cut very simply, but with a deep v in the back which showed off her angular shoulder-blades. It had been thrown in the back of her wardrobe the last time she saw him, and it had stayed there, to be packed up for storage with her formal gowns when she moved to Florida with Jerry. New partner, new dresses, that was the rule.

She held it in her hands, feeling its heaviness, and imagined it on Katie, falling in drapey folds over her neat hips and slim waist. She had good legs, Katie, and with that boring blonde bob slicked back or held with some glitzy diamanté headpiece . . .

Maybe.

Angelica smiled, then sighed.

It would be something else she was bringing full circle. And that was the point of coming back to

CHAPTER TWENTY-NINE

Lauren woke early on Sunday morning, and her first thought, almost before her eyes were open, was about Bridget's worry-lined face last night. She'd seemed old and anxious. Not her reliable, ageless mother, but a middle-aged woman with a huge problem.

That was closely followed by her wedding, and the realisation that matching white horses weren't just a possibility—they were now totally out of the question.

Lauren lay motionless in her warm bed, and struggled yet again to work out how she felt, and what she should do.

There was no sound from her parents' room next door, and she wondered if her mum was lying there too, unable to sleep for worrying.

Were they too old to remortgage? What if her parents had to sell the house to pay those bills? Move somewhere smaller?

She closed her eyes as her heart sped up and her chest tightened.

Deep breaths, she told herself, as Dr Bashir had trained them to say at the surgery if a patient started to come over too emotional at the desk. Deep breaths. Focus on the breath going in . . . and out. And in . . . and out.

It was fine going out, but as she breathed in, she saw her mother's drawn and worried eyes, and that file of cold red bills, and the slashes of misery it would put through their happy, loving marriage when it came out that Mum had kept all this from Dad.

Then on the out breath, she saw the croquembouches and the beautiful fairy-tale dress, and the gold plates at the buffet, everything being swept away and replaced with—well, with what? Her dream wedding, the one she'd planned in her head since she was fourteen, gone, just like that. Never to be had again.

Her throat tightened just thinking about it and her eyes snapped open.

They fell immediately on a brochure for a local castle venue, one with a real maze where you could have your wedding pictures taken.

'Come on, Lauren,' she said aloud. 'It's going to be fine. I'll tell Chris everything, and he'll know what to do.'

She was still a bit annoyed with him after that face-off at the pub the previous night, but on balance, the thought of sinking into the comfort of Chris's warm arms, and feeling his hands stroking her hair, tipped the scales in his favour. Plus, she reckoned, he'd be desperate to show how supportive he could be. She and Chris didn't argue. Not for long anyway.

*   *   *

Once Lauren was in her car on the way to Kian's flat, things started to look brighter. Chris was doing well at the dealership; maybe he could get an advance on his bonus and they could pay for more of the wedding themselves? Or better, he could ask Irene for some money to pay for some stuff? She was always offering to chip in for the cost of things.

Then there were her brothers. I could ring Billy, she thought; he'd just sold his house, so he'd have some spare cash to lend Mum—and then we wouldn't have to cancel quite so much.

A few gold plates slipped back, and her mental wedding dress flounced up from its scaled-back Monsoon stand-in state, to a bridal shop one, with an extra ruffly skirt.

For a second, Lauren remembered the look on her mother's face when she'd suggested talking to Irene, and she felt a bit uncomfortable. And there was always the off-chance that Billy might tell Dad. But what was the point in being so proud? Mum was in trouble, and Irene was only too happy to pay. What else did Irene have to spend her money on anyway?

I can sell my car too, she thought, nobly, parking outside the flat and locking her little Clio. It's not worth much, but it's a start.

A bell rang in the back of Lauren's mind that the handmade wedding dress currently under construction cost exactly three and half times more than Chris had paid for her car, but she didn't pay too much attention to it.

'Chris!' she called, letting herself in. 'Chris?'

The curtains were still drawn in the flat, but she could hear the shower running.

They must have had a late one after I left last night, she thought, picking her way through the pizza boxes in the sitting room. The whole flat stank of lager and stale smoke. Lauren felt bad about storming out of the pub like that, but Chris needed to know that she wouldn't stand this stupid competition between her and Kian for his

411

attention.

He was an adult now, a fiancé. And now they had adult-sized problems to deal with.

Lauren was just about to go through to Chris's room, through the sitting room, when a small girl with an even smaller towel wrapped round her Fake Baked body, and another round her head, stepped out of the bathroom, and right into her.

They stared at each other in mutual shock, as the girl clung to what Lauren knew was actually a hand towel.

She must be Kian's pull from last night.

The poor thing, thought Lauren. No wonder she wanted a shower.

'Hi,' she said, with a friendly smile, dumping her handbag on the sofa, where various clothes still lay crumpled as they fell. Lauren tried not to look, as did the other girl. 'Don't mind me, I'm not stopping. Kian up and about yet, then? Or is he still sleeping it off?'

'Kian?' The girl's face was blank.

'Oh, my God, you mean you didn't even get to exchanging names?' exclaimed Lauren. That was bad, even by Kian's standards. Still, the girl was pretty cute: dark hair and eyes, no visible tattoos. Not very Longhampton. Whatever it was that Kian had, he certainly knew how to use it. 'For future reference, his name's Kian Matthews, and he sometimes talks about himself in the third person, so I'm surprised it didn't register, to be honest. He must have been really plying you with booze!'

'I wasn't that drunk!' she protested, angrily. 'I didn't come back with a Kian! I came home with *Chris*! Excuse me, but I have no idea who Kian *is*!'

'What?' Lauren's knees went weak, as if

412

someone had tripped her up. Her body suddenly felt completely empty, and she could barely form words through her shock. 'Chris? You're sure about that?'

'Yes, Chris. Chris Markham, works at the Jaguar dealership. I'm not some *slapper*!' The girl pouted, and through her rising hurt and anger, Lauren couldn't help noticing that she was one of those small, sexy pert girls who'd always made her feel so galumphing and lanky. The girls who always ended up with cool guys like Chris.

All of a sudden, Lauren felt fourteen again; gangly, red cheeked and, worst of all, the last to know *anything*.

'And who are you?' the girl demanded. 'Do you live here?'

'I'm his fiancée!' yelled Lauren, drawing herself up to her full five foot ten. She towered over her. 'I am Chris's *fiancée*!'

The fury of Lauren's words knocked the wind out of both their sails.

'Oh, shit,' said the girl in a small voice. 'Shit.'

Lauren might have looked fierce, but she was falling to bits like a jigsaw inside. Am I asleep, she wondered, frantically. Am I in the middle of some horrible, cruel dream? First Mum, behaving so out of character, and now Chris. It's just wrong.

So that's why Chris hadn't answered his phone after she left the pub! Her mind filled with excruciating images of him chatting this girl up with that flirty little twinkle in his eye, buying her drinks, laughing at her jokes, then taking her home in a taxi, with Kian egging him on, telling him he was too young to be settling down—she could just hear him now.

413

And then, undressing her, and kissing her, doing all the intimate things that he'd learned to do with *her*! In their bed! Lauren's skin crawled and she couldn't think any further.

Just then a bedroom door opened, and Chris's bleary figure emerged, a hand over his face to shield his eyes from the light. His bare chest was visible under the dressing gown he'd hauled on over his boxers, and Lauren felt physically sick at the sight of his pale golden chest hair. This girl had been kissing that moments ago, touching him . . .

'What the hell's going on out here?' he demanded, rubbing his eyes. 'Some of us aren't feeling so great . . .'

Lauren marched over, and before she knew what she was doing, she gave him an angry shove.

Chris roared in surprise, staggering back into the sofa with the impact.

'You bastard!' she sobbed, raining down blows on his chest with her balled-up fists, shock and humiliation fanning the flames of her fury. 'You cheating, lying bastard! Is that why you didn't want me to come out with you? Is that why you were so keen to move in with Kian? So you could see other girls on the side, without me knowing? Is it?'

Chris looked dazed, and tried to grab hold of her flailing hands. 'Slow down, Loz. What are you talking—'

'Don't try to get out of it! She told me! She told me you took her home! She . . .'

Lauren stopped, and looked round, but the girl had slunk off, and the clothes were missing off the sofa.

'Loz,' pleaded Chris, 'I can explain everything, it's not what it looks like, honestly, it's—'

'Don't bother,' spat Lauren. 'Tell Kian—tell him he's got what he wanted. You can have as many single nights out as he wants now! Because you're not having any with *me*!'

She would have said a bit more, but the thick tears were already choking up her throat, making it raw, and her heart was beating so hard she was surprised he couldn't see it, banging away in her chest.

Chris was still yelling, 'Lauren, Lauren!' as she stumbled down the stairs, her feet slipping on the nasty carpet, and she had to cling onto the banister to stop herself falling as tears blurred her vision.

She knew she wasn't really safe to drive, but yanked open the car door anyway, wanting to be gone before Chris could run out and give her some cobbled-together 'explanation' straight from the Kian Matthews Book of Slimy Male Behaviour. As she turned the ignition the CD player came on, and it was the compilation of songs Angelica had made for them to practise to.

'Once Upon a Dream' from *Sleeping Beauty*— she'd been singing along to that only yesterday, thinking how amazing it was that a guy as good looking as Chris wasn't a dog, like some of the men her girlfriends were always being messed around by.

With a groan that seemed to come straight from her stomach, Lauren ripped out the CD and hurled it into the back seat, before pulling off the hand brake and driving away.

*   *   *

She didn't know how far she drove round

415

Longhampton but for once Lauren didn't mind its bossy one-way systems and endless traffic lights. It left her free to concentrate on crying and feeling numb. Eventually, she found herself driving down the broad old road that ran alongside the park, where every seventeen-year-old went to do three-point turns.

She saw a large space, pulled into it, and turned off the engine. It ticked in the silence as she stared through the windscreen at the painted spike railings and leafless trees. She and Chris used to go to the park a lot when they were at school, to be 'alone'. They even had their 'special bench'. A few brave dog-walkers were up and about, being hauled round the ornamental duck pond by their pets. One couple was juggling a spaniel, a toddler and a double buggy, but seemed to be enjoying it.

That's not going to be us now, thought Lauren, as her heart contracted in pain. Me and Chris, we're never going to have a toddler and a spaniel. He's ruined everything.

She grabbed her coat and got out. It really was cold, and she had to set off walking at some pace to keep warm. Longhampton's park was surprisingly big, built for the town by some Victorian factory owner who felt his minions should have somewhere to go for their daily sunlight ration, and Lauren had covered nearly a mile of winding path before she suddenly ran out of energy and slumped on the bench, where she and Chris used to snog until their lips were sore, and sat staring miserably into space.

She probed her broken heart ruthlessly, making herself picture Chris with that girl, whose name she didn't even know, wallowing in the pain of it

416

all. How could he do that to her? When they were so far down the line with the wedding? He knew the deposits were paid!

Well, it was all off now. And he'd be lucky if her dad didn't go round there and thump him.

From nowhere, Lauren suddenly thought of her mother. Mum's gone into all that debt for nothing, she realised, horrified, and even though she didn't think she could feel any worse, she did.

The town hall clocked chimed the half-hour, then the hour, and Lauren still couldn't find the energy to move. Footsteps came and went, sometimes slowing, as well-meaning passers-by peered to see if she was OK, and despite feeling as if she were filled with broken glass, Lauren somehow managed to mumble, ''M fine, thanks. Really, thanks,' and force a twisted smile until they walked on.

After a while, though, she heard a voice she recognised. A man's voice.

'Lauren?' it said, tentatively.

The accompanying footsteps slowed, then stopped in front of her.

Slowly, Lauren parted the fingers covering her face, and saw two pairs of trainers standing on the pathway. Two pairs.

She looked up. It was Chris, and he had Kian with him. Both looked as if they'd only just stopped yelling at each other; Chris looked furious while Kian just looked weaselly.

'Kian's got something he wants to tell you,' said Chris, and gave Kian a shove.

'Chris didn't pull that girl,' admitted Kian. 'It was me.'

'You're just saying that to cover up for him,' said

Lauren, dully. 'I'm not stupid.'

'No, really,' said Kian. 'It was me. I told her my name was Chris because . . . well, I'm lying low for a while, put it like that. Not exactly . . . off the leash at the moment.'

A tiny glimmer of hope flickered in Lauren's heart.

'Sorry, mate,' he went on. 'I didn't think it would cause problems. I mean, come on! How was I meant to know you'd come over?' He gave Chris a side look. 'Didn't even know you'd got a key.'

'Shut up, Kian,' snarled Chris. 'It's not me you should be apologising to.'

'Yeah, sorry, Lauren.' Kian tried his winning smile, but neither Lauren nor Chris responded. 'Look, you've obviously got some making up to do, so I'll, er . . . I'll . . .'

'Shove off,' supplied Lauren.

'Yeah. I'll . . . shove off. See yiz later.' He turned on his heel and ambled off. He'd only gone a few steps when he turned round and shouted, 'Still on for best man, then?'

Chris looked at Lauren, and she saw something weird in his eyes. Embarrassment, she decided. And probably he was annoyed with her for lamping him like that, and he was entitled to be, really.

'Get bent, Kian,' she yelled. He flicked a cheerful v-sign and carried on walking.

Chris didn't move. For a moment, Lauren wasn't sure what to say; you couldn't just slam big emotions like that into reverse, and be all nicey-nicey again.

'And *is* the wedding still on?' he asked.

'I don't know,' she said. 'Is it?'

Lauren knew she should feel relieved, but

somehow she didn't. Something else had been dislodged from a dark part of her mind—was it the pissed-off expression in Chris's eyes last night, when she'd asked him to come home with her, and he'd looked daggers at the thought of cutting his evening short? Was it that she'd never be able to enjoy the wedding now, knowing what trouble her mum was in? Or was it something else? Like, doubts?

Lauren stared at her feet, shocked at herself.

Chris sat down next to her, and fiddled with the sleeves of his hooded sweatshirt. Lauren loved that Gap sweatshirt. It made him look like a blond jock from *The OC*, or the clean-cut hero of some American teen film.

'Loz, we need to talk,' he said without looking at her, and as soon as he said it, she knew it wasn't going to be good.

'I know,' she said, and took hold of his hand. OK, so Mum had told her not to tell anyone about the credit-card bills, but she had to tell Chris. They'd have to scale back on the plans, and he'd need to know why. It was only fair. 'Listen, let me go first—it's about the wedding.'

To her surprise, relief seemed to flood Chris's face. 'I'm so glad you said that. I'm so glad it's not just me, Loz.'

'What?' she began, creasing her forehead, but he was gabbling on.

'I think we've got rushed into it, you know? It's not like I don't love you because I do, well, as much as I know about it, but sometimes, specially lately, I've felt like it's really the wedding you're into, not getting married to me.' He turned to face her, and to Lauren's horror, she could see from the tightness in his face that he was serious. He meant what he was saying.

'But you know that's not . . .'

'Isn't it? You're always going on about how it's something you've dreamed about since you were little—well, you've only really known me since you were seventeen. It's the first proper relationship for both of us. And the wedding hasn't changed since we've been going out, has it? It's still the same plans you've had for years—to be honest, I sometimes feel like you're just slotting me into it, that anyone else would do.'

'Chris, don't say that.'

'Why not? It's true, isn't it? Look, I'm not saying it's your fault. I know my mum's just the same— she's been wanting to plan some kind of huge wedding to make up for her own, but, you know . . .' He shrugged. 'It makes me wonder if this is going to work. I mean, I don't want a big do, but no one's even asked me! If you want a big fairy-tale party, then just have one. But don't let's pretend it's the same thing as getting married.'

'What?' Lauren felt blind-sided. 'Are you saying you don't want to get married?' she asked, weakly. 'But you asked me to marry you!'

'I know,' said Chris, miserably. 'And it wasn't like I didn't want to at the time, but, you know, it was Christmas, and we were both a bit pissed, and I just got . . .' His voice trailed off. 'A bit carried away, maybe. I didn't think it would all start happening so fast.'

Lauren closed her eyes as his words sank in. It had seemed impossible that today could get any worse, but apparently not. 'Oh my God,' she said. 'Oh my God.'

Seeing her shock, Chris started back-pedalling. 'I do love you, Lauren, honestly . . .' He grabbed her hand, but she pulled it away. 'I'm twenty-three! You're only twenty-two. We've only ever been on one holiday alone together and that was four days in Ibiza. Shit, are you crying?' He leaned forward, and tried to see under her hands. 'You are. Oh, Loz, please don't. I hate seeing you cry.'

Lauren pushed him away.

'Please don't. I'm trying to be honest here,' he pleaded. 'I don't want to let you down.'

'How can you let me down any more than you are now?' she sobbed, and Chris put his arms around her. She didn't feel angry enough to push him away again.

'Just now,' Chris said softly, into her hair. 'You really thought I'd slept with that girl, didn't you?'

Lauren bridled at the accusation beneath his words. She knew exactly what he was saying. 'And? What else was I meant to think? She *told* me you had, and your phone was turned off when I tried to call you last night.'

'Well, I didn't.'

'Yeah, I know that now,' she conceded, reluctantly.

'But that's what I mean—it doesn't show a whole lot of trust in me,' Chris went on, hurt. 'If you could think that.'

That, thought Lauren, was a bit much. She sat up and glared at him. 'And you think you've deserved it since you moved in with Kian?' She counted on her fingers. 'Out most nights, acting like you're single, spending money we're meant to be saving on beer and takeaways? While I'm at home with my mum and dad?'

421

'God, at least save the nagging till we're married!' Chris rolled his eyes. 'Yes, living with Kian has made me realise I don't want to settle down just yet. I'm not saying I don't want to marry you ever, but I just don't know what I want. I do know, though, that I really don't want to hurt you. So I think we need to step back and think about this. Yeah?'

Lauren was silent, and she turned away from him, staring out at the park while his words sank in. Her brain went on to automatic, as her eyes followed two joggers round the outside perimeter railings.

She felt Chris take her hand, wrapping his fingers round hers but she couldn't bring herself to move her head and look down in case she saw the engagement ring that apparently didn't mean as much to him as she had thought.

'It doesn't mean I don't love you,' he said, softly.

Lauren was so paralysed with unhappiness that she couldn't speak.

They sat in silence, listening to the wind blowing through the indestructible shrubbery of the park.

'So what do you want to do?' said Lauren eventually. She was amazed at how steady her voice sounded when she was churning up inside.

'Can we just have time-out for a week?' said Chris. 'Just to think?'

'You want me to *think* about how much I want to get married, so you can come back in a week's time and dump me?' she replied sarcastically. 'No, Chris.'

'No!' he protested. 'I just want to press pause for a moment, just to be sure I know what's happening! Don't you feel that? That it's all kind of running ahead of us? What with the house and the big plans and everything?'

Lauren nodded, very slightly, and cast a glance sideways. She couldn't help hurting at how relieved Chris looked.

Relieved at what, she wondered. That she hadn't kicked off? Or that he was on his way out of their relationship?

Lauren's head ached. Chris didn't let go of her hand. He didn't show any signs of moving.

A jumble of thoughts crowded into her mind, all tied together so tightly she didn't know how to start untangling them: her shattered wedding dreams, Chris's half-rejection (what did he *mean*?), her mum's nightmare debts, how she could start explaining any of it to anyone?

Lauren squeezed her eyes tight shut and when she opened them, the windswept park was still there, bleak as it ever was. She was filled with the need to be left alone, to work out what exactly she felt. These aren't thoughts Mum can help with, thought Lauren, and a depressing sense that she'd finally reached adulthood hit her.

More than signing the mortgage, more than choosing the wedding dress. Having a problem you could only solve on your own—that was being grown-up.

'Can you go now, please?' she said.

'What?'

'Can you go? I need to be on my own.'

Chris looked surprised. 'But . . .'

'I can't think with you here. Ring me on Wednesday, OK?'

'You're sure you don't . . .'

'I'm sure. Call me then. Text me to tell me

you're calling. Whatever.'

'OK.' Chris got up and started to walk away, his hands in his pockets. He'd gone four or five steps when he turned, and almost ran back to the bench.

'You mean so much to me, Lauren,' he said, urgently, taking her hands and crouching so their eyes were level. He hadn't shaved in his rush to catch up with her, and an acrid morning smell lingered on his skin. But his eyes were lovely, she thought, randomly. Blue-grey, and honest.

He gazed into her eyes as if hoping she could read more there than he could say. 'I just don't want to mess it up and have us hating each other in two years.'

'I don't either,' she said, in a small voice.

Chris leaned forward, cautiously, then closed his eyes and touched his lips against hers. They were warm and soft, and as he kissed her, with painful gentleness, Lauren's heart was submerged by an aching wave of loss. How could he be so kind, and so cruel at the same time?

Taking her kiss as a positive sign, he started to curl his hand around the back of her neck, but she pushed him away.

'Go,' said Lauren, biting her lip, and this time he did.

She sat motionless for a while, trying desperately to lay one problem flat long enough to follow it through.

She could cancel the wedding.

Just thinking that made her stop breathing for a second, but she forced herself to carry on.

If Chris wasn't sure, then there was no way she was going to force him down the aisle, especially not if it was going to put her mum in debt. He

424

hadn't said anything about splitting up, after all, just that he wasn't sure about the wedding.

But how could you carry on with someone who reckoned they loved you, but not enough to marry you? When everyone would know he'd called it off? Her heart cracked with shame, and then cracked again at the very idea of losing the beautiful, magical day she'd planned so carefully; something twisted inside at the thought of her satin wedding shoes, perfectly broken in now, and all for nothing.

But if the wedding didn't happen, then her mum would get some of that money back—and she wouldn't have to spend more. They could sell some of the centrepieces and silk decorations on eBay (even though she felt ill just imagining parting with all the clever little knick-knacks she'd found), maybe even sell the dress, although most of those deposits were non-refundable.

Lauren hesitated as the problem twisted once again in her head. What if her mum thought she'd called off the wedding because of the money? She'd blame herself. She'd think Lauren had done it to save her face.

She pressed her hands to her eyes. And what if Chris calmed down by Wednesday? What if this was just some Kian-inspired panic attack—pre-wedding nerves, like you read about in the magazine features. That happened. At least it showed he was thinking about what it really meant. What was the point in getting her mum's hopes up (or down) and then having to tell her it was all going ahead?

And then there was the house. They wouldn't get any of that deposit back. Chris hadn't said what he wanted to do about that.

But how do *you* feel? she asked herself. What do *you* want?

Lauren let her eyes drift around the perimeter of the park, hoping the answer would just pop into her mind.

It didn't. It was like being trapped in a room with crowds of people all shouting at once, and the only voice she couldn't hear was her own.

CHAPTER THIRTY

Katie never thought she'd be glad to leave for work on a Monday morning, but there were moments on Sunday afternoon when she wondered if the clocks had stopped, the hours were dragging by so torturously.

Something had definitely changed, since Ross quietly moved his clothes into the spare room. Katie didn't even know he'd done it until she took a basket of ironing up to put away, and when she pulled open his underwear drawer in their room, it was empty, apart from one forlorn bar of soap. It had been there so long, she noticed automatically, the Body Shop had changed their packaging.

Holding her breath, Katie opened the wardrobe, and saw his shirts had gone too. And his books from his side of the bed, and his iPod, and his guitar that he hadn't played in years. Things she hadn't even registered were there before.

Her stomach contracted painfully. This was what she'd wanted. This was the no-pain solution for the children, and yet it felt more of a rejection

426

than if he'd packed his things and left altogether. He was closing himself off to her, just like she'd closed herself off from him. Until that moment, she'd had no idea just how much it must have hurt him. He still wouldn't really talk to her. Whenever she tried to ask him how he was feeling, he just turned away.

Katie put the basket down and sank onto the bed, fighting back tears, then wiped her eyes hard, with one of Jack's soft T-shirts. This is the tough part, she thought. Get used to it; it'll pass.

It might just have been her own paranoia, but she was sure the kids sensed something was up. Maybe she and Ross were being *too* normal, agreeing *too much* with each other. Jack was whingey, and wouldn't settle for his Sunday afternoon nap, and Hannah's eyes seemed to follow her around the room. Once or twice, Katie went through to the kitchen to make some coffee, and when she turned round, Hannah was standing by the door, half in and half out.

The second time it happened, Katie said, 'Are you OK there, Hannah Banana? Can I get you a drink?'

Hannah scuttled over to where Katie was standing and grabbed her hand tight.

'Mummy,' she asked in a wheedly voice, 'why did Daddy sleep in a different bed last night?'

How did she know? panicked Katie.

'Um, because he snores, and keeps Mummy awake!' she said, brightly, making a mental note to tell Ross, so at least they'd be peddling the same unconvincing lie. 'So I asked him to snore in the spare room.'

'Don't you get lonely without Daddy?' asked

Hannah.

'No, darling.' Katie smoothed back Hannah's hair from her forehead. 'You sleep on your own, don't you?'

She looked dubious. 'Don't you love us any more? You didn't want to come to Center Parcs with us.'

Katie tried not to notice the way Hannah lumped her, and Jack, and Ross in as one, but picked her up and gave her a tight squeeze, bursting with protective love as Hannah's arms and legs wound round her, clinging like ivy. 'I love you more than anything else in the whole world,' she said, fiercely. 'And sometimes mummies have to work, but that doesn't mean I'm not thinking about you and Jack all the time.'

'I wish you didn't have to go to work, Mummy,' said Hannah, and she sounded much younger than she had done for a long time.

'I know, sweetie,' said Katie. 'I wish I didn't have to, too, but that's what grown-ups do.' She tried to tell herself that her daughter, at least, had a strong female role model, but it didn't fill in the answering silence from Hannah.

*   *   *

Just before she left for work on Monday morning, Ross said, off-handedly, 'I won't be in tonight, just so's you know.'

'What?' Katie stopped stuffing papers into her laptop bag.

'Monday nights. It's going to be my night off from now on.' He coaxed Jack into taking another spoonful of porridge. His swollen cheekbone had

428

gone down, leaving him with just a little cut on his lip. It added a touch of Jack Sparrow roughness, which Katie found oddly attractive.

Though obviously she didn't approve of him and Greg fighting.

'And I'd like to take Thursdays off. The whole day. Jo says she can get Jack and Rowan into this nursery near her house on Thursdays, because she wants to start retraining. She's thinking of going back to work, part-time.'

'Really?' said Katie, surprised. 'She didn't mention that to me.'

'Well, she was thinking about it before Greg dropped this on her, and now she definitely wants to. We talked about it while we were away. I'm thinking of doing some retraining too, actually. Get up to speed with the new Photoshop software, that sort of thing.'

'Are you? That's great!' Katie's heart bumped ambiguously in her chest. Was Jack really ready to be left at nursery? And how much would it cost?

Ross wants to start working again, she reminded herself. That's what you wanted. Focus on that.

Ross gave her a side look. 'It's a chance to get my own life back, now Jack's old enough to be left on his own at nursery.'

She couldn't stop herself. 'Are you sure he'll be all right?'

Ross glared at her. 'For one day a week? I think so, Katie. It'll do him good to meet other toddlers. Do both of us good, come to that.' He softened a little as Jack grabbed for the porridge spoon. 'It's a nice nursery. Jo's been looking into all of them locally, and she's pulled some strings to get them both in. Come on, they're friends, Rowan and Jack.

They'll know each other.'

'Of course. Course.'

Something twisted in Katie, at the thought of Ross and Jo discussing their break-out plans from the tyranny of childcare. Was that why Jo hadn't mentioned it to her, in case she didn't understand?

'It's a great idea,' she said, trying hard not to sound patronising. 'Great.'

But all the way to work, she had to keep pushing away the mental image of Jo and Ross, two heartbroken survivors, the nurturers, thrown together, their friendship taking on more significance every day.

There's nothing you can do, she told herself. If you can't love him properly, you should let him go.

I can't, she thought, miserably.

*   *   *

There was the usual stack of paperwork in her in-tray when she dumped her coat and bag in her office, plus an enraging Voicemail message from Eddie, wondering where the evidence for the 'problem' with the Memorial Hall was.

'I've been on to Historic Buildings and they've no records of any letters demanding listing protection.' His voice turned faux-concerned. 'Are you sure you were looking at the right building, Kate? Or was it just one of those time-of-the-month blips? Sort it out, my love—don't want them thinking my team can't tell the difference between a community hall and a cathedral.'

She seethed and deleted the message.

Why's he taking such a personal interest in this, she wondered, then answered her own question:

there's something going on with the developers.

Well, two can play at that game, she thought, and looked up the number of her contact at English Heritage.

*　　　　*　　　　*

Katie left work dead on time, and drove home via the big toy superstore where she assuaged her guilt with a couple of bags of toys, trying not to think about Greg as she did so.

Ross was changed to go out when she arrived, and his appearance, rather than the usual scene of domestic devastation behind him, made her stop in her tracks.

He'd had a haircut, and was wearing his smarter jeans, and a long-sleeved T-shirt. Clearly he was making an effort that he couldn't normally be bothered to make for her, and it stung a little inside.

'Off somewhere nice?' she asked sarcastically, as Hannah clamoured for her presents. She'd had a haircut too, Katie noticed. So had Jack.

I wanted to do Hannah's next haircut, she thought. She made herself push the thought away: from now on, she was going to make every effort not to nag.

'Just out,' he said, airily, and then added, because he was so unused to not telling her things, 'some parents from Hannah's old playgroup are getting together.'

'The one in the Memorial Hall?' asked Katie, half her mind still in work mode.

'Yes.' Ross looked closely at her. 'Why?'

'Well, could you maybe suggest they write some

letters to English Heritage, asking for it to be listed? I've got the address. There are plans to build a big block of flats right over it—but obviously if it's being assessed for protection then . . .'

'Do you ever stop thinking about work?' demanded Ross. 'Seriously?'

'This isn't just about work!' Katie took off her coat. She didn't know how to say, if I can save the Hall, maybe I can save us too. And she didn't like to say, is there a reason you don't want to talk about *your wife's job* tonight, out with these yummy mummies?

'I can't do much about it myself,' she pressed on. 'There's too much office politics and money tied up. But if local people who use it make a fuss—'

'I'll mention it,' Ross said, curtly. 'Now, I've left supper out, and what, Hannah?'

Hannah was clinging to his leg, gazing up with puppyish eyes. 'When are you coming back?'

'Later.'

'When later?'

'After you've gone to bed, madam.'

He exchanged a look with Katie, who clapped her hands, and said, 'OK, Hannah—who wants an . . . ice cream?'

Hannah looked at them both, slowly and carefully, then stuck out her lower lip. 'Not me,' she said, and ran away.

*   *   *

Katie tried everything she could think of short of letting Hannah run riot with the fairy-cake cases, but she remained in a foul mood all Monday night, delaying bedtime with every trick she knew. Hannah was, Katie thought grimly, her mother's daughter. Ross didn't get back until 10.30 p.m., and right on cue, Hannah trailed downstairs and insisted on him taking her back up.

Katie couldn't help earwigging as Ross was tucking her in, and heard him say, 'Yes, Mummy loves you. And I love Mummy. And Mummy loves me.' He sounded more convincing than she did, Katie had to give him that.

When Hannah didn't spring out of bed at 6.30 a.m. the next day, as she usually did, Katie went in to wake her up, and felt a guilty flicker of relief amidst her concern when Hannah moaned about her sore throat and funny tummy.

'She's not well,' she told Ross, in the kitchen. 'Might explain why she's been extra clingy these past few days.'

'Maybe,' said Ross, non-committally.

He didn't say much else. He'd stopped talking about anything that didn't directly involve the children, or the house.

'Must be something she picked up while she was away?'

'It's just a bug,' said Ross. 'Jo was saying last night that Molly's got a cold. I'll see how she is after breakfast, and if she's really poorly, I'll keep her at home.' He looked up from sorting the laundry; according to the new list of chores he'd drawn up, he would load and wash, while she had to iron.

Katie paused at the door. 'So Jo was there last night? How is she?'

'Fine,' said Ross. 'Coping, you know. She's still in shock. You're going to be late for work.'

I should phone Jo, she thought, but what can I say? She and Ross are their own little club now, it was impossible to talk to her, not knowing what Ross had said.

'I'll call her,' she said, as much to herself as Ross, then paused again.

Ross didn't offer any more conversation, but continued loading the machine.

Silently, Katie turned and left the kitchen.

*   *   *

'Where's Ross this week?' asked Bridget, kindly, as she and Katie changed their shoes in the vestibule.

'Oh, he's looking after the children—Hannah's got one of these bugs going round,' Katie replied. It was what she'd rehearsed in the car on the way over. Dancing was the last thing she felt like tonight, but the thought of spending an evening in the house, full of recriminating echoes and reminders of the kids was unbearable.

As soon as she'd arrived, she was greeted by Bridget and Frank, and Baxter, and Chloe, who'd had her hair cut and coloured by Trina's niece at The Hair Academy, and needed reassurance that it didn't make her look like a cocker spaniel.

Bridget and Katie both struggled to find the right words, but the best Bridget could come up with was, 'It's lovely and bubbly.'

'She did her best, Chloe,' said Trina, in an aggressive manner. 'It's not the easiest hair to work with, is it?'

'What are you saying, Trina?' demanded Chloe. 'That my hair put up a *fight*?'

Despite her grey mood, a little buzz of warmth

had crept underneath her numb exterior. Their familiarity, and their welcoming smiles were comforting. Katie didn't know how long she could keep up the casualness, but the idea of having some gentle contact with people, without having to talk too much, or think too much, made her feel a little less alone.

'Hannah's not well?' said Bridget at once. 'There's been a bit of a bug going round school . . . That must be it. Once one of them gets it, you know.'

'Really? I mean, I don't think it's too serious, but we didn't want to leave her with a sitter. Ross volunteered, so . . .'

Katie trailed off, now worried that Bridget knew something she didn't.

Bridget patted her arm reassuringly. 'Don't worry, it's amazing how quickly they get over these things if there's someone there to cuddle them into bed with a hot drink and a story. She'll be fine in a day or two. Good for Ross, letting you come out!'

'Well, you know . . . No Chris tonight?' she asked to change the subject, as they went into the hall. Lauren stomped past them both, heading towards the ancient loos at the far end of the main room. She wasn't, Katie noticed, wearing her white satin bridal shoes to dance in.

Bridget waited until the banged door confirmed that Lauren was out of earshot, then checked to see where Frank was: chatting about lawnmowers with Baxter. She dropped her voice. 'Oh, not so good, I don't think. They've had a bit of a falling-out about something, but she won't tell me what. Says nothing's up, but you know . . . Mothers know, don't they?'

'Oh no!' said Katie, genuinely sorry. 'Surely it's just the usual pre-wedding nerves?'

Bridget's gaze flitted back and forth towards the door, anxious not to be seen talking in a low voice—which could only be about one topic. Concern was written all over her face, in the sad eyes, and twitching mouth. Katie could see that every part of her was thinking of Lauren, wanting to take away the hurt.

She's like a mother lioness with a full-grown cub, thought Katie: still protective, even though Lauren towers over her. They have a proper mother–daughter relationship. She thought of Hannah's fierce, knowing eyes, and felt useless.

'I think it's all getting on top of her, with the house, and the wedding plans and everything,' said Bridget. 'Nothing more than that. She's only twenty-two, you know. Still a baby, really.' She sighed. 'Oh dear.'

'Everything OK?' said Frank, coming up and putting one arm on his wife's back.

Bridget's smile snapped back into place. 'Yes, fine! Everything's fine!'

'Good,' said Frank, and winked at Katie. 'No Chris and no Ross, eh? That means I've two smart young ladies to myself this evening!'

'Yes,' said Katie, with a crooked smile at Bridget. 'That's one way of looking at it.'

*   *   *

Lauren didn't want to be at dancing tonight, but her dad had asked her if she was coming, and she couldn't say no. She'd only just managed to get herself through three whole days at the surgery, with Sue asking questions about whether it was worth her cousin's daughter getting a wedding cake made professionally, and bloody Kathleen making personal remarks about whether the vicar would need a stepladder to marry her and Chris. Like she was the wedding expert now.

Chris hadn't phoned. She hadn't phoned him. Or texted. She could hardly bear to think about what Kian would be saying to him, or what they'd be doing together. She didn't even know if he'd told Irene; presumably not, since Irene had called her twice to ask whether she'd consider having her hairdresser's toddler daughter as a flowergirl. She didn't even know if that was in exchange for a wash and bridal put-up—a thought that wouldn't even have crossed her mind before she found out about her mum's credit cards.

If the actual wedding happening or not wasn't enough to worry about, a sneaky fifteen minutes at lunch on the internet hadn't exactly put her mind at rest about debt problems either. If anything it had made it worse, some of the horror stories she'd read about old people losing their homes and never being able to get a credit card again.

Worst of all, it was weird not being able to spill it all out to her mum, like she normally would. Lauren couldn't remember ever having some major problem and not being able to come home, burst into tears and tell Bridget everything. Now she was fighting to keep everything inside because she didn't want to add to her worries—which were all her fault anyway.

It was so bad, she could barely concentrate on her steps and she trod on her dad's toes twice during the first few bars of their social foxtrot practice.

'Don't be doing that at your wedding, Laurie!' he joked as they tried to dance to some old-style tune she didn't know. 'Or you'll be having me in tears as well as your mum!'

'Sorry,' she mumbled. Great—she couldn't even dance any more. Now she wasn't going to have her gorgeous dress and first dance, she was going to go back to being Lauren the lanky klutz, knocking everything over.

A fat tear slid out of her eye and ran down her cheek.

'Close those feet, Lauren!' shouted Angelica from the other side of the room. 'Or else Frank'll be tripping over them!'

'What's up, love?' said her father in such a kind, comforting voice that Lauren felt about seven years old again.

'Nothing,' she managed.

'I don't think so,' said Frank, gently, holding her a little bit closer, so her forehead could rest on his shoulder. 'Your old dad knows when something's up.'

Lauren struggled not to cry, but Frank seemed intent on making her howl.

'I've seen you moping around the place these last few days,' he went on, in the same well-meaning murmur, 'and you know, if you're having doubts about marrying Christopher, then you just say. Don't be worried about your mum and me being upset—all we care about is your happiness, love. You're married a long time, and if you're not going into it a hundred per cent . . . Well, it's not fair on Christopher, is it?'

Lauren couldn't say anything. It was typical of

438

her dad to assume it would be *her* having doubts, not Chris. Chris, in his eyes, was bloody lucky to be marrying Lauren in the first place.

'And better you say something now,' Frank said, 'before the invitations go out, eh? Give him the chance to save some face. You've got to be honest . . .' He turned them round a corner, although they were doing such small steps that Baxter whisked past them with a surprised-looking Katie. 'Your mother and I have always been upfront with each other, right from day one. No secrets.'

If only Dad knew, Lauren thought desperately, that Mum's got a *huge* secret, for the first time in their lives, and it's because of me!

'You know, I'm an old romantic,' said Frank, warming to his theme, inspired by the sentimental music, 'when you set out to get married, you have to think, I'm only going to do this once. You have to be sure that this is the man you're going to have by your side for the rest of your life. You're setting off on a journey, and you've got to go down the same roads, together, even when those roads get rocky and you're fed up. When one of you's ill, or you have children, and money's a bit tight. I know you don't think about those things when you're picking out your dress and the flowers, but that's what hitching yourself to another human being's all about.'

That sounds good, thought Frank, making a mental note to add it to his Father-of-the-Bride speech.

'The wedding's only one day, but you've got to think what's on the other side of that. The rest of your lives. It's why I've always thought I'm the luckiest man in the world, with your mother. If you and Chris are as happy as we are in forty years' time . . .'

Lauren gulped. Forty years? Suddenly she had a flash of understanding, about what Chris had been getting at. The rest of her life. Already.

She let out a loud, shoulder-shaking sob, and Frank stopped in shock.

'Lauren?' he said, holding her at arms' length. 'Lauren, love, what have I said?'

'It's nothing you said!' she sobbed, as he cuddled her into his shoulder.

I don't want to be married yet, was all she could think. I'm not ready for this to be it for the rest of my life.

'Lauren?' Now Bridget had come rushing over, anxiously peering up, pulling Lauren's long hair out of her face so she could see her properly. 'What is it, darling?'

'I'm sorry, Mum!' wailed Lauren. 'I'm sorry!'

'Sorry about what?' asked Frank, bewildered. 'I don't know what I said. We were fine a moment ago, weren't we?' His face creased like a worried bloodhound. 'Weren't we, Lauren?'

'Is everything OK?'

Angelica stopped the CD, leaving Lauren's sobs to resound around the carved oak rafters of the Hall. Katie and Chloe came over, offering hankies, stroking her back. Peggy, Baxter and Trina hovered, not sure what to do for the best, but looking sympathetic nonetheless.

'I'm fine!' hiccuped Lauren, unconvincingly.

Bridget and Frank exchanged worried glances, but it was Angelica who took charge of the situation with brisk compassion.

'Now, Bridget, why don't you take Lauren

440

outside into the vestibule, and help her calm down? Hmm? That'll be better, won't it? There now.' She put her arm round Lauren and began leading her out, with Bridget following. Their heels clicked on the polished floor, punctuated by heaving gasps.

'What's that about?' Chloe mouthed to Katie, who shrugged and raised her eyebrows.

'Is she all right?' asked Trina, not bothering to drop her voice beneath the usual dull roar. 'Is she up the duff or something?'

'No!' said Katie and Chloe, even though neither of them had the faintest idea.

Angelica came clicking back into the Hall, a wide dancing smile on her face. It didn't disguise the concern in her eyes. 'OK!' she said, brightly. 'Let's carry on. And this time, shall we put a promenade step into that social foxtrot? I know you all remember the promenade step. Baxter, if you could partner Chloe this time, and who was dancing with Bridget?'

The music started up again and the dancing resumed as if nothing had happened.

*   *   *

Outside in the tiled vestibule, Lauren sat on a bench beneath the plaque listing the names of the Longhampton Fallen 1939–45, with Bridget's arm round one side of her, and Frank hovering next to them, until Bridget waved him back into the Hall.

'Just you and me, now, Laurie,' she said, tenderly, and the floodgates opened.

'I don't know what to do!' she said finally, for the fifth time.

Bridget put her lips against Lauren's hair. 'This hasn't got anything to do with . . . what I told you about paying for the wedding, has it?'

Lauren shook her head. 'No, I promise. It's about . . . I just don't know. But then I think that you and Dad were the same age as we were, and you've done all right, so I *ought* to know . . .'

'Laurie,' said Bridget, slowly. 'I'm going to tell you something I've never told anyone. And I'm only telling you, because I don't want you to feel that you're under pressure to do *anything* you're not ready for.'

Lauren raised her head, and realised her mum was gearing herself up to be very honest. Her heart sank. She wasn't sure she'd got her head round the credit cards yet.

Inside the Hall, Angelica had moved the class on to a vigorous cha-cha, loud enough to drown out any potential crying. The Latin rhythm clacked and shuffled through the glass doors, with Angelica's voice yelling instruction over the top.

'Move your hips, Trina!' she bellowed. 'Your hips! Don't your knees bend at all? You're too young to have replacements!'

'Your dad and I very nearly eloped, on my twenty-first birthday,' Bridget began. 'We'd been planning it for months—he had the ring, and the licence, and we were going to go up to Gretna Green on the bus. I even went out and got myself a white mini dress and matching knee-high boots. It was *very* romantic and secret, because your grandad wasn't very keen on your father, you see— thought his hair was a bit long, because he'd not done National Service. Dads don't change, do they?'

442

Lauren shook her head.

'Anyway,' sighed Bridget, 'I don't know why we'd got it into our heads that we *had* to be married, but in those days people didn't live together like they do now. Not round here, anyway. So the day started getting nearer, and we'd come up with our clever cover stories as to where we'd be, and then I woke up the day before my birthday, and I thought no. I can't get married yet. I haven't met Paul McCartney.'

'What?' Lauren stopped gazing at her feet and looked up at her mother. 'Were you *likely* to meet Paul McCartney in Longhampton?'

'No, I mean, I hadn't been to London.' Bridget widened her eyes as if it was perfectly obvious. 'Paul was the only Beatle still not married, and I hadn't had a chance to go to London and bump into him in a pub in St John's Wood and be swept off my feet. If I married your dad, that would never ever happen. Obviously, yes, it was a bit of an outside chance, me bumping into Paul, and him not minding the fact I've a tin ear, but I still didn't want to rule it out. I was terrified of hurting your dad, though. I didn't want to tell him, but I knew I couldn't marry him. Not yet.'

God, thought Lauren, I'm seeing a whole new side to Mum this week. Paul McCartney! Of all people. And she's not been to London my entire life so it's not like it made much difference.

'So how did you tell him?' she asked, curiously.

'Well,' sighed Bridget, spreading her hands on her knees, 'I didn't need to do anything, in the end. I made myself so sick with worrying that my mother had to call for the doctor, and I was told to stay in bed for three days, no visitors. Your dad came to pick me up—although we'd had a code for that, I mean, talk about planned like a James Bond film—and my mum told him I'd got bad nerves and he should come back at the weekend.'

'And did he?'

'Oh, yes. But we never spoke about eloping again. I think he'd gone off the idea as much as I had. Not that he ever said as much. No, it was the planning that was so lovely, you see. Having a secret just the two of us knew.' She sighed again. 'They were more innocent days. But happy.'

'But you got married in the end?' Lauren pressed her. 'You did want to?'

'Of course! Well, we had to. I found out Billy was on the way. But the funny thing is, it wasn't a case of *having* to—soon as I knew I was pregnant, Paul McCartney didn't so much as cross my mind.' Bridget held her daughter's hands and looked hard into her eyes. 'That's what I'm trying to say, not very well, I know. I just knew your dad was the right man for me, for ever. But it was because I was ready. Our wedding wasn't anything like the big romantic plans we'd made—we arranged the whole thing in about a week. Then Billy was late, thank God, by over a fortnight, so it didn't look so bad.'

'Oh, is *that* why Gran looks so lemon-faced in the photos?' asked Lauren, as the penny finally dropped. 'Not because of your dress at all!'

Bridget nodded, then her wicked grin turned serious. 'Now, your father doesn't know any of that. I don't think he'd want to anyway. But you know what I'm saying here, don't you?'

'If a part of me still wants to marry Justin Timberlake then I shouldn't marry Chris just yet?'

'I'm not sure I know which one Justin

Timberlake is, but yes, that's the gist of it. And,' Bridget went on, patting her hand, 'turns out I got the better of the two in any case. I don't see your dad dyeing his hair, do you?'

Lauren laughed, then bit her lip and looked up at her mum, her eyes wide with fresh distress. 'But what about the money?'

'I keep telling you, Lauren, we'll worry about that later. The main thing is you. Your happiness. Now, I think you and Chris need to have a proper conversation—not about the wedding, not about the house, just about what you two feel.' She squeezed her hand again, feeling how slender Lauren's fingers were. 'Be honest with each other. It's the only thing that matters in the end.'

'I know,' said Lauren, getting to her feet, and wobbling like a newborn giraffe. 'I'm going to ring him now. I think we can wait a while.'

They paused for a moment, enjoying the bubble of tenderness that surrounded them. It made Bridget's heart lurch, seeing how much like Frank Lauren was: his pointed nose, his kindness, his reassuring solidity. She adored Billy and Dave, but Lauren was her little girl, still. I'd have given up *all* of the Beatles to have my beautiful daughter, she thought with a fierce tug of pride.

Next door, Angelica instructed everyone to change partners and locate their sense of rhythm before she came round and started bending their knees for them.

'I won't get to dance at my wedding,' said Lauren suddenly, in a small sad voice. 'If Chris and I call things off, I mean. *If* we do.'

'You'll get to dance at the social night instead!' said Bridget, trying to sound more cheerful than

Lauren's crestfallen face made her feel. 'With your dad, and all the other chaps lining up to dance with you. And you've got to admit, Chris could do with a bit of extra practice before he does anything in public . . .'

Lauren managed a brave smile. 'Yeah. I suppose.' She leaned down, hugging her mum tightly. 'Thank you,' she said, her voice muffled. 'I love you. You and Dad.'

'I know,' said Bridget. 'We love you too.'

Lauren unfolded herself, then pulled her shoulders back. 'Right,' she said, and with a final crooked smile, she marched across the tiles to the heavy front door.

Bridget watched her go, and sent up a silent prayer to whichever helpful deity was in charge of dodgy relationships that Lauren found the right words. Or, failing that, that some random act of God would spare her the awful conversation, just as she and Frank had been saved from theirs.

Then she heaved herself up off the bench (When did I get so creaky and ancient? she wondered) and went back into the main Hall, to find the husband she'd loved every day since then.

It was easy enough to tell Lauren to be honest, but she wasn't looking forward to the confession she knew had to be made that evening.

CHAPTER THIRTY-ONE

After Lauren left, the class never really got going again properly; Frank and Bridget danced together in the sort of close hold that suggested they were

446

engaged in a conversation they didn't want anyone to overhear, while everyone else pretended not to look curious as to what that might be about. Angelica, the seasoned pro, maintained her glossy smile and cheerful encouragement, but even she seemed distracted, and Baxter had to take her to task about her definition of a *fleckerl*.

At half-eight, Angelica finally called it a day, and Katie hurried over to catch Bridget before she left.

'Is everything OK?' she asked. It didn't come naturally to Katie to interfere in other people's problems, but there was something in Bridget's eyes that she couldn't stand to see.

'Oh, I think it'll be . . . I don't know.' Bridget shouldered her handbag like a soldier and smiled wonkily.

'Well, if there's anything I can do . . .' Katie knew it was a lame thing to offer, but Bridget seemed to be grateful for it. Her eyes turned more animated as she seized on a distraction.

'I've written a letter to your boss at the planning department, about this place. And I've suggested we do it as a school history project too—which'll be a nice local interest feature for the paper, don't you think?'

'Clever!' said Katie. 'I mean, you've obviously got lots else to be thinking about but—'

'I'm happy to think about this,' said Bridget. 'Believe me.'

Then Frank came back from the loo, and Katie saw a new determination come over Bridget as she waved goodbye.

As she was changing her shoes in the entrance hall, she heard Angelica's heels clicking over to her.

'Katie, are you dashing off?' Angelica's red dancing courts were standing about a foot away from her.

She straightened up. 'I've got to get back to Hannah,' she said, feeling rather fraudulent. 'She's not too well.'

'Oh, right. Of course. Um, I'd like a quick word, if you've got a moment,' Angelica went on, then glanced around the vestibule where the class were slowly getting their things together to drift out into the cold evening. 'If we could just wait a second until . . .'

Oh God, thought Katie, as her heart sank. It'll be about Ross and what we're going to do for this display. Everyone else had chosen their songs, apart from them. And Jo and Greg, of course.

'Night, all!' called Baxter. 'Another lovely evening! Your footwork's really coming on, Katie!'

'Thanks.' Katie raised her voice a fraction too loud. 'Night!'

Angelica watched, smiling, as Baxter helped Peggy on with her coat, then she turned and walked over to the chair where she put her own bag and coat.

Katie watched her walk, fascinated by her grace. Each step was a mini dance, thought Katie, admiring the flex of her calves and the way her skirt swung like a bell. Angelica was just the right side of cartoon womanly. It was the sort of womanly you could see at a distance.

'I hope you don't mind,' Angelica was saying, returning now with a large paper carrier bag. 'But I've been watching you and Ross and there's something I wanted you to have.' She handed

Katie the bag. 'I'm having a clear-out,' she added. 'Everything must go.'

It was from Fenwicks, in London, and much heavier than Katie was expecting.

Cautiously, she looked inside at the glittering folds of dark fabric, with a red lining like strawberry jam and dotted with heavy layers of hand-stitched jet-black sequins.

'Angelica,' she said, lifting it out slowly. 'It's . . .'

'I think we're about the same size,' Angelica was saying, 'give or take an inch or two. It's one of my old competition dresses, a bit elaborate for practice, perhaps, but you're really never going to get *into* dancing until you let a little femme fatale break through those boring office suits. Short of marching you to the shops and making you buy something to do justice to those legs of yours, I thought this might help you find your inner drama queen.'

Inner drag queen more like, thought Katie.

She paused when Katie didn't respond, and added in a kinder tone. 'Don't take it the wrong way. You only have to let her out on the dancefloor if you want. Pack her up at the end of the evening. Maybe Ross might appreciate a bit of feminine glamour when you're dancing? Men aren't as subtle as us. Sometimes they like a bit of obvious. Make him feel he's dancing with his gorgeous wife, and not his bank manager?'

Katie said nothing, but held up the dress by its sequinned shoulder straps and let it fall past her chair to trail its handkerchief hem on the floor. It weighed a ton, but the dress seemed to wiggle on its own.

Angelica was right—the bias cut looked as if it

would slip over her curves perfectly, although it was handmade and didn't have a size label inside. It was far too stagey to wear outside, but she knew that under the right lights, like the mirrorball at the social, it would come to life in a different way. It was a dress that danced with you. A dress that made everyone turn to look at you and the man who was guiding you proudly around the floor.

'It's lovely, Angelica, but it's not really me,' she said, and her voice wobbled. She pressed her thumb and forefinger against her eyes to stop the tears starting.

'Well, yes, it's pretty nice,' Angelica agreed after a pause, 'but not enough to make you weep over it.'

Katie let the dress fall into her lap and blinked hard.

Come on, Katie, she told herself. Don't let Angelica see you upset.

But it was all bubbling up inside her, all the pain and despair she'd felt in the last week, and pressed down so the children wouldn't see, so the team at work wouldn't see. There had been no one to tell—no Ross, no Jo, no one.

'It's too late. Too late for me to find my inner dancer. Ross and I won't be coming any more,' she gulped, straining under the control. 'He's . . . we're not . . .'

'You don't want to do the demonstration?' Angelica's skinny eyebrows shot up her forehead. 'But you're my star pupils!'

Katie screwed up her face. It was so stupid she almost wanted to laugh. Part of her did feel bad about missing the class's moment of glory, but a bigger part suddenly realised how much of her life she'd wasted worrying about exactly that sort of thing. Doing well. Jumping through hoops. 'No, we're going to separate.'

'Oh my God. Not you as well.' Angelica crossed her arms, then raised them heavenwards. 'What *is* it about this class? What am I doing wrong?'

'We tried. We really tried but it's over.'

'Are you sure?' Angelica pccrcd at hcr, hcr eyeliner making her narrowed eyes seem feline. 'Because you don't look that over to me.'

Katie looked up. 'Angelica. We were only *coming* to class as part of our relationship counselling. We've been having crisis sessions for the past couple of months.' She swallowed. 'But I said some things I can't take back, and now, we're sharing a house but that's it. He's cutting himself off from me. And . . .'

She closed her eyes, and heard her own worst fear come out of her mouth.

'I think he's fallen in love with someone else. Someone who probably suits him more than me. And I don't know what's going to happen now.'

There, she thought. I've said it. Somehow it made her feel slightly better.

Angelica took a few deep, thoughtful breaths, then looked at her sideways, tipping her smooth dark head to one side like an exotic bird.

'Mind if I give you some advice?'

Katie shook her head.

'I've seen hundreds of couples dancing. Learners, amateurs, pros, the lot. I see them dance with other people, and, sometimes, I see little fires starting where they shouldn't.' Angelica leaned forward and tapped Katie's knee so she'd look up. 'Sometimes I see little fires go out. But in all the classes you and Ross have had, and in the social dances too, his eyes have never left you, whether you've been dancing with him or not. He watches you when Frank's giving you a turn around the floor, he watches when you go to the loo, he watches when you're dancing together and you refuse to look him in the eye. Not all the time, not in a possessive way, but now and again, to check you're all right. When you're dancing with him, he dances differently—his back's straighter, his step's bouncier. I promise you, he isn't having an affair with Jo.'

'Jo?' Katie froze, and immediately backtracked. 'I never said anything about . . .'

'You didn't need to. It's obvious from your face. They're not, though,' she assured her. 'They're friends.'

'But I think they are!' protested Katie. 'It's my fault—I've pushed him around and made him feel like I don't appreciate him when I *do*. He's great with the children, and I understand now how much he's given up to look after them. I just . . . I just don't feel what I did.'

Angelica sat back in her plastic chair and crossed her legs. 'Katie, do you think it's over? If you could get in your car and drive away, tomorrow, would you?'

Katie paused, and thought hard. 'No,' she said, after a moment or two. 'I can't imagine a life without him. But I just don't see how I can see the old Ross again—I can't tell whether he's stopped being sexy, or whether I've just shut down all that side of myself.' She raised her eyes sadly. 'Isn't that sad? I've forgotten how to be a woman.'

Angelica abruptly changed her plans. The dress

clearly wasn't going to be enough.

'Katie,' she said, 'I'm going to teach you a dance, on your own, that'll help. I promise. It'll make you feel better about yourself, for a start.'

'Really?' asked Katie, doubtfully. 'I'm not that good at dancing.' She looked pained. 'Ross is the dancer.'

'No, but you're good at standing up for yourself, and that's what this dance is all about.'

'What is it?'

'The Argentine tango,' said Angelica.

Katie's hopeful expression dropped. 'Oh God, not that one with the stomping up and down, and the whiplash-neck thing? No, I don't think that's going to help.'

'No, no—you're thinking of the *ballroom* tango.' Angelica shook her head. 'That's totally different, that's all about the man. This is something much sexier, much more sensual.' She smiled encouragingly at Katie. 'It's about two strong people, dancing together. You learn this, and I promise you, you'll remember how to be a woman.'

'You say that as if you've tried this yourself.' Katie suddenly realised how little she or anyone else at the class actually knew about Angelica, aside from a few snippets about professional competitions and cruises. Did she have a husband? A lover? A dancing partner? Children?

It was almost impossible to imagine Angelica having parents. She was such an individual, self-possessed entity. And yet, thought Katie, her whole career has been about being the perfect partner.

'I have,' said Angelica, simply. 'And it changed my life.'

She hesitated for a second or two. 'I can't come in the evenings, though, with the children and . . .'

'You get a lunchbreak?'

Katie nodded.

'Then meet me here. Tomorrow lunchtime. We'll start then, OK?'

There was something about the confident, brisk way Angelica spoke that Katie agreed.

* * *

'Here we are,' said Frank, jovially, as he parked the car. 'I'm about ready for that cup of tea!'

It was now or never, thought Bridget. Now. Do it now. After you've had such a lovely evening.

'Frank,' she said, before she could stop herself. 'Frank, there's something I need to tell you.'

'What?' he said, unbuckling his seat belt and turning easily to her. 'You've told our Lauren she can get me all togged out like a footballer in a cravat, haven't you? Well, the answer is no. Not even for Princess Lauren. If she needs a Disney Beast, mind you . . .'

He looked at her with such affection that Bridget wanted to cry.

'No,' she said. 'I've got myself into some trouble. With money.'

Frank hesitated for a moment, as if she were joking, then when he saw she was serious, his face fell. 'Oh, Bridge. How much?'

She knew he'd be expecting her to say a couple of hundred, and when she told him the full amount, the shock he couldn't disguise, though he tried, was painful to her.

He wasn't just shocked at the amount, she knew,

but at how she'd let him down. Bridget screwed up all her courage into one tight little fist and confessed everything.

'I feel such a fool,' she said. 'I ignored it for too long, but I've done what I can, I've sold some things, but . . .' She took a deep breath. 'That money you gave to Lauren for the deposit—that wasn't the bond you took out when you started work, that was money I'd been saving for a rainy day. I didn't want to tell you because I didn't want you thinking I'd been hiding our money away. I thought you might think I'd been cheating you of it.'

'You? Cheating me? Don't be daft!' Frank started, but Bridget had to carry on.

'That was the money I was going to use to make up for the extras Lauren wanted. And I know we've both been a bit spendthrift lately—that camcorder you got, for instance, and my lovely ring—and without your salary coming in . . . It's added up.'

There, she thought. I've said it. It's out.

They sat without speaking in the dim streetlight. Bridget noted there weren't any lights on inside the house, so Lauren must still be round with Chris.

Poor love, she thought, wishing it could be her taking the hurt for her.

'No, it's me that's the fool,' said Frank eventually. 'I feel a right idiot. It's my fault for just handing over that cash without checking it through with you first. I'd no business doing that. I should have known you'd not let a sum of money like that just sit there. Well, she'll just have to give it back.'

'Frank! She can't!'

He turned to her. 'She'll have to, love. What else can we do?'

Bridget rubbed her forehead. 'No, don't. I think she and Chris might decide to put off the wedding. That's where she is now, talking to him. He's . . .' She hesitated, not sure how much Lauren would want her to say. 'She's not sure if she wants to go through with it. It'd be too mean to take this off her as well. Maybe we can do some kind of buy-to-let arrangement, I don't know.'

'Really?' Frank looked stricken, and the money worries vanished, as the awful vision of a heartbroken Lauren filled his mind. He thought of some of the things he'd said to her, not realising what she must have been hiding. 'Is that what tonight was all about? Oh, I could cut out my stupid tongue.'

Bridget took his hand. 'You wouldn't hurt her for the world. She knows that.'

'I still feel . . . Oh, God.' Frank shook his head, as if that might break through the fog of emotion and let him find words. It didn't. All he could see was his little girl, weeping on his shoulder over something he couldn't make better for her. 'I'm a stupid, insensitive man,' he said, thickly.

'Come here,' said Bridget, seeing tears shine in his eyes. She pulled his body into hers over the handbrake, something she hadn't done since they were courting. 'I'm the one who should be crying. Keeping secrets from you, like that.'

'Why didn't you tell me, Bridge?' he asked. 'I wouldn't have bellowed at you. I wouldn't have thrown you out!'

'I didn't want you to worry. And I was too proud to have you think less of me. After forty years!'

456

Bridget gulped. 'You'd think you'd grow out of silliness like that!'

Frank held her at arms' length so she could see how serious his face was. She couldn't remember the last time she'd seen Frank cry. He didn't cry when the children were born, or when his dad died. He didn't even cry when England won the Ashes. But now there were silvery tear tracks down his cheeks, shining in the orange streetlight, picking out the craggy, weathered lines of a face she knew as well as her own. Better, in fact.

His skin might be more wrinkled, she thought, but those are the same gentle eyes that smiled at me in our English O-level class. Did he still see the teenager in her face? Behind the glasses and the crow's-feet?

Frank gazed at her in the dim streetlight, and finally said, 'There's nothing you could do that'd stop me loving you, Bridget. We're a team, you and me. We'll sort out this debt, and we'll help Lauren, and we'll have no more secrets, eh? No more.'

Then he pulled her into his chest, and they kissed each other like teenagers, albeit teenagers with dodgy hips and bifocals, glad of the other's warmth and familiar, comforting smell.

The daft bugger, she thought. It couldn't be put right that easily, Bridget knew, but for the moment, all she wanted was to hear Frank say it would be, and to feel his arms round her, forgiving her, reassuring her that they'd face it together.

CHAPTER THIRTY-TWO

The next morning, Ross was changed into his smarter clothes again for his 'day off': a dark pair of jeans and the cashmere jumper Katie had given him for Christmas, over a T-shirt. He was making an effort, clearly, but not for her. Even more heartbreakingly, he had a buoyancy about him that had everything to do with getting out of the house on his own.

'I'll take Hannah to school, then drop Jack at nursery,' he informed Katie, slicing up Hannah's toast into soldiers. 'Jo's going to pick everyone up from nursery and school so they can go off to an early bonfire party, so if you want to collect the kids from hers on your way home, she's happy to give them some tea.'

'We're having sparklers!' Hannah informed her.

'Wow! Lucky you!' said Katie, then asked Ross, 'What time are you going to be home?'

It felt weird, even asking.

'Not sure,' said Ross.

'Well, can you *be* sure?' she asked, tetchily. 'I mean, will it be before the kids go to bed?'

Ross gave her a sarcastic look, and she realised he was getting her back for all the evenings she hadn't been able to put an exact time on her return.

She changed tack, trying to keep her voice cheerful. 'So, what are your plans?'

'Oh, you know, I'm going to talk to some people about work, then Jo and I are having lunch.' He dumped the toast on the plate. 'Hannah, jam or

458

marmalade?'

Katie had the feeling that was all she was going to get, and left it, miserably, at that.

*   *   *

At work, she waited until Eddie was hovering around the office opposite hers, exchanging golf-related pleasantries with Nick Felix, and then called the office that dealt with listed-building applications.

'Yes, it's about the Memorial Hall,' she said in a loud voice, watching as Eddie's ears pricked up. 'I was wondering if there was . . . Oh, you have? Seventeen letters? I had no idea . . .'

Eddie marched in and glared at her.

'Well, that does put a different complexion on things,' said Katie, pulling a clownish frown. 'I'll have to filter that back to the information gatherers. Who's applied for an events licence? For what?'

'What?' mouthed Eddie, leaning over her desk.

'For a charity ball?' She raised her eyebrows in a 'fancy that!' gesture. 'Really? Historic significance . . .'

Bridget had been busy, obviously; it sounded as though she'd done everything short of calling the BBC.

Eddie didn't waste time. 'What the hell's that about?' he demanded, almost before she'd put the phone down.

'Looks like there might be problems getting demolition orders on that Memorial Hall,' said Katie.

'But the roof's rotten!' exploded Eddie.

459

'Well, apparently there's now some Friends of the Hall fund-raising group been set up,' said Katie, innocently. 'To fix it. For posterity.'

'Really?' He gave her a suspicious look. 'In the last few weeks, perhaps? That's a coincidence.'

'Oh, I think it's more in use than the initial surveyors realised,' she said. 'Probably been meaning to do something about it for ages. It's a lovely old place, Eddie, very romantic. Have you ever had a look round?'

'No,' he snapped. 'It's just an old building, Kate. And one that's in the way of a very important new housing development.'

'The new housing can go in several different places, though,' she heard herself say. 'Can't it?'

Eddie's expression wobbled in surprise.

I've been so wrong, thought Katie, running myself ragged getting my self-respect from pleasing morons like Eddie. That's what you do when you're twenty, and you don't know any better. 'People obviously love it,' she went on. 'Sometimes it takes a big crisis to get them galvanised into writing these letters.'

'And how would they know there is a big crisis?' Eddie's eyes narrowed. 'Unless someone leaked plans of the development?'

'Who knows?' said Katie, and smiled, sphinxishly. 'I'll look into it.'

*   *   *

At lunchtime, Katie skipped her usual egg mayo baguette and headed straight for the Memorial Hall, her silver shoes in her bag.

Although she was thinking about the councillors

460

and the developers as she walked, she certainly wasn't expecting to see them standing right outside the Hall.

Nick Felix was tapping dubiously on an outside wall, clipboard in hand, with a couple of men in suits. They were all wearing hard hats.

When he saw Katie, a furtive look spread over his face.

'Kate?' he said. 'I, er, did Eddie send you?'

'No,' she replied, 'I'm here to use the Hall.'

'You're not here to do the assessment, then?' one of the developers asked.

'No.' Katie refused to feel guilty. Let Nick report back on her. So what if she had an interest in the place? So did lots of other locals—that was the whole point.

'Don't let us keep you,' Nick said smoothly, making a 'do go in' gesture with his hand, and, pushing her suspicions to one side for a moment, Katie marched through the doors.

Angelica was already there, wearing her red dancing shoes as she stepped slowly around the Hall, staring up at the stained-glass windows, lost in her own thoughts.

When Katie coughed, she spun round with her usual grace, and smiled to see her, then smiled directly at her silver shoes and the red lipstick Katie had hastily swiped on in the vestibule, using the reflection in a framed Coronation Ball programme as a mirror.

'Wonderful!' she said. 'I did wonder if you'd come.'

'The new me,' said Katie. 'As of today, I fit work round my commitments, not the other way round.'

'Let's not waste any of your lunchbreak, then,

eh? Now, the first thing I want you to do,' said Angelica, standing next to Katie and taking her hand, 'is put everything you *think* you know about tango right out of your head. The rose between the teeth, the silly head-flicking—that's not what this is about. That's just tea-room nonsense, really, no sex, please, we're English. Tango Argentino is the real thing—think about gauchos and prostitutes, and hot, steamy rooms. It's not about falling in love, like the waltz or the foxtrot, it's about *making* love. But you've got to commit yourself to it, otherwise it just doesn't work.'

She gave Katie a stern look. 'No half-measures, Katie. Tango is a dance you have to lose yourself in. Be someone else.'

'Right,' said Katie.

Although, it might be easier after a few drinks. Already this was seeming less of a good idea.

No, she told herself. You've got to try.

Angelica seemed to see her hesitation, and shook her hand encouragingly. 'I know you can do this! Now, I want you to imagine you're like a big cat, with nice loose limbs, prrrrowling for a man.' She stretched out her long leg, making a languorous line as she drew her foot slowly back to close. 'Seductive. Body conscious. Yes?'

'Yes,' said Katie, obediently, though it felt stupid.

'Now, there's not much to learn, you'll be pleased to hear. The basic step is called a salida.' Angelica took one slow step forward on her left foot, drew her right foot slinkily next to it, slowly slid back past it with her left foot, then closed with two quick steps and a slow. 'Like a backwards c shape. And again.'

462

She did it again, this time with Katie following her, mirroring the sway of her hips.

'Slide your feet,' said Angelica, 'sloooower, slinkier. And again.'

They did it over and over again, until Katie was sure she had the pattern right. It wasn't hard, and with Angelica teaching just her on her own, she didn't feel as self-conscious either.

'Fabulous, I think you've got that. Now, the hold.' Angelica put her arm round Katie, and took her hand, keeping eye contact as she pulled them close together. 'This is where it's a bit of a disadvantage learning with your female teacher, I'm afraid. There isn't a formal hold, because it's not a formal dance, it's very improvised. You're much more intimate, much more connected to your partner's body. It has to be close, because most of the steps involve you playing around with your partner's legs.'

'Really?' said Katie. 'Don't you fall over?'

Angelica laughed. 'No. No, it's part of the struggle of the dance. Anyway, he'll be very focused on keeping upright. So let's try those steps together . . .'

And she set off, walking outside Katie's backwards steps, counting the slows and the quicks. They went round and round, then Angelica angled them off to the side, and round again and back, and soon Katie was remembering to slide her feet, and when Angelica tipped her backwards, she actually felt herself lean into it.

Like she was doing her own thing, not following instructions. And that was something she'd never felt in any of the other dances. A flicker of excitement rippled through her.

463

Katie crooked her neck up and saw that Angelica was beaming with delight.

'Well done!' said Angelica. 'That's lovely! I think it's time for some music, don't you?'

She went over to her CD player and Katie checked her watch. Half-one already. It would take her five minutes to get back to the office. She didn't have that long.

But as soon as the distinctive staccato tango rhythm started, with mournful accordion squeezes, Katie felt a sudden desire to fit it all together. She started moving her feet in the salida even before Angelica came back.

Angelica said nothing, but took her in the hold and began to move, stepping around while they did one, then two, sets of the basic pattern.

Katie looked up, and couldn't stop smiling. 'This feels really easy,' she said.

'No, it's not easy, you've just found a dance you can do.'

'Really?'

'Yes, really. Stop fishing for compliments. Now in the Tango Argentino the man doesn't make *all* the decisions. Here, he might put you into a little extra step,' she motioned for Katie to step over her foot, 'but you can decide how many of them you do. Now twirl, flick your foot up, but keep your knees together so you're turning yourself round, that's it, and now the other way. That's called an ocho—a figure of eight.'

Katie carried on spinning on her toe, flicking her foot up. It took her a couple of goes to get it right, but then she couldn't stop. It felt wonderful.

'Is this right?' she asked, but as soon as she asked it, she realised she didn't really care if it was or not. She just enjoyed doing it.

'You've found your dance,' said Angelica. 'I knew you would.'

'Do you think?'

'I do.' Angelica gave her a firm look. 'The tango isn't for wallflowers. The woman needs to be strong, and definite in her moves, just as strong as the man. And there aren't so many rules as for the other ballroom dances, so it's really up to the dancers to decide how it goes. Ideally, you should forget there's anyone else in the room when you're dancing this. It's about seducing your partner, making the audience feel the heat sizzling between you.'

Katie had been feeling encouraged, but as Angelica finished, she deflated again.

'I don't see me and Ross sizzling,' she said.

'Katie, let me tell you something,' said Angelica. 'You've got to stop worrying about how good you are, and just enjoy it for what it is. Enjoy the feeling of moving, enjoy the compliment of a man wanting to dance with you. Stop letting that brain of yours run things.' She gave her a pointed look. 'Ross is better than you at the moment because he's not so hard on himself. I promise you, if you stop trying to mark yourself out of ten, *everything* will get better.'

Katie opened her mouth to protest, then stopped, knowing Angelica could see through the stiff holds to their cold and lonely bedroom.

'Everything,' repeated Angelica, meaningfully.

She blushed and looked down at her shoes.

'Anyway,' Angelica went on, to spare her embarrassment, 'once you get into the tango, you won't want to do anything else. It's the sort of

465

dance that just takes you over. I mean, when I . . .' She stopped.

'You what?' asked Katie.

Angelica gave her a sad smile. 'When I first learned the tango, my partner and I didn't bother with waltzes or foxtrots for months. Our ballroom teacher was furious. We went round the milongas just dancing this. Learning the moves, making up new ones, letting it get right into our blood. It was like learning to dance all over again. I loved it.'

'Was that your dancing partner or your . . . romantic partner?' asked Katie.

'Both.' Angelica brushed some invisible lint off her skirt, and Katie saw a glow of something soft come over her face. 'He was called Tony Canero. We were brilliant together—on the dancefloor at least. We won everything we entered, pretty much. I've never seen a man who danced like him, then or since. He really found something in me that I didn't know was there—great partners do that.'

'Was he your husband?'

'No.' She made a tsking noise with her tongue, her face still vulnerable. 'No, we didn't marry. It's better to learn to dance with your husband than to marry your dancing partner, I think. We danced together, all over the world, every competition going, and we were together the same amount of time, but it all came to a head. It all ended. No, I haven't seen him in years.'

'You didn't stay in touch?' asked Katie, curiously. How could you achieve that much with someone, live through an experience like that, and let them just vanish from your life?

'We didn't exactly part on Christmas-card terms,' said Angelica. 'He ran off with a younger

466

woman. Just before we were about to compete in a national championship, actually—not the greatest timing.'

'What a bastard!' said Katie, her eyes widening in sympathy.

Angelica opened her mouth to say something, then closed it again. When she looked at Katie, frankness made her eyes even more piercing. 'I was about to say something very flippant there, but if I'm being honest, it was as much my fault as his. I was very insecure in those days, thought that I was only as good as our last competition. I had this obsession about winning every title. I thought Tony would only want me so long as I could be the perfect partner, as long as we were learning new things together.'

She looked down at her hands. 'In the end, he said he didn't know whether I really loved him off the dancefloor as much as I did on it. Which was rich, because I could have said the same about him. I think the reality was that we were both scared of having to be honest with each other, when we didn't have the dancing to do the talking for us. We were really hot stuff on the floor, you know. I couldn't bear the thought of us stagnating into slippers and cocoa when he found out how dull I was underneath the sequins.'

'You're hardly dull, Angelica!'

The ballroom smile didn't cover the regret in Angelica's face, and standing there in the empty, daylit Hall, she seemed older than at class, and more worn out. 'Tempestuous relationships are all very well when you've got the energy for fighting and making up, but . . .' She shrugged. 'It ended very quickly, but I'd rather have quick endings than drag things out. And then I went off to America and was married for a while to a very sweet man, Jerry, and I was very happy.'

Katie wasn't convinced by her bright smile or her verys. 'Tony's never tried to get in touch since?'

She shook her head. 'No. I've moved around a lot. I've never believed in going back, in any case.'

'You're back here, though, aren't you?' Katie pointed out.

Angelica sighed through her long nose. 'Seems so.'

The tango music seemed to have unlocked memories that she couldn't pack away, and Katie was conscious that she was intruding.

Not intruding, she thought, sharing. I'm sharing my own relationship woes with her, without speaking, and she's sharing with me. It was a bittersweet feeling, but not completely sad.

'Sorry,' she said. 'I didn't mean to be nosy.'

'You're not,' said Angelica. 'It's just . . . It brings it all back, teaching you this, being back in this Hall again. You know, I came back here to sort my mother's house, and really it's been *me* that's needed the sorting out.' She looked up at Katie and twisted her mouth wryly. 'Don't put things in storage, that's my advice. In life and in relationships. One day you have to unpack it all, whether you like it or not.'

Angelica slapped her hands on her knees to indicate that the melancholy break was over. 'And when you unpack your old dresses, you're absolutely depressed to think you were once that skinny.' She smiled. 'You have to find slim young women to pass them on to. Now, don't you have that job of yours to get back to?'

'I do.' Suddenly Katie was in no rush to get back to work. It had slipped down her priorities. 'Can I have a CD of tango music to listen to in the car?'

Angelica smiled, and her face lost thirty years in a flash. 'Of course. At last!'

*   *   *

As she left, pulling her coat tightly around her against the chill November wind, Katie looked back at the Hall, and was startled to see one of the outer stained-glass windows was broken. Not smashed, but definitely damaged. Slowly, she walked back, and realised that deep cracks split two other windows, and the wooden window frames had been pulled away, as if to prove they were rotten.

Her chest contracted with outrage, and in an instant, she knew what Nick had been up to—she'd heard about shady stuff like that before, contractors 'discovering' irreparable deterioration in staircases when they examined them with sledgehammers, or accidental damage done to historic façades, meaning the whole building may as well come down.

That was the last straw, thought Katie, and instead of feeling bad, she felt thoroughly elated as she stormed back to the office.

*   *   *

Jo's house was as tidy as ever, but, later that evening, Katie could sense a hum of chaos as she walked through the door to pick up the children.

469

Ross hadn't called to say where he was, and she was too proud to phone him to see what he'd got up to on his day off.

The television was on very loud in the sitting room, for a start, which Katie didn't remember ever hearing in Jo's house, and the girls were screeching about something in the kitchen. She couldn't tell what; they were making a high-pitched keening noise that, in her house, usually signified extreme pleading for sweets.

As she walked in, Katie realised she'd been proved right for once.

'No more Haribo!' Jo was yelling back as Molly and Hannah made hysterical praying gestures. 'Molly, I promise you, even if I had any more, you wouldn't be getting any! Look,' she added, spotting Katie, 'Hannah's mummy will back me up. Isn't that right—too many sweeties before tea makes your hair fall out?'

And I thought Jo was way above scary stories, thought Katie. Thank God it's not just me.

'Absolutely right,' she nodded, seriously. 'And I was thinking of taking *some* little girls to Claire's Accessories to buy new hair bobbles this weekend, but obviously there's no point taking you two if you don't have any lovely hair to put in them?'

Hannah and Molly looked shocked, then ran off, screeching, to the sitting room again.

'Thanks for that,' said Jo. She let her face fall back into its exhausted state once the girls had left and Katie realised that it was only copious concealer making Jo look normal. 'I promised myself I'd never do blatant sweetie lies like my mum did, but they haven't let up all afternoon. I'm on the verge of running amok with that sleeping

470

stuff Leigh Sinton drugged her kids with last summer.'

'What?' said Katie, putting the kettle on before Jo felt obliged to hostess her. 'I missed that.'

Ross might have told her, but she couldn't remember. She could barely remember who Leigh Sinton's child was. I've been missing too much, she told herself fiercely. No wonder Ross thinks I don't care.

'Delphi's mum. She couldn't be bothered to play i-Spy all the way to Brittany, so she knocked them out before they got to the motorway. Everyone pretended to be shocked, but Boots sold out of whatever she used in two days.' Jo gave her a weary look. 'The scandalous world of the under-fives, eh? We have to make our own entertainment.'

'It's more entertaining than my day at work.' Katie sank onto a kitchen chair. 'One passive-aggressive argument with my boss about this regeneration project and now I discover they're trying to sabotage the whole thing. Hence a sneaky mobile-phone call to English Heritage about getting the key building in that very same regeneration project listed so my boss can go berserk and possibly fire me.' She watched Jo make them both a cup of coffee. 'The woman at English Heritage even asked me if I wanted a job with them, seeing as I was so concerned with historic buildings. I might as well write my own resignation letter, save Eddie the bother of sidelining me back to car parks.'

Jo put a mug down in front of her. 'Why not? I think it's a great idea. You should talk to them— it's just the sort of thing we need round here, more appreciation of what the town's already got.

471

What's happening with the Hall?'

'Well, Bridget suggested we have an awareness-raising evening before Christmas—she and Angelica are organising an old-style ball, where everyone comes in vintage clothes? Bring the place to everyone's attention, get them fired up about saving it. Angelica's promised she'll ring some of her old big-band contacts about the music . . .' Katie cupped her hands round her coffee, not caring that it stung her hands. She looked up at Jo, and added, tentatively, 'You must think I'm just like Greg, always obsessing about the office when I should be worrying about stuff nearer to home.'

'Katie, you're nothing like Greg,' said Jo. 'Nothing at all.'

'I am.' Katie stared into her mug. 'Work's taken over my life, I know. But it's because I want the kids to have everything they need, and it's down to me to provide that. I just want to be a good mum. And I'm not.'

'You're an amazing mum, Katie,' said Jo, very seriously. 'You're far, far too hard on yourself. Do you think Hannah would be doing as well as she is if you weren't? You work hard, and you set a great example about being independent. And it's not like you don't spend time with the children—you do! You're there for them when you get in, and all weekend.'

'Not enough,' Katie began. 'It's not the same as you being at home every day with them . . .'

'What? Fitting them in around everything else I have to do?' demanded Jo. She put down her coffee and folded her arms across her chest. 'Look, you've got to stop this idea that it's some kind of *Play School* idyll being at home twenty-four seven.

472

Yes, it's lovely sometimes. But you ask Ross—it can be like solitary bloody confinement, when it's just you, a squealing baby and the *Fimbles* for hours and hours on end. You'd go mad within a week. You need a seriously high boredom threshold, and yours is down here somewhere! Face it, Katie—and I say this as your friend—Ross is great with the kids. Of the two of you, he's the right one to be at home with them. So stop beating yourself up about it, and just get on with it.'

'But I feel like I'm letting them down!' Katie burst out.

'How?' Jo stared at her. 'I don't get it. How are you letting them down?'

'By not being there.'

'Well, that's about *you*, then, not the kids,' said Jo, robustly. 'That's about you feeling guilty. Because let me tell you, they're just fine. You spend proper, focused, positive time with them when you're home, and they love you. Anything else is just you setting yourself yet another impossible hoop to jump through, that no one else gives a stuff about.'

Katie was taken aback by the breezy way Jo was dishing it out. 'Are you saying I'm neurotic?'

'No!' said Jo. 'I'm saying you're missing the point of how good a mum you already are! You're being the best parent possible by giving them a roof over their heads and everything they need. That. Is. Enough.'

She relented a little, seeing Katie's dazed face. 'This is just now, Katie. You've got *years* of parenting ahead of you. Years! Think of all those mother and daughter shopping trips you'll have with Hannah when she's older. You don't know

473

how things'll turn out—Ross might go back to work in a few years, and you can go part-time when Jack's at school. *You* can be the one going to football matches and sitting through endless recorder recitals.'

She reached over and grabbed Katie round the waist, shaking her for emphasis. 'I mean it, Katie. Why are you so angry with yourself? You're a great mother. I admire what you've done enormously and it breaks my *heart* that you can't see what everyone else can. Give yourself a break.'

Katie felt her lip tremble. 'No one's ever said that to me before,' she admitted, wobbling a little. 'Sounds stupid, doesn't it?'

'Really?' Jo looked astonished.

She shook her head. 'No. I always thought I'd be a mum like you—you know, all warm and cake-baking, and cosy. That's what I wanted, to stay at home like my own mum did with me, *doing* stuff. Being responsible for my children. And it hasn't worked out like that, and I just feel . . . like I've failed.'

'Then you're daft,' said Jo. 'Because it's not just about how well you can make your own play-doh. I'd say you've done a better job than me.'

'And I've taken it out on Ross,' Katie went on, suddenly realising. 'I've been angry at him for doing what I wanted to do, and maybe I've just been jealous that he's done it so well. You're right, I don't have his patience, or his niceness.'

'Oh, you do,' insisted Jo.

'No, I don't. For a couple of hours, yes, but not for day after day. And I've been so wrapped up in hating myself that I've let it destroy our marriage.' She looked up at Jo miserably. 'I've pushed him away because I hated myself. How stupid is that?'

'Pretty stupid,' agreed Jo. 'But it's not too late.'

Katie shook her head. 'He's just not talking to me any more. I keep trying to tell him how I feel, but he won't listen.'

'I don't think it's too late,' said Jo again. 'Trust me.'

She scrutinised Jo's open face. What did she mean by that? What had Ross told her? It stung, not just that Ross found it easier to talk to Jo than he did her, but that Jo had a faith in her marriage that she couldn't see.

'Why? What's he said?' she demanded immediately, but Jo's mouth had closed in a firm line.

'He hasn't said anything,' she insisted, but Katie didn't believe her. 'I just know. Are you still going to that counsellor?'

'He won't, not now.'

'Well, maybe you should go,' suggested Jo. 'On your own? It might be helpful.'

Katie thought of Peter, and the things Ross had probably said about her after she stormed out of their last session. Going on her own was like admitting it had failed.

At least her private tango lessons with Angelica would be good exercise, even if they didn't have the magic effect Angelica seemed to think they would. 'Maybe,' she said, to agree more than anything else.

'I'm going to start going,' said Jo, starting to stack the dishwasher. 'On my own. I don't see why you and Ross and my mum should be the only ones stuck with my moaning.'

The shrieking continued from the sitting room,

475

but Jo carried on loading plates calmly and ignored it. For someone whose husband had walked out days ago, she seemed unexpectedly serene.

'Jo, don't take this the wrong way, but are you on tranquillisers?' asked Katie. 'Did you go to the doctor or something?'

'Oh, this isn't what I'm like all the time,' said Jo. 'Inside, I'm furious. It's sort of the fury that keeps me calm. I keep thinking, how dare Greg leave me, how dare he treat me so appallingly, and that allows me to let the kids do whatever they want, and not be round there begging him to come home. It's a sort of weird balance. And he's paying for a cleaner to keep the house tidy so I can focus on the children, plus he's not here giving me a hard time about the mess. Or the size of my arse. I don't have to worry about where he is, because he's not meant to be here. So that's a few things less to get stressed about.'

Jo's composure slipped, just enough for Katie to see the strain around her eyes, and her heart ached in sympathy. At least she was angry. At least she wasn't blaming herself. But was it really good for the girls to have their mother boiling away inside?

'Jo,' she said, carefully, 'if you need some time out, I can always take the kids, you know. I mean, I'm not saying you can't cope on your own, but if you need to let off steam . . .'

Jo saw Katie's concern and touched her arm. 'Listen, don't get me wrong, I'm not furious all the time. Sometimes I'm really scared, and that's when it goes to pieces. But I keep telling myself that it's better like this, than if I'd forgiven him over and over, and my beautiful, bright daughters grew up into terrified fembots who think the only way to

476

make a man love them is to be thin and let him screw around.'

'And you're right,' insisted Katie. 'If you need someone to tell you that, call me. Any time. Twenty-four hours a day.'

'I will.' Jo managed a weak smile. 'I've hired my solicitor, and my mum's constantly on the phone, so they'll be telling me too. But I'm so glad I've got you and Ross.' She paused, and lifted her eyebrows significantly. '*Both* of you.'

It was weird, thought Katie, how Jo and I've suddenly got something back in common, now we're both struggling again. Or maybe, she corrected herself, it's just that I've managed to take a step back from my own navel-gazing and seen she needs some support.

'You're going to be fine,' she said, wanting it to be true with a strength that made Jo blink with emotion.

A thunder of small feet in the hall stopped either of them from saying any more, and the sadness vanished from Jo's face to be replaced by convincing cheerfulness as Molly rushed in, with Hannah close behind.

'Come and see, Mummy! Come and see!' Molly ordered. 'Come and see our magic horse!'

'It's a game,' explained Hannah, pointedly directing her attention to Jo. 'Jo! You have to play!'

'*Both* Mummies have to play,' said Jo, firmly. 'Now what does this horse eat?'

'How about these lovely carrot sticks I've brought with me from the supermarket?' Katie suggested, waving the bag of lunchbox crudités that—fortuitously—was at the top of her supermarket shopping. 'Horses love carrots.'

'Remember the ones we saw on our holiday?' Jo added. 'Are you going to show us how they munched up the carrots?'

Hannah looked suspiciously at Katie, then grudgingly conceded. 'All right. You can bring the carrots, Mummy. But be very quiet, he's sleeping.'

She and Molly crept off, shushing each other loudly.

'I hope your horse impression is up to scratch,' sighed Jo.

'It's better than you think,' said Katie.

CHAPTER THIRTY-THREE

The drizzling dampness of autumn turned into a crisp, cold winter chill as November wore on, and Ross continued to vanish off on his own on Thursdays, and Monday evenings.

He was vague with Katie about where he was going but she noticed, from little things Hannah said, that he was spending lots of time with Jo, and that he'd had another haircut that sharpened up his face, bringing him into a new, fresh focus. He was sparkier round the house, not letting Hannah's new clinginess set into habit, and reminding her, with scrupulous fairness, how lucky she now was to have Mummy all to herself on Thursday evenings. It made Katie try even harder to show him how much she appreciated what he did, but though he was as kind as ever, the distance between them still echoed.

Jo came along to the ballroom lessons again,

and Katie felt a new sympathy for Trina and Chloe, as she and Jo often had to dance together, for lack of male partners. Frank and Baxter had never been so popular. It was nice, though, feeling like two old ballroom ladies. They had a laugh about each other's bosoms getting in the way, and how Katie still tried to lead even when it was Jo's turn.

As they were leaving at the end of the evening, Angelica caught Katie putting on her coat.

'You and Ross, you will dance at the gala night?' she asked, although it was more of a statement than a question.

'I don't think so.' Katie shook her head. 'I mean, things are OK, but . . .' She shrugged. 'Maybe I could do something with Jo? A jive or something?'

A determined expression set on Angelica's face. 'Katie, you're still coming to our lunchtime session tomorrow, aren't you?'

'Yes, but I . . .' She was going to say, I don't see what the point is, but the fierce look in Angelica's eyes stopped her. 'Yes,' she said. 'I am.'

'Good,' she said, and swept off to tell Lauren she would be having her big waltz moment after all.

'I heard that,' said Jo. 'I can't believe you're trying to wriggle out of dancing with me.'

'Well, if it's just us four girls, maybe Angelica can work up a can-can number for us.'

'*Moulin Rouge!*' said Jo. 'With Trina and Chloe!'

'That's a cha-cha,' deadpanned Katie, and was pleased to see Jo's shoulders shake.

Katie was happy to make Jo laugh, because Greg's solicitors weren't making it easy for her. Their suspicions about the secret girlfriend turned out not only to be true, but she was both pregnant and a junior employee, and Greg wanted a divorce quickly, but with as much as he could cling on to.

As soon as they were in the car, Jo spilled out the details, and hot tears spilled out at the same time, running angrily down her face.

'He's putting a price on what I brought to our *marriage*,' Jo sobbed. 'I can't believe he's valuing me, like he's valuing the house!'

It was the same most weeks. Katie comforted her the best she could, and then Jo cleaned up her face with a baby wipe and went back to teach Molly how to rumba or cha-cha or whatever Angelica had put them through that week. Molly and Hannah had abandoned ponies in favour of pleas for ballet lessons, but only with Angelica.

Angelica was 'thinking about it'.

*   *   *

A few weeks later, when Katie arrived for her lunchtime tango lesson, she guessed Angelica was already there, because as she pushed open the front door, loud tango music was soaring through the Hall, the haunting accordion chords gliding against the staccato drumbeats. It made Katie stop for a moment. There was something insistent about the way the melody surged between light and dark, and it raised the hairs on the back of her neck. It isn't music to tap your feet to, she thought, not like the pretty waltzes; it's music to strike poses and act out parts.

Slowly, she was beginning to see why Angelica thought it might be good for someone who needed permission to step out of their everyday life; music like this demanded something more than just a series of learned steps.

As she hung her coat up on the hook, Katie glanced through the glass panes into the Hall, and caught a glimpse of Angelica's lithe body arching like a black cat as the music slowed to a keening crescendo. She was wearing a simple red dress, and had tied her hair in a loose ponytail. It shone like a ripple of black treacle down her back.

Katie had never seen Angelica's hair down before and she stopped, captivated by how striking it was, as it swished and flicked from side to side, not one thread of grey in it.

You'd never think she was nearly sixty, marvelled Katie, as she watched her syncopate her gestures against the beat, stretching out long arm gestures to double time, and slowly drawing her pointed toe around. She had the sort of natural rhythm that would make her look like the greatest dancer in the room, even when she was eighty and only dancing a quarter of the steps she used to. Each one would count, and you'd see the ones she wasn't dancing as clearly as if she had.

She was about to go in when she realised Angelica wasn't on her own; there was a man in there with her, dressed in black. He'd been standing to the side while she did some kind of semi-Flamenco stamping step, and now he took hold of her again, stepping back into the salida as their cheeks touched. The music changed tempo, and he walked around her as Angelica spun on the ball of her foot, her leg flicked back at a perfect right angle.

Katie's heartbeat quickened as her nerves took hold. Was that Angelica's own partner, or someone else she was giving private lessons to? Did she

481

expect her to dance with him? They were pretty good together, and when Katie saw what the tango should look like when it was done properly her old despair that she'd ever learn to be that good flooded back.

I don't really want to dance with anyone but Ross, she thought suddenly. I don't want to meet new people dancing, I just want him to dance with me like that.

Angelica stopped and demonstrated a new step to the man, darting her foot in and out between his leg, so her red shoe flashed against the black of his trousers. He held her close, his long white hand low on her red dress, as the Argentinian music rattled and yearned in the background.

'You've got it!' she heard Angelica exclaim, with a delight that she rarely displayed in group class. 'Perfection!'

Feeling like a voyeur, Katie sank back onto the bench and put on the shoes she danced in. She'd bought a new pair especially, gold leather with good slippy soles—as much glitz as she could manage to change into on her lunchbreak.

Katie looked at her feet and tried to imagine them doing the same haughty, sexy steps that Angelica had been showing off. It would have helped if she'd had time to give herself a pedicure; tango Argentino was the sort of dance that demanded bright red toenails peeking through fishnets.

For the first time in years, Katie actually wished she'd had time for a pedicure, and she shocked herself by wondering if the salon next to Sainsbury's did lunchtime appointments. Maybe that was what Angelica meant about rediscovering her inner woman.

'Come on, feet,' she said, as she pushed herself off the bench and prepared to go in. 'Do it for me.'

When she opened the door to the Hall, the music was still playing, but Angelica was on her own, sketching out a shape with her arms, stepping back and forth thoughtfully as she explored a new step in her mind. Her head bounced up when she saw Katie, making her ponytail flick. Up close, she didn't look quite so young, with feathery lines around the eyes, but the unbounded pleasure in her face and the flush in her cheeks gave her a radiance that was more than beautiful.

'Ah, hello!' she said. 'I've got a surprise for you!'

'I saw,' said Katie.

Angelica looked caught off-guard. 'Did you?'

'Yes, I saw through the glass—you were dancing with someone.'

'That's *part* of the surprise,' she said, recovering quickly and wagging her finger. 'The first bit is this.' She stepped lightly over to the chairs and picked up a yellow Selfridges bag. 'I think it's time to take your tango lessons on a stage, now you know the basics, so first of all, I want you to pop into the loos and put this on.'

'Another dress?' said Katie, thinking of the amazing red encrusted number still hanging in her wardrobe, a kidnapped butterfly amidst her drab office suits. 'But you've been far too generous already. I thought . . .'

Angelica shook her head. 'No, that's a ballroom tango dress. Far too stagey for what we're doing here. This is a real milonga dress, for the tango Argentino. Much sexier, easier to dance in. Go on, put it on.'

'But that man,' Katie said, taking the bag nervously. 'Do I have to dance with him, because I'm not sure that . . .'

'You're not my only student,' said Angelica, sternly. 'Now, off you go.' She tapped her watch.

Reluctantly, Katie went into the chilly loos.

If the worst comes to the worst I could get the council to hire this place out to film crews, she thought, looking round at the cobwebby pipes coiling round the walls. Even the plumbing had been done with an eye to elegance, and the institutional blue-grey paint didn't spoil its neatness.

The dress didn't look very big in the bag, just a little puddle of black jersey, but when Katie pulled it over her head, it fell over her body and hung perfectly where it hit her shoulders and hips, flattering her white throat and the curve of her shoulders with the deep v shape in the front.

She looked at herself in the mirror, half amazed and half horrified at how sensuously it clung to her body, highlighting every inch of what little shape she had. The fabric was heavy and swung as she turned to see her back exposed in a matching v.

It swung so sexily that Katie found herself swinging back the other way, just to see how it would feel. It felt fabulous, rippling against her knees, so she swung back again, this time turning her head over her shoulder to peep coyly at herself in the mirror.

A sultrier Katie peeped back, and she nearly laughed in surprise.

There was a big silky red rose on a comb in the bag too, which Katie pushed into her hair, holding her fringe up at one side. The music had started up again in the Hall, and with a final check in the mirror (where had all those curves come from?) she stalked back out, already holding herself differently, so her post-Jack tummy bulge wouldn't draw more focus than her shoulders.

Angelica clapped her hands when she saw her, although Katie detected something else in her face too—a shadow of something that she tried not to let Katie see, but it must have been quite a strong emotion because it showed in her eyes, even though her red lips were smiling generously.

'You look stunning!' she said. 'Stunning! From now on, that's your tango outfit.'

'But I can't possibly . . .'

Angelica waved her hands. 'I'm getting rid of a lot of my old gowns. I've got a whole box for Lauren to dress up in. Now then, as I said before, you can only learn so much dancing with me. You need some tension to play with, so you can find that inner vamp we talked about.' She patted Katie's hand to temper the words with kindness.

'So I've found you a partner.'

Katie's heart began to beat more quickly. This was it. This was taking it a bit further, and she wasn't sure she even wanted to practise moves like that with someone other than Ross.

'He looked pretty good to me,' Katie started to say, 'I hope you've warned him that I'm a total beginner . . .'

'He's a beginner himself,' said Angelica, and pulled the door to the ante room open. 'We're ready for you now.'

The man in black stepped into the Hall, running a familiar hand through his dark hair, and in that instant, Katie realised it was Ross.

It took her a second to match her Ross with Angelica's self-assured partner from a moment ago. Ross, dancing with that sort of assertiveness? Really?

Angelica was smiling as if her face would split, and turned her back very deliberately while she went over to the CD player, leaving them staring at each other, as if they'd only just met.

'Katie?' he said, lifting an eyebrow.

Katie couldn't think what to say, but she could feel herself blushing, though she didn't know why. Ross looked masculine and unfamiliar, in a black polo neck and tight trousers. Another man's clothes. He'd done something to his hair too, because it was gleaming and pushed off his face, showing off his eyes, and he walked with a confidence that bordered—she couldn't quite believe this—on a swagger.

The effect made her skin prickle with excitement.

I really fancy him, thought Katie, as shock and attraction and delight ran through her like a massive jolting shot of espresso. He is a *gorgeous* man.

Ross narrowed his eyes, and said, '*Bailamos*?' as he held out his hand.

He didn't say it entirely seriously, but there was no trace of his usual self-deprecating humour, and it only added to the delicious strangeness of the situation.

'*Si!*' said Katie, in the same pretend Spanish accent, and without warning, he swept her into the closest possible hold: his arm tight around her back, his hand clasping hers right up by her cheek. She felt her whole body melt into his as he tipped

486

her slightly off balance, but his leg was strong against hers, bearing her up, and she let him feel the weight of her against him, so their bodies touched the whole length of her thigh.

Their noses were almost brushing and his breath was warm on her face. They were so close to each other that she had no choice but to look deeply in his face, and for a moment the rest of the room blurred into nothing as the shock of being so intimately connected after months and months of physical detachment swept through every nerve ending in her skin.

Ross gazed into her eyes with a passion that made the colour flood into her cheeks; his eyes were nearly black and it was obvious that he was seeing a different Katie, just as she was seeing a different Ross.

She stared back, not letting herself smile and spoil the drama of the moment. So this is what those magazines mean when they tell you to dress up as different people and meet in a bar, she thought, dazed. It's Ross, but not Ross. Tango Ross. I know he's going to be seductive and masculine and everything else the dance tells him to be, and he knows I know. He knows I'm going to be sensual and defiant, and he can't wait.

Their lips were still inches apart, and neither of them could look away, for fear of breaking the electric tension crackling between them. Katie knew she couldn't hide anything from him, and a kind of fearlessness spread through her at the dare in his eyes.

Yes, sure, it was pantomime, but Katie couldn't remember ever feeling so attracted to Ross, and because she could tell he felt the same way, an old sexiness crept over her. The same tingle she'd felt when they first met, and she couldn't believe he fancied her as much as she fancied him. I want him to feel that again too, she thought, desperately. And if he won't listen to me at home, he's going to listen to me now.

The music started, and without speaking, he led her into the basic salida. Their hips brushed as he stepped around her backwards step with a deft confidence that made her trail her left foot with more vampishness than she'd summoned up with Angelica. They did it again, neither varying the steps as they measured each other up, like two cats prowling in a circle.

Just when Katie thought they were going to get through another basic—with a touch of disappointment—Ross suddenly led her into the figure-of-eight spin that made her swivel first one way, then the other, up on her toes, as he stood back, watching motionless apart from his eyes, which followed her as her hips turned to push into the spin.

'You dance this step to tease your partner,' Angelica had told her, demonstrating with a provocative flick of the knee that Katie had thought she'd never master. 'You're flirting with him, making him wait to carry on the dance. *You* decide how many ochos are enough.'

Her skirt began to flare the first time she turned, and Katie knew it was rising up around her knees, showing off her slim calves. She spun once, twice, then as Ross started to lead her back into the basic, she flashed a stern look at him from under her eyelashes and did another spin, then a fourth.

Then, and only then, she let him step around

her to finish the salida, and without thinking, her head arched back proudly, just like Angelica's had in the lesson.

She met Ross's gaze, and a thrill of excitement shivered through her as he let a small approving smile tug at the corner of his mouth. Not the puppyish, eager grin he usually gave her, but something much more sexy, more difficult to please. She'd pulled off that move perfectly, and he was impressed, she could see in his face. And in his eyes, and his hands which stroked her back, and his breath, which was quick on her neck, much quicker than their slow pace required. Katie slid her feet languorously along the floor as they stepped round once more in the basic pattern, and Ross led them off at an angle, into the centre of the room.

Katie was vaguely aware of the door swinging shut as Angelica left, but she wasn't really listening any more. Every part of her tingled when it came into contact with Ross's body, when their legs grazed against each other in the close steps, when he pulled her so close that their chests touched, when she trailed her ankle teasingly against the inside of his calf in the darting hooks and flicks while he stared at her with his dark, hungry eyes.

They were moving without thinking, and Katie had never felt so inside herself, acutely aware of her movements, and of the breath rushing in and out of her lungs. She had no idea where the steps would go, whenever they started the basic pattern. Sometimes Ross let the steps linger, going doubly slowly on the long beats, and sometimes he would speed up, and the blood raced around her veins as she followed his lead.

The Spanish accordion soared above the rattling percussion, while a woman sang words Katie couldn't translate but understood perfectly: they were about needing, wanting, loving someone. She was racing with adrenaline. Being able to move inside the music, in harmony with another person, was the most astonishing feeling in the world, and a million miles away from the classes they'd stumbled through before. With this dance there were no rules to get wrong, or right—where they went around the room was as much up to her as Ross, and the excitement of knowing that her steps would guide his steps kept her on the very edge of concentration as she scanned his face for clues.

He held her at arms' length, so she could spin one way, then the other, in an ocho that only lasted two swivels, because she wanted to be in his arms again, and their eyes didn't leave each other's face.

I have no idea what he's going to do next, she thought, giddily, and as if he could read her mind, Ross pulled her right up close to him, so their mouths nearly touched, sending electric tingles into her lips. He held her there for a moment, so she could feel the hardness of his body against hers, then, still holding her gaze, he dipped her right back.

Katie didn't even resist, trusting him absolutely to hold her safe. The blood rushed to her head as her spine arched and the music rushed and crashed into a final scratchy pinnacle of guitars and drums.

I've never been so happy, she thought. I feel like a thirty-something woman, with so much behind me, and so much ahead of me, and this handsome, surprising man to do it all with.

And then she felt Ross's arm pull her back up,

490

and before she could even take a breath, his hands were in her hair, and his lips were on hers, searching and kissing.

Katie forgot everything else, as she wrapped herself around him, kissing him as hungrily as she used to when they first met, and every touch and murmur was fresh. How could she have got so close to this man that she'd forgotten to see who he was? The thought of losing him now was unbearable.

It wasn't about him, she realised now. It was about her. It was about being happy to be herself, and right now, she didn't want to be anyone else.

Ross pulled away so she could see his face. 'I've been having lessons,' he said. 'On Thursday evenings. Angelica's idea. You're so much better than me, though.'

Tears filled her eyes and she smiled through them. 'I'm not. I'm sorry,' she whispered into the soft skin on his cheeks. 'I've been so stupid. I've let everything get between us, and I'm sorry for hurting you.'

'I've been just as bad,' Ross murmured back, serious now. 'But not any more. You're what makes my life right, and I don't want to lose you.'

'You won't.' Katie covered his cheekbones, his eyelids, his lips with quick kisses. 'You can't.'

The rain poured down outside, hammering against the stained-glass windows. It didn't sound like an English downpour to Katie; it sounded like a steamy Latin American monsoon.

CHAPTER THIRTY-FOUR

When Bridget set her contact network in motion, in aid of getting more publicity for the Memorial Hall campaign, things really started moving in ways that surprised even her. Teaching virtually every Longhamptonian under the age of fifty—all of whom were happy to do what they could for lovely Mrs Armstrong—meant that within days, the Gala Ballroom Dance evening went from a discussion over coffee with Angelica and Katie to the local social event of the year.

'A quick phone call' to the deputy editor of the Longhampton weekly newspaper led to a whole-page spread about the Memorial Hall, with full details of tickets, and an interview with Angelica about her career as Longhampton's most famous daughter. That was just the start. Such was the public response that they had to follow it up the next week with a fashion special starring Lauren modelling Angelica's old dresses, while Trina's niece at the salon was drafted in to advise on how to achieve the *Strictly Come Dancing* ballroom hair styles. And although Chloe couldn't be persuaded to model for her a second time, she did a lovely job of making Peggy's grey hair look like the Queen's. If the Queen had gone in for diamanté butterflies and 'pink flashes', as well as roller sets.

Bridget explained in her interview that it wasn't so much about raising money for the Hall, as raising awareness of its threatened state, but even at £25 a head (drinks and live music included, courtesy of another old pupil who ran the local wine merchants and a semi-retired band leader contact of Angelica's, from her London days), the tickets were flying out. The interest was quite astonishing. Frank hadn't been able to tend to his garden for days, what with having to answer the phone constantly, and Lauren couldn't sell enough tickets at the surgery. Even Kathleen grudgingly admitted she wanted one: 'Just to see you dance, Big Bird,' she added, as if some additional explanation was required. Before long, Ross and Jo had set up a website to answer all the questions, and the on-line petition racked up daily, with interest from as far away as London.

'You've done a lovely job on that,' said Katie, looking over Ross's shoulder one evening as he uploaded some more photographs he'd taken of the glitterball. The children were both bathed and in bed, and the house was peaceful. She dropped a kiss on his hair. 'Beautiful photos.'

'Thanks,' said Ross.

He turned and smiled up at her. Giving praise and receiving praise without making a big deal of it was something they were working on—at Peter's insistence. Two sessions on their own helped, and now they were going together again. It had felt a bit forced at first, but the more they did it, the easier it got. Now everything seemed a little warmer.

'Stop being so hard on yourselves,' he'd told them, when they went back. 'If you don't cut yourselves some slack, you'll both be looking for criticism where there just isn't any. That's where the rows come from, not each other.'

Even though Peter looked very fairly at both of them as he spoke, Katie knew he was talking to her, more than Ross, but she didn't bridle. She thought of what Jo had said, and Angelica, and simply agreed. Three genuine compliments a day, that was their new goal. It was easier than getting Hannah to eat her five bits of fruit and veg, anyway.

'I was talking to Jo,' Ross went on, 'and one of her friends needs a new website. I said I'd meet up with him, have a chat about maybe designing something.' He clicked on a spooky detail of the stained-glass windows and made it link to the details Frank had researched about the designer—quite famous, it turned out. Another tick on the heritage list.

'Jo says?' Katie began, before she could stop herself, but Ross didn't rise to the bait.

'Yeah, some estate agent going it alone. We've been talking about it for a while, actually, since Center Parcs? That's what we've been meeting up about—making plans for a web design business we can run together. From home, so we can fit it round the kids.' He turned back to check Katie's reaction.

'Oh!' she said, rearranging her face into approving surprise. 'Right. Was that what you were going round there for?'

'Yeah. Jo's been giving me some advice about costings, marketing, that sort of thing. Why? What did you think we were doing?' he asked, amused. 'Having an affair? Don't be so ridiculous.'

He spun back and carried on clicking. 'Why would I look elsewhere when I've got the best tango dancer in the world right here?'

Katie put her arms around Ross's shoulders and buried her face into his neck: he smelled of Jack's bath, and Persil. She didn't say anything, but little throwaway compliments like that meant more to her for being so freely, honestly given, reassurances that they weren't taking each other for granted. She didn't envy Jo for the expensive empty bunches of roses Greg used to bring her, not now she knew they were excuses. Ross's tea in bed was worth a thousand times more.

'It'll be nice to put some money into the kitty,' Ross went on, casually, changing the portrait of Bridget in front of the door. 'Means maybe you can think about going down to four days? Have a day at home with the kids while I get my nose to the grindstone in Jo's shed. That's where we're planning on setting up our design HQ, by the way. Unless you can swing us some development office deal.'

'I'll talk to work,' said Katie.

And that's all I've ever wanted, she thought, watching as Ross's mouse meandered over his web page, doing amazing, creative stuff she didn't understand.

'If you want me to sort out some . . .' she started, but then stopped herself. Let Ross run his own business. She had to knock the control-freak thing on the head.

'What?'

'Nothing,' she said. 'Just proud of you.'

Ross turned away from his computer and wrapped his arms around her waist. 'Then we're a very proud couple.'

*　　　*　　　*

The one person who wasn't particularly impressed

by Longhampton's upsurge of interest in the Memorial Hall was Eddie Harding.

It put him in 'a difficult position, on-message-wise', as he explained through gritted teeth in a pre-meeting tête-à-tête in Katie's office. It could hardly be a more difficult position than the one he was currently occupying, one buttock perched on the edge of her desk with what he obviously saw as relaxed casualness.

'Where are we on the benefit see-saw, Kate?' he asked rhetorically. 'Are we backing the people who need housing, or the conservation nuts? Who are, obviously, equally valid?'

Whichever end the voters were on, she thought, what with the council elections coming up. She said nothing, though. It spooked Eddie when people didn't agree with him immediately.

'It's tricky for me,' he added more menacingly, leaning forward so far she could smell the coffee on his breath. 'When one of my key team is on the front of the paper in a fancy dress, talking about bloody sprung floors.'

'With Amanda Page, MP,' Katie pointed out, calmly. 'Showing how the town planning department is in tune with the town's history as well as its future.'

'It shows partiality.'

'Quite right. I'm very passionate about the Hall, and I've already made recommendations about negotiating with the developers to work the regeneration around it,' she said, uncapping her pen to show how unintimidated she was. It would cost them extra, of course, which was why they were dragging their heels. All over Eddie, she was willing to bet.

She looked up at him, and smiled brightly. 'But if you feel it compromises your integrity, that's fair enough. I was hoping to have a chat with you after the meeting—I've applied to set up an Historic Environment Champion post.'

'What?' Eddie's face darkened as various implications occurred to him. 'What sort of nonsense is that?'

'Don't you think we've got a duty to safeguard our historic civic buildings?' Katie looked reproachful. 'Amanda Page thinks it's terrible we haven't appointed one yet.'

Eddie changed tack, and dropped his tone confidentially. 'Doesn't sound like a career-advancing post that, Kate. Not for an ambitious girl like you.'

Katie met his toady eye straight on. He didn't need to know she'd already drafted the job description for a four-day week, and more or less been told she could start in the new year. He definitely didn't need to know that part of her remit was protecting sites from exploitative new developments, and that certain people already had their eye on certain other people.

'There's all kinds of ambitious, Eddie,' she said. 'Now, how's your foxtrot? Can I sell you a ticket to the gala dance night?'

*   *   *

Bridget had breezed through the preparations for the dance with her usual efficiency, setting everything up at the same time as planning the Christmas play and buying most of her Christmas presents.

This year, they were on a strict £15-a-head gift budget. But at least there were no credit-card bills left.

It had been Lauren who'd sprung into action, charming the local suppliers into refunding the various big deposits, and selling on every single wedding item she'd collected so carefully, including all five pairs of her shoes. It helped that she and Bridget knew most of the people they'd dealt with, through the school and the clinic, but even so, Bridget had had to admire the way Lauren had swallowed her mortification and got on with it.

'You know I'll be back,' she'd promised them. 'Next year maybe—we haven't set a date, no, but I'll let you know as soon as we do!'

That had brought back a couple of thousand pounds. And then Frank had surprised her too, by getting over his male pride, and having a chat with Irene about the house.

'If you're going to pay for the wedding, then let my Ron do this for them,' Irene had said (blinking back tears, according to Frank, who'd not known where to look). 'He left Christopher some money in trust until he was twenty-five, so he wouldn't buy some silly car with it, I suppose. Between you and me, Frank, I've often thought about giving it to him, but I've worried he wasn't really mature enough to spend it wisely. But these last few weeks . . . Well, I think they've both made a very adult decision about their future, don't you? It can't have been easy, postponing the wedding when your Bridget was so obsessed with it. Will you let me give Christopher that money now, to make up the deposit for the house? Please? I can write you a cheque for your half right now . . . ?'

Frank had already been nodding in agreement, when Irene had added, mistily, 'Because I know how proud Ron would be to consider Lauren his daughter-in-law. She's a very special young lady . . .'

And then they'd both had to blink back tears, and after that, Frank had come to the generous conclusion that Irene 'wasn't as stuck-up as I reckoned'. He'd even insisted she come to the Christmas ball with them.

The final money had come from quite an unexpected but welcome source.

Frank and Bridget had gone out to see a film one evening, leaving Lauren at home packing up the parcels of wedding knick-knacks she'd sold on eBay. When the doorbell rang at about eight, Lauren was surprised to see Angelica on the doorstep, staggering under the weight of several enormous suit carriers.

'Merry Christmas!' she said from somewhere underneath them. 'Are you going to let me in?'

Lauren ushered her into the sitting room, hoping against hope that Angelica hadn't decided they were all going to wear matching outfits for the display, like drum majorettes or something.

'I've brought you an early present,' Angelica said, throwing the bags over the sofa as she started to unzip them. 'Before you say a word, I'm having a clear-out. I don't need them and I want you to have them. I want them to be danced in again— they deserve another lease of life.'

Sumptuous flashes of crimson and scarlet sequins began to emerge, like butterflies from the carrier chrysalis. Ballgowns. Beautiful, shimmering skins, far too lovely for me, thought Lauren, touching them reverently. 'But when am I . . .' she began.

'Now, Lauren, I heard about the wedding,' Angelica said, gently. 'And I understand why you were so wrapped up in the white dress, and the petticoats, and everything. But you're every bit as elegant on that dancefloor as you will be one day in a wedding dress. It's not quite the same, I know, but . . .' She left the sentence unfinished and instead turned back to the dresses, freeing them from the drab carriers until the sofa gleamed with lavish, netted drapery.

Angelica wanted to say, I never had the big white meringue, but it didn't stop me being the centre of attention. Eventually, dancing would give Lauren that glow of self-confidence she was missing. When she realised she'd never have to sit down at a dance again.

Lauren didn't respond and Angelica wondered whether she'd crossed the line.

Her round blue eyes were drinking in the dresses, but her smooth forehead was tense with worry. 'Angelica, no one's ever given me anything as amazing as this. I don't know what to say.'

'Thanks would be fine. And a promise that you'll carry on dancing in them.'

Lauren clutched one to her chest—the lucky foxtrot dress, Angelica noted, with the floating crimson feathers. 'It's just that . . . They're gorgeous, like something a princess would wear but . . .'

They were gorgeous, but how would she feel about wearing these to dance in when she knew her mother had her eternity ring for sale on eBay?

'What?' asked Angelica, and the whole story of

500

Bridget's money worries spilled out of Lauren in a torrent of guilt.

'Well, then you should sell the dresses!' Angelica said at once. 'They're only dresses! They're worth a fair bit.'

'But they're your . . .'

'They're *costumes*.' She put her hand on Lauren's arm. 'And that part of my life is over. Keep one, for being glamorous in, and sell the rest. Believe me, nothing's more important than your mum's happiness. And you've got a wonderful mother.'

'I suppose you've only got the one,' sighed Lauren.

'Well, yes,' said Angelica, 'usually.'

*　　　*　　　*

Bridget was thrilled to end her auction early and get the ring back, but even so, she was determined to keep Christmas—and her new emergency plans—under control. 'No going overboard with gifts this year,' she said to Frank, over supper one night. Lauren was out with Chris, 'practising' at Kian's. 'Not after . . . what happened.'

'There's nothing I need anyway, love,' Frank replied, as if she'd made an eminently sensible suggestion. 'Apart from a new pair of dancing shoes. We're tackling the quickstep again next year—I want to get my footwork back up to speed.' He winked. 'You don't know what you started.'

Bridget did know what she'd started all right. It was Frank who'd made the extra lesson with Angelica to brush up their waltz technique. Originally, Angelica had wanted them to

501

demonstrate the foxtrot at the gala night, with Lauren and Chris doing the waltz on their own, but Frank had refused, before Angelica had even got the words out.

'No,' he said, firmly. 'Lauren'll be a bag of nerves if it's just her up there, everyone watching, specially with that great flatfoot, Chris, hauling her about. Much better if we do it with her, eh, Bridget? Make it a family affair!'

Angelica had caught the protective glance that flickered between them. Lauren might be giving Chris another chance, but he was obviously only back on probation, as far as Frank was concerned. She made a mental note to give Chris an extra private lesson herself. Or get Bridget to. 'What a good idea!' she said.

'Perfect,' said Bridget, and glanced up at her husband. He wasn't just holding himself upright for the waltz these days. His stoop seemed to have vanished altogether.

He looks even better now than he did when we were jiving, not waltzing, she thought, happily.

CHAPTER THIRTY-FIVE

The night of the Gala Evening was cold but clear, and the inky December sky twinkled with pin-sharp stars, as if in tribute to the spangled circle skirts and freshly cleaned suits parading into the Memorial Hall, to the pulse-quickening sound of the big-band numbers blaring through the windows.

Before the doors opened to the public, Angelica

502

stood inside the Hall and savoured the last few quiet moments, on her own while the band were getting changed. She felt as if she had one foot in her past, and the other foot firmly in the present. She didn't want to look into the future. She was just going to concentrate on enjoying tonight as she'd never allowed herself to before. Finally, after years and years of changing and struggling, she was happy to be herself, dancing with whoever asked, appreciating the efforts of her students, letting the music flow through her.

You can't really go back in time, thought Angelica, running her eyes over the old friezes and dancing ladies. She stepped in a slow waltz across the spotless floor, under the tickertape of the mirrorball. That's why it was so important to tie up those loose ends while you can. Tonight, she thought. I'll tie them up tonight.

Her scarlet lips curved in a smile as she admired what she, Katie and Bridget had put together in record time. Even in its heyday, the Hall hadn't known a night like this one: instead of orange squash, chilled champagne bubbled in flutes on trays in the vestibule, and tiny silver balls hung from the rafters, like a constellation around the huge mirrorball that revolved slowly over the polished floor.

The tickets—printed on stiff card and gold-edged, to Angelica's specifications—requested 'dressing up' from all attendees, and as the guests began to arrive, she realised she had unlocked an unexpected passion for glamour in the town. There wasn't a ballgown left in any attic, department store or charity shop in the area, fake tan sold out in Boots, and the hairdressers were booked solid for the whole day with women requesting 'big dos'. With so much coverage in the paper, every local grandee was there, eager to be seen posing for the cameras, alongside the regulars from the social dance night. Skirts were so huge that there was barely room for more than five women to freshen up their lipstick in the echoing loos at any one time.

The dancing got underway at 7.30 sharp, after a nervous but moving speech from Bridget about how important it was to protect the beautiful things in the town, and none of the dance class was short of partners. It was Baxter who'd hit on the idea of selling dance cards for the ladies to fill up, with Angelica charging a restoration donation per dance, already she'd raised enough to get the boiler fixed properly.

The class display was due to take place at 9.30 p.m., in the interval—'to give everyone a chance to get their breath back', explained Angelica, and from the flushed faces filling the dancefloor at 9.25 p.m., it hadn't come a moment too soon.

'Everyone ready?' asked Angelica, as her tense pupils stood outside in the hallway, ready for their big entrances like chicks behind a mother hen. The band was playing 'Moonlight Serenade', and when it came to a close, it would be time for them to start.

She tried to keep her voice light, but she could see the goosebumps on Lauren's pale arms, and Katie's shallow breaths making her new green dress rise and fall. They were all nervous. Even Baxter kept fiddling with his hair, smoothing it back with his hand until it gleamed like a penguin's head.

Angelica knew the metallic nerves they'd be feeling; it didn't matter whether you were stepping out in the Tower Ballroom or your own front room, when other people were watching, everything was different. Already her subconscious was measuring out the verses, counting down the choruses left.

'I know it's not the time for big speeches,' she said, over the muted trumpets crooning inside the Hall, 'but I want you all to know that you've made me very proud already, even before you go out there. You're going to be wonderful. I wish I could dance with you all tonight, and I hope you'll make room for me on your cards.'

'Don't!' said Lauren, wiping at her eye with the back of one hand and waving the other frantically. 'You'll make me smudge my mascara!'

'Yeah, don't,' said Trina, whose extensive eyeliner collection had seen her in charge of make-up. 'It took me ages to do.'

Trina and Chloe were dancing a cha-cha together, 'seeing as how we've done without men so far anyway'. Sensibly, they'd applied the Latin theme more to their hairstyles than to the traditionally skimpy wisps of sequins: Chloe's hair was frizzed into a blonde afro of curls, stuck with gold flowers, while Trina's short dark crop was gelled into what her niece optimistically called 'the elfin look'. They both had more glitter glued to their cheekbones than the cast of *The Rocky Horror Picture Show*, but had stuck to simple tiered skirts beneath.

'Don't think about anything else other than the music,' Angelica went on, looking around the group. 'Just let it flow into your head, and your feet will do the rest! Enjoy having that floor to yourselves for once—and remember to smile!'

Automatically, everyone's lips curved into the ballroom-dancing rictus, just as the music slowed to a close in the Hall.

'It's finishing,' said Katie, her voice disappearing in a little upward gasp and Lauren turned pale underneath her liberally applied tan.

Angelica began to bustle, to take their minds off it. 'Now, then, who's first? It's Trina and Chloe, isn't it, for "Lady Marmalade"?' She began lining them up in pairs. 'And then Baxter and Peggy, for your wonderful foxtrot, and then all my Armstrongs for the waltz, and then the lovely big finish . . .'

She turned to Katie and Ross and smiled. 'You two are going to steal the show. Ready?'

Ross squeezed Katie's hand and answered for both of them. 'Can't wait.'

*   *   *

Angelica stepped out onto the stage and took the microphone. It was an old-fashioned flat one, like a carpet beater, and as she looked out from behind it into a sea of black and white suits, mingled with shimmering sugared-almond frocks, time seemed to shiver in front of her. The flushed faces lifted up to her, pink with effort and pleasure, didn't look modern, and with the vintage curled hair, and red lipstick on every woman's mouth, it could have been a black and white photo come to life, as if the old ghostly dancers of the Hall had slipped back amongst the living, unable to resist a live band and a party atmosphere.

A ripple of applause greeted her appearance and she had to flap her hands to make it stop.

'Ladies and gentlemen,' she said, her voice ringing confidently through the Hall. 'It gives me more honour than I can possibly express, to present to you tonight, the Angelica Andrews School of Dance!'

She stepped back as the band swung into the irresistible swagger of 'Lady Marmalade', and Trina and Chloe sashayed on to the floor, taking it in scrupulous turn to dance the lead, as they twirled in almost perfect time. Trina and Chloe could have spent their lives on a Vegas stage, not in a Midlands tax office, as they tossed their hair like showgirls, strutting and posing and flicking out their hips, until the whole room was clapping along with them.

No sooner had they run through their routine than the music changed into 'Night and Day' and Baxter and Peggy strode out on to the floor, their joined hands held high so Peggy's floating chiffon sleeves could catch the air and trail elegantly behind her.

Peggy still looked like a pepperpot, thought Katie, peering through the doors, but a beautifully self-assured pepperpot in a midnight-blue dress glittering with thousands of hand-stitched stones that must have come from her old dancing wardrobe.

Bridget was watching too, but she wasn't seeing Peggy the old lady any more. She'd had a conversation with Peggy, just before they went on, which left her unable to see anything other than Peggy the young dancer of sixty years ago, when she was still a teenager.

They had been putting the final touches to their make-up in the ladies' loos, or rather, Lauren had been fussing about affectionately, adding 'a little something' to Bridget's basic mascara and blush. Bridget was busy trying to tone the results down so Frank wouldn't have a heart attack.

'You're very lucky to have a daughter,' Peggy had said, when Lauren had dashed off, and Bridget was surprised by the wobble in her voice.

'I am,' she agreed. 'Especially after two lads. Lauren's always been my baby girl.' She dabbed at her lipstick. 'You and Baxter have sons, don't you?'

'We do. Graeme and Ray.' Peggy pressed her lips together. 'But I had a little girl too.'

Bridget turned slowly from the mirror. She'd never heard anything about a daughter before, and Baxter was more forthcoming about his sons (and their sporting achievements) than Peggy was. In fact, this was more conversation than she'd ever had with quiet Peggy. She got the feeling that she had to get something off her chest. People often got things off their chest with her, usually at parents' meetings.

'Really?' she said, gently. 'Did you lose her?'

'In a manner of speaking.' Peggy stared at her stout reflection, as if she was trying to find the young girl in her own lined face. 'I fell pregnant for the first time when I was only young myself, younger than your Lauren. Baxter had gone off to do his National Service, you see—we weren't even engaged. My father didn't trust him, thought he was too much of a fly-by-night with his dancing and that.' She smiled sadly, showing her little teeth. 'Which he was in those days, I won't deny it. My mum was furious when she found out, called me every name under the sun. She wouldn't let me tell Baxter. He wasn't due back from Germany for a year, and she said she didn't want me tied down so young. I don't even think she told my dad, she just sent me off to her sister's in Wales, saying I had rheumatic fever and needed the air.'

She made nervous nibbling gestures with her lips, as if it felt strange to be talking about something she'd kept silently in her head so long.

Bridget felt terribly responsible for the secret Peggy was offering her. Obviously she had no one else to tell, but for some peculiar reason, she felt she had to let it out, now. 'And you had a little girl?'

She nodded, hard. 'Beautiful little thing, with his dark hair and eyes like a pussycat. They had her adopted. I wasn't allowed to write to Baxter but I told him anyway, as soon as he came back, I mean, how could I not? But it was too late. My mother said it would be cruel to try and find our baby, now she had parents who loved her. And sometimes I think Baxter only married me because I was so sad, and it was his responsibility. I wasn't his only girlfriend, I know that.'

'Peggy, no!' Bridget exclaimed. 'No, I'm sure he didn't!'

Peggy shrugged, as if she didn't care now either way. 'I've never stopped thinking about her. I loved the two boys, but we never had a girl. I wanted one very badly. I did meet up with the mother once, you see, after my own mother died, and I could make some enquiries, like, but I could tell she loved my little girl like her own. We could have had her back then, but it would have been a cruelty to

509

take her away. A cruelty.'

She looked up at Bridget, and her small eyes were wet beneath the shimmery shadow. 'Sorry, dear. It's been bringing it all back, you know, coming along to dancing here. Especially tonight. It reminds me of what this place was like when Baxter and I first met. Anyway . . .' She plucked a tissue from up the sleeve of her ballroom-dancing dress, and patted her nose with it. 'Here we are. Still together.'

'Still together,' agreed Bridget, because she couldn't think what else to say.

Then as they left the bathrooms, she saw Angelica sail across the floor with the Mayor, making him seem like Gene Kelly, and the quick spark of pride that lit up Peggy's face told Bridget what Peggy hadn't quite brought herself to confess.

Angelica was their little girl. So that was why Peggy and Baxter, the two experienced dancers, had come along to a beginners' class. Did Angelica know? Would Peggy tell her? Did she need to?

Bridget thought of Lauren and the wordless bond they had, and shivered inside with an emotion she couldn't put her finger on.

She watched Peggy now, sailing around the empty space with Baxter, their feet seeming to float above the floor. They put the rest of the class to shame, really, with their lightness of touch. Peggy was good, and had years of practice, but Baxter really had a tremendous natural gift. Someone who danced that well couldn't help but attract the ladies, she thought, but he must have loved Peggy to have stayed for so long, she thought. Maybe he missed his daughter too. Maybe staying together, with their secret, kept their

510

daughter alive to them. Maybe dancing did.

What difference would it make now, after nearly sixty years?

'Are you ready, love?' Frank whispered in her ear.

Bridget jumped. 'Yes!' she said, turning round.

Lauren stood behind her, her willowy body encased in the poppy-red sequins and floating tulle of Angelica's longest gown. It had been almost floor-length on Angelica, but the feathered hem hovered around Lauren's shins. Lauren didn't mind that. 'Something less for Chris to trip over,' as she pointed out. 'Plus, you can see my new shoes better.'

'How are you feeling, Chris?' asked Bridget in a whisper.

Chris looked extremely handsome, but quite some way beyond nervous in his black tie. He cast an anxious glance towards Frank, looming behind him.

'Fine,' he said. 'Be glad when it's over.'

'You just concentrate,' Frank said, ominously.

'We know, Dad. Just keep it simple,' said Lauren, serenely. 'We're going to take it slowly. Right, Chris?'

Chris nodded, and, with a final swallow, he took her hand, seeing Angelica's cue from the stage.

She's grown up so much in the last few months, thought Bridget with a burst of pride. And she looks lovelier in that ballgown than she ever did in those bridal shops. Besides which, red sequins made Lauren's blue eyes sparkle far more than those blank white dresses. And she could wear them any Friday she wanted.

Angelica's voice was cutting through the

applause as Baxter and Peggy swept off the floor.

'And now, dancing the waltz, Frank and Bridget Armstrong, and Christopher Markham and Lauren Armstrong!'

The band struck up the lilting introduction to one of Bridget's favourite songs—'True Love' from *High Society*—and they set off, not needing to speak.

Bridget gazed up at Frank as they began their basic pattern, moving as one, their close hold never breaking as they floated around the space. She didn't see the banks of watching faces, because her eyes were fixed on the familiar face in front of her, her husband holding her steady, leading her firmly and standing up ram-rod straight. A simple, easy smile acknowledged the many times they'd played this as one of 'their songs'.

His attention was divided, though, between her, and Lauren, trying not to tread on Chris's toes, on the other side of the room.

Lauren was doing all right, Bridget could tell, but Chris wasn't letting her turn with the same confidence that Frank did. Their circles were small and cramped, instead of the generous arcs that they were making.

It wasn't Chris's fault, thought Bridget. It would come. It was all down to practice.

'Go on,' she said to Frank, with an understanding nod. 'I know you're dying to do a father's excuse me.'

And so Frank tapped Chris on the shoulder, just in time to catch Chris mutter, '. . . more beautiful than anyone else here,' and he warmed a little towards the lad.

Then, as Lauren's face lit up, he took his

daughter in his arms, as proudly as he would have done on her wedding day and they began to waltz. Frank swung her round in a head-spinning series of open turns that made the feathers of her hem float up in a leisurely cloud.

In the distance, beneath the noise of the band, Lauren could hear the ripple of admiring applause as their tall figures sailed down the centre of the floor, as if they were Astaire and Rogers, dancing on a Hollywood cloud of dreams.

Lauren had never been applauded for anything before, and it felt lovely. I'll never be Big Bird again now, she realised, her heart lifting up like a balloon inside her stiffly beaded bodice, not now I know my feet can do this. And if Chris and I could still be dancing together when we're Mum and Dad's age . . .

She caught sight of Chris on the other side of the room, gamely leading her mother into a promenade step. He looked almost competent, but then Mum was a great backlead.

One step at a time, she told herself. Don't miss how incredible you feel right now. And it was all down to her own gangly, awkward self. How amazing was that?

Frank caught her smiling, and thought his heart would burst with pride.

'You're the star turn,' he said.

'You and Mum are, you mean,' said Lauren. 'Well, we all are. We're the von Trapps of Longhampton.'

'We are,' said Frank, and hummed the melody as they dipped and swayed. Bridget loved this song. He remembered her singing it to the boys when they were tiny babies, rocking them back to sleep when she thought he couldn't hear her singing. But he could hear, standing on the stairs, looking at his wife, and his children, and knowing there was nothing else in the world a man could wish for.

What the hell, he thought, I'll sing if I want to.

'Love, forever . . .'

'Da-aa-aad,' said Lauren, grimacing.

'. . . true,' sang Frank, and the song drew to a close.

*   *   *

'Just us now,' said Katie, watching the Armstrongs' light-as-a-feather waltzes sending the crowd into a flurry of romantic sighs.

Ross gripped her hand. 'Katie, just so you know . . .'

Katie's heart started racing as the Armstrongs bowed and curtsied to each other. Any moment now the tango beat would start and then they'd be on.

She pulled up the straps of her new dress—her own, this time, bought on a shopping trip with Jo. It had done them both good, booking a wardrobe makeover. New women, the pair of them. Hannah and Molly had some of the clothes they'd thrown out for their dressing-up box, and Lauren the internet expert was helping them eBay the rest. Very lucratively, in Jo's case.

'What?' she asked, distracted.

'We're not doing the tango.' As he spoke the band started playing, Angelica announced them, and Katie turned in panic.

'But we *practised* the tango!'

Ross grabbed her hands. 'That's just for us. It's

514

like Angelica said, some things are private. We're going to do a social foxtrot, nothing fancy. Just you and me.'

Katie opened her mouth to object, and Ross put a finger on her lips.

'I asked Angelica for this song,' he said. 'It's the wedding dance we couldn't do when we got married. Trust me. Let me lead.'

Before she could protest, Ross led her out onto the dancefloor.

He looks so handsome, she thought, her heart banging even faster in her chest, as she admired him in his dark suit and buttercup-yellow shirt. Ross wasn't a suit person, but he knew she loved to see him in one. Last year, she would have said nothing and hoped he'd somehow guess, while he'd have taken any hints as a dig about his lack of a job.

Now, though, they'd found a compromise: he'd got himself a casual new suit—not too formal—for the meetings Jo was setting up for their web design business, and she'd promised not to nag him about ties. He looked good enough without one.

'What's the song?' she asked, as he put his arm around her, pulling her tightly to him. Butterflies jostled in her stomach, not just because everyone was staring at them, but because if the song was wrong, somehow, it would be a million times more embarrassing than her falling over his feet.

'Wait,' said Ross, and tipped his head forward so his forehead touched hers.

Then the romantic Gershwin melody began and she recognised it straight away. She looked up into Ross's brown eyes and hoped he could see in hers how full her heart was at that moment. Too full to speak.

'It's very clear . . .' sang Ross, just in case she hadn't got it.

But Katie had. 'Our love is here to stay,' she replied.

And he led off in their simple social foxtrot, nothing fancy or showy, just the basic romantic steps that let you hold someone close enough to whisper in their ear. Steps that had led to so many weddings in Longhampton since the Hall opened. Steps that let a very modern man and wife borrow some old-fashioned stardust, for as long as the song lasted. Their love was there to stay even when the Hall was being swept and the doors were locked for the night.

As Katie and Ross smooched around the floor, the mirrorball spun above their heads, showering them with white diamond confetti.

Then, as at all the best weddings, the tiles of the sprung maple floor vanished from sight as the rest of the dancers took their partners and joined them.

One of those couples was Angelica Andrews, dancing a slow foxtrot with Peggy, their heads tilted in gentle conversation as they stepped and turned in their own private world, letting the years blur and vanish around them.

EPILOGUE

The national papers picked up on the quirky story of the old building being brought back to life by ballroom dancers. It had 'film potential', according to one over-enthusiastic feature writer, which set Trina and Chloe off into a long, heated discussion about whether Gwyneth Paltrow could learn to dance well enough to be Lauren. Baxter had Roger Moore down for himself, although Ross and Katie thought David Suchet would be a better fit. Especially if he still had his Poirot moustache.

One paper ran a whole page on the gala night, finding couples who'd met at the Memorial Hall, and interviewing Angelica at some length, about her starry past and her feelings about coming home, now ballroom dancing was big news again, thanks to the television. They sent a photographer, who did a gorgeous portrait of her in her mother's sitting room, long legs crossed, in her red jersey practice dress.

'Oh my God, you're so photogenic,' Lauren had gasped at the paper, when she and Bridget came round with Katie to discuss the next move in the 'Save the Hall' campaign. 'Look at you! Not a line on your face!'

'I have a portrait in the attic,' Angelica said, with a wink at Bridget. 'It's a wreck, believe me.'

That was true, too, in a way, she thought, as she cut around the photograph from the newspaper and stuck it carefully in the last page of her mother's last album. A whole history of myself, sitting here in a box in my parents' old house, while

I went round the world trying to get away from it. And now here I am, adding to it.

She looked approvingly at the final picture. Angelica, at home. Happy. For good measure, she stuck her wedding photo of Jerry in there too, but took out a picture for herself: one of her and Tony at the National Championships in 1977, mid-air in some complicated jive move, eyes black with liner and fixed entirely on one another.

Angelica didn't even remember seeing it at the time, and now it could have been someone else.

Maybe it was better that way, remembering Tony as he was then, dark and sleek and handsome. She had no idea what he'd look like now—gone to seed, probably, with a string of divorces and a clapped-out Porsche.

She looked at herself in the photograph again, curled up on the sofa, raising her chin to the photographer as the light fell on her cheekbones, and shadowed her long slanting eyes. It had been weeks now since she'd needed a sleeping pill to get through the night; even her creaky old knees seemed to be loosening up again.

I've done all right, though, she thought, and allowed herself a gentle smile.

*   *   *

In the days before Christmas, Angelica decided two things: she would get a new puppy, whom she'd love, housetrain, and not treat as a substitute baby-husband, and secondly, it was time to put 34 Sydney Street on the market.

In her truthful moments, she wasn't really sure that she wanted to sell, but she believed in setting things in motion and seeing what happened.

If someone offers and I'm sad, then I'll stay, she reasoned. But with house prices in Longhampton getting to what they were, she'd be mad not to take what she could and get back to her lovely white house in Islington, and her friends, and the cafés, and the life she'd put on hold.

Yet, to her surprise, she found herself thinking, I could always keep it going. It's not like it would cost much to run. I could come up for weekly lessons, keep Peggy and Baxter company at the social nights. Maybe get the formation team going again, if there was enough interest. And Jo and Katie were still on at her about children's lessons—that was something to think about.

It made her smile that she could even be bothered to tell white lies to herself about it, when she was honest about so many other things now.

While everyone else was scurrying round the precinct doing their last-minute Christmas shopping, Angelica tidied what little there was in the house, ready for the estate agent to come round to value it. She'd made a pot of coffee and put croissants on to warm, as Jo had advised. She was pouring cream into her mother's saved-for-best milk-jug when there was a knock at the door, and, straightening her skirt, she went to answer it.

Whatever's to be will be, she thought.

'Hello!' she said, with a warm smile for the estate agent on the front step, and her smile broadened as she thought, he's not the spotty youth I spoke to on the high street. So there *are* attractive older men in Longhampton after all.

And then her smile wavered, and broadened, and wavered again as slowly old memories clicked

519

together in her head, waking up from a long, long sleep.

She swallowed, suddenly conscious of her hair, her feet, her posture, everything. Surely it couldn't be? Really?

'Hello?' she said again, this time with a touch of disbelief, as the man standing in front of her gave her a slow, appreciative smile that reached all the way up to his jet-black eyes.

If it was who she thought it was, he hadn't gone to seed. He'd just matured, his youthful swagger mellowed into a rakish older charm. The red scarf hanging round his neck, over the cashmere coat, didn't say multiple divorce, and neither did the lack of silver in the dark, swept-back hair.

'Saw you in the papers, and I found you at last,' said Tony Canero. He extended a tanned hand, with one gold signet ring on the little finger and no pale tan line on his wedding finger. 'You're a difficult woman to track down, Angie.'

The gesture was so poised and balanced, so redolent of his perfect timing, that Angelica felt her feet go light, as well as her head.

She didn't miss the irony that he'd eventually found her here, the place she'd been running away from all the time she'd known him.

That wasn't irony, though. It was right.

'Well, here I am,' she said.

'And you look as beautiful as ever,' he said. 'Are you dancing?'

'If you're asking,' said Angelica Andrews, and he took her hand, the promise of many dances in one easy motion, and kissed it, never letting his dark eyes leave hers.

13